Call
the
Lightning

LAURIE OLERICH

DEDICATION

Thank you to my amazing son Taylor for putting up with my whiteboard drawings and crazed mutterings about plot twists. I couldn't do this without you!

ACKNOWLEDGMENTS

A special shout out to the wonderful people who've been helping me get my writing career out of fantasy and into reality! I'm so lucky to have friends who share my enthusiasm.

Angela Bauer: Her artwork is amazing! She's the genius behind the book cover. Thank you for your endless patience!

Angela Gulick: My oldest friend and website guru. Thanks for listening, nodding politely and then steering me towards reason. The Primani glyph and my logo are her designs. Very cool!

Dr. Charles Mount: Project Archeologist in County Kildare, Ireland. Thank you for helping me with Bronze Age research. The site visits were instrumental in building Killian's world.

Prologue:

THERE WASN'T MUCH LEFT. Piles of blackened stone dotted the lot like burial cairns now. The entire house was gone. A small rusted shed leaned sadly to one side. Green vines had begun to swallow it whole. But now on the verge of winter, the vines had shriveled and hardened to brown. They might've been the only things holding the shed together. The garage still stood. Part of it had burned but it wasn't completely destroyed. The yellow police tape had come loose and waved cheerily from the locked gate at the driveway. Shivering in the cold, I stood with my back to the tree line above the compound and scanned the property for others. Out of habit, really; or maybe my training was paying off and it was an instinct to look for the enemy. Either way, I looked. It was lonely here, in the middle of the mountains, and right on the verge of a winter storm. It would snow soon if I was reading the clouds right. Swollen and grey, they lumbered overhead as the cold wind howled down from Canada.

Even as the first fat snowflakes began to fall, my mind was very far away…remembering, remembering, always remembering. Behind closed eyes, every detail was seared into my memory. The fire had branded the vision into my mind. I *couldn't* forget that day even if I wanted to. And I didn't want to. I had to keep it alive. There was meaning to it…something I was supposed to see. But I hadn't been able to move beyond the horror and pain that hit me as soon as the vision came. I had to try though, it felt important...So I braced myself again and let the vision come. I flinched as the brilliant light of the first explosions flared behind my eyes. Again the scene played out in slow motion.

I watched as Dec landed against a pallet of guns and one of the demons lunged at him, tumbling them both into the darkness. One by one, the timers went off and the explosions rocked the foundation. The house rumbled ominously as it shifted off of its moorings. Plaster fell from the ceiling in chunks as smoke blackened the basement. They should have left by now but they were still in there. What were they waiting for? I held my breath as Sean turned to help Dec. Separated by flames, Killian yelled at them to go. He could leave but he wouldn't as long as they were still inside. Horrified and helpless, I couldn't look away. After shoving the burning pallet to the side, Sean grabbed Dec's arm as the big demon aimed his weapon at Sean's back. He fired just as the barrels of chemicals exploded in a blinding burst of white fire.

"Sean!"

With a deafening roar, the house erupted, the blast so intense it seared my eyes. Stunned and blinded, I staggered upright as half of my soul was ripped away. Sean! Oh, my God! No! Still screaming his name, I was barely aware of Dec's arms around me or our flight away from the men with guns.

That was a year ago.

Here in the present, I hugged myself as tears washed away the vision. My eyes had healed but my heart was still broken somewhere under the crumbled foundation of this house. My skin prickled and I knew I was no longer alone with my memories.

"Why do you come here?" he asked with a sad smile.

Wiping away the icy tears, I straightened my shoulders. "I could ask you the same question."

"I come for you." He reached for my hand.

Chapter 1: Stakeout

MY STOMACH GROWLED in bossy demand for food. The aroma of baking bread drifted into the window and my mouth watered in response. Across the street, the night shift was busy running the ovens in the bread factory. My butt was asleep and I had to pee. Stakeouts were overrated.

"God, I'm starving!" I whispered. I dug my hand into my stomach in hopes it would stop growling. It just made me have to pee more.

My partner, Dec, slid a piece of gum across the seat. Oh yeah, that would do it. I stuffed it in my mouth anyway and counted the minutes until we could leave.

He said, "Okay, they should be here any minute if our intel is right. Keep watching the side door and I've got the front."

A shadow moved just outside my line of sight and I shifted my night vision binoculars to the right. There they were. Two men were coming up the cluttered alley and headed into the metal door on the side of the old brick shop. This wasn't the nicest of neighborhoods and most people would avoid it after dark. We, however, weren't most people. In fact, I was the only *people* here. My partner wasn't, strictly speaking, human at all. But he passed himself off as human and his supernatural powers came in handy during fights with thugs. At the moment, we were slouched inside an old crappy pickup truck staking out the brick shop.

I snapped a couple of pictures and said, "Two men headed inside."

Dec whispered, "Uh-oh, what do we have here? Delivery truck pulling up to the front."

We watched as four men unloaded several white barrels and some crates from the back of the panel delivery truck. Carefully, I snapped pictures and hoped I was getting their faces in focus.

"Human?" I asked.

"You tell me."

"Nice try." I could see into buildings if I tried. The CIA called it *remote viewing;* I called it a curse. I refused to try since Sean's disappearance a year ago. Some might think having psychic abilities was a gift. I would disagree. It was a curse and I didn't want any more visions branded into my memory.

He closed his eyes for a moment and muttered, "Humans. I don't sense anything else."

We waited until the driver came back to the truck and pulled away and then we followed him. Dec was driving and kept a good distance behind the truck. I knew my job and used the binoculars to keep track of the truck. It was very late now and the streets were empty. We had to stay pretty far behind so the driver wouldn't notice us. Eventually he pulled up to a grey brick warehouse and parked the truck outside. After finishing his cigarette, he went inside.

"Watch the door. I'll be right back." Dec disappeared and reappeared next to the truck.

I stared at the door as he crawled under the truck and attached the tracking device. I held my breath and worried. In a second, he was back in the driver's seat and we headed back to the farmhouse. Mission accomplished. We were done for the night. It was 2 a.m. by the time we got home. Killian, as usual, was waiting up for us.

"These barrels look familiar. Did you smell anything?" he asked and flipped over the picture he was scrutinizing.

"Yeah, bread," I answered without thinking.

He didn't crack a smile. "Bread? Good job, Princess."

I groaned and rolled my eyes. I wasn't stupid. Really, I wasn't. Somehow I always seemed to stick my foot in my mouth when Killian was around. He made me twitchy and kept me off balance. He was the undisputed leader of our group; and yep, he was the boss of me. We were monitoring demon operations in the area and I was trying to help out. It was a combination of police and super-secret agent work. I wasn't a cop or a secret agent, but I was trained to kill bad guys and had excellent instincts. My intuition was nearly always right and that made me useful. Killian decided whether or not I went on missions or stayed home. So far, I only went on missions he considered safe. Tonight was one of those. Stakeouts were both safe and boring.

Tonight's stakeout was related to an investigation we started more than a year ago in Manhattan. A pain-in-the-ass demon named Dagin was using his job as an arms dealer to spread chaos and destruction around the planet. According to Killian, that's what demons did. To further that goal, his evil engineers had developed a weapon that was selling like crazy on the black market and terrorists were putting in orders from all over the world. We had slowed down progress by blowing up a large stockpile of weapons and the research lab in a farmhouse in Vermont earlier this year. That was the first time I used my new powers and worked with Declan, Killian, and Sean.

They call themselves Primani. They're the good guys: they protect humans and hunt demons. They're an elite group of warriors with amazing abilities and somehow I'd joined them. In the beginning, I was simply another of Sean's charges. He was assigned to keep me safe and to correct my destiny. When my mother died, my destiny took a swing off track and he started watching out for me from a distance. That would've been enough if it hadn't been for Scott Flynn. Scott had beaten me half to death. His attack sent my attitude, faith, and destiny into a downward spiral that was apparently unacceptable to the powers that be. Sean had to take a more active role in keeping me safe. It was a simple mission that didn't stay that way. We fell in love and nothing was the same after that. My destiny was wrapped up in his and we were connected in ways we were still trying to understand.

Drooping with exhaustion, Dec filled Killian in on the stakeout and we went over the rest of the pictures I took.

"Good shots, Mica. You're getting good with the camera. We'll need to follow up with the owner of that truck and keep watching the shop. I don't like the looks of those barrels."

Dec offered, "I'll send the pics to Alex. Maybe he can ID the men we saw tonight. It would help to know who we're dealing with."

Alex was Killian's boss. He ran the entire east coast special operations division. Killian ran our little cell but Alex supervised a dozen of them up and the down the eastern seaboard. He had all of the resources and technology available to investigate people and solve crimes. Probably we had better technology than the CIA. It helped to be supernatural too. Mind reading and teleporting, or traveling as they called it, were very useful when fighting criminals. Unfortunately, I didn't have the power to teleport so I had to hitch a ride or take a real car.

I yawned hugely. "So can I go to bed now? I'm beat."

Killian barely glanced up from the stack of pictures but waved me out of the room. Domino trotted after me. The room I shared with Sean was big and airy in the sunniness of the day. At night, however, it was shadowy and empty. I hated being alone in the dark. I kept a small nightlight burning near the closet to keep the shadows at bay. Once upon a time, I had been afraid of the demons in my closet; now I've learned there are far scarier demons roaming the streets among us. My closet had little appeal to the demons I'd met so far. Domino, my little Dalmatian, protected me from all things creepy. As we entered the room, she walked a circuit around and paused at the windows and the closet door. Satisfied there were no human or demonic intruders, she hopped up on the bed and curled up on her pillow. With a last brown-eyed glance at me, she yawned hugely and went to sleep with her head between her paws.

I stroked her velvet ears and stared at the ceiling. Her little furry body kept me warm in the big empty bed and I was grateful for her. She was a peace offering from Sean and I smiled at the memory. It was the day he'd finally given up trying to fight his attraction to me. He had remained elusive and secretive still, but he had unbent enough to let me in. From that day forward, Sean was mine and I was his. Domino still wore the St. Christopher medallion around her neck even though it was meant for me. It was his way of saying I needed protecting and I didn't have the heart to take it off of her collar. It was part of who she was.

The dream came nearly every night now. It was always the same. I walked down an endless hallway filled with many doors. The doors were locked and unmarked. It was quiet and dark. I didn't feel afraid here. Mostly I felt numb as I drifted through the dream. There was nothing around me and I wondered what the point was. Eventually I heard someone calling my name. At first it was barely a whisper, but it grew louder as I wandered further into the darkness. The voice gained strength until I recognized it. I pressed my ear against the nearest door and listened. The voice came from behind the door. I pulled on the handle but the door wouldn't open. Louder and louder the voice called me. It was scared and the sound twisted my guts. I pulled on the door until I was exhausted and sagged against it.

There had to be a way inside…

Chapter 2: Spring Awakening

A STORM WAS COMING. Angry thunder rumbled in the distance and cold gusts of wind bent the branches of the maple trees around me. Unconcerned with Mother Nature's snippiness, I focused on my breathing and relaxed my body. The smell of green things filled my head as I opened my mind to what would come. When I meditated, I tuned out the world and found peace. The tiny room I visualized in my mind was empty and calm at the moment. I wanted it to stay that way and made no effort to reach out for a premonition.

Today I sought only peace.

A gust of wind blew my hair into my eyes and scattered my thoughts like leaves. I shoved my hair back and tried to regain my earlier sense of peace. A drop of chilly rain splashed off of my outstretched palm and yet I continued to breathe slowly and deeply. Gradually I drifted into my happy place and tuned out the storm completely. I floated among the trees with feet that didn't touch the mossy earth. Warm air caressed my skin as I made my way into the forest. Fine tendrils of mist swirled at my feet as I wandered. No light guided me, no darkness stalked me. Today I merely wandered free and alone. I'd found the peace I longed for, but something was missing.

Someone was missing.

Rain sluiced down my back as a bolt of lightning struck a tree nearby. The loud crack barely penetrated my consciousness. Another sound held my full attention now. Beginning softly and growing louder, I heard someone calling my name. The next flash of lightning lingered brilliant cobalt long after the sound of thunder faded.

"Mica!" Killian's sharp voice against my ear brought me out of my dream world and back to reality.

I blinked rain out of my eyes and accepted his hand. As he pulled me up, I shook my head to clear it. His familiar touch steadied me as I came back to the moment. The heavy rain softened the lines of his face and made him look more human than usual. His thick black lashes were clumped together around those brilliant blue eyes that still startled me with their intensity. Today they were fathomless midnight; other days, the wild color of the ocean. I sighed wistfully. He was gorgeous and I'd be blind if I didn't see that.

"What did you see this time?" He searched my eyes.

Indifferent, I said, "Nothing new. No light, no dark. Just me and the trees."

"And that troubles you?" He took my hand and tugged me towards the house.

"Yes. I guess it does. It's peaceful, but I wanted…" I slowed down and sighed. There wasn't any point in talking about this again.

His hand tightened around mine and he said, "I know, babe. I want the same thing, but--"

"Just stop! I won't give up on him. I can't!"

He stopped abruptly and I ran into him. He squeezed my shoulders and said, "I'm not asking you to give up on him, Mica! We all want him back. It's just been so long now. I don't know what to think anymore. No one has any answers." He cupped my face in one of his big paws and added more softly, "I wish I could take away your pain."

I rubbed my cheek against his hand and leaned into his chest. How had I ever thought he was cold? After a moment of hesitation, he wrapped his arms around me and we stood in the stormy woods lost in our own memories.

Sean's beautiful face teased me. It was mostly lean lines and sharp cheekbones. His eyes were his most striking feature. Large and slightly turned up at the edges,

9

they were a moody blue with heavy black lashes and feathery eyebrows. His mouth could go from a grim line to a soft sweet smile that melted my heart. He was serious and intense but his eyes knew my heart and his smile was only for me. A powerful and lethal soldier, a Primani, he had softened only for me. I was his balance. I missed him with an ache that stopped my breath sometimes. He was my other half; my soul mate. It was his power that had awakened my own powers. I was trying to help when I used my vision that day in Vermont. After Sean disappeared, I spent months cursing my vision and refused to use it. Even after all these months, I had nightmares about it. I could still see Sean's face contorted with agony as the explosions ripped him away from me. We never found his body. None of us could sense him anymore.

He was just…gone.

"We'll find him. Don't give up." Killian whispered against my ear and tucked my dripping hair behind one ear. His calloused fingertips left a trail of heat across my jaw and down my neck.

I forced a watery smile for him. Tenderness was totally out of character for this one. Out of the three, Killian was the oldest, the most experienced, and the deadliest. He was my protector in Sean's absence. Before he disappeared, Sean made him promise to take care of me. Like everything else he did, he did it with complete commitment. He had a lot of very good qualities, but he was bossy and impatient with humans. He was also intense, gorgeous, and scared the hell out of every human he came into contact with. Despite, or perhaps because of all of this, I was irrevocably tied to him in ways I no longer questioned and I loved him completely.

Later, I was cleaning up the kitchen when a familiar sunny face popped around the corner.

"Hey, darlin'!" Dec was back.

With a very girly screech of joy, I flew to him and he swung me around in a bear hug. Domino jumped up and wrapped her legs around him too. There wasn't a Primani alive who she wasn't crazy about. Laughing at her antics, Dec scooped her into his arms and gave her some love. With her brilliant black freckles and petite little face, she was pretty irresistible and she knew it.

"Oh, my God! It's been months! I've missed you!" I held him out at arm's length and drank in the sight of him. "You need a haircut!"

His blond hair was curling around his ears and was streaked white by the sun. Like Sean and Killian, he was beautifully made with a lean face, golden skin, and hypnotic eyes. His eyes were the same brilliant shade of blue they all had, but he had a ready smile with adorable dimples. The dimples hadn't made many appearances since Sean disappeared. None of us smiled very much anymore.

"Are you back for a while, Dec? It's been *hard* without you." I smiled and gazed into his face. It was so good to see him.

His eyes were shadowed and he needed to shave. He rubbed a hand over his scraggly beard. "I don't know. I hope so. I've missed you too, darlin'." His Irish accent slipped out every now and then. He winked at me.

"Tell me what's been happening here." He dragged a chair around and straddled his lean body around it.

"I'm working at the mall again. I don't seem to have an allowance from Alex like you guys do. I have to earn my money. Plus I can't stay cooped up here all day. Killian and I need a break from each other."

He chuckled darkly at that. "I bet. Are you still training?" His eyes traveled over my body taking in the muscles that I'd worked hard to maintain.

Sean had drilled me relentlessly on hand-to-hand combat and Krav Maga last year. He was adamant that I be able to protect myself from whatever might happen. I also had a gun and a knife that I carried on missions. I insisted Killian keep up my training to keep from getting out of shape. He didn't like it.

"Oh yeah, he hates it though. He says I'm obsessed and it's not healthy. That--coming from Killian. I think it's funny."

Killian walked in just then. "You are and it's not. Don't act like you're innocent here." He nodded at Dec and added, "She nearly ripped my throat out yesterday. She forgets she's supposed to be *practicing*." He rubbed his neck idly.

I flushed. "Well, it's a good thing you've got superpowers then! I'm not letting up. I *will* be ready."

Killian rolled his eyes at Dec. I couldn't read their minds and they knew it. I tapped my foot on the tile.

Dec peered closely at my face. "You're not sleeping again?"

I started to deny it, but there's no point. He knows me better than I know myself. "No, not really...the nightmares are back. And lately, I've been...hearing him."

His eyes widened. "Hearing him? How?"

I straddled one of the kitchen chairs. They weren't going to like this. I should've told them as soon as it started. "I have these dreams...Dec, he's calling to me. I hear his voice. It was faint at first...barely a whisper. Now though...it's clearer and more...insistent...he's scared." I shivered and wrapped my arms around myself.

Dec gripped my hand and said roughly, "Does he say anything else?"

"No, he's just...calling to me."

"And you think it's Sean?" Killian's expression was guardedly hopeful.

I met his eyes and nodded. "It's his voice, Killian. I *know* his voice."

"And when you meditate? Do you hear him then?"

I hesitated. "Yes, today I did. This is the first time though. It's only been happening for the past few days."

For the first time in a long time, there was a light in Killian's eyes. Like me, he'd been on autopilot for these months and the spark was gone. He stared out of the window for a few minutes and seemed to make a decision.

"Okay, we're going to try something. But I need some time to think it over first. You need to go to bed and take a nap. I need you to be rested for what I'm thinking. No dreaming! Just sleep. Let it restore your balance. Have you learned to recharge your energy yet?"

Excited now, I jumped up from my chair and asked a million questions. What was he thinking? What plan? Why wait? Recharge? Let's just do it! He finally held up a hand and I lost audio to my voice. My lips moved but no sound came out. I glared at him. I hated when they did that! He shrugged and gestured to Dec. Time to work his magic.

Grinning with full dimples, Dec said, "Come on, sweetheart, let's take a nap."

He draped an arm around me and I felt the warmth of his body seep into mine and let the drowsiness take over until my knees gave way. A delicate woodsy smell drifted through my mind and I closed my eyes. He scooped me up like a child and carried me to my bed. With a kiss on my forehead, he told me to embrace the oblivion. I slipped into a deep dreamless sleep for the first time in nearly a year.

Twenty-four hours later, I woke up a new person. I bounced into the kitchen in search of my menfolk and food. Both were conveniently located within arm's reach. They made me lunch: tuna salad on toast and a bowl of cut up cantaloupe. I gave them both a grateful glance and devoured my food. After gulping down a glass of milk, I sat back and asked about the plan.

Dec, the best healer of our group, picked up my hand and closed his eyes. After a minute, he declared I was healthy again. Apparently my *saol*, or energy force, was back in balance. I still felt like half a person without

Sean, but I didn't want to spoil the moment by sharing that little piece of information. I actually did feel better than I had yesterday, at least physically.

Killian's plan was a complicated one. I was a little leery of it after last year's exorcism in Manhattan. That plan was *simple* and we both nearly disappeared. It was almost a disaster...

"Are you crazy? What makes you think this will work?"

He actually grinned at me like a normal person. "Possibly, yes. It's been a rough year, babe. But I think this'll work. We're just going to explore and see if my hunch is right. If I'm right, we'll figure out how to bring him back."

Dec squeezed my hand and said seriously, "I'll be right here to pull you back. Don't worry at all about that. My whole focus will be keeping *you* safe. I know I can do that. I might lose *Killian*, but I won't lose you." He'd nearly lost us both last year and had been inconsolable over it. I knew he'd leave Killian hanging in purgatory if he had to make a choice this time.

I blanched and cried, "What? No, you can't lose him either!" I swung around to Killian who just lifted a shoulder in a half shrug. He seemed to agree with Dec on this point.

"Kidding, kidding! Let's do this before we talk ourselves out of it."

The three of us formed a circle on the living room floor with our hands joined and resting on our knees. The afternoon sun was fading and the light was dim. I wore the gold locket they'd made me for Christmas last year. I quickly said a prayer over it and kissed it for good luck. I'd grown a little superstitious about it...It contained a golden drop of blood from the four of us and I hoped it would help draw Sean back to us. The circle wasn't complete without our fourth person. Killian looked over at me and I nodded. I was as ready as I would ever be.

I closed my eyes and visualized the small open room I used for meditation. Dec's energy flowed in a steady stream from his hand into mine and the gentle current traveled through my bloodstream. His was pure supernatural energy and contained power that far outshone my own hybrid human-Primani energy force. The burst of energy sent my blood singing and pulsing in time to the rhythm of his heart. My muscles strummed and vibrated and I tingled all over. If left unfocused, I would probably float away. I was feeling lighter already.

I murmured, "Not so fast...slowly."

Deliberately, I drew that energy to my brain and used it to amp up my psychic powers. We hoped the Primani *saol* would give me the extra strength to do what we needed today. At the same time, I felt Killian's mind prodding mine.

Are you ready for me now? he asked silently.

Yes, slowly though.

I relaxed and mentally allowed him into the room. For the first time, I could see myself and another person standing within the imaginary room inside my head. He turned to me and smiled tightly. I gave him my hand and the two of us walked towards the small door that I opened in the back of the room. Breathing deeply, I focused on keeping the image steady. It was easier now than it was a year ago. I was stronger, much stronger. I opened the door to the misty forest and together we stepped into the unknown.

Now what? I asked Killian.

Call him. He squeezed my hand.

Reaching out with my mind, I called Sean.

Silence.

A few minutes went by and I called him again. Three times I called him; three times he didn't answer. It wasn't working. Damn it! Why isn't it working? A sudden spike of Dec's *saol* hit me like adrenaline. My arm went rigid with the force of it and I tensed against the pain.

He whispered, "Focus, darlin'. Keep going."

The *saol* spike came again.

I steadied my breathing and reached out to Sean again. I called him louder as if he was lost in a vast wilderness and could not hear me. Over and over I called him to me while sending out emotional memories of us. I visualized his face when he gave me the locket. His eyes glowed with pride as he watched my blood join theirs and turn to molten gold. I saw his body hovering above mine on the sailboat the first time he kissed me and my heart nearly stopped. Unleashed for the first time, his raw power flowed around us like a cocoon. I lay frozen while his eyes read my heart and knew I loved him.

And still I called him.

Sean, I need you. I love you. You have to come back to me.

Calmly, I waited.

Killian's strong fingers linked through my own as we wandered through the forest. He called to Sean too. They were like brothers and their bond was strong. He joined his psychic energy with mine and amplified the power of my voice and my projections. We hoped this would help Sean hear me and find his way back to me. This also meant Killian had to see everything I projected and I'm sure he didn't enjoy it. But he loved Sean too and would do anything to bring him back. I stopped calling his name and waited again. Killian grimaced when I pushed out my memory of the night we became lovers. More than our bodies were joined that night. Our energy, our essence, our souls were joined. There could be no separating us after that. And yet, the explosion had ripped him away and I was still stinging with the loss. I called him to me and waited.

If he's out there, he'll come. Killian's eyes were distant as he tried to reassure me.

After an eternity the faint sound of my name drifted on the breeze and disappeared. It was barely audible but we both heard it. Killian froze, listening. My heart pounded so loudly it drowned out the sound.

"Mica! Stop. Breathe." Dec jolted me again and pressed my fingers to stop me from shaking.

Careful to not break the spell, Killian wrapped his hand over mine and gripped the locket between us. He smiled into my eyes and told me to call Sean again.

Now he channeled all three of our energies through the locket and out to wherever Sean was waiting. Golden rays of light streamed from the locket and disappeared into the mist. I stared into Killian's eyes and saw universes yawning in front of me. Sean was out there, somewhere, in those universes. This time when I called Sean it echoed through the forest like a lightning strike.

Again!

Sean!

Louder! Killian's eyes glowed cobalt now and he stared past me into the forest. He sensed Sean; felt him out there.

Sean! Come back!

As the last echoes of my voice faded into memory, a movement caught my eye. My eyes followed the motion. There, in the mist, a swirl of golden light motes danced between two trees. Sean! Killian murmured words over the locket in the strange language of theirs. The locket glowed in our hands but I didn't take my eyes off of the light in the trees. Killian's voice grew stronger and his words were clearer. As he spoke, the swirl of light gradually formed a solid core of *saol* that hovered in the air. He commanded, compelled, insisted...the words were nonsense to me, but the power of his voice sent chills down my back. The more Killian spoke the hotter the locket got until it burned my skin. I tried to let go but Killian instantly squeezed my hand against it.

No!

I gritted my teeth against the pain and kept my focus on the vision.

Come on, baby! I turned my eyes to where his face should be and waited. After another moment, the core of *saol* shimmered and settled into the shape and features of a man. As I held my breath, Killian's words rang through the trees and the locket burned into my hand. I blinked and when I opened my eyes a pair of cobalt eyes bored desperately into mine from across the clearing. I started to move but Killian froze me in place.

Don't move! Go slowly. We need to back out of this and bring him with us. Focus, don't lose him!

Holding hands in a death grip, Killian and I slowly backed up until we leaned against the door to my room. All the while, I kept my eyes glued to Sean's and pulled him with us. He followed like a man in a trance, but at least he came. One step at a time, he followed us. Once we got back to the little room, I stopped and reeled Sean in. He came forward slowly until he stood in front of us. Afraid to startle him, Killian and I slowly released the locket and each took one of his hands. Killian withdrew from my mind at the same time I mentally left the room.

When I opened my eyes, I sat with Dec and Killian in our little circle. I blinked in a daze and sagged against Dec. His face was red and he was sweating from the effort to keep us grounded. His body was pale gold and the glow was just fading as he retracted his *saol*. Killian's eyes were black against the chalkiness of his skin. Mine must've been pale too because he looked alarmed when his eyes cleared enough to see again.

"Are you okay?" His voice was shaky and his eyes still unfocused. He opened and closed them trying to reset his vision.

It took me a second to find my voice. I wasn't sure if I was okay or not. What just happened here? My brain felt like tissue paper and my hand burned like fire. I opened my hand and held it up. Killian held his up too. In the center of both of our palms was a perfect imprint of the heart-shaped locket. It was branded into our skin.

Where was Sean?

"We were so close! I saw him. I *felt* his hand. What happened?" I was thrashed. This sucked.

Killian slowly shook his head in confusion. "I don't know. It should've worked."

"Damn it! This sucks!" I stalked to the window and bounced my forehead against the glass. Oh God, what happened to him? Where was he? We were so close. I swiped at the tears that threatened to fall and sighed. I wanted to get angry, but there was no point in railing against fate now. It didn't change things. We were close so we would try again. I would never give up on him. He was my other half. I wouldn't be whole again without him. The click of the door closing told me I was alone with my thoughts and I sagged against the window.

Suddenly the atmosphere in the room changed and a blue charge of electricity zigzagged along the outline of the window frame in front of me.

A sheer reflection took shape.

I whipped around to see him hovering unsteadily in the doorway. He wasn't quite standing on the ground but he was solid. His eyes blazed with familiar blue fire but they were unfocused. He was holding out one hand trying to balance. Shrieking his name, I threw myself into his arms and knocked him into the wall. Completely unchecked, the current inside of him careened through me nearly stopping my heart. I gasped at the pain in my chest but kissed every inch of his beautiful face.

"Oh God, it's really you!" I repeated over and over again.

The more I kissed him the more he seemed to steady himself. He wobbled a bit as his body became more solid, more real. The fire in his eyes dimmed to the normal midnight blue and his skin to a healthy golden tan. Still wobbly, he shook his head from side to side and sucked in a deep breath. With his *saol* under control and his feet on the ground, he finally smiled his heartbreaking smile at me and I dissolved in happy tears.

"Killian! Dec! Come quick!"

They ran into the room and skidded to a stumbling halt. Breaking into huge grins, they swept us both into a group hug. Poor Sean was so overwhelmed with sudden life he couldn't control his *saol*. He flickered on and off like a lightning bug.

"Oh, man, it's a miracle! I am *so* glad to see you!" Dec vibrated with happiness and hugged Sean so hard he lifted him off of his feet.

Killian pulled me aside. "Put him to bed before he falls down. He's going to need some time to recover."

I grinned like an idiot and he broke into a rare smile. I swear he winked at me but I'll never be sure. It happened too fast.

"Good job, babe. I knew you could do it," he added with look of respect.

Sean took my hand and I led him back to the room we'd shared last year. He was really quiet. In fact, he hadn't said a word yet...I shut the door behind us and drank in the sight of him. It was a miracle.

"Come on, let's lay down. You're exhausted." I gently pushed him to the bed. His movements were stiff and awkward as if he wasn't familiar with his body.

I curled against his side and ran my hands over him. I couldn't stop touching him. He was real! I'd imagined him and remembered him a million times this year, but my imagination wasn't up to the real thing. He was muscular and strong and even totally exhausted, he was incredibly beautiful and sexy. I couldn't stop touching him just to be sure he was really here. Up on my elbows, I smiled into his eyes. I was ridiculously happy. Grabbing him by both cheeks, I kissed his whole face again.

Stiffly, he pulled my lips to his and kissed me softly. "Mica?" he whispered before falling into a deep sleep.

Two days later, he was still asleep and I was back in bed with him. It was nearing midnight and I couldn't fall asleep. I was too happy. Instead, I sat on the bed and stared at Sean. Pale moonlight drifted across his face and highlighted the strong cheekbones and heavy lashes. His face was softer in sleep and his body was relaxed. I lightly traced the shape of his face with my finger and held my breath as the faint glow followed my touch. Years ago I'd discovered the quirky little reaction. When his guard was down, as in sleep, the energy flowed close to the surface. He controlled it when wearing his human façade but the golden light was always just below his skin. Inspired, I trailed my finger around the hard muscle of his bare shoulder and across his chest. I kissed the tiny freckle under his collarbone and smiled. He was perfect and he was here. I would never want anything else. I meant to kiss him and go to sleep but when I touched my lips to his, his mouth held mine and deepened the kiss. Little lights flashed behind my eyes as my head swam and I melted against him.

Sometime later, he held our joined hands behind my head and smiled down at me. The amazing connection was still there. Our individual bodies were gone and there was only one.

There was no *Mica* and no *Sean*.

There was only *us*.

"You're so beautiful. I must be dreaming," he murmured sleepily. Tightening his arm around me, he kissed me one last time and fell asleep.

The sounds of birds singing woke me the next morning. Sunlight streamed into the room and a soft breeze trickled in through the screens. I stretched lazily across the bed and reached for a sheet. Mm, I was so comfortable and closed my eyes for more sleep. Then I remembered today was a new day. I sprang out of bed so fast I stumbled into the dresser and ricocheted off of the door jam.

Running to the kitchen, I called his name. Did I imagine the whole thing? It wouldn't be the first time that I'd dreamed about him…I skidded around the corner and stopped dead at the sight in front of me. Dec and Sean sat with their heads together at the kitchen table. From their expressions, they were talking seriously about something and I hesitated to interrupt. Instead, I hovered just outside the doorway and chewed my lip. Should I go in or not?

"Spying, Mica?" Killian observed behind me.

I jumped with a squeak and Sean glanced over at me. I elbowed Killian in the ribs and bounced into the room. Sean stood and met my eyes. Smiling, I went to him and kissed him good morning.

"Are you all right, Sean?"

"Considering where I've been, I'd say I'm much better!" He laughed but there was an edge to it. He was still freaked out.

"Where *have* you been? We've been looking for you for a year," I said.

He frowned and looked sharply at Killian. "A year? What do you mean?"

It was my turn to frown. "You've been gone for almost a year. We've been crazy without you."

Shaking his head in denial, Sean sat down. "That's impossible! What day is it?"

Concerned, Killian answered him with narrowed eyes, "She's right, Sean. It's been nearly a year. Where have you been?"

"I don't know...everywhere? Maybe nowhere?" His mouth was set and his eyes reflected his pain. He looked out the window and reined in his emotions.

My heart squeezed in sympathy. "What happened to you?"

He hesitated. "I don't really know. One minute I was in the basement of the farmhouse and the next I was...scattered."

Dec blanched. "Scattered?" He shuddered and shut his eyes in sympathetic pain.

Killian inhaled sharply and said, "No!"

I looked uncertainly from one to the other, but none of them would meet my eyes. They were all in their own private hell as they absorbed Sean's words.

"I don't understand. Someone tell me what you're talking about." My voice trembled as I tried to resist the strong emotions swirling around me.

Sean shrugged off the shock and started his story. "Being *scattered* is bad, Mica. We can only die if our *saol* core is vaporized. We call it being 'scattered' because all of the particles are scattered into the winds. A lucky demon can kill us this way...and apparently other things can cause it too."

I interrupted him, "You can't heal yourself?"

"No, we don't survive it because we can't usually find all of the scattered particles. Our core is unique to each of us, Mica...like your DNA is. Without all of it, we're missing essential parts. It would be like you losing a chunk of your brain or an organ. You'd have a hole there. You might be able to function like that. But what if you lost vital strands of DNA suddenly? You would have serious problems. It's the same thing with us. As far as healing ourselves goes, well, when the *saol* is gone, we have no way...no energy source...to heal ourselves. It's just too overwhelming for us to do."

I paled and swung around to Killian for confirmation. He grunted his agreement. "Oh my God! It's a miracle we got you back then," I said through fresh tears. It *was* a miracle.

Dec got up and hugged Sean hard and sniffed back tears. Hesitantly, he asked, "What was it like?"

"At first there was nothing and I just floated. I didn't even know what had happened. My thoughts were scattered too and I couldn't remember anything. There was nothing...just mist. But then after a while, I felt Mica out there, somewhere. I didn't realize it was her though. I just felt a connection...an anchor...to a place." He paused, thinking of something more. "Did you cry for me?" He cupped my face in his hands searching for the answer.

I was crying now. "Yes! I cried and I prayed and I pleaded and I begged for you to come back to me…It was a…dark time."

"I felt you…your sadness."

Killian scowled at the memory and got up to pace. "It was…difficult…especially for Mica. She saw everything that happened inside the house that night. She watched you explode and disappear. She relived the nightmare every night."

And he had been beside me for most of this, but he didn't need to mention that now.

"And we couldn't find you. We searched for you everywhere, but no one knew what happened or where you went," Dec added. "Killian and I took turns looking but you were gone." His voice broke and he coughed to cover it.

They had been gaunt with fatigue and lack of food. They hadn't slept or eaten for days at a time while traveling all over the world trying to sense Sean. I finally convinced them to slow down and eat; to take care of themselves too. When Dec collapsed one night, I put my foot down and demanded they eat. After that, they still went out looking but they ate and slept in between trips. Traveling, as they call teleporting, takes a huge toll on their energy stores and it was only a matter of time before one of them burned out.

Sean turned to Killian and said in a voice swelling with emotion, "I *felt* her, Killian. Like a chain holding me to this plane, I felt Mica's hold on me even when I floated. I wanted to let go and drift away but Mica, I heard you. I felt your pain. I don't know how, but it's true. Your voice anchored me and I couldn't let go. Then I heard you call my name and it was irresistible. Every part of me was drawn to you--I guess you really are my other half."

I fingered my locket and considered Killian's plan, his magic. He was a genius; there was no other explanation for him. He always knew what to do and how to use our powers. We would be lost without him here. To his intense surprise, I grabbed Killian and kissed him on the mouth before he could say a word of protest.

"I love you! You're amazing!"

Dec explained to Sean, "It was his plan that brought you back to us. We're all grateful that it worked." He grinned at Killian's scowl.

Killian just grunted and said, "It wasn't just me. It took all of us to bring you back. I'll fill you in later. For now, why don't you two go do something outside of the bedroom? I don't need any more of Mica's porno memories in my head!"

"Killian!"

He laughed at my outrage and pointed to the back door.

An hour later, we left the house and wandered off into the woods. There was a pretty creek nearby and we used to hike to it all the time. We headed towards it now. Shyly, I peered up at him from under my lashes. It was no use. I was going to cry again. Damn it! I was really trying to get a grip on my emotions, but they were all over the place since he came home.

Sean gently tugged me to him and wrapped his arms around me. I sank against him and took a deep breath. He rubbed my back and rested his chin on my head.

"You're scared of me," he observed quietly.

"No, I..." I started to protest but stopped. He was right. I was afraid. I didn't know how to act after all of the pain I'd been through this year. I didn't really believe he was actually here. Surely this was another dream.

"Why don't we just take things slowly? We can get to know each other again."

"Slow is good." I pulled back and gazed into his eyes. I could feel the imprint of his hands against my back. He was definitely real and he was here. "Kiss me?"

He hesitated for a split second and lowered his mouth to mine. I wrapped my hands around his neck and kissed him back until I ran out of oxygen and had to gasp for air.

I pressed against him like a cat and he groaned against my neck. Every thought in my head disappeared until there was only him.

Later, I commented, "I'm so glad we're getting to know each other again. I feel better already."

A cross between a laugh and a groan greeted me. Sean stretched and said, "You're going to need to work on your shyness, Mica."

I laughed and flopped down across his stomach just to hear the air whooshing out. He rolled me over and pinned me on my back with his nose pressed to mine. "I love you." He kissed me with a smile. "Near or far."

"Don't leave me again. I couldn't breathe without you. My heart was broken."

"At least it wasn't every molecule in your body."

Chapter 3: Reunion

DINNER WITH FRIENDS should be fun. Unless your boyfriend was a supernatural being who had been in limbo for a year. My friends weren't too happy with him at the moment. After the, uh, accident, I couldn't bring myself to tell them he had died. For one thing, I didn't know that for sure; and for another, I didn't want to jinx him. So I had to say he left me. If I had been cheerful about it, there might not have been a problem. As it was, the past year sucked; and I was by turns, depressed, militant, and secretive. Once in a very great while, Dec or Killian made me socialize in public. Dec nagged at me and bribed me with pizza. Hanging out with Killian was fine for me, but he tended to clear entire rooms with just a glance. Besides, he didn't really like people. He thought humans were annoying. We didn't go out too often.

Our little group of friends had shrunk to a couple. Ricki and Kevin were in college in Ohio as was Tyler. Dani and Aric still lived in town and went to the Plattsburgh campus of New York State University. Dani helped out in her mom's little shop Zen. Aric worked on his dad's farm and at Peabody's as a bartender. Everyone was very busy these days. Dani was still mostly my best friend but I didn't see her too often. What with my new career as super-secret special agent for the Forces of Good...I was a little busy training to kill bad guys and learning to use really cool gadgets like night vision binoculars or NVBs. These were not activities I could share with Dani.

"Are you sure this is a good idea?" I asked for the third time. We were sitting in the car waiting for the others to show.

Sean chuckled at me and said, "Sweetheart, you love Dani and want to see her. I'm back for good now. You'll need to tell her eventually. Don't you think?"

"Yes, but let's put it off--"

"Chicken!" He pulled me up for a kiss and I gladly joined in.

He set me away from him and scanned my face with curious eyes.

"What's wrong?"

"You're not glowing anymore. Remember when you used to glow every time I touched you?"

"Oh, yeah, that was awesome. So glad that's stopped. Don't worry, I still *feel* like I'm on fire!" I smiled seductively and fanned my cleavage.

Killian joined us in the car. "She's really mastered her powers this year. You'll be amazed when you see what she can do now."

I blushed at the compliment. "Wow, that's so sweet. Thanks, Killian. I didn't think you'd noticed."

Dec snorted from the back seat. "You'll never get another compliment, darlin'. Are you recording this?"

Killian added, "Well, she's worked hard and she doesn't complain. I'd say this compliment is earned."

We pulled into the parking lot and I immediately spotted Aric's car. Damn, they were here. I was hoping they'd forget. I fidgeted with my locket chain until Sean's fingers closed over my hand.

"She loves you, remember? She's not going to be upset with you about this."

"No, she'll be upset with you!"

"I've been through a lot this year. I think I can handle one pissed off female. Give me some credit, okay?"

"Okay, okay. Let's get this over with."

As usual, Killian went in first and Sean and I went in next. Dec brought up the rear. Old habits die hard and none of us went anywhere without practicing security measures. Scanning the room for bad guys and exits was second nature to me now. Correction: usually I did it too. Tonight I only had eyes for Dani. I sought her out from across the room and held my breath as she discovered Sean. Dani's face went through a series of expressions when she spotted me and then saw Sean with me. Her eyebrows went straight up and her clear grey eyes narrowed. Aric flinched as she dug her nails into his arm. Mouth set and eyes hard, Dani marched over to me and hauled me off to the patio for a little chat. I looked helplessly behind me at Sean who just shrugged and waved me out the door.

"What is *he* doing here?" she demanded as soon as we were alone.

I unhooked her fingers from my arm and answered, "Uh, he's back."

"Back?"

"For good." I smiled really big to show this made me happy.

She scowled. "You didn't tell me you were seeing him again. When did this happen?"

"Recently. Very recently…like a couple of days ago. It was a surprise for all of us." I took her hands in mine and pleaded, "Dani, I love you. You're my best friend…my sister. But you have to trust me on this. Sean and I are okay now."

She started to respond but then paused and glanced down at my locket. "What on earth…?" Distracted, she reached out and picked up my locket. She dropped it like it burned her and shook her fingers.

"Ouch! What's with the locket? It's glowing."

Her fingertips were red.

"Uh, magic?" I laughed it off with a joke and a shrug.

"Uh-huh."

She narrowed her eyes doubtfully and added, "You know I'm not stupid. Don't bullshit me."

"It's no big deal. It's just a locket."

"Yeah, sure it is. I don't believe you, but go ahead and keep your secrets. One day you'll regret it. Let's go back to the others. I'm sure Aric is ready to be rescued," Dani said.

"Oh, you bitches don't need to leave so soon. We just got here." A familiar cold voice froze me in my tracks and I rolled my eyes. Again?

I turned to see Scott Flynn and three others spread out across the back entrance to the patio. Scott's smile was hard as he pushed off from the wall and stalked towards us. His thick dark hair and deep-set brown eyes were still the same. The expression on his face was new though. Psychopath? Newborn vampire? Demon?

Pick one; they all fit.

I hadn't seen him for a long time. He looked even more unstable than he did last year. I hadn't been in town much and he'd been in and out of jail. Unfortunately he'd survived his latest stint in jail. Damn, his timing sucked. I swiveled to the other exit and it was blocked too. Not a surprise. We were trapped on the enclosed patio. Instead of screaming for help, I faced Scott as he made his way towards me. I planted my feet and got ready to hand his head to him. I was more than ready and it showed in my face. He took a good look at my expression and lost a little of his swagger. He slowed down and moved with more caution. I cracked my knuckles and stretched.

Purring obscenely, he said, "I've missed you. You and me have some catching up to do. You're looking good." His eyes raked my body and settled insolently on my crotch. He spread his hands in a gesture of goodwill and added, "You might want to play nice."

One of his thuggy friends barked a mean laugh at that. "Yeah or we all get a crack at you when he's done!"

I looked at that one and said, "Shut the hell up, moron." Dani gasped and dug her nails into my arm. Out of the side of my mouth, I said, "Let go of me and stay back. I've got this. Yell for Aric."

Dani opened her mouth to scream, but one of them grabbed her around the waist and clapped a hand over her mouth. She struggled and kicked at him, but he pressed his arm against her throat and she froze. I watched out of the corner of my eye as he held her against him and groped her with his free hand. Her eyes were spitting fire but her face was turning red as she lost oxygen. I wanted to yell for Dec but didn't want Dani to learn their secret so I sent an SOS to Killian instead. Oh, please be paying attention!

Killian! It's Flynn. Hurry!

Scott took advantage of my hesitation and lunged at me. I stepped to the side and he lumbered forward missing me completely. I swung around to face him and kicked him squarely in the jaw. His head snapped back and he staggered. I sensed another guy coming from behind me and dove forward to take Scott's legs out from under him. He landed hard on his back with a whoosh. Before he could react, I kicked him in the face, hopefully breaking his nose. Blood splattered everywhere. The sound of screaming broke through my adrenaline rush. Dani's captor had pinned her against the ground and was trying to shove his hand down her shorts. She was screaming bloody murder so he punched her in the face.

In seconds, the patio was crowded. Sean, Killian, Dec, and Aric all burst through the doors at the same time. Aric took one look at Dani and went berserk. He threw himself into the guy and knocked him sideways onto the ground. Dec had to drag Aric off the guy to keep him from killing him. Once the guy was out cold, Dec and Aric led a sobbing Dani out to Aric's car. Two of the smarter criminals melted into the darkness while I held Scott Flynn in place with a boot against his throat and Sean stood behind his head. Blood was pouring out of his nose and his eyes looked up at me furiously. He wasn't afraid. He was waiting me out.

I put a little pressure on his throat and he grunted in pain. "Not so tough now?" I mimicked Killian's feral smile and dug my heel in a little harder. His eyes showed fear then.

"That's what I thought!" I smirked and put a smidgeon more weight on my heel.

"Mica! No killing!" Killian ordered, amused.

Sean squatted down and snarled, "Yeah, don't kill him. I have a promise to keep." He leaned into Scott's face and said something too low for me to hear. Whatever it was, it had the desired effect; Scott frantically turned his face away.

I laughed out loud. Scott was getting a very close up view of the unusual eyes that announced, without a doubt, that Sean wasn't wholly human. His eyes burned in their sockets when he was in killing-mode, or soldier-mode, as I called it. It was a Primani thing. It happened when they were fighting demons, teleporting, or just really mad. It was an involuntary reaction to the *saol* that they used. It still scared the hell out of me even though I was perfectly safe with them. Apparently Scott didn't feel safe if the kitten sounds he was making were any indication. I laughed harder.

"Get the fuck up." Sean hauled Scott to his feet with one hand. He shoved him into Killian who pulled both arms behind his back. Before I could say another word, Sean pulled me to him and kissed me with such intensity that my whole body glowed and threw off waves of searing heat. My eyes burned like fire and everything seemed oddly bright like I was wearing sunglasses. He'd turned me into a road flare…Scott's eyes went huge and he started shaking violently. He tried to turn his head away but Killian forced him to look.

Understanding the game now, I leisurely turned to face Scott again. "Touch me again and I'll light you on fire."

He blanched and fell to his knees.

"Oh, you'll burn."

Killian laughed at Sean's horrified expression. "Dude, you've got no idea!"

Chapter 4: Scented

SUNNY DANI WASN'T SMILING today. A shadow passed over her eyes as she stared out the window. She had no bruises on the outside, but I sensed her pain and my heart twisted in sympathy. She was the sweetest soul I knew in this crazy new world of mine. I wanted her to stay innocent. I hadn't told her anything about the earlier run-ins with Scott to keep her from worrying. She'd had no idea that we had a history. She turned back to me and sighed.

"How are you feeling?" I whispered.

Her mom was listening outside her bedroom door. I didn't want to say too much. Instead, I handed her some cookies I baked and tried a smile.

She frowned back at me.

"I know you're worried about me. Don't be. I'm not the first girl to be attacked by a stupid guy. I'm just glad Aric got there before he could...well, you know." Her hand fluttered and dropped back to her lap. She tapped her fingers against the side of her leg and pressed her lips together.

Her sadness was breaking my heart.

"I'm so sorry! It happened so fast! I can't believe they dragged you into this."

Usually Scott and his merry band of psychopaths tried to drag *me* someplace private for their entertainment. His thug friend must be new in town.

Dani looked me in the eye and said, "This has happened before, hasn't it? You and Scott seemed to have a rhythm going." Her voice was soft but laced with underlying steel that sent an alarm bell off inside my head.

I squirmed in my chair next to her. "Uh, no, it's not. He just won't leave me alone. Sean and Killian have beaten the shit out of him a couple of times but he keeps coming back. The guys have been training me for the past few years. I was ready for him this time. I don't need help any more. One of these days I'll probably have to kill him."

Dani's eyes narrowed. "You say that so casually; like you've done it before."

"I'm not trying to be casual. But I'm not going to let the psychopath kill me. That's what he wants and I'm not going to let him do it."

"Okay," she paused and asked, "And what about Sean? And Dec? There's something not right about them."

Yeeeeah...so *not* going to go there with her.

Stiffening, I sat back and crossed my arms. I knew I looked defensive but I had to draw the line. This wasn't something I could share, even with Dani.

"They are who they are. Nothing more, nothing less."

Suddenly she leaned forward and grabbed my wrist. "You're still lying to me! Do you really think I can't tell? You're my best friend; I know you better than you think I do. How can you keep secrets from me?"

Okay...not sadness after all.

As her nails dug into my palm, I realized I had let her down. I was wrong...I'd put her in danger and not even thought about it. I sucked. Damn.

"Okay! I'm a horrible person! I'm sorry for getting you hurt! I'm not trying to lie to you, but there are things I can't tell you. They're not my secrets to tell. Please try to understand that."

Unpeeling her fingers, I got up and looked out the window. It was beginning to get dark outside. Dani's mom was making dinner down in the kitchen and I should be getting home. This conversation couldn't go much further anyway.

"Look, I hate this. I love you but I can't say anything else. Is there anything I can do for you? Other than spill my guts?" I hugged her and she stiffened but then hugged me back.

"I love you too, but I'm still pissed at you. I don't care about that idiot guy. I care that you're involved in something that you won't tell me about. That hurts and I don't like it. I'll let it go for now, but you're gonna have to tell me sooner or later."

I looked into her pretty grey eyes and sensed she was more disappointed than angry now. That was better, but not much. I still felt like a bitch.

"We'll see. Let Aric spoil you for a while. That's what he thinks he needs to do. If you don't let him help you, he'll be crushed." With that last piece of advice, I headed back to the farmhouse.

As I pulled up to the driveway, I noticed all the lights were off. Hmm, that's strange. Where was everyone? I parked the car and shut the door quietly. Before heading inside, I looked around the outside. No sign of an attack-- no shattered windows, nothing blown up, nothing unusual at all. Huh. Reassured, I went in through the kitchen door. Domino greeted me and trotted along beside me, her tail low to the floor. The house was quiet. The kitchen was spotless. No one had cooked in it today. That was odd. The guys ate a lot. It wasn't like them to clean up the kitchen so well. Uneasy now, I crept through the living room back to the bedrooms. I listened for voices or music but the house was deathly silent. I was getting more nervous the further into the house I walked. I peeked into the bedrooms as I passed by. Dec's was empty of life but a disaster as usual. He never worried about putting clothes away or making his bed. Life was too short.

I hesitated at Killian's door with my hand on the knob. I hadn't been inside this room in a very long time and the last time had been disturbing. I opened the door and peered into the darkness. His scent stopped me in the doorway. Woodsy and musky, it was unique to him and conjured up a vivid image of the last time I was here. I groaned and closed my eyes to stop the memories. They came anyway.

That night, I had been dreaming about walking down the endless hallway again. In my dream, I tried to open the doors and they were locked. They were locked until I came to this door. The door had swung open and I had walked blindly into the room. In front of me was a soft glowing light and I reached out and touched it with my hand.

Minutes later, I woke up flat on my back with stars in my eyes. My brain struggled to adjust to being smacked against the wood floor. On top of that, my skin tingled unpleasantly all over and I was drooling. Killian, with a sheet draped loosely around his hips, crouched beside me looking worried. He was shaking me by the shoulder.

"What happened?" It felt like I was hit with a stun gun.

"You were sleepwalking. You, uh, startled me. I'm so sorry, babe."

He pulled me up and I flopped over. My legs didn't seem to work just yet. The natural response to falling is to grab onto something, right? Is it my fault I missed Killian altogether but did manage to snag a fistful of the sheet on my way to the floor?

My face flamed again just thinking about it. Good Lord, was there no escaping the memory? It took months to get the image of Killian's amused face out of my mind. Then there's the rest of him...Focus. Focus. I took a deep breath. Where is he now? Not in the room; that's for sure. I backed out of the room and went to my own. It was empty too. I switched on the lamp and saw a note on the nightstand. It was from Sean. I read it once quickly and then again more slowly. It was signed, 'Always, Sean.'

Well, hmm. What to do now? They would be gone for a while and I was to stay put and not get into trouble. Huh. Why do they always assume I'm going to get into trouble? It's not like I go looking for it! Domino had been lying on the bed watching me with interest. Now she straightened her ears and focused her attention on the note.

Well, now what?

"You want to know what the note says?"

She wagged her tail.

Tapping the folded paper against my leg, I explained, "Mission. Alex says they've got a lead on Dagin's new lab and they need to go check it out. They'll be out for a week or more. It's status quo for me and you, Princess. Looks like we get to hold down the fort again. Are you up for it?"

She yawned and daintily stepped down from the bed. She stopped under the alarm pad and looked up. *I can't do it alone.*

Breathe in, breathe out...I sucked in hot thick air and grimaced. Mile three was going to kill me today. I was struggling to keep my pace and finish. Sweat ran into my eyes and burned like acid. Damn, it was freaky hot today! Domino loped easily beside me as we passed the mile marker. She wasn't even panting hard; that's all the proof I need. She's not a real dog. A real dog would be hot too.

"You know you're not a real dog. Admit it!"

She rolled her eyes at me and kept trotting along. *Amateur!*

Laughing and sucking at more air, I slowed to a walk and slugged some water. I poured her a bit in my palm and squatted so she could drink. Out of the corner of my eye, I noticed a man watching me. He was standing next to a dark blue car in the parking lot. Nonchalantly, I turned so I could see him better while I poured some more water out.

"Keep drinking," I ordered the dog.

She licked at my palm and lifted an ear.

"The guy in the khaki shorts and red polo is watching us."

I poured more water and glanced up under my lashes. Yep, he was still there and still looking our direction. His mouth was moving just a little bit. Ah, he was using a mic. Okay, either he was a cop, a terrorist, or someone on Dagin's payroll. None of those options were great. He was dressed in pleated khakis and a polo shirt. He didn't fit my image of a terrorist, so that left cop or demon. Would a demon bother with designer labels? I wasn't sure. Either way, not good. Would he follow me openly or try to hide it? Let's see.

I led Domino back to my car and took my time getting situated. I glanced around to see if he was still paying attention but he was gone. I swiveled around in all directions but he wasn't there. Did I imagine that whole thing? No, surely not. I pointed the car towards the house wishing the guys were home. They hadn't come back yet, and I wasn't expecting them for a few more days. I drove the long way home and kept an eye out for a tail. If someone was following me, they were very good. I didn't see anyone. Finally I headed home and parked inside the garage for once. Slipping inside, I set the house alarm and called Sean. He answered on the third ring.

"What's up?" He sounded distracted.

"I love you too! And oh, by the way, I think someone was watching me today."

"Don't be a smart ass. What happened?"

I explained about the polo shirt guy in the park. After listening to my story, Sean was quiet for a minute. "Well, what do you think?" I asked.

"It's possible that you're under surveillance. But the question is by whom. Dagin? Maybe...but that would be unusual for him. The truce is over so he'd probably just kill you if he saw you by yourself. His business partners shouldn't know about you. Um, my guess would be feds."

Yikes!

"Feds? What would they want with me?" I checked the mirror for a sniper beam in the middle of my forehead and stepped away from the window.

"You told me about the men who were at the house in Vermont. They wore uniforms and had NVGs and night scopes on their rifles. They were planning to raid the compound while we were inside. Bad guys wouldn't do that. They would've just stormed it and shot the place up. So those guys you saw were most likely legitimate law enforcement. Local cops wouldn't have jurisdiction over arms dealing ops. Could be FBI or even Homeland Security...hmm..."

The silence stretched.

"Sean?"

No response.

The line went dead. No signal. Crap. I needed more than 'hmm' from him! I hit the redial button and got voice mail. I left him a message and got to work. If someone was watching me, I needed to be ready to dash in a hurry. I pulled out a backpack and filled it with things I'd need if I have to bug out: a couple of changes of clothes, toothbrush, extra ammo, cell phone charger, extra cell phone, and some other important things. I packed a real suitcase with stuff for a longer stay and put that in the trunk along with Domino's food and extra bowls. I added some blankets and first aid stuff and some big bottles of water. Lastly, I rummaged through our stash of protein bars. There. I could leave in a hurry by car or by foot. I loaded my Sig Sauer P229 and put it in the holster on the small of my back. There. Now I was armed. I felt loads better already.

I had the whole afternoon to kill and was too edgy to do anything productive. Instead, I practiced the Krav Maga techniques that Sean and Killian taught me over and over again. I could disarm an attacker who had a gun or a knife. I could kill an attacker if necessary. I really hoped it wouldn't be necessary. I had to shoot two men last year and I still felt guilty about it. Oh, they deserved it--they were trying to kill me at the time. It was self-defense, but that didn't make me feel good about it. I would do it again if I had to though.

It was 2:00 a.m. and I was restless. Domino rolled over and grumbled at me for waking her up. She was relaxed so I should be too. After all, she's the canine with super hearing. I finally gave up pacing and checking the windows and went to sleep.

My alarm went off at 8:00 and I fell out of bed in a panic. I had my gun out and pointed at the closed bedroom door before I realized it was the alarm clock, and I had to go to work. Smacking myself in the forehead, I put the gun down and took a shower. The day was uneventful. I watched for a tail everywhere I went. I didn't see anyone suspicious. By the end of the day, I had a splitting headache from the tension and actually hoped someone would knock me out.

"Okay, Princess, it's your turn to play lookout. I need to get rid of this headache." I rubbed my face against Domino's soft fur and gave her a pat.

I lay down on the couch and closed my eyes. Dec had taught me to heal myself, and I needed to practice. This headache was killing me so I was going to give it a shot. With careful deliberation, I visualized the warm *saol* inside of me as it flowed gently through my veins into my muscles and organs. I saw it flow under the fragile skin that covered me. It was pale gold as it moved along. Slowing my breathing as much as possible, I gently urged it towards the back of my head where the pain was the worst. A faint light glowed behind my eyelids as I did this. My body was relaxed and yet taut with the current. The feeling was both soothing and invigorating. I felt like I could float away or run forever. It was powerful. *I* was powerful. The pain gradually receded and then disappeared completely.

Domino growled a warning deep in her throat and I slowly opened my eyes. She stared at the door to the kitchen with ears cocked and tail wagging slowly. I sat up and moved to pick up my gun from the table.

"What?"

In response, she jumped forward and ran towards the doorway. At the same moment, the air was sucked out of the room. Killian and Sean appeared and Domino skidded to a stop in front of them. Laughing with real pleasure, Killian reached down and rubbed her ears. Sean's eyes found mine instantly and widened in surprise. He stiffened and Killian looked up.

"Well, damn," Killian said in wonder.

"What's wrong with you two? Did I grow another head?"

Sean cautiously moved towards me and turned my arm so I could see into the mirror. What now?

"Look," he ordered softly.

The eyes that stared back at me weren't mine. They were backlit with a soft white light. It wasn't the vivid blue fire that defined the Primani. No, the light was barely there, but faintly shining just behind the midnight blue of my iris. What did this mean? Even as I watched, the light dimmed and faded away again.

"Cool." No witty comments popped into my head just then.

Sean shook his head and silently communed with Killian. Both looked over at me and smiled.

"You're becoming high maintenance, Princess," Killian commented and then laughed. "I don't know what to do with you anymore."

Sean asked, "What were you doing? I could feel your heat before we traveled. We knew you home."

"That's cool! You felt me?"

Killian snorted with impatience.

"Sorry! It's interesting! Okay, I had a bad headache and decided to practice healing myself. It worked. I felt like I could fly away and run for miles. It was amazing!"

"Hmm. It sounds like you healed yourself and recharged yourself at the same time. *That's* different."

"Really? It doesn't feel that way to you?"

"Not quite, darlin'. I think we might feel it differently because it's always been a part of us though. I *always* feel like I can fly," Sean explained with a cocky grin.

"Of course, you *can* fly so you'd know! Why can't I travel too?"

Killian came back into the room and paused by the hallway.

You've been in my room? He sent his thoughts to me.

I jumped guiltily and flushed. How did he know?

Your scent lingers.

I flushed a deeper red as the memories from that embarrassing night flashed into my head. There was no escaping it. He was never going to let me live it down.

I pouted and shot back, *It was an accident! A real friend would let this go and stop embarrassing me!*

Not a chance!

You're such a jerk! Turning my back on him, I said aloud, "Come on. Let's go up to the room." I grabbed Sean's arm and dragged him up the stairs. Domino took off with Killian.

When we got into the room, Sean said, "Do you want to tell me what's going on with you two? Or do you want me to guess?" His shoulders were stiff and he leaned against the wall with his arms folded in front of him.

I sighed. I guess I could lie but that would surely backfire on me. So I stalled for a minute and tried to come up with the right words. Images of my falling to the floor dragging that damn sheet with me overwhelmed me again. Ugh! Killian had been surprised, and then amused when I rolled onto my stomach and covered my eyes with both hands. He simply laughed and walked away naked.

"I saw Killian naked!" I blurted out. "But I closed my eyes!"

Sean's mouth dropped open and then snapped shut again. "What?"

My face flamed and I started babbling. "It was an accident! I didn't mean to. I thought he was you...When I touched him; he shocked me and knocked me out. When I came to, he was really sorry! You have to believe me. It was an accident!"

His mouth twitched. He finally yelled, "Killian!"

A few minutes later, Killian lounged in the doorway. "What's up?"

The smirk was adorable but completely uncalled for.

As if he didn't know what was up...he could read my mind for crying out loud! He was probably listening to the whole embarrassing conversation. The rat!

"Do you want to tell me why you were naked with my girlfriend?" Sean's lips were twitching as he held back a grin.

"It's all her fault. She came into my room and assaulted me while I was asleep. You know what can happen when we're startled? Well, she ended up on the floor, drooling. Completely her fault, but I did feel bad about it."

Killian's explanation left a lot to be desired.

"What? Are you kidding me?" My voice went up several octaves. "I was sleepwalking! I was having a nightmare! You practically electrocuted me! It's no wonder I fell down." I jabbed my finger into Killian's chest and added, "And I didn't drool. You're mean."

Intrigued, Sean said, "So when were you naked, exactly?"

"Oh, after she yanked the sheet off of me," he said with a perfectly straight face.

"Out! Get out!" I snapped and pointed to the door.

Laughing, Killian sauntered out the door and I slammed it behind him. I jumped up and kicked it for good measure. "Jerk!" I yelled at the door.

Sean's laughter finally penetrated the haze of fury surrounding me, and I stopped muttering under my breath and looked at him. He cocked his head and said, "Temper, temper."

With a gleam in my eye, I advanced on him. He backed up still laughing. I advanced. He backed into the wall and held up his hands.

"Now, come on, sweetheart! You don't want to hurt me! You love me, remember?"

"Not at the moment!" I gritted out between my teeth.

He grabbed my wrists in one hand and hauled me against him. It was hard to wiggle out of the way with my arms extended above my head and my breasts thrust forward against his chest. I stopped wiggling and he stopped laughing. Instead, he dipped his head and kissed me until I forgot why I was mad.

"So would you like to see *me* naked?" he whispered against my lips.

Chapter 5: Ancient History

"MMM, THAT FEELS AMAZING. I'll die if you stop now."

He stifled a laugh and kept rubbing my shoulder. His brisk movements stretched my tight muscles and relieved the pain that had been bothering me for days. I shifted my position slightly to give him better access to my arm. Lying face down on the living room floor, the only thing I could see was the dust bunnies nesting underneath the couch. Wow, guess one of us should drag out a vacuum and evict the little guys. Come to think of it, I couldn't remember the last time anyone cleaned the house.

"Sean?"

"Yeah, babe?" He straightened my arm and firmly pulled his strong fingers down my forearm to my wrist. After pulling each of my fingers out straight, he was done. He sat back and stretched his own fingers.

Groaning with contentment, I sat up. "When will you take me to Ireland?"

He grinned at me. "Ireland? Where did that come from?"

"I don't know. I just want to see where you grew up. Er, sort of grew up. I guess."

I had to laugh at myself. I wasn't even sure he was technically 'born'…We hadn't gotten around to talking about how one became a Primani. Were they born as people first? Or did they just adopt a hot human form and wing it? So far, every Primani I'd met had been pretty hot. Maybe it was a job requirement.

He didn't answer me right away. Instead, he bent over and stretched.

Dec interrupted us. "Hey, what are you guys doing sitting around the house? It's beautiful outside. We should go climbing."

The clock said it was only 9:00 and it *was* beautiful outside. Even though it was summer, we were enjoying a cold snap. It was going to be in the 60s today. It was perfect for a trip to the mountains.

"I'll call Dani! She'll want to come too. She's been bummed since Aric left."

An hour later, the four of us were heading down the highway towards Keene. As we got further into the mountains, my spirits soared. I squeezed Sean's hand over the console and leaned back in the seat.

"Wild thing." He winked at me.

"Yep." I winked back.

As soon as he steered the car onto the shoulder, Domino climbed over the seats and stood in my lap. I got a mouthful of tail before I could open the door and shove her out. Dani and Dec climbed out of the backseat and grabbed their backpacks. Dani had amused herself by braiding her pale blond hair into randomly spaced braids. She was very cute in a hippy girl kind of way. More importantly, she was actually smiling for the first time in a while. Aric had gone to visit his sister in Florida and was not coming back for another month. Poor thing drooped like a flower without him. I hoped today's trip would cheer her up. If nothing else, close proximity to Dec all day would raise her spirits. He had that effect on humans.

The forest around us was lush and green. It smelled like heaven. I raised my arms above my head and inhaled deeply. Ah! I was home! Sean was right. I *was* a wild thing--a creature of the forests, of the mountains. I felt most at home here. Maybe I was a wood nymph in another life. I'd have to ask Dani about that...I danced a little happy dance and started up the trail. Sean kept pace with me, but Domino ran in front. She insisted on herding her humans lest any of the flock wander off. I turned to grab Sean's hand and paused to stare at him. Damn. I was such a lucky girl! The sunlight peeked through the leaves and dappled his face with golden color. His hair was longer now and curled just over his ears. The military cut was long gone, but it was still black as night. With black hair, vivid blue eyes, golden skin, and an incredible body, he attracted me like iron to a magnet. Unwilling and unable to resist, I arced towards him and wrapped my arms around his neck.

"Geez, don't you two ever take a break?" Dani busted us when she rounded the trail.

Dec felt compelled to add, "You should try living with them. It's nauseating."

"Oh, ha ha. Someone's just jealous!" I responded and took off up the trail like a billy goat.

After happily tramping along for more than an hour, the sound of running water drew me towards a ravine off the main trail. Domino slowed her gallop to a more careful walk and we picked our way through some low sycamore branches to the source of the sound.

Pushing one last leafy branch aside, I stopped, mesmerized and delighted. "Ooh! Look!"

It was breathtaking! Sunlight streamed into the waterfall like a sign from God. It was one of those rare sights that make you believe in magic. Well, other kinds of magic…

To Sean's amusement, I threw down my backpack and shrugged out of my hoodie and shoes. Calling the dog, I hopped over the rocks until I found a good spot. Leaning in from the side, I stuck my head under the current. The water was shocking as it streamed over my head. I shook my head to clear the water out of my ears and leaned back into the water again. No way could I resist the call of the waterfall. Domino splashed into the stream and drank about a gallon of water. With tongue lolling, she bounded over to Sean and shook out her fur. Laughing, he jumped easily to a higher rock out of her range. Numb with cold, I dried myself off with my hoodie and wandered over to Sean's rock.

Unconcerned with the time, Sean and I settled into a comfortable position and stared up at the clouds that just peeked through the leaves above us. I shivered with cold and curled up against his side. He was always hot. It was like having my own personal furnace. We shared the silence and peace with our hands clasped over his chest. His heartbeat was strong against my palm and I was thankful.

"This is Heaven."

He sighed quietly and kissed my knuckles. "No. This is better than Heaven."

Surprised, I peeked at him from under my lashes. His eyes were closed and his lips were curled up in a natural smile. I leaned over and kissed the corner of his mouth just to see him open his eyes. Nose to nose, his eyes were soft as they met mine. Maybe he was right. This was better than Heaven.

"Tell me about Ireland."

He sighed a bit wistfully. "It's green and wild. It's a magical place. You'd be at home there. Like a fairy, you are."

I smiled at the image of me with fairy wings. "When did you live there?"

He was quiet for a few minutes. Finally, he said, "A very long time ago."

I traced a heart shape over his heart and whispered, "Tell me."

He pulled me closer against him. "I was born there. My father came from Germany, but my mother was Irish. Her family had been in Ireland for generations. I can still remember her smile..." His voice trailed off. His eyes were far away.

"She must have been beautiful."

He smiled up at the clouds. "Yes, she was. She had a mane of wild black hair and wicked blue eyes. When I was older, my father told me she was the most beautiful woman in the land. She died when I was still a child. My father raised me alone until he died. I was 16 then."

My heart skipped a beat and I asked, "What happened to her?"

He hesitated and finally warned, "It's not a pretty story, Mica. She was killed by soldiers--My father's men. You see, they were afraid of her...of what she could do...of what she *might* do. There were things happening in the village. The livestock were dying from no apparent reason. Crops failed because the rain refused to fall. People started to go hungry. Children got sick and died. My baby sister died. Things were very bad. Then one day, one of my father's men came into my house and saw my mother performing a ritual."

I stiffened in surprise and he hurriedly went on. "Not an evil ritual! She was simply praying for rain to heal the land. But the soldier misunderstood. His hysterical ranting sealed her fate among the ignorant and frightened." He stood up and stretched, knuckles cracking with the effort.

"What happened then? You can't leave me hanging!"

"Okay, but then we have to head back. It's getting late." He took my hand and pulled me up to stand with him.

"My mother was killed by one of the soldiers. There was a struggle and she ended up dead. The man tried to say it was an accident, but his sword had gone straight through my mother's body. It was no accident." His eyes glittered with anger as the memories swamped him.

"I saw everything that day. My mother...knew things...she sent me to hide as soon as the soldiers came towards the house. I climbed a tree and hid. My mother tried to lead them away from the tree, and he ran her through from behind. I *hid* in that tree and memorized the face of the man who killed my mother." His voice was harsh and cold, remembering a child's pain that still hurt the man he'd become.

Tears glittered in my eyes as I pictured the scared black-haired boy desperately clinging to a tree branch. I couldn't even imagine his fear and rage. My own mother had died in her sleep three years ago and the loss still stung. Sean was lost in his memories now and didn't see my tears.

"His name was Maedoc and he was the first man I killed. It was no *accident* when I ran him through. I felt...better...somehow after that." His eyes cleared and he added in a matter-of-fact tone, "My father buried her near an old Druid site. After that, we moved to another town and we stayed there until...until...well, until I became a Primani."

"What did your dad do when they came for her? Didn't he try to protect her?" I was angry for him.

"Of course he did! But it's complicated." He tapped his fingers against his leg, searching for the right words. "My mother wasn't praying to God. Christianity didn't exist there. She was a Druid priestess. Her family grew up in Northern Ireland and embraced the old ways. My father and most of the soldiers came from Europe and didn't believe in the same things. My mother and the others kept the practices of their religion hidden as much as possible to keep from losing it altogether."

"How on earth did they get together in the first place?"

He laughed out loud at my question. "Destiny? He was a Celtic warrior and she a Druid priestess. He took one look at her and couldn't walk away. Put them together and you get me. Raphael tells me I have a special purpose--up until now, I didn't believe him. Since I've met you...I'm beginning to think he's on to something!" He kissed me quickly and started to pull me towards the trail.

I dug in my feet and he stopped. "You left something out."

He raised an eyebrow at me.

"What *year* were you born?"

"112 A.D. Give or take a year."

Chapter 6: Unwanted House Guests

"OKAY, DANI, TAKE CARE! See you later!" I
practically threw her out of the car when we pulled up to
her house. She was speechless as we drove away.

Dec said, "What on earth is the matter with you? Are
you crazy?"

I swung around to face him. "Not a chance! Spill it,
you. When were you born?"

He jumped like I'd scalded him. "Sean? What's she
talking about?"

Sean rolled his eyes and turned down the music.
"The day you were hatched! You might as well just tell
her. She won't let it go."

"Did you, uh, tell her when you were born?"

"Yep. The whole story."

"Really? You told her everything?" He seemed
skeptical and looked at me with a frown.

"Come on, Dec. Just tell me! What will it hurt?"

Resigned, he said, "Okay, fine. I don't know exactly,
but sometime around 426. We didn't keep good records
back then so I'm not positive."

For the second time today, my mouth dropped open
and I was speechless.

"And Killian?"

They looked at each other, unsure. We were pulling
up in front of the house and the car was silent as Sean
shut off the engine.

"And Killian?" I repeated my question.

"920 B.C.," Killian said from behind me.

Shocked, I repeated, "920 B.C." and fainted.

Someone dragged a cold wet rag over my face and I
sputtered indignantly and pushed myself up onto my

elbows. My audience wore identical amused expressions. Killian looked vastly more entertained than the other two though. He just smirked, smiled, and shook his head.

"Okay, so I was surprised. Don't laugh at me. I'm new to this magical lifestyle, you know." I studied their faces and felt the bond we shared.

My locket twitched against my chest and I smiled. Yes, we were connected by something extraordinary.

Killian broke the extended family bonding with an announcement that we had a new problem.

"So what's going on now?" I asked.

Instead of answering me, he turned on the television and switched the channel to local news. After a short piece on the rising price of gas, the anchorman cleared his throat and put on his serious news face. A woman's body was found in a cemetery near the old Plattsburgh Air Force Base. The local police department had not released her name, but she was described as an athletically-built brunette between the ages of 17 and 25. She had been raped and beaten. The cause of death was strangulation.

"That poor woman! That's awful. But what does she have to do with us? Was she one of your charges?" I asked.

Dec's face was white as he absorbed the news. Killian waited for me to catch up. I glanced between them for a moment before slowly sitting back down.

"I should've killed him when I had the chance!" Sean said harshly.

Killian raised a hand to settle everyone down. "We don't know for sure it was him; could've been anyone. Let's not jump to conclusions."

Sean looked incredulous. "Who's jumping? I'd say it's pretty obvious."

Killian said, "Look, our instructions are to warn Mica and keep her safe. That's it. We have other orders that have priority. We need to follow up on some intel about Dagin. Rumor says he's acquired a new supply of chemicals and two new scientists to resume production. Alex has the whole east coast looking for the new lab."

"And Flynn? What do we do about him?" Dec asked.

"Officially? We do nothing. Not our focus." He held up a hand again when we all protested at once. "Unofficially, however, we take him out if an opportunity presents itself."

Sean's smile was feral. "I'm counting on it."

"Well, I'm totally freaked out now. I'm going to bed." I yawned hugely and stood to go.

"Good idea, Princess. We should all get some sleep. We've got a lot to do tomorrow. Everyone meet up at 8:00 and we'll go over the plans." Killian searched my face for...what? Stress? Fear? Something else?

Setting my jaw, I gave him a look that he understood. We'd shared this look a thousand times while Sean was gone.

It simply said, "I've got this. No worries."

And I did.

I was humming "Chasing Cars" in the shower when the clear curtain slid back. Sean leaned against the sink letting his eyes drift lazily down my soapy body. He still wore jeans but the button was undone and they rode low on his hips. He'd already stripped off the t-shirt he wore today. I licked my lips and tried to say something sexy but nothing came out. My tongue got stuck in my mouth. Instead, I stepped back to make room. The jeans hit the floor in a blink of an eye and his hands were everywhere at once. With my back against the warm tile, I closed my eyes and let the sensations overwhelm me. He dragged his lips away from my mouth and smiled wickedly. Nonplussed, I started to ask what he was up to, but it came out as a yelp when he scooped me up and wrapped my legs around his waist. His arms cushioned me from the hard tile as he impaled me with one quick thrust.

"Oh. My. God."

Moving against me now, he bit my earlobe and murmured, "Not quite."

After using all of the hot water, we stumbled to the bedroom to work out the bed. Exhausted and limp, I trailed my finger through the fine black hair that formed his happy trail and said, "There is no way that you've never had sex before me. You're like a porn star."

"A porn star?" He propped himself up on his elbow and frowned at me.

He looked so disgruntled, I started to giggle. "Baby, wait. I meant that as a compliment! You're just so amazing when we…uh, do it." I blushed.

"You're a mess, you know that? Of course it's amazing! Hello? Supernatural beings here! Our souls are connected; we share the same *saol*. God Mica, when I see you my brain and my body go into hyper-drive with awareness. I'm aware of every breath you take, every heartbeat, every emotion. When I touch you, I feel your blood flowing under your skin. I feel it under my fingertips. I have the power to draw it to the surface anywhere I want. Do you know how hot that makes me? I want to lose myself in you." He gently traced the pale blue vein on my chest with his thumb. "I can give you pleasure because I feel what you want when your breath catches just so."

My breath caught as he nipped my collarbone with his teeth. I felt my bones turn liquid again and knew he was right. I felt the same things when I touched him. I was turned on just standing close to him. He hummed with energy that I felt on every inch of my skin. I assumed everyone in love felt this way, but maybe he was right. Our souls were entwined as much as our bodies. Maybe this was special.

He peered up from the vicinity of my naval and asked, "Besides, whatever made you think I was a virgin?"

Whoa! What did he just say? I started to sit up when a loud crack of thunder sounded close by, and I jumped out of my skin. The glass in the window rattled, and a bright flash of lightning lit up the room. Domino jumped up and barked madly at the window. In a flash, Sean was up and dragging on his shorts. He stood near the window and listened. Not tonight! I knew the drill. Freaking demons again...

I threw on shorts and a tank top and combat boots. I'd rather fight naked than barefoot. I hated fighting barefoot. I always ended up hurting my toes. I didn't hear anything unusual but Domino continued barking madly. She was in anti-demon mode. Dec rematerialized next to me and tapped my arm to let me know he was there. Grateful for another body, I squeezed his arm in response.

"Where's Killian?" Sean asked.

"Out. It's just us. Who is it?"

"I'm still listening. I can't pick up his thoughts in this rain."

"Mica can. She does it all the time."

He whistled softly. "That's new. Give it a try, would you?" Sean nudged me.

I moved closer to the wall and closed my eyes. The rain and wind could be distracting, but I'd learned to tune them out. I did that now. I sent my mind out to probe for any other mind that might be loitering on the property. At first there was nothing. But as I focused on the back of the house, I sensed two others: one human, one demon. Hmm. That was interesting. Without breaking my connection, I held up two fingers--one on each hand. That was the code Dec and I came up with this year. Right hand for demons, left for humans.

"Back door," I whispered and finished scanning. "Only the two."

Sean said, "Let's go then."

He took the lead and we made our way through the house. All the while, I listened for more intruders. Finally, I stood still again and probed the human's mind. It made me queasy.

This motherfucker better not stiff me my money. I don't know why I had to bring him at all. I don't need help to snuff a couple of losers.

"Jesus! He's here to kill us." I repeated the human's thoughts.

Sean smiled whitely in the darkness. "He can try."

Dec chuckled and tensed. I sensed rather than felt their bodies prepare for the fight. I called it going into soldier-mode. They called it "supernatural flight or fight response" minus the flight part--they never ran from a fight. They didn't know how that would feel. We were spread out a bit so we couldn't all be shot at once. Sean was closest to me so I glanced at him and suppressed a shiver. His body was taught like a wire, and I could already feel the waves of heat coming off of him. Dec's eyes were gleaming hotly when he turned to look at me. I knew they would be fully ready in another second or two. Suddenly my vision wavered oddly. The room brightened like I had on night vision goggles. I wasn't wearing them now, but I could see everything clearly, including the two bodies that were approaching the door on the porch. I could see straight through the walls. I bounced on the soles of my feet and glanced around. It was the oddest thing. I felt light as air...I wanted to fly.

Sean gave the signal and both of them disappeared and rematerialized behind the intruders. The human took one look at Sean and bolted for the road. Dec's hand whipped up and he hit the demon right between the eyes. The demon screamed shrilly and disintegrated into ash. Okay, well now I had nothing to do. There was no one to fight. So I waited while the adrenaline, and whatever new fluids I had, flowed through my jerky muscles. I sat down heavily and focused on trying to breathe. Dec strode inside covered with ash and paused when he spotted me.

"Whoa, darlin'! You don't look so good. What's going on with you?" He came over and looked closely at me.

His eyes still blazed and they hurt mine when he looked into them. I winced and squeezed them closed.

"Sorry! Hang on a sec and I'll help you." Completely unselfconscious, he pulled the ash-covered t-shirt over his head and tossed it in the corner. He stuck his head under the kitchen faucet and rinsed off the ash. Demon ash burned the hell out of human skin. I learned that the hard way...

My muscles were settling down again, and I was only sporadically jerking now. My arms were twitching uncomfortably like I had been hit with a stun gun. I really, really needed a pair of rubber shoes. He came over dripping wet and knelt in front of me. His hair hung in wet clumps in his face.

"You...lllook lllike a drown...ed rrat," I stammered out.

"Yeah, yeah. Hush. I'm working here." He studied me and then ran his wet hand down my arm from shoulder to fingers. He repeated this with the other arm. His touch quieted the twitching. Then disaster happened. It always did. I'm not sure why I didn't expect it. Just as he reached up to feel my forehead, my leg shot upward. His mouth made an "O", and he rolled over into a fetal position.

"Oh, Dec! I'm so sorry!" Mortified, I kind of fell out of the chair and crouched next to him.

He wasn't in the mood for help though. Through stiff lips he said, "Go away!"

I was still hovering when Sean walked in pushing the human in front of him. I nearly jumped out of my skin. I needed to talk to these guys about sending me telepathic warnings. Constant surprises couldn't be good for my heart. Holding my pounding heart, I checked out our would-be killer. He didn't look so hot. To start with, he was blindfolded and blood was running out of his nose onto his faded Metallica t-shirt. Unfortunate, that; I loved Metallica. His hands were tied behind him and he was limping badly. He was missing a shoe and his baggy jeans were ripped and bloody in several places. Domino peered around his legs and smiled an evil doggy grin. *I told him not to run...*

"He's getting blood on my kitchen floor," I commented to Sean.

He shrugged. "I'll be in the basement."

Dec moaned and tried to straighten up. "Wait for me, bro. I'm coming."

Sean tilted his head curiously at me. "It was an accident!" I cried.

"It always is."

Chapter 7: Vanishing Act

"WELL, THAT SUCKS." I rubbed my burning hand and started for the sink to wash it.

Killian watched from the doorway. "What are you doing with that shirt?"

"Demon guts."

He peeled away from the wall and crossed to me. "Demon? When? Are you okay?" He grabbed my shoulder and held me at arm's length. Scowling, he looked for injuries. Finding nothing obvious, he relaxed his grip on me and asked again, "Want to explain about the demon?"

He seemed cool, but I sensed his tension. He was afraid for me. I patted one of his biceps and gave him a reassuring smile. I filled him in on the night while I scrubbed the ash off of my hand.

"So do you think my powers are evolving again? I was hoping to be immune to the ash, but that isn't the case."

He thought for a minute before answering me. "Well, it sounds like your *optical* vision is evolving to give you greater sight like your telepathic powers. That would make sense if your vision is your greatest power. We have the same ability to see things in the dark, and the fight response works to sharpen that. It makes us more powerful." He tented his fingers and considered me with new intensity.

He stared at me for so long I squirmed uncomfortably. What was he doing? Was I giving off some kind of weird psychic vibes?

Finally he shook his head a little and said, "I'm just not sure about your description of feeling like you could fly. Have you felt like that before?" He paused and said urgently, "Tell me you haven't actually *tried* to fly?"

"What? No, I'm not an idiot!"

He snorted like he could argue that point but didn't. Smart man. We stood there for a minute just looking at each other until a muffled scream drifted up from the basement.

He smiled nastily and headed to the basement door. "I'm glad you're okay. Do me a favor and stay that way."

The lights were off in the basement, and I had to pick my way carefully down the stairs. No one had bothered to finish this side so the concrete walls and floor were bare and cold. The only things down here were the furnace and hot water heater. Even the washer and dryer were upstairs. There had been two tiny windows, but Killian covered them over to keep anyone from getting in. Sean turned to greet us when we rounded the corner.

"Good, you're here. Meet our houseguest, Ramon. He's been very cooperative so far."

"Is he conscious?" I asked skeptically. He didn't look conscious...his head was lolling against his chest.

Sean nudged the man with his boot and ordered, "Don't play dead. Say hello to your target, asshole."

Ramon immediately raised his head in our direction and woodenly said hello. Huh. He *was* being cooperative. That's a surprise. He also looked very, very stoned.

"Uh, hey killer, can I talk to you for a second...privately?" I asked Sean.

Patting Ramon on the top of the head, he said, "Don't go away."

I pulled Sean into the other side of the basement and hissed, "What are you doing to him? He's like a zombie over there!"

Firmly dragging his hand out of mine, Sean crossed his arms. "Nothing painful, he's just groggy. But I could *torture* him for information if you'd prefer that."

"No! That's sick. Don't hurt him any more than necessary."

"Make up your mind. Do you want me to torture him or not? We don't have all night."

I threw up my hands. "Oh, do whatever it takes. I just don't want to hear the screaming!" I said the last part as loud as possible. Hopefully our houseguest had good hearing.

It was still dark in here, but my eyes had adjusted so I could see pretty well. Killian had spent the last few minutes stalking around our guest. The poor guy was shaking in the chair and moaning pitifully. I stomped down a wave of sympathy for him. After all, he *was* trying to kill us. Killian hadn't touched him, but he didn't need to. I felt the wave of heat from here and knew the man would feel it like an open furnace. His terrified eyes were blank and staring. His mouth opened and closed in silent screams. I shuddered and wrapped my arms around my chest.

Killian paused behind him. He put both hands on Ramon's shoulders and Ramon twitched violently. The chair rocked from side to side. He groaned like a trapped animal making my skin crawl. Killian calmly closed his eyes and whispered in his ear. His words echoed inside my head.

Neaon dagon a stlaya, neaon dagon a stlaya

Fascinated, I couldn't look away. Hypnotized, Ramon sat frozen while the whispering went on. The tone was at times cajoling and then harsh. Killian's knuckles were white on Ramon's shoulders and he bent closer to his ear. His lips barely moved as the whispering continued. It sent chills down my spine, but I still couldn't look away.

Ghara a dagon stlaya ul cthuli? Neaon dagon a stlaya

Killian's voice boomed inside my head and cold sweat trickled down my back. The ancient words made no sense to me, but the power behind them was unmistakable.

His power was unmistakable.

His voice, his words, his power…his insistence was impossible to resist. I was captivated and would have done anything he asked at that moment. *My* will was crumbling into tiny little pieces, and I wasn't even his target. What was he saying to Ramon? His face was frozen in a mask of horror.

Ghara a dagon stlaya ul cthuli?

As the last of the words echoed inside of me, I started to back away. I didn't want to see any more. I didn't want to hear any more. I backed into Sean and turned to leave. But he stopped me and held me in place. I tried to struggle with him, but he was too strong and I couldn't move away. Frustrated, I blinked back tears and bit my lip. Refusing to watch, I shut my eyes.

Taking my chin in his hand, Sean forced my head up and said, "Watch, Mica." His voice was hushed with awe and his eyes glowed with reverence.

Killian stopped whispering and I heard him sigh in my mind. He stood perfectly still for a few seconds and then let go of Ramon's shoulders. Nothing happened at first, but then Ramon's face was transformed. The mask of horror melted away and an expression of profound peace took its place. He nodded in my direction and slumped in the chair.

"It's done," Sean said against my hair.

Numb, I stared at Killian in horror. Oh, my God! What did you do? His head snapped up and he started towards me and I backed away. Shaking my head in denial, I wrenched away from Sean and stumbled back up the stairs. Dec caught up with me halfway down the driveway. Instead of stopping me, he matched his pace to mine. The moon was low and covered with stringy clouds that seemed sinister above the trees. The rain had stopped but lightning still streaked the sky. Thunder grumbled in the distance. I ran until I was out of breath and slowed to a stumble by the side of the road. Dec waited patiently while I bent over sucking in air. When I was breathing normally, he tentatively offered his hand. Automatically,

I reached for it but then stopped. What did I really know about him? Any of them? What power was he hiding from me? Would he take away my will? My life? Was it that easy for them? Oh, God! I'm a part of this now. What does that make me? Would my powers evolve until I could kill with my mind? Jesus…it was unthinkable.

With haunted eyes, I bit my lip to stop its trembling.

Like approaching a dangerous animal, he circled me with hands out. His eyes were soft, but his mouth was set in a firm line. He was worried and it showed.

"Just leave me alone, Dec. I don't want any of you near me."

He flinched and dropped his hands to his sides. "Mica, please," he pleaded.

Something in the tone of his voice made me look up at him. He was standing so close, but I felt a chasm yawning between us. His expression was pained as he watched me struggle. What was I doing to him? Dec was my friend, my healer. He'd been the one steady rock in my life for two years. I was hurting him now. Damn. My lip trembled and I bit it again. I needed to get a grip. He must have sensed the change in my mood because he took a tentative step in my direction and held out his hands again. Sniffing, I lifted one hand.

He pulled me into his arms and kissed the top of my head. "Let me help."

I nodded against his chest and relaxed as his body grew warmer around me. My fears slowly disappeared and my heartbeat returned to normal. I sighed and pulled back. His beautiful blue eyes were grave as he gauged my mood.

"You're afraid. Again." He ran his fingers through his hair in frustration. "Damn it! What's happened now? You're not supposed to be *afraid* of us. We're here with you…because of who you are!"

He laughed bitterly and added softly, "Somehow, we keep failing you. I'm so sorry, darlin'."

"No, Dec, stop it! You haven't failed me. I've failed you." I whirled around and faced the trees. I couldn't look at him anymore. "Don't you see? I'm the weakest link...I'm afraid of what I don't understand because I feel vulnerable, weak. Killian's power..." My breath caught in a sob and I bit my lip.

Turning me around, he said furiously, "You are *not* weak! You're a human; and an amazingly strong one too. Over the past few years, you've evolved from a typical teenager into a scary bad ass member of our team. You're a natural. You scare the hell out of me sometimes, especially when you're pissed. You're handling your new powers like a pro." He stopped to suck in some air and said more patiently, "I know it's hard for you. But damn it, Mica, you are strong and capable. You're one of us." He shook me by the shoulders to make his point.

"But I don't want to be!"

He flinched as if I'd slapped him. "What makes you say that?

I hesitated and inhaled sharply. "What Killian did to that man..." His whispering voice still echoed in the back of my mind. "I don't want to be like that. That's not who I am."

"That man is better off now."

Shocked at his callousness, I backed away from him again. "I can't believe you'd say that!"

His silence was deafening.

The sound of the wall going up between us was not.

I closed the door softly behind me and steeled myself for the argument to come. But the living room was empty when I walked in. Good. I just wanted to go to bed. My brain hurt from thinking so hard and my heart felt tender in my chest. Hugging Sean's pillow to my chest, I lay there staring out the window. Sleep wouldn't come. Instead, I relived the scene in the basement again. Sean's face had been...admiring, even awestruck, when Killian finished with Ramon. He'd made me watch! What was the point of that? Was I supposed to swoon over Killian's power? Did they want applause? Were they getting off on it? It made me sick.

Maybe they're not as good as they say they are. A soft voice commented in the back of my mind.

Ignoring it, I turned my thoughts to Sean again.

I couldn't understand his obvious admiration of Killian's actions. I mean, Killian killed that guy, didn't he? Was it the way he did it that was cool? Was twisting his mind until it imploded cooler than, say, slitting his throat? It was *cleaner*; maybe that's the point. I wasn't squeamish about killing in general; sometimes you had to do it or be killed yourself. I got that. I just didn't get how he could so coldly kill that guy for really no reason. So he tried to kill us. Big deal! A lot of people have tried to kill me this year and no one killed them because of it. Scott Flynn's heavy brow and deep-set eyes leered into view and I rolled over to avoid the picture. I loved Sean and Killian. I loved Dec, too. Maybe I was so used to seeing their caring or protective sides that I forgot they're warriors first. Sean once told me that other Primani weren't as *friendly* as these three. Maybe they're just doing what they need to do, and I'm too much of a wuss to blow it off.

The dream was insidious. It crept up on me while I lay in that vulnerable window between consciousness and the early stages of sleep. My body was floating off into oblivion when the first images tickled my sight. Caught in the paralysis of sleep, I was helpless as the dream unfolded. I watched from above as Sean walked into my mind. He was bloodstained and weary as he crossed a clearing. Early morning mist softened the harshness of the bare trees. The silver light cast no shadows as he slowed to a stop. Stretching tiredly, he sat down on a rock and dropped his head into his hands. He was heavily armed with an automatic rifle and extra ammunition looped over his right shoulder. His shoulders drooped and he rolled them tiredly. A shadow moved behind him, but he didn't see it. My heart pounded in my chest as the darkness moved closer to him. Run, Sean! I tried to warn him, but my voice had no sound. Sean sat perfectly still, unaware. The shadow moved closer and a tingle of recognition crawled down my spine. Sean slid his hand to the sheath strapped to his calf and tensed as the shadow took human form. No! Wait! I screamed at him. But it was too late. He couldn't hear me anyway. He'd whipped around and thrown the shining knife without hesitation. I gasped in shock and the dream world wavered out of focus.

With a cry of anguish, Sean dropped to his knees and pulled my body into his arms.

"Forgive me, Mica! I had no choice. I had no choice," he cried as he rocked me against his chest. My eyes stared unseeing into the branches above us.

Two more shadows slid out of the trees. With identical expressions of pity, Killian and Dec joined him in the clearing. They were also heavily armed and dressed for combat.

Killian's eyes blazed hotly as he said, "This was foretold by the angels. You shouldn't have loved her."

Dec added, "Her weakness was dangerous. You know that." He touched my face with something like revulsion and wiped his hand against his pants. "Burn the body now. We have to go."

No! My cry of protest broke the spell and I sat up in bed. The bed was empty next to me. Where was Sean? My heart was still galloping in my chest as I shoved the remnants of the dream out of my head. Where on earth did that come from? I must be going crazy. Sean wouldn't kill me. He loved me more than anything else. Didn't he? A small niggle of doubt argued the point.

Yes, he loves you, but you'll always be second to the greater cause he serves. He'll kill you if you get in the way.

No! That's not true. He's my soul mate!

But that doesn't mean you get to live...your destiny is still evolving, remember?

Oh, shut up!

Dragging on a shirt, I stalked out of the bedroom calling for Sean. Domino padded silently behind me. Dawn was just bringing its pale yellow light when I stopped at Killian's door. Knocking softly, I waited for him to answer. I knocked again and waited. If he was here, he would have answered the door. He sleeps so lightly it could barely be called sleep. I cracked open the door and looked inside. His scent was very faint this morning. I inhaled deeply and his face came immediately to my mind. I saw him as he looked at me so many times...mouth compressed in disapproval and eyes mocking. He was a hard man to please, but he loved me, didn't he? I thought he did. Exhaling, I pushed his face away and continued my search. Dec's room was empty too. They were all gone. They'd left without me. They'd left me here alone. Why? What did that say?

It says they don't trust you.

Of course they trust me! I'm valuable to them. I've been on a lot of missions. I kick ass too.

Yes, but nothing important. Not since the farmhouse. Not since you failed them.

What? I didn't fail them! It wasn't my fault there were demons that day!

You didn't fail them? Really? What happened to Sean? You know that was your fault. Deep inside, you know it. They know it, too.

No! It's not true...I leaned against the wall and closed my eyes, letting the truth wash over me like acid. This was crazy. I'm losing my mind here! I need to go. I need to get out of this house and get my head together. Rushing now, I showered and packed. I loaded my things into the car and waved Domino into the shotgun seat. I had no idea where we were going, but it didn't really matter as long as it was away from here.

Three hours later, we sat at a picnic table in a rest stop near the interstate. Gazing into the distance, I idly petted Domino. She sat in guard dog position on the bench next to me. What was she protecting me from here? Remembering my training, I scanned the park around me for threats and allies. There were about a dozen cars parked in the lot, but nothing seemed threatening at the moment. A middle-aged blond woman with two little kids unwrapped sandwiches at the table next to me. They dug in and giggled as their puppy rolled around in the soft grass. They didn't seem like much of a threat. I continued my scan. A grey-haired man slowly made his way out of the bathroom and headed towards his car. He was slightly misshapen and limped across the parking lot. One shoulder was higher than the other and his head was bent awkwardly. His shapeless overcoat seemed a little out of place here. It was warm and sunny at the moment. I peered under my lashes and watched him carefully. He paused next to his car and Domino growled softly. The man straightened and looked right at me. I tensed as his eyes turned yellow in their sockets.

Like a mad dog, Domino barked viciously and went airborne. With paws barely skimming the pavement, she threw herself in his direction. Screaming in panic, the little family next to us sprinted towards their car. The demon's eyes brightened and he lightly bounced a fireball in his hand. He grinned evilly and aimed at the little girl.

"No!" I jumped up and yelled at him just as he released the fireball.

He exploded into a cloud and the fireball vanished before it struck the child. Time stopped. Stunned, I gaped at the spot where he'd disappeared a split second ago. What the heck happened? Where did he go? Expecting Primani, I whirled around. I saw no one. The parking lot was empty. Looking front again, I searched for the little family, but they were gone too.

Everyone was gone.

An icy gust of wind sent me running for the car. Domino continued to growl but had stopped barking. Shaking with adrenaline, I jumped into the car and slammed it into gear.

Driving much faster than the speed limit, I pulled onto the Tappan Zee bridge before rush hour. Traffic moved steadily along as my thoughts cleared. How did I get here? I asked myself for the hundredth time. I must've been on autopilot. Thankfully the hot Australian GPS voice guided me flawlessly to the parking garage and I parked in the penthouse slot. I slipped the leash on the killer dog and walked into the lobby like I belonged there. I smiled beguilingly at the concierge as the golden elevator doors swept closed. The foyer of the penthouse was painted a beautiful royal blue and had black marble floors. The bright geometric paintings still hung on the walls, but the tiny golden cherub was missing from its alcove near the door. The niche was empty now. That was odd. I knocked on the door and waited.

No one opened the door. It was the middle of the afternoon; maybe Jordan had gone out. Jordan was the very sweet angel who managed the house for Alex. He was unfailingly kind to me and I looked forward to seeing him again. I tried the knob and the door swung inward without a sound. Domino growled. Something was wrong. My spidey-senses were tingling…I might not have super powers, but the smell of fresh blood is always a big sign that something bad has happened. Wait…there was a heavy stench lingering behind the blood. My nose curled in on itself in protest. Vaguely familiar, I carefully inhaled and tried to process it.

It was the smell of hell.

Demons? Here?

Freezing outside the door, I listened hard. I heard soft footsteps inside. Closing my eyes, I looked into the penthouse and searched for the source of the sounds. There was a body on the tiled kitchen floor. Oh, please don't be Jordan! I prayed silently.

The apartment was empty, but the French doors were open onto the rooftop garden. A figure stood in the garden looking down over the wall. Wishing I had my Sig handy, I slid inside the door. I glided through the kitchen and picked up a knife from the rack. It would have to do if things got physical. My breath caught as I looked down at Jordan's unconscious form. He was bleeding heavily from a gash in his forehead but was still alive. Peeking up at the doors, I grabbed a towel and wrapped it around his head. His eyes fluttered at my touch.

"Shh. It's me," I whispered.

With surprising strength, he gripped my hand and said, "James! Where's James?"

"I'll find him. You rest now." I gently removed his hand.

I slipped out to the garden and let out a sigh of relief. James.

"James? Thank God!"

He whirled around at the sound of my voice. Grief distorted his handsome features into something ugly. His eyes glowed angrily and his hands were clenched into fists. Upon seeing it was me, he relaxed slightly. "Mica? Why are you here? Did you see…Jordan? He's…" A sob tore from his throat and he bowed his head.

"James, he's not dead. We have to help him right now though. Come on." I grabbed his hand ignoring the jolt of current that made my head spin.

Rushing back into the kitchen, I skidded to a stunned stop. "What's going on here?" I asked James. The pool of blood was gone as was the towel. The kitchen was spotless.

He looked puzzled too. "I don't know. I came in a few minutes ago and found Jordan on the floor. He wasn't moving…there was so much blood…I thought he was dead. Then you showed up."

"What did you do with Jordan?" He asked me with a strange gleam in his eye.

I didn't like the tone he was using. "What did *I* do? I just got here. Maybe I should ask you that question." I fingered the knife in my hand.

He smiled tightly and said, "Are you planning to use that on me?" He glided imperceptibly closer. There was something oily about his expression and I took a stronger grip on the haft.

Domino snarled and moved between us. He stopped and casually leaned against the island with hands raised.

"You want to call off Cujo there? She must be confused. I'm not the bad guy." He paused and added, "I need to call Alex."

Trusting the dog, I didn't call her off. I let her growl. I told him to call Alex though. He pulled out a cell phone and placed a call to Alex. After explaining what happened to Jordan, he hung up.

"Well? Is he coming?" I asked.

"Yeah, he's on his way. He'll be here shortly. I have to go to another meeting though. I'll be back a little later." He gave me a little smile and vanished.

Domino barked once and rubbed her face against my leg. Well, that was creepy. Assuming Alex would be here in a few minutes, I stood in the kitchen.

"Hey Cujo, do me a favor and use your super-dog senses and sniff around. We're looking for blood and the smell of a stranger. Someone who shouldn't be here, maybe."

Like a very hairy CSI, she went to the front door and started from there. Meanwhile, I searched the kitchen. No sign of blood. I stuck my nose down to the floor and peeked into the seams between the tiles. Nothing. I know I saw Jordan...Where did he go? What gives? This was really weird.

Alex was a no-show. It had been three hours since James called him and he hadn't showed. I paced up and down the hallway and ground my teeth in frustration. Damn it. What was taking him so long? Surely this was important? Jordan had to be okay, didn't he?

There's nothing wrong with Jordan. You've made a mistake.

I know what I saw. Jordan was hurt.

The little voice continued. *Are you sure that's what you saw? You're tired. Maybe you didn't see anything.*

I did see it! Jordan was bleeding...

Then where is he?

I whispered, "I don't know."

Chapter 8: A Momentary Lapse of Reason

THE WITCHING HOUR and I couldn't sleep.
Millions of city lights muted the stars as I stared out into
the night. I leaned against the brick wall on the rooftop
and tried to let my mind drift. It wasn't working for me
tonight. My thoughts rambled disjointedly. I couldn't
organize them into anything remotely coherent. Every
time I tried to meditate, little voices of doubt intruded.
Random images from my past flitted around like
hyperactive butterflies. I must be really stressed; my
concentration was shot and meditation was light years
away. There was just too much going on right now.
Cursing in frustration, I stomped back inside and locked
the doors. I didn't know what to do. I couldn't call Alex
myself because I didn't have his number in my phone. No
one had given it to me. Sean always had it though, but
calling him wasn't an option at the moment.

My heart caught painfully. I missed Sean. But this
was necessary. Getting away from him for a little while
was my only option if I wanted to sort out my
thoughts...my memories. I needed to understand what
happened that day in Vermont. Something nagged at me,
there was some clue I was overlooking. It was important,
but I couldn't find it. My stupid brain wouldn't cooperate.
Curling up with Domino, I fell into a restless sleep full of
dreams. I woke suddenly with no idea where I was.
Blinking in the morning light, I looked around in
confusion.

Oh. That's right--the penthouse.

Yesterday's events came rushing back and I sighed. I
was alone. I sensed no one else in the apartment. After
dressing and eating, I shouted for Alex. Well, he's
supernatural, right? Maybe he can hear me. I tried

shouting for Raphael and Zadkiel too. No one magically appeared. I left a note on the table, just in case, and took Domino for a walk. We rounded the corner onto Broadway where swarms of people marched to their destinations. New Yorkers had that look of purpose about them. Everyone knows where they're going and they don't mess around. The energy of the city recharged me and I joyfully joined the swarm and let it sweep me along. I had no particular place to go.

After grabbing two hot dogs from a vendor of questionable cleanliness, the dog and I perched on the steps in front of the Metropolitan Museum of Art. I slid Domino the rest of my bun and licked spicy brown mustard off one of my knuckles. Leaning back, I closed my eyes against the caressing breeze and breathed in the exhaust fumes.

"You must be my soul mate," a deep voice said in front of me.

I scrambled to my feet blinking against the slant of sunlight. Oh! There in front of me was a beautiful male with sparkling blue eyes. He was perfectly marked and regarded me regally. What muscular haunches he has! Oh, and the human attached to the leash was not so bad either. It was no surprise that Domino hadn't warned me, she only had eyes for…

I asked, "What's his name?"

"Domino. And yours?"

"Domino."

"Wow, we really are soul mates!" The man held out his hand and said, "I'm Balin."

He had warm golden brown eyes and thick brown hair that was just a little too long. Curling against his collar, it gave him the look of some kind of model. Italian maybe? His nose was crooked as if it had been broken, but it added character to an otherwise flawless face. His mouth looked soft, sensitive even…more of a poet than a fighter. But was he harmless? Looks didn't always show the truth, did they? He could be a demon for all I knew, but it couldn't hurt to be polite.

We chatted for a few minutes and he invited us to walk with them to Central Park. Seeing no real reason to say no, Domino and I joined them. The trees were thick and the path was shady and cool in the afternoon sun. It felt good to breathe in the semi-clean air of the woods. Joggers ran by with their iPods humming making me wish I'd brought my running shoes. Balin was a natural entertainer and told story after story until I found myself laughing in spite of the weight on my mind. But by the time the sun cast long shadows over the park, I was ready to get back to the penthouse. My stomach growled alarmingly and I blushed.

"Wow! It's late! No wonder you're starving. Listen," he said, "do you want to grab dinner? I live pretty close. We can leave the dogs in the loft and go out."

Alarm bells tinkled in the back of my mind. Something was a little off. Hoping to appear nonchalant, I looked indirectly into his eyes but nothing but steady brown irises met my own. There was no wall of fire, no blackness, and certainly no kaleidoscope of color showing his innermost thoughts.

Still not comfortable with going to his flat, I made excuses. "I'm sorry, Balin, but I need to get back. My uncle should be home by now and I need to see him. But thanks for the offer."

His poet lips grazed my knuckles as he said, "Until we meet again then." He winked broadly and turned away.

My skin tingled like a raw nerve when I pulled my hand back. I resisted the urge to wipe off his kiss and practically dragged the dog four blocks before I slowed down and stopped. Breathing like I'd run four miles, I rubbed the back of my hand viciously against my jeans. It was still there. My skin felt raw where his mouth had touched it…it burned like the skin had been scraped off the top. I held it up in the fading light, but the skin wasn't broken. It was tan and taut like the rest of my body. Still, it stung like hell and I stuck it in my mouth automatically. Bitter acid curled my tongue back and I spit it out. Ugh. Gross!

Who is this guy?

Better question: *What* is this guy?

Alex was still absent when we got back. Disappointed, I poured a glass of water and scrounged for dinner. Apparently, Jordan hadn't been shopping. The fridge was sadly empty. I managed to find some crackers and a tiny wedge of cheese though. There was a carton with three eggs in it and a box of cereal. I flipped a coin. I lost. Domino got the eggs for dinner. Tapping my fingers absently on the bar, I had a minor epiphany. I was bored. I marveled at the idea for a few minutes. I couldn't remember the last time I was bored. There was no help for it though. I had to do something. I flipped on the television and caught the news. The news anchor was in the middle of a story about the body of a homeless man. A picture of a burned warehouse filled the screen. Intrigued, I turned up the volume.

"And the unidentified man was found outside of this abandoned warehouse near the East River. He was reported dead by an anonymous caller earlier today. Cause of death has not been determined."

A close up of the warehouse flashed on the screen. The building itself was mostly destroyed but the front entrance was still intact. The pale red siding was streaked with grime. I know that place! I've been there before. Hmm. What would a dead homeless guy be doing there? Cause of death? Hmm, I would bet my right arm cause of death had something to do with chemical poisoning. Dagin? Again? Or maybe, *still* would be a better assumption. He was still operating in the area and I'd bet his men never cleaned up the crap in the old warehouse before moving on...

What would it take to get rid of this demon?

Ignoring Killian's rule of never going off alone, I was making my way to the other side of the East River. I was pretty sure I could find the warehouse again. It felt good to do something useful. I had memorized the street map and tucked it into my jacket pocket. I was wearing the darkest things I'd brought, but felt oddly unprepared for a fight. Killian had rules for our ops. Every time we had an op, we went over the plan and the weapons we'd need. Keeping to my training, I went over my own simple plan, but I felt naked now without NVGs or a headset. All I had was my Sig and a knife strapped to my calf. Sean had given me the silver-bladed Primani knife a few months ago. Unlike the heavy military-issue weapon we usually carried, this one was more a stiletto than combat knife. It was also simply engraved around the haft with two intertwined circles. A small cross bisected them through their center. The symbolism was clear: my blood, their blood, our blood together. Together, we were stronger. I fingered the blade and hoped I'd be strong enough going solo.

The sun was down completely and as usual, the streetlights were mostly broken. This area was a wasteland, and no one seemed to care about keeping the lights on. Pausing on the same bridge I'd crossed with Dec so long ago, I felt a crushing sense of déjà vu. I let the feeling wash over me and absorbed the images. I'd been here before and was here now. There was nothing weird about that. Shaking off the creepy feeling, I took a breath and kept moving forward hugging the tree line instead of walking down the rutted dirt road. The same broken-down 18 wheeler greeted me around the bend. Geez, didn't anyone clean up? That thing had nearly crushed me flat the last time I was here. Probably I wouldn't need to worry about any explosions tonight so it was safe to go hide behind it. The weeds climbing up its windows would provide excellent cover for a nosy secret agent like me.

Disappearing in the shadows, I looked for any other signs of life. Not sensing anyone, demonic or otherwise, I slipped over to the far side of the warehouse. The homeless guy was found near the water. It was super creepy here in the dark so I was going to move through this like lightning. Get in, get out! A branch scraped against the side of the building and I jumped. Suddenly this wasn't the best plan ever...I was really alone here. Even the sounds of cars were very far away. No one would hear me scream...

Hello, what do we have here?

Using the toe of my boot, I rooted a piece of melted white plastic out of the dirt. I pulled out a plastic bag and carefully put the bit of plastic inside and sealed it. I shoved it into my backpack and kept looking. Tapping a toe, I racked my brain for ideas. During last year's raid, the chemicals had sidelined me and James when they blew into us. I was coughing up blood for hours until Raphael healed me. If the barrels leaked into the ground...and the homeless guy slept near the building out of the wind...What would Sara Sidle do? I scooped some dirt into the plastic bag and sealed that up. I searched around the rest of the building and didn't see anything weird. I was just turning to leave when I thought I saw a movement in the brush.

Slowly pulling out my gun, I turned towards the brush and nearly dropped it in surprise. The biggest rat I've ever seen came out from under it and sauntered towards me like I was dinner. It was almost as big as Domino! With tiny rodent eyes gleaming hotly in the moonlight, it looked like a demon from hell. It lifted its nose and sniffed the air catching my scent. Emboldened now, it picked up its pace and shuffled closer. Holy shit! I took off in a dead sprint back up the middle of the road. If I was attacked by another person, I would shoot him and let the rat eat him.

Thanks to all the running I've been doing, I survived long enough to find a corner grocery store. I was happily putting groceries away when my cell phone rang. Tossing Domino a cookie, I checked the caller ID. It was Sean. I guess he's finally noticed I'm not there...my heart did a little flip-flop in my chest and I considered the phone. It kept ringing.

"Sean?"

Pregnant pause.

"Where are you?" he asked with a heavy sigh. "Mica? Do you have any idea how worried I am? Where are you?"

"I'm fine. I'm okay and I don't need your help."

Long silence. I could hear his teeth grinding together through the earpiece.

"Okay...would you at least explain this...note you left me? Was this supposed to explain things?" He sounded like a man trying very hard not to shout. I could picture him counting to 10 before speaking.

Grimacing at his tone, I said, "I was mad."

I had been really angry when I wrote it, but it seemed like a lifetime had passed since then. Probably I should tell him about Jordan and James...

"That's it? *You were mad*? That's your explanation for tearing out of here in the middle of the night without even talking to me? What the hell were you mad about?"

His frustration came through loud and clear. A little embarrassed now, I tried to remember what I wrote. I couldn't quite remember...It seemed like so long ago, maybe I had overreacted. What was I angry about again? Something to do with Killian? No, that wasn't right. Sean? No, never him. What was I upset about? I chewed my lip as I racked my brain for memories. A warm fog settled over my brain.

The quiet voice of memory whispered to me. *They left you alone. Remember? They left you. They walked away and left you alone. They didn't take you with them because they don't trust you.*

Realization dawned as bright as the sun through the fog. That's right! They left me without a word and took off. My Primani left me alone. They didn't trust me to go with them. Why couldn't I go? I was a strong fighter now. I've proven myself. There's no reason to make me stay home! What were they up to? More secrets? They were probably killing someone else who irritated them. Ramon's terrified face slammed into view. His face twisted in pain as Killian stood behind him...whispering those evil words, killing without even touching. Talk about keeping his hands clean! Maybe I'd be next? I'm always irritating them. Even Dec gets tired of me sometimes.

No wait, that's not right. I shook my head to clear it. I was confused. I hadn't been that angry, had I? I came here to get my thoughts together. I left for some space...the fuzziness returned. Shaking, I lowered myself to a chair. My head spun in a slow spiral as I pictured Sean's blue eyes snapping at me in anger. He was always angry! What was his problem? Couldn't he just leave me alone for a change? He doesn't own me. I have a right to my own life. That's right, to *my* life. I'm not Primani! I don't have to answer to them. Staring groggily at the kitchen counter, I saw red behind my eyelids and my blood steamed as it raced through my body. My skin burned and glowed like a lamp in the dark kitchen.

Knuckles white against the counter, I slurred, "Oh, go to hell!" just before sliding into darkness.

Domino's cold nose nudged me awake sometime much later. My face hurt. As if moving through wet cement, I dragged my arm to my face and pulled my cell phone out of the crease in my cheek. I must've been lying on it for a while because there was a deep impression in my skin. What happened? Why am I on the floor? My mouth felt like cotton and my eyes burned. I shifted to sit up and my head exploded. With both hands gripping my skull, I stared up at the skylight. Any little movement brought excruciating pain. My eyes watered with it and I drew in a careful breath. Domino whined helpfully and I slowly cracked an eyelid. Her eyes looked into mine. *Declan?*

Of course! I lay very still and focused my healing energy on my splitting head. Breathing slowly, I guided the gentle current and felt its warmth surround my neck and flow into my aching face and around my skull. The pain subsided slowly and I felt refreshed again. I sat up gingerly and then stood up and stretched. I picked up my phone and groaned.

The screen was shattered.

Hundreds of itty bitty ant cars crawled along the city streets 18 stories below me. Leaning out a bit further, I could barely see the people walking by. I'd been staring blankly at the scene for a while and still no magical solution had presented itself. I had to make a decision. I was alone in the penthouse and I was lonely. I had $5.82 and had to use my credit card for everything. I had no way to get more money. There was a dead guy at the warehouse where we accidently blew up a stockpile of toxic chemicals that were stored inside white plastic barrels. I now had samples of said plastic and contaminated dirt. My hand ached.

Problems were many; options were few. I could call Sean…that would solve the loneliness and money problems. He'd know how to send the samples to their lab too. Good idea except my phone was destroyed. I flexed my fingers and frowned. They seemed stiff to me…absently, I rubbed my hand and wondered if we had any drugs here. Maybe aspirin would help?

The wind nearly knocked me over as I turned the corner and hit an open space in the sidewalk. Clouds roiled high above the buildings as I rushed up the street. I zipped up my jacket and pulled up the collar. The air was wet with a threat of rain and it would be cold when it finally hit the sidewalk. I was rushing to get back before that happened. The bottle of Tylenol rattled in my pocket.

Only two more blocks...My hair blew into my eyes again, and I shoved it back for the hundredth time. As I did, I caught a familiar reflection in the plate glass window next to me. My skin prickled at the exact moment I crossed the opening to the alley. I didn't have time to scream when I was yanked off my feet and thrown into an open car door. Struggling madly, my boot connected with something soft, and a surprised grunt was the last sound I heard before a sharp pain burned into my neck.

Chapter 9: The Puppet Master

BURNING AIR SWIRLED around me as light as butterflies. Naked, I stood with my arms spread wide as the flames licked my skin as a lover might. First nipping sharply, playfully, but then warm and tender, the flames caressed me. I welcomed them with a soft smile. The flames brought pleasure...and power. My skin glowed like phosphorous as I rose above the firestorm. White hot incandescence, powerful...my *saol* blazed towards the heavens. The winds howled with the sons of Hell calling my name. They called to me in supplication, in worship. They stoked the fires that grew hotter around the pillar that was me. My eyes blazed with white fire as I turned them on my servants. Come to me, I called them. Come to me!

Rough hands yanked my arm and a searing pain raced up my shoulder to my chest. I cried out in protest and then sank into blackness.

And still the fires raged.

The fire changed me, ruined me, my skin melted and oozed away. My human body was gone. Cut open down the middle, there were no organs or bones...only a core of molten *saol*. It raced through my veins rushing to strengthen, to heal, to save my life. But the demons' fires were melting me...they were too hot. I didn't have time to heal. The gentle life force boiled under my skin...it was cooking me from the inside and I screamed as my skin melted off in sheets. Golden sheets, light as parchment, floated to the floor until nothing but the thick molten *saol* of my essence, my soul, remained. My human shell was destroyed. Slowly, my soul overflowed the table I lay on and dripped to the floor.

Suddenly, a great cold wave washed over me and the searing pain stopped. Shaking with cold, I thrashed and moaned. Teeth chattering, I bit my lip and tasted blood. I was freezing now, no longer burning. Voices murmured from a great distance, but I heard them through the haze of unconsciousness.

"Bring the bitch around. Do it now!"

"I'm trying! I can't just bring her out of it. Her brain will shut down."

"No one gives a fuck about her brain. Wake her up!"

"Don't you want her to answer questions? If you do, you need to give me some more time to bring her around. I've got to get these drugs out of her system or you'll have nothing but a pretty little vegetable."

I heard them clearly now but decided that discretion really was the better part of valor. Not sure if this was the bravest soldier move or not, I played dead. One of the men leaned into my face. I nearly gagged on his rancid breath. He reeked of old cigarettes, rotten teeth, and a lack of soap. Laughing meanly, he shoved a pillow over my face and raked his nails up my leg. My eyes watered instantly.

"I'll be back later. Hurry up. The boss is waiting for her." Footsteps echoed and disappeared up what sounded like metal stairs. The clank of a gate banged above me.

"Asshole!" the other man said quietly. He moved the pillow and paused. I tried to look comatose. Sighing, he commented, "I don't know what you know, little girl, but you'd be better off dead."

After an eternity of rustling papers and clanking glass, the man finally left me alone in the dimly lit room. After the gate clanged shut, I waited for several minutes before cracking open an eye. I knew the room was empty but I didn't want to sit up too quickly. What the hell was going on? Barely lifting my head sent daggers of pain down the back of my skull. Red light erupted behind my eyes like fire. Shit. Gasping, I lay back against the pillow and willed the fireworks to stop going off inside my eyes.

I was going to puke. Taking slow deep breaths, I ignored the pain and looked around. I was in a small concrete room. There were circuit breakers on one wall and pipes crisscrossing the ceiling. It was damp and smelled like sewage. Where was I? Warehouse? Subway? I couldn't tell. It was damp and smelly so my guess was underground. But where?

I counted down the seconds and no one came back. Leaving me alone was a dumb idea, an amateur move. Don't they know who I am? I'm so outta here! Intending to slide off the table and make a sneaky exit, I swung my legs to the side and moved a whole half an inch. Alarmed, I looked down at my legs and saw harnesses holding me to the table. My arms were strapped as well.

Well, this was *not* good.

I closed my eyes and blinked back tears. Okay, I was still alive so there was time to find a way out of this. The gate opened and heavy footsteps pounded down the stairs followed by lighter ones.

"Well? How much more time?" Bad Breath Boy was impatient. He nudged my leg.

"Another hour? Two? That's probably it. Check back then."

"You better be right." He stomped back up the stairs. In the silence that followed, the clock ticked loudly from the makeshift desk.

"I know you're awake. You can open your eyes if you want." His voice was soft, nasal. "I won't hurt you."

Startled, I flinched and he turned my wrist to take my pulse. "Your heart is racing and with good reason." He leaned over me and added, "Come on, it'll be easier if I don't have to give you more drugs. You won't like the side effects."

My eyes snapped open to see a pair of clear green eyes looking down at me. Heavy lashes surrounded them but a large purple bruise kept them from being pretty. I blinked and the man stepped back. His nose had been recently broken and was swollen and slightly off center.

He made a face that wasn't quite a smile, and glanced up at the stairwell. Eyes warning me to be quiet, he spoke loudly to me as if I was still asleep.

"Okay, enough games. This oughta bring you around." In a whisper, he added, "The door's open."

Frantic, I hissed, "Untie me!"

He shook his head, "Are you crazy? They'll kill me!"

Furious, I growled at him. He backed away from me. "Coward!" I jerked on the restraints but they just cut into my skin. My toes were already numb and I didn't want to lose them. I'd need them to escape. The doctor, if that's what he was, came over and pulled the sheet back across my chest. Oh, God! I was naked! Cringing at the idea that any of these…criminals…stripped me while I was unconscious, I snapped, "Pervert!"

With another nervous look at the stairway, he hissed into my ear, "There are worse things than being naked, believe me."

A phone buzzed and he answered it. "Yes, she's awake. I'll have her ready. Yes, I do understand. Five minutes."

My heart froze in my chest when he turned around, his face ghostly white. Twin spots of anger stood out on his cheeks. He stood clenching and unclenching his fists before turning to a small box. I blanched and tried to squirm away when he filled a small syringe.

"No! Please, don't!" My eyes were pleading as I tried to scoot out of the restraints.

Without hesitation, he slid the needle into my arm. "This will help. Trust me."

Heavy boots crashed down the stairs, and he tucked the syringe into his lab coat. Two big men came to escort me. Feeling oddly detached as the drugs kicked in, I waited as they stalked over to me. One of them threw a robe at me and told me to put it on. Doctor Green Eyes released the restraints and I sat up and rubbed feeling back into my ankles. My head felt light and I closed my eyes to stop the dizziness. An odd humming distracted me and I paused to listen. It was a pretty sound…like angels singing.

"Hurry up, bitch!" He backhanded me out of my daze.

"Piss off!" I spit blood on him and wiped my mouth with the back of my hand.

Grabbing me by the hair, he pulled my head back and pressed a razor against my throat. "I'm gonna skin you alive, you stupid bitch!"

His partner snickered at him and grabbed his arm. "Later! She's got an appointment. Let's go."

Half dragging me between them, they pulled me up the stairs and into the hallway. My shins banged painfully on the top step, and I bit my lip to keep from yelping out loud. These guys were getting on my nerves. The hallway was only barely lit with dying emergency lighting that was twitching with its last life. Brick? Interesting, that. There weren't too many underground places that had brick walls. Good clue. The trip down the hallway didn't take long and I was shoved into a wooden chair in the middle of an empty room and left alone. Lone chair? Empty room? This was so clichéd I almost laughed. I started to until I saw the tiny red LED light near the ceiling.

Instead of laughing, I rubbed my hands together and tightened the belt on my robe. I felt naked sitting here. Keeping my face blank, my thoughts ricocheted around my brain. I was having a hard time forming complete thoughts. I tried to fight the haze of drugs but it was hard. What was I doing here? Who snatched me? What was that pretty music? Why were the walls moving? Minutes ticked by and my butt went numb. Cautiously, I stood and stretched. I studiously avoided looking directly at the camera but I felt the eyes on me. My head still felt strange and light. The humming continued on and off. My legs were heavy and I was having a hard time moving around without stumbling. No way was I going to make a run for it. Damn it. Why couldn't I travel like the Primani?

The door burst open and bounced off the nearest wall. I froze and slowly turned around. My heart stopped for a minute as I looked into the face of nightmares. He *looked* like a human, but the skin wasn't quite right. His face writhed slowly like it was alive under the thin brown skin. A webbing of white scars stood out in sharp relief across the right side of his face. His right eye drooped as the scar pulled it downward. His other eye gleamed brightly with anticipation as he stalked into the room. It was all I could do to stand still and not back away.

Sean's words came back to me and echoed in my head.

Demons feed on fear, Mica.

He stopped so close that the material of his shirt brushed against my chest. The acrid stench of sulfur watered my eyes and sent me into a coughing fit. Satisfied, he nodded at the camera. The LED light blinked out and the door closed behind him. We were alone. He stepped closer and every instinct screamed at me to move away.

Demons feed on fear.

I could feel whatever was pulsing inside of him crawling against my arms as he leaned into me. It felt like hundreds of snakes struggling to break out of a sack. Sweat ran down my back, and I stared straight ahead. Inside my head, I was chanting *I can't see you, I can't see you.* Staring through him, I focused on breathing, in and out, in and out...

He smiled then, an ugly approximation of a human smile, and said silkily, "Nice try, pretty human."

He lifted a hand, and I flew backwards into the wall and collapsed on my knees. Groaning, I pushed myself into a sitting position and glared up at him.

"Son of a--"

He flicked a finger and, like a puppet, my arms lifted above my head and I was pulled upright. Horrified, I tried to resist but I had no control. In the blink of an eye, he stood pressed against me again. My arms were stretched painfully above me forcing my back to arch and my breasts to thrust forward. The belt of my robe was gone and the material hung away from me leaving me naked to his eyes. He took one hand and raised it to my chin. Unable to refuse, I looked at him and saw Sean instead. It was Sean's strong beautiful face that swam in front of me now. It was his hand that caressed my body and pulled me against him. Every voice in my head screamed in denial as he lowered his mouth and kissed me savagely. His hands groped me even as he forced my head back into the wall. Unable to push him away, I retreated into my head and closed my mind.

I can't see you. I can't hear you.

A brutal slap snapped my brain back to reality. The demon was back. Blood ran down my nose and I reached for it. Surprised I could move on my own, I flicked my eyes to the demon and pinched my nose to stop the bleeding. My chest was still bare and now covered with bright red blood. I dragged the robe around me and tied it tightly. Not that that would help…

"What do you want, demon?" I snarled at him, using the rest of my bravado. My brain was mush and I just wanted to sleep.

He didn't bother to answer me. Instead, he smiled again and snapped his fingers. My robe was gone. Stunned, I gaped at him.

"You are in my world now." He snapped his fingers again and my robe was wrapped around me. He glanced up at the camera and nodded. The LED light blinked to life.

"Sit down. We have much to discuss." He waved a hand towards the chair and waited politely.

Stiffly, I staggered over and sat down. No sense in antagonizing him…

Demons feed on fear…

I was terrified.

Oh, God, Sean! Where are you? Primly, I crossed my legs and tucked the robe around me and faced him with an expression of polite interest.

"So, what's on your mind?

"Wake up! Come on!" a voice whispered harshly in my ear. "You can't be dead!"

Hands shook me and the frantic whispering continued until I finally opened my eyes. Well, one eye. The other one was glued shut by caked blood. Waking up was a bad idea as the pain registered. Everything hurt. I moaned and even that hurt. I squinted and saw Doctor Green Eyes hovering above me looking worried.

"Who are you?" I croaked.

"Not now. You're a mess and they'll be back." He paused. "I can't believe you're still alive." Heavy footsteps sounded on the ceiling above us. Panicking, he injected me with something and a warm feeling of oblivion washed over me.

The dream swirled into the blackness of my mind, and I was blinded by its light. Squinting into the dream, I saw a white shape take form. Gradually it became clear. The farmhouse! Inside, Sean and Killian were arguing. I couldn't hear the words, but they were nose to nose and pushing at each other. Faces white with anger, they shouted at each other. A pale light glowed briefly and Dec appeared to shove them apart. His face was thin and dark circles stood out in sharp contrast to his pale skin. His eyes were bleak as he pleaded with his brothers. Sean stalked back a step and pointed a finger at Killian.

"This is your fault!"

"My fault? Really? You're the one sleeping with her," he said between his teeth.

Sean exploded and threw Killian into the nearest wall. They moved so fast I couldn't see everything clearly. It was a violent, ugly fight. They were trying to tear each other apart, and Dec was yelling at them both. The dream began to fade and I struggled to hold it.

"Sean! Sean! I'm here! Please...please...Killian! Wait!"

Staring up at the swaying camera, I trembled and bit my cheek to steady myself. I was back in the room again. I lost track of how many days I'd been here. Five? Ten? Between the doctor's drug cocktails and the savage beatings that left me unconscious, I hadn't been able to escape or call for help. During one fleeting moment of lucidity, I'd tried to yell for Dec but I had no audio...guess they figured that out and put me on mute.

My hair was hanging in front of my eyes and hurting my cheek. The gash was deep and puckered. Red and swollen too, it itched with infection. It was making me nuts, but I was too weak to move my hair and it hurt to shake my head. I could barely lift my hand, but I didn't need to move. The demon moved me when he wanted me to do something. That was good, I supposed, since I wasn't cooperating. I closed my eyes and tried to remember my middle name. Did I have a middle name? I'd lost huge chunks of my life...I was terrified I would slip into a coma and never wake up. Whenever I was even a little lucid, I'd been playing little games inside my head, forcing my brain to stay awake...trying to remember things about my life or lyrics to my favorite songs. Lately though, I'd been losing the memories and the will to keep playing the game. I prayed it was just the drugs.

Come on! Let's just get it over with! Making me wait was part of their game. It increased fear, my fear. It was the same thing each time; the same questions. I had no answers and my resistance was crumbling. I resisted by blocking him out of my mind. I simply closed the doors to those memories. It worked to keep them from getting information about the Primani, but wasn't healthy for me. Every time I retreated inside my head, the demon beat me...and worse.

Demons feed on fear...
Yes, Sean. They do.

But they enjoy pain more.

Broken, I let a tear run down my face. I was exhausted. I hadn't eaten. They didn't offer me food. I would starve to death soon.

"Shall we try again, human?" The silky voice was back.

Very deliberately, I raised my face and struggled for some emotion, any emotion at all, when I looked into the scarred face. The room wavered like it was underwater. His face swam in and out of focus. The grin stretched into a rictus. I flipped him off.

He just sighed and lifted his hand. Expecting to be thrown into the wall again, I stiffened. This time, though, was different. He pulled me upright like his own personal puppet.

Angry today, he circled me. "You don't respond to me. How are you resisting me? What is your magic?" His eyes burned in his face and his skin crawled restlessly. He studied me with an expression of concentration. "Not Primani...I would know it. There is *something*..."

With a wave of his hand, the blood-stained robe was gone and I hung naked like a broken mannequin. My matted hair hid my face. It was a shield of sorts, and I tried to retreat behind it. He was different today: more intense and angry. He paced like a caged animal. Something was wrong and my stomach clenched in dread.

There *were* worse things than being naked.

Suddenly he yanked my head up and shoved a long thin dagger against my throat. My eyes dimmed as I retreated again.

"Oh, no you don't! Not this time!" He grabbed a fistful of my hair and hacked it off. Working up to a hellish rage, he snapped his fingers and flung me to the floor. My knees were already raw and scabbed and pain shot through them when I landed.

Pulling me up, he switched faces. Oh, God, no. Not again. I couldn't resist him when he changed into Sean. Frantic, I backed away on my hands.

"No, no!" I pleaded, vision dimming to a pinpoint.

Most of my broken bones were from retreating when he turned into Sean. He made me feel things I knew were wrong. He made me want him even though I knew it wasn't Sean. The demon was convincing...and I was weakening.

It was only a matter of time.

"Take my hand, darlin'," the demon demanded in Sean's voice. The lilt was perfect.

"No, no, it's not him. Not him..." I curled into a ball and cried.

He lifted me up and held me against his chest. My mind swirled with images of Sean...real memories. No!

It's not him. It's not him.

Even as I chanted my denial, his hands gently stroked my back. There was nothing sexual in his embrace; there was only comfort. This touch was familiar, soft. It *could* be him...My body was racked with pain but he soothed it with his touch. Gradually, the animal panic faded and some rational thought broke through. The demon wasn't trying to have sex with me? What was he after? He had an angle...there was no way he wanted a hug. I realized he wasn't controlling me now. He thought he had weakened me enough to get me to cooperate. Frantically, I struggled to think clearly. My brain was overwhelmed with drugs and pain. Desperately, I tried to clear my head. There had to be something I could do...Raphael's face shimmered behind my eyes...he stood in the pale room I used for meditation. His lips didn't move, but I heard him say "Remember..." before he vanished like mist. Then a memory came to me...so long ago...we sat in the kitchen and he talked to me about my future.

With serious eyes he'd said, "I'm afraid your destiny isn't written in stone, little one. It's still evolving, as are you. You continue to surprise us with new abilities and these will continue to shape your destiny."

"What are you saying, Raphael? I'm not going to be with the Primani? With Sean?"

He shook his head. "No, child, that's not what I'm saying at all. Your true destiny is forged by your abilities and how you choose to use them. It comes down to choices. I'm saying you must harness these abilities now. Work to understand and sharpen them. Use your strengths to become stronger. Use your wisdom to become wiser. Use your sight to see farther."

He smiled gently at me then. "You will be challenged and you will be hurt. There is great pain on your path, Mica."

The demon tensed and dragged me closer to him. Still masquerading as Sean, he whispered into my ear. "I need your help, Mica. Will you not help me?" He stroked my back. "It's such a little thing." His lips branded me just under my ear and my flesh crawled in revulsion. My brain started to freeze up in resistance, but Raphael's words echoed.

Use your sight to see farther...

Stalling, I asked, "What can I do? I have no answers." Forcing myself to act cowed, I dropped my head down.

The silky voice was back and strong hands held me up when my knees gave out. No force, just strength. He purred in my ear, "Where is *Sgaine Dutre*? Where is it?"

"I told you, Sean, I don't know what that is."

Waves of heat erupted from him as the human façade crumbled with his fresh anger. His clawed hands dug into my neck as he squeezed. Blood streamed from the jagged holes he made. The mask of Sean melted away and revealed his true face. Black scales replaced the soft human skin. I strained to move away from him, but his power was absolute. He hissed at me and produced a short black blade. He pressed the tip against my collarbone.

"Your convenient memory loss is getting tiresome. My patience is done."

He pressed the athame into my skin and carved a symbol across my chest. It didn't even hurt. I was surprised to see blood streaming down my stomach. Little red rivers…dazed, I tried to raise my head.

"At this rate, you'll bleed out soon. I suggest you search your memory once more. Call me if you remember anything useful." He snapped his fingers, and I was abruptly in my cell.

Collapsing to my knees, I struggled to keep my eyes open. This was really, really bad. There was no coming back from this. I was already losing too much blood from my throat, there was no way I could heal myself now. Sean would come. He had to. He had to…I just had to call him…The room grew dimmer and I struggled to stand up. I fell on my face instead.

"Oh, God! What did they do?" Doctor Green Eyes scooped me up and sat me on the bed.

With more strength than I thought possible, I grabbed his hand and gritted out, "Inject me, *now.*"

Confused, he hesitated. "Inject you?"

"Wake me up!" I ordered. "I can't…pass…out. Please…" My voice trailed off as the room dimmed to a single stream of light.

Shaking off the confusion, he filled a syringe and pushed it into my arm. I leaned back on the bed and let it work. I closed my eyes and let the drug overrun the haziness in my mind. Like adrenaline, it pushed aside the fog of pain and starvation and shock and gave me clarity. I have to stay awake. I have to call him. Taking a deep breath, I called to Sean. If I could bring him back from other planes and universes, surely I could call him to me now. He was connected to me. He would hear me. He had to. There was no time to be careful as I'd been before. The consequences couldn't be any worse. My mind was too fuzzy to form a precise image; instead, I projected out my own image...lying bloody and dying in this bare room.

Sean...Sean, please! Come now...hurry. I'm dying...dying...

I was vaguely aware of Dr. Green Eyes wrapping me in bandages and pressing on my wounds, but the wounds in my neck were deep. He couldn't stop the bleeding and swore desperately at me. He was begging me to hold on, to not die, to let him help. With the rhythm of my heartbeat, the blood flowed steadily and soon my legs were cold, my fingers tingling. My heart began to slow.

Sean...I can't hold on...can't hold on...

The doctor opened my mouth and kissed me. "Come on, come on!" His voice was harsh but I barely heard him. He was very far away.

My fingers were cold. I shivered violently. So cold...My heart fluttered like a trapped butterfly inside my chest. It would stop any second now.

The doctor kissed me again and my heart stuttered. It tripped and stuttered. I gasped for oxygen, my back arching off the bed.

I'm sorry, baby, I'm... My heart stuttered one more time and stopped. *Done.*

"No! No, you can't die. Hang on!" He pressed his lips against mine and blew air into my lungs. Counting breaths, he pinched my nose and blew again.

Not kisses after all...

"Mica! No!"

I hesitated. I had been drifting, but the command stopped me. Sean?

Oh, Sean, it's too late. I'm already dead.

"Oh, no you don't! Get back in your body now. It's not your time." Sean's angry demand gave me pause.

Confused, I looked around and realized I'd been hovering just above my body. I looked at him and he met my eyes. His beautiful eyes glittered with fury as they locked onto mine. Fury and something else. Fear? Pain? Desperation?

"You can see me?" I asked.

"Of course I can see you! Now get your ass back into your body before I strangle you."

Dec added impatiently, "We can't move you without your body *and* your soul. You'll need them both. Hurry up!"

I must have hesitated because Sean growled and lunged at me.

Chapter 10: Grounded for Eternity

COLD...SO COLD...I shivered. My heart tripped and stuttered inside my chest. I wasn't going to live. Even Sean couldn't stop death. He might be an angel, but he wasn't God. I sucked in a breath of air and Sean's arms tightened around me. I would be okay with dying in his arms though.

"Dec, you've got to fix this." His voice was shaking.

Gentle hands lowered me to the bed, and someone pulled the robe off of me. Twin gasps of shock. My heartbeat grew fainter again.

"Mica, baby, can you hear me?" Sean's voice was gentle, pleading. "We're here now. We've got to fix you up. Hang in there--No floating." He squeezed my fingers so tightly my knuckles ground together audibly.

Dec said, "I'm going to heal you. Just keep breathing. Please..." Warm fingertips closed around my neck sinking into the ragged tears. I writhed beneath him as he reached into each tear and sealed the ripped arteries. It burned like fire, and I whimpered and tried to move away.

"Hush now, it'll be okay. I have to do this to stop the bleeding." Something warm and wet dripped onto my cheek. He sniffed and murmured, "Almost done..."

Sean wrapped me in a blanket and stroked my hair. "Dec? How's it going?" He was barely controlling his panic; his hands were shaking while he held my hand.

Dec finished with my throat and though it still burned like fire, the bleeding stopped. My heart stopped twitching and turned over a more regular beat. He moved to my chest and covered the carving with one of his big warm hands. I looked into his face, just inches from my own, and saw the tears in his eyes as he focused inward.

Such pretty eyes…blue and soft…gentle…I drifted off to sleep again.

"No sleeping!" Sean gripped my chin between two fingers and forced my eyes open. "Stay focused on me. Look at my face."

I blinked and tried to focus on him. He was blurry and swam in and out of my sight. My eyes were very heavy, but he squeezed my chin. I blinked and his face was steadier.

Dec said, "I think the bleeding's stopped. We need to clean her up though. There's too much blood to tell…" His voice cracked. "I'll get some water."

After he left, Sean dropped to his knees and murmured in a low angry voice. "*Saogin dea, saogin dea. Deone' culpae satrinae.*"

When Dec came back, they got to work cleaning me up. Using wash cloths, they carefully washed away the blood to see the destruction underneath.

Gasping, I tensed when someone lifted my right arm. "Ow, that hurts."

There was a pause. "Well, it's broken…" Dec said, "…in three places."

"That hurts," I said when someone rubbed the washcloth over my right thigh.

Another pause. "It's broken too."

When they lifted my left leg, I broke into a cold sweat. "This one too?" Sean asked softly.

Dec confirmed, "In two places." His voice was terrible.

"I'm okay, I'll be fine. I just need some sleep…"

Ignoring my protests, they finished with my front side, and carefully rolled me onto my stomach and froze. Not a sound from either of them. "What?" I managed to ask. What was wrong with my back? I lost track of everything the demon did…

It was Killian who growled in response, "There is no hole deep enough."

Sean finally found his voice and choked, "My God."

"What...is that?" Dec asked.

It was Dec who began washing away the blood and I sucked in my breath. "Ow." He froze and his face crumpled into sobs. He dropped to his knees and buried his face against the bed and cried.

"Oh, Dec, no. Don't cry for me. It's nothing. I'll be okay." I tried to turn over and he gently pressed me back down.

"You shouldn't move." His voice hitched with a sob, but he cleared his throat.

Sean knelt down by my face. "His name. Did you get his name?"

He reached one hand out and very carefully slid my hair out of my eyes. He touched me as if I would shatter into crystals. The gentleness of his touch was so at odds with the promise of vengeance in his eyes.

"*Sgaine Dutre?*" I whispered.

His howl of rage sent shivers down my spine. He'd barely held onto his control and now it snapped. Jumping up, he put his fist through the mirror and yelled for Raphael.

I awoke feeling disoriented and sat up in a panic. My sudden movement brought Sean's head up and he quickly tried to smile. It was a good attempt, but the result was iffy.

"5.5," I said.

"What?"

"That's a half-ass attempt at a smile. Aren't you glad to see me? And alive too?" I wiggled fully functional fingers at him in a jaunty little wave.

His mouth curved into a genuine, though fleeting, smile. "You're grounded, young lady. You're not allowed out of my sight for...I think...eternity is an appropriate amount of time."

"How do you feel?" he asked seriously.

I carefully moved my arms and legs and touched my nose. The pain was gone, but my head swam alarmingly and I swayed with dizziness. They might have healed my broken bones, but they couldn't heal weeks' worth of starvation, no matter how powerful they were. He reached over and helped me lay back down. He stayed perched on the side of my bed and stared at his hands. Strong, beautiful hands...I reached out and traced the blue vein that pulsed on the top of his hand. In response to my touch, his *saol* flowed faster and rose to the surface. It left a reassuring trail of golden light under my finger. He covered my hand with his and brought it to his heart. The warmth and steady beat soothed my jangled nerves and I closed my eyes. I felt his heartbeat against my palm and it glowed behind my eyes and was echoed with my own. He was my heart, my soul. He was my 'forever and always'. He didn't have to ground me. I wasn't going anywhere.

"I am yours, you are mine. Do you remember that night?" I pulled his face to mine, and he kissed me gently, his lips barely grazing my own. Inhaling his scent, I felt warm again for the first time in a long time. "I love you."

His arms shook from holding himself back. But he slid them around me and pulled me close. Kissing my hair, he murmured, "I love you more."

We sat wrapped in each other's arms until a tap at the door interrupted us. Raphael poked his head inside and his smile was radiant as he exclaimed, "Little Mica! How good it is to see you so pink again." With the attitude of a professional healer, he felt my pulse and took my temperature. After listening to my heartbeat, now back to normal, he proclaimed I would live.

"You frightened us quite badly, you know. These young Primani saved your life. If they hadn't found you when they did, you would have been far beyond our help. As it is, shoving your spirit back into your dead body was stretching the rules a tad."

He smiled mischievously and added, "On the other hand, I don't think we can force you to vacate your corpse until you're ready--lack of heartbeat aside."

102

CALL THE LIGHTNING

"Raphael, thank you for saving my life *again.*" I squeezed his arm and looked down, embarrassed.

"I didn't save your life this time; you were out of danger when I got here."

"No, you did." I cleared my throat and told him about the memory that came to me when the demon was torturing me. Sean was leaning against my side and I welcomed the solid feel of him. He whistled softly when I finished my story.

"Well, you've had more than your share of pain now. I hope destiny is satisfied." Sean raised an eyebrow at Raphael. His look said 'it better be.'

Raphael shrugged elegantly, "Who's to know? I certainly do not." Turning back to me, he added, "I do, however, know that you have a great future with us and we cannot lose you so soon." He held out a hand and pulled me to my feet. "Alex is here and he's called a family meeting since you're up to it."

"Mica! You look so much better!" Dec greeted me first. Bounding over to me, he scooped me up into an enthusiastic, but oh-so-gentle, bear hug. Kissing my cheek, he searched my eyes for signs of pain. "Are you strong enough to be up? Don't lie. I know you."

I pressed my cheek against his shoulder and hugged him to me. Tears sprang to my eyes and I sniffed. He held me away and wiped a tear from my chin. "What's this? Why are you crying?"

So much for bravery..."I'm just a little...overwhelmed I guess." My eyes overflowed and he pressed me into him again.

"It's okay, darlin'. You've had a rough time. Give yourself a break. Not *all* of your wounds can be healed with *my* hands." He rubbed my back and I felt calmer as his magic went to work.

"Oh, Dec! I thought I'd never see you again! I couldn't stand that...knowing that I left like I did. I was

103

so angry with you guys. I left and didn't tell you I love you."

He smiled down at me and a single tear slid over his perfect cheekbone. "You don't have to say the words; I know your heart." Playfully, he held out a familiar shiny chain.

"But how did you find that? They took it from me."

"Your doctor friend had it in his pocket. He was more than eager to hand it over when I asked *politely*." He slipped it around my neck and locked the clasp. The small gold heart settled over my own and glowed like a firefly for a moment.

"That's much better. You're lucky he carried it around with him. When Sean heard your call, we used the locket to zero in on you. It's like a little GPS."

"It's all very touching, but can we get on with this meeting?"

I whirled around. "James? What are *you* doing here?"

Alex considered the two of us thoughtfully and cleared his throat. "Mica, come and join me on the couch." He patted a soft cushion near him.

Sean took my hand and walked over with me. He draped himself over the arm of the couch closest to me. I guess he wasn't letting me out of his sight any time this century.

James scowled as Sean rested his hand over my shoulder. Narrowing my eyes, I threw him a stare. What was his problem? I pasted a fake smile while I thought over our last meeting. I needed to talk to Sean about that. There was something wrong with *this* Primani...

Something you'd like to share, Princess? His tone was sarcastic, but the look he gave me was anything but.

Killian. Perfect and perfectly annoying, he stood casually with arms crossed in front of him looking down his nose at all of us. That was classic Killian. In spite of his bad attitude, it was good to see him. I drank him in. He looked tired and pale. His jaw was shadowed and eyes hollow in their sockets. Dec and Sean had the same air of exhaustion about them. What happened to them while I was gone? There must've been a mission, a big one, from the looks of them. They all looked like hell.

You're an idiot. You know that, right? He was subtly shaking his head.

So we're back to insults, are we? That didn't take long. Glad I didn't cry all over you.

He huffed and his silent laughter warmed my heart. Who was I kidding? I was exceptionally glad to see him any time I could.

But what about Ramon? Look what he's capable of. You can't trust him. The doubting voice whispered to me.

His laughter abruptly stopped, and I glanced up expecting to see him smirking at me. His eyes held mine in a look that spoke volumes. His eyes widened, letting me in, challenging me to look if I dared. Did I want to look inside and see the real Killian? Could I handle the truth? Not now...

I was so scared that night.

Of me. His tone was flat, almost angry. Oblivious to everyone else, his eyes bored into mine, an electric spark from across the room.

I couldn't meet his eyes and lowered mine. *Yes.*

Damn it, look at me! Why didn't you talk to me? After all we've been through? You know you can talk to me!

You killed that man...Ramon. For nothing! How could you?

He pushed away from the wall and stalked over to me, face white with fury. Startled, Sean leaped to his feet and Killian stopped. "Get up. It's time for you and me to have a *real* conversation."

"What do you think you're doing? Let her be." Sean and Dec both spoke up at once.

Killian shrugged off their objections and pointed at me. "We have unfinished business, her and I. Let's go. Now!"

I wasn't afraid of him, usually. But at the moment, I was weak and he was pissed at me and I was just a tiny bit afraid of his power. I stood up but didn't move towards him.

Holding out his hand, he exhaled through his nose and said in a more reasonable tone, "I can't make you. I'm asking you. Please."

"I'll be right back." I kissed Sean on the lips and held out my hand to Killian.

He gripped my hand securely in his. I heard him say, "Don't count on it!" as we vanished into the dark.

Chapter 11: Healing and Forgiveness

ONE SECOND WE WERE IN THE PENTHOUSE in Manhattan and the next we were….here. Curious, I looked around at the green hillside and was lost. There were no houses or buildings of any kind in any direction I turned. There was nothing but green hills to the east and flat rocky land to the west. Cold wind swept down on us blowing my hair in my eyes. As I automatically tried to put it in a ponytail, I remembered my hair was gone and lowered my hand slowly with a sigh. I was still holding Killian's hand and let it go.

"Where are we?" I whispered. It felt like holy land.

He laughed loudly and threw his hands out. "You don't have to whisper. Who's going to hear us?"

He looked so happy I thought he might have come unhinged during our flight.

"Afraid not, babe. I'm just free here."

"Okay, can you *please* stop reading my mind? Here, at least? I need to know my thoughts can be private. I might have secrets…from you."

He considered that for a minute and said seriously, "I *do* have secrets from you. But maybe I can share a few of them while we're here." He stepped closer to me and lifted my chin so he could look into my face. "Can you keep another secret? Mine?"

I wasn't sure of his mood just then. Was he serious? Was he joking? I said, "You'd ask me that after what that demon did to me? I died protecting your secrets."

His eyes clouded and he let go of my chin. "That was thoughtless of me. I'm sorry. I didn't mean it that way."

Turning away, I said, "I know…I'm a little raw right now. Can we get out of this wind before I freeze to death?"

"I know just the place. Come on." He grabbed my hand and led me down the hillside into a jumble of ancient rocks. The grey rocks were leaning on each other like the ruins of an old castle. As we approached the pile, a feeling of complete calm settled over me and I felt light and warm. It felt oddly holy here. The very air seemed to shimmer with life.

"Killian, what is this place?"

He turned and spread his arms. "Home sweet home." Smiling hugely, he added, "Dip your hands in the water before you cross the threshold. It's custom."

He gestured to a shallow basin that formed the top of a stone near a crack in the rock. It was little more than an indention in the stone; it could've been carved out by dripping rainwater over centuries. But I had a feeling it was made by the hands of men. Looking closer, I could see the crack was wider than it looked. I looked sideways at him and he gestured with a sweep of his arm.

"Go ahead. Hell, I'm an angel. What kind of trouble do you think I'd get you into?"

He had a point. I carefully dipped my hands in the basin and sluiced water over my hands and wrists. I felt compelled to clean myself completely before entering this place. Killian noticed and nodded with approval. He did the same and ducked inside. A minute later, he pulled me in after him. It was dark as a cave. Afraid to move, I hovered just inside the entrance.

"Wait there." I heard a scratching sound and a small light appeared. Killian held a shallow bowl that was full of light so I could see. It put off a surprising amount of light.

"What's in the bowl?"

"Moonlight," he said with a perfectly straight face.

"Uh-huh. Yeah, sure." It was like a temple inside. There was a stone altar and carved pots sitting around it. Painted runes lined the altar and the walls. I had no idea what the red markings said, but I knew this place was very old.

"You might as well get comfortable. We'll be here for a while." With a gracefulness I've never possessed, he slid to a reclining position on the floor. He patted the dirt next to him.

"Let me get this straight. We're alone, in the middle of nowhere, in God knows what time, and you didn't pack blankets or food. And you accuse me of being flighty?"

"You'll be warm and I can get food when we need it. We'll be okay, I swear. Now sit."

He was lying on his side propped up on his elbow. I lay opposite him so we could talk face to face. The moonlight did interesting things to the planes of his face though and I had trouble listening to his words.

After a few minutes he said, "Why are you staring at my face? You're not hearing me, are you?"

I blushed to the roots of my pixie hair. "It's the moonlight. I can't concentrate."

"Fine. Come over here and you can look the other way."

I ended up lying on my side with my back against his chest. I could feel his breath tickling the back of my neck while he talked. Every time he breathed his chest expanded against my back and a tingle of electricity spiraled down my spine to my toes. I knew exactly how hard the muscles of his chest were and how far down the happy trail went...Oh, Jesus.

"I have to sit up." I hopped up and sat cross-legged a safe distance away. I didn't care if I froze to death or not. His nearness was killing me. He seemed completely unaffected by me. Was he so immune? Maybe he was. He was ancient, after all. Did they make Viagra for 3,000-year-old soldiers-of-Heaven?

He eyed me strangely but didn't comment. Instead, he said, "Enough small talk. I brought you here because I care about you and I hate fighting with you." He raised an eyebrow and added, "Yes, I said it. Tell anyone I did and I'll just deny it. You'll only look stupid and lovesick so you should probably keep your mouth shut." The eyebrow came back down.

"You don't understand everything you probably should about us. So let's talk about some things. First of all, I didn't kill Ramon." He held up his hand and my audio cut out. My mouth moved in argument, but no sound came out.

Eyes throwing daggers at him, I clamped my lips together. There was no point in pushing it; I'd get audio back when he was ready to hear me.

"Ramon is perfectly happy living a new life. He's working at a Best Buy selling cell phones in Houston. I swear!" He crossed his heart and waved his hand imperiously. "Go ahead, you have questions. Ask."

"But you were hurting him. I saw you."

"True statement. The process isn't easy but it's worth it. In simple terms, I reprogrammed his memory. I retrieved all of the memories of his criminal activities so we could figure out who hired him to attack us. I've been told that it is...unpleasant...to have your memories siphoned off. He didn't seem to like it much so it's probably painful." He shrugged a shoulder. He didn't really care if it hurt or not.

"After I retrieved the memories, I erased them from his mind. I erased each memory of every evil or even criminal act he'd done. In his case, there were a lot of memories. That's what really hurts--the erasing part. Most people faint from the pain."

My mouth hung open, and he reached over and closed it with a long, lean finger. "But--"

"He's got his other memories, and he'll move ahead in his life doing good things or at least, not doing bad things. He won't recognize his old criminal friends and get into trouble. He's in a new city with a fresh start. And, we've got a lot of helpful information. It was a win-win. Now, isn't that better than killing him?"

He was so smug.

I wanted to smack him in the head.

He burst out laughing and said, "Come on, babe. You made a mistake. It's all right. You're only human, after all."

"You are such a...such a..." I was at a loss. He was right. I'd made a mistake and what a colossal mistake it was. If I hadn't jumped to conclusions, if I would've trusted Killian, I wouldn't have been so freaked out. I wouldn't have left them.

"All of this pain...it's my fault. I should've asked what happened. I jumped to stupid conclusions. I'm sorry. I'm so, so sorry." I walked over to one of the walls and stopped. I wanted to lean against it, but that seemed disrespectful, so I stood awkwardly and let my shoulders slump. "You guys could've died because of my stupidity, having to rescue me again! I'm an idiot."

In the space of a heartbeat, he was standing behind me. He eased me back and rested his chin on my head. Rubbing little circles on my arm, he said, "This isn't your fault."

Turning me around, he asked, "Do you blame yourself for this demon snatching you off the streets?"

When I didn't answer him, he shook me and said harshly, "*Not* your fault! This is what evil is, Mica! Demons prey on people. They use people for their own agendas. They tried to use you to get to us. My God, if it's *anybody's* fault, it's ours. Primani and demons are ancient enemies. We've fought each other since Adam and Eve got thrown out of Eden. It's the nature of things. Good and evil will always be enemies. But it's our job to protect humans and it was our job, *my* job, to protect you."

Oddly formal, he declared, "It is I who needs to beg for *your* forgiveness." His eyes reflected the moonlight as he looked steadily into mine.

Searching his face, I saw the lines and the dark circles under his eyes and I knew them for what they were. They were scars from his self-inflicted wounds. He was in agony when I disappeared. He hadn't slept, he probably hadn't eaten. He worried and he accepted the blame like he did when we lost Sean. How many nights did we sit in silence touching our fingers together, just to share the guilt, the feeling of bone-deep grief? There had been no words of comfort. Just the barest touch of physical contact to remind us we still lived. How many days did we bury the grief and rage by throwing ourselves into training and hunting so we could be exhausted enough to sleep without nightmares?

And how often did that work?

I whispered, "You give too much; let me give something to you."

I reached out and cupped his face in my hand. He sighed softly and closed his eyes as I traced the strong lines of his cheek and jaw. Light as a feather, I erased the circles under his eyes and soothed the sharp crease between his brows. My fingertips were warm and strong as I took away the tension that banded his forehead.

Then, very gently, I ran my thumbs over the silky skin of his eyelids. Soft and delicate, the skin protected his most dangerous weapon. He stiffened when I slid both palms down the tight muscles in his neck but then relaxed when I stopped. Breathing slowly and deeply, I released my energy into his shoulders. I let my mind wander as my *saol* flowed through him. I felt the rise and fall of his chest as his breathing slowed. His heart beat against my chest, its rhythm powerful and steady.

Looking down, I saw the faint glow had already encircled us both, and he was asleep on his feet. Satisfied by the very tiniest hint of softness in his expression, I lifted my hands and pulled my *saol* back to me. As the last of the glow faded to moonlight, I tugged his hand and pulled him down to the floor. He was so tired, he simply followed me. Curling up in front of him, I shivered with the sudden chill of the earth floor. Without a sound, he draped an arm around me and pulled me back against him. Like all males, including supernatural ones, he burned with his own private furnace. His heat made me drowsy and I started to drift off. Maybe it should worry me that we fit together like a lock and key, but it didn't. Completely sure of him, I closed my eyes and slept like the dead.

"Come on, there's something I want you to see!" Killian paused at the top of a slope and waited for me to catch up. The noon sun glinted off of his black hair and caught the sparkle in his eyes. He was so happy here and his happiness was infectious. I grinned and picked up my pace.

"You're getting slow!" he commented when I finally caught up to him.

"You've got supernatural powers. It's an unfair advantage."

The view from here was pretty incredible. The slope was covered in purple heather and ended at the sea. "Oh, it's beautiful! Can we get closer? Please?"

Laughing at me, he said, "Sure, why not? It is beautiful, isn't it?"

We picked our way to the rocky shore, and only one of us managed to stay dry. I was wringing out my socks and vainly wondering if my butt looked fat in my wet yoga pants. They were cotton and clung like second skin. Since I didn't know I was taking a Tolkien-like journey, I was wearing black yoga pants, a tank top and a hoodie. I had tennis shoes on my feet. These weren't the best shoes for hiking the heather, but at least I wasn't wearing flip-flops.

Back from rock hopping, Killian draped himself on top of a dry rock and leaned back into the sun. Waves crashed incessantly against the rocks as they tried to reclaim the land. I closed my eyes and gave my senses to the ocean. Salt tickled my tongue, waves crashed in my ears, fine cold spray dotted my face and the blue, oh, the blue of the water was heaven. It was the exact shade of Primani eyes. Was it only Irish-born Primani? Hmmm.

"Killian? Do you get your eyes from the ocean?" I asked sleepily.

He snorted and said, "Aye, lass, and my luxurious hair from a wee silkie."

"Your eyes are the exact color of this water."

He sat up and blinked at me. "Really? Funny, that. Yours are too."

"No, they aren't. Mine aren't that...uh, blue." I blushed and turned away.

"That's not what you were going to say. I thought we had no secrets here?" His voice teased like a caress.

"I was going to say 'beautiful,' but I didn't want to stroke your ego any more. God knows it's big enough." I stuck out my tongue for good measure.

He just laughed and said, "You used the words 'stroke' and 'big' in the same sentence. Did you have something on your mind?" He leaned back enticingly and patted his lap in invitation.

"Pig!" I couldn't help laughing at the exaggerated leer on his face.

Slipping over to my rock, he made himself comfortable. "Something's bothering me." I nodded and he continued. "The demon had to know you were in the city. The usual trackers either physically follow you around or they use a tracer. Tracers can be physical or psychic."

"How would someone put a psychic tracer on me? Wouldn't I know?"

"No, you wouldn't unless you know what to look for. Have you noticed any changes in your thoughts? Any ideas that might push you away from home, something that isn't quite you? If they wanted to get you to the city, pushing you there would be the easiest way. You come on your own and you're easier to get to. With us around, well, that's a harder way to go."

I thought back to the little voices I'd heard. I'd thought they were my own thoughts, insecurities..."Well, the night of the break in, I had a really, really bad dream where you guys made Sean kill me and burned my body. "I described what I remembered of the dream. "I felt betrayed when I woke up."

His face blanched, "That's some dream." He thought for a minute and asked about voices in my head. "Not schizophrenic voices, but the little nagging doubts that aren't really true to your nature. They'd hit you when your defenses are down."

Slowly, I said, "Maybe. I regretted leaving as soon as I got to the penthouse. After the weird scene with James, I wanted to call Sean, but something kept telling me you guys didn't care about me. I argued about that. I *know* you guys care about me. But the little voice was convincing enough that I decided not to call that night. Then I wanted to call later, and the voice hinted that you didn't really want me on the team or trust me with anything important. After all, you'd all left me there alone and gone out on a mission without me. It hurt my feelings and I decided not to call."

Amusement glittered in his eyes, but he smothered a smile with his hand. "So, let me get this straight. You had a mental argument with *yourself* and you lost?"

"All I can say to that is *wow*," he added.

"Oh, funny. That's not exactly how it went. The voice wasn't so obvious. There were just little suggestions that played into my fears. I'm already insecure. It wasn't hard to play on that." I stretched and yawned. "Wow that really pisses me off when I think about it. Do you think it's the same demon who tried to kill me?"

"Not sure yet. We'll work it out though. We can't let this go without a reaction. It would tip the scales in their favor. Not to mention, none of us will rest until we've blown that demon back to Hell."

Totally changing the subject, he asked, "Are you getting hungry yet?"

"Yes! All this fresh air is wearing me out and making me hungry. What's on the menu? Seal steaks or sushi? I think I see some fish out there…"

"Even better. Close your eyes and don't move. I'll be right back." He vanished with a grin.

I sat up and looked around. "Killian?"

"Over here!" He'd reappeared behind me with a basket in his hands.

Curious, I grabbed my clothes and hopped over to him. "What's that?"

Holding it above his head, he said, "Not yet. Let's walk a bit and find some grass. You can call it a picnic."

The sun was burning just over the horizon. Everything was red and gold as the sun set to the west. Even the water burned like the sun. Killian came up behind me and asked if I was cold.

I rubbed my arms. "A little, but it's such a long journey for the sun, it's almost rude to leave before it's finished."

"You have an odd way of looking at things. Are you sure you're human?" He lifted an arm in invitation and I curled under it to lean into the furnace of his body. My goose bumps vanished immediately. We stood in companionable silence while the sun sank beyond our sight. Millions of pinpricks of lights replaced the sunset and I craned my neck to see the night sky.

"Can we lie down?" I asked.

"What did you have in mind?"

I smacked him in the stomach and he grunted. "You have a surprisingly dirty mind for an angel."

"I asked an innocent question. I think you have the dirty mind, which makes more sense since you're the *human*."

He bent close to my ear and said, "Okay, what do you want to do?"

A little breathless, I said, "I want to look at the stars, on my back."

"Ask and you shall receive. Come on."

Five minutes later, I was still smiling. Shaking my head, but smiling. Ask and you shall receive, indeed. We were lying side by side on the grassy hill above the stone ruins. I was using his arm for a pillow and sucking up his excess body heat to stay warm. If anyone saw us, they'd think we were aliens, lying here in the dark, glowing with our own personal starlight. I giggled at the image and he grinned. The night sky was like black velvet, the stars brilliant against it. I felt like we were the only two people in the world.

That begged the question.

"Are we the only people in the world?" I whispered.

"If we were, why would you whisper?"

He had a point. "I don't know. It's rude to shout?"

"Well, are we?"

He turned to his side and pulled me closer. My body responded with a mind of its own and I arched against him. He cupped my head and lowered his mouth to mine. The kiss was so soft I might have imagined it. He lowered my head to my makeshift pillow and leaned back to look at the sky.

"Yes. Does that frighten you?"

Not really; at the moment it sounded like a good thing. There was no way to deny what my body wanted. At the first touch of his lips, my blood heated and my heart pounded in anticipation. I knew perfectly well he could feel my reaction to his kiss, but he was choosing to behave. I groaned and took a deep breath. I'm a terrible person. Geez, he could have me right now if he wanted to. All it would take was one more kiss, one more touch, one simple *word* from him.

No matter how many calming deep breaths I sucked in, I couldn't deny the attraction I felt, and I wouldn't lie to him, if he *asked*...probably, I shouldn't volunteer this information. Sean's face popped into my head. He seemed to scowl at me. Yes, it's better if we don't take this to another level. Unless of course we somehow get trapped in this dimension and have to repopulate the earth from scratch. Visually, that was an interesting thought. I could picture Killian lifting me up against a tree or in the pounding surf of the ocean intent on creating babies. Our bodies would move together, slamming with the rhythm of the tides. The hard muscle of his shoulders bunched as he held me in place, the ripple of movement across his abs...sea spray glistening over my breasts. My body warmed at the idea and I spent a minute playing that through inside my head. The surf could be very useful.

"You do know I can read your mind, right?" He leaned over me and looked into my eyes. His expression was a mix of amusement and pain.

Oh, shit. I was so busted. My face went up in flames.

"Still reading your mind," he teased. "Would you like to finish your fantasy though? At this point, we'd both feel better."

"You're evil!" I snapped and stomped into the ruin.

Laughing incredulously, he said, "I'm the one with restraint here! Do you have any idea how much I want to throw you to the floor and yank those pants off of you?"

He was kidding, sort of, but a wave of dizziness washed over me at the word 'yank.' I stumbled and he steadied me. "I don't need your help!" I said just as I tripped on another stone.

"Going to take care of yourself?" he whispered next to my ear.

"You have such a dirty mind! I knew it!"

He spun me around and said sternly, "And you, Princess, are having impure thoughts about your Primani. *That* is a punishable offense." As he said the words, his hand traveled down my back to rest just inside my waistband. His fingers idly played with the fabric.

My heart thudded in my chest, and I clutched his shirt and pulled him closer. "What's my punishment?"

He smiled wickedly and licked his lips. My mouth watered at the sight and I swallowed hard. Every nerve in my body tensed when he slowly dragged his fingers through my hair to expose my neck. Breathing unevenly, he whispered against my ear, "A spanking, of course."

"You are such a jerk!" I glared at him from across the altar. "I can't believe you did that!"

"Oh, come on, it didn't hurt! It was just a tap." He was grinning broadly at my outrage. He moved my direction.

Stepping to the other side, I said, "That's not what I meant, and you know it!" I huffed and crossed my arms.

Brandishing an apple, he said, "I've got food. Come and sit down. You can't sleep on the altar." He actually shuddered at the thought.

"Oh, how appropriate, Satan, you brought an apple," I said snidely.

He looked appalled. "Don't speak that name in here! Are you crazy?" He knelt at the altar and murmured words and crossed himself.

He moved so fast I missed his intention. Before I could blink, he scooped me up and deposited us both on a heavy rug that must've come with the apple.

"Just sit, all right?" He held my hand and refused to release it even though I tugged on it. "No way. I'm keeping your hand for the moment." I tugged harder and he smiled his feral grin.

"You keep pulling like that and it'll come right off at the wrist."

I gave in with bad grace. "Fine. What's your point?"

"Babe, we've been through hell together. Haven't we?" He squeezed my hand.

I nodded and relaxed my hand in his.

"We've known each other for four years now. In the beginning you were just another charge…and not even *my* charge. You were a pain in the ass, but you had *such* courage and strength. I didn't want to like you, but I couldn't help respecting you. You were a warrior in your own reckless, human way. Then you and Sean got together." He paused and took a bite of the apple.

He absently stroked my fingers while he talked. His voice was compelling, and I leaned closer to him. "It wasn't exactly forbidden, just very uncommon. We Primani don't allow ourselves to feel anything other than responsibility towards our charges. But Sean…well, I don't blame Sean. I never have." He smiled wolfishly and pointed at me with the apple, "I've always blamed you."

I yanked my hand and nothing moved. "Me?"

"Yes, you! You've been different from the beginning. It took me a while to see it, but I've known for years now." He paused and chewed another bite of apple.

"Aren't you going to share that, Adam?" I joked with a real smile.

"Of course, here take a bite." He held it to my mouth. I took a small bite and licked juice off my chin.

"So, you were saying how I've coerced Sean into falling in love with me? Do continue."

He chuckled and continued, "No, babe, you haven't done anything wrong. You never could. I'm trying to say you're meant for Sean and he's the key to you. We all know, and I mean *all* Primani, know there is the rare moment when a human becomes eternally entangled with an angel. This isn't the first time, but it is really rare. *You* are really rare." He sighed and paused to collect his thoughts.

He reached over and touched my cheek with the backs of his fingers. "You've shown me love, *real* love, and I will treasure your gift to me. Always." His eyes grew distant and the silence stretched.

"I love you. That hasn't changed." I kissed his knuckles and smiled a wobbly smile.

"You just want my body."

Chapter 12: A Serpent in the Garden

"WE'LL HAVE TO LEAVE HERE SOON. The others will be angry with me as it is." He offered me some water and stared over the waves. The gentle breeze ruffled his hair, and I thought he'd never been more relaxed.

I sighed wistfully. "Do we really have to go back? It's so peaceful here. I feel better here."

"It has a special magic of its own. You're feeling better under its influence. It affects me too."

"Really? How does it affect you? Do you feel happy here? You seem so relaxed." That was a good thing.

"It's a long story, but I'll just say it recharges me in ways that my own *saol* could never do." He reached over and drew me against him suddenly. I stumbled and fell into him. Standing this close, I was vividly aware of our feelings for each other and my arms curled around his neck.

Uncurling my fingers, he said wryly, "And *that* is another effect of the magic here."

"You lost me."

He grinned down at me and said, "Fuck it, one kiss won't hurt."

Before I could react, he kissed me with an intensity that made my head swim. His mouth claimed mine. There was no gentleness this time, no butterfly wings. He was a warrior and he took what he wanted. My body melted against him. I wanted him. I needed him. His power, his heat...There was *only* him. My mind whispered his name like a prayer. Killian, please...I tugged his shirt up and buried my hands underneath it. He was scalding hot but I was used to it. Whispering his name, I dragged his mouth back to mine. In one fluid movement, he set me down on the ground. Before I could blink, his body covered mine completely and I screamed in agony.

"Mica! Wake up! You're dreaming!" Rough hands shook me awake. "Wake up!"

Shrieking, I thrashed away and stumbled to my feet. I had to get out of there. I bolted into the fading light.

The sky was dark when I finally stopped running. Huge sobs tore through my chest and I collapsed to my knees. Oh, my God. It's not possible. It's not possible. He'd never do that. Not Killian, not ever.

A hand touched my shoulder and I screamed and jumped up. It was Killian. Wasn't it? His face swam in and out of focus. Of course, it was only him. We were alone here, weren't we? Who else could it be? Shaking, I tried to breathe but I couldn't get enough oxygen and my vision dimmed.

"Here, drink this." He held a cup to my lips and poured a bitter liquid down my throat. It burned on the way down but I swallowed it.

What happened? Everything was a little fuzzy and I dug around my head for the memory of the last few hours. Vaguely, I recalled the demon and the dream. It seemed far away though and I had no fear of it. Bemused, I squinted into the room and noticed a fire near the altar. The bluish flames sent undulating shadows crawling over the crooked stone walls. They reminded me of ghosts drifting along a cemetery. It was beautiful and primal. Something about the fire called to me and I started to rise.

He laid a heavy hand on my bare shoulder and said, "Not yet." His voice was strangely harsh. Familiar, yet strange, it had an underlying heaviness to it that I'd never heard before.

He moved purposely to the altar where he had laid out things I'd never seen before. "What are you doing?"

My voice sounded strange too. It was like talking under water. I shook my head to clear my ears. My head felt heavy and I gave up trying to shake it. Instead, I gazed at Killian as he moved around.

He was focused entirely on what he was doing. Without looking at me, he said, "I'm preparing the altar. I have to hurry."

With some ceremony, he carefully laid out two gleaming knives. There were identical in length and shape and had been carved with strange symbols. I thought they might be runes, but I couldn't tell from where I sat. One had a round ruby in the haft while the other held a large blue stone.

Faintly, I said, "The color of your eyes..." I swayed on my feet but didn't move. I seemed to be rooted in place.

He glanced up at me then and smiled tightly, "Exactly the color of my eyes."

The room swam in and out of focus, but I wasn't dizzy. My brain was working, but my senses were distorted. The walls wobbled and trembled. The blue flames slithered up the altar itself and I leaned towards the fire again.

What was in that cup?

It couldn't be bad. This was Killian. He was my protector, my hero. I giggled at the thought of him being anybody's hero. Okay, I was a little dizzy.

He loomed over me and announced, "It's time."

He lifted me up and carried me to altar. He laid me down with unusual gentleness. The stone was rough against my skin. I couldn't remember taking off my clothes. The air vibrated and undulated with waves of energy. There was an odd humming sound coming from the ruby-handled knife. Killian stood over me, his expression impossible to read.

He looked into my eyes and stroked my cheek with the backs of his fingers. "I'm sorry," he whispered.

His chest was bare except for a medallion around his neck. It was made from hammered gold and gleamed dully in the firelight. A single blue stone pulsed with light in the center. The fire bounced off of the gold and spread across the muscle of his chest. He was beautiful...

He chanted softly and picked up the blue-handled knife. Swiftly, he carved a rune onto his right hand. Blood welled from the cut and slowly leaked over his wrist. He picked up my left hand and quickly carved the same rune into it. I watched in fascination as the blood welled up. I hadn't felt the blade.

"*Sgaine Dutre dia en saled.*"

He said the words while clasping his hand over mine. Our blood flowed together onto the altar. His voice rumbled with power as he spoke the ancient words. He held the knife in front of him as he commanded it to do his will. The blade reflected the firelight, but the blue stone pulsed to the rhythm of Killian's heart, strong and powerful. I could hear the steady rhythm and feel its vibration against my chest. The weight of his heartbeat pressed against my skin even though we were inches apart. My own heart slowed to match his. His eyes were focused inward, not seeing me. Instead of blue fire, they were clear as the crystal blue of the stone. It was like looking into the ocean.

Leaning over me, he drew the knife across my forehead and down the center of my face in the shape of a cross. My face warmed at the touch. I felt my *saol* flow towards the cross. And still, the beating of Killian's heart overwhelmed my senses. It was all I could hear and feel. My skin vibrated with it.

"*Sgaine Dutre a dios.*"

A sudden pain crushed my chest; my heart stuttered and skipped a beat. With delicate precision, Killian carved a small rune over my heart.

"*Sgaine Dutre a dios.*"

The stone blazed to life and lit his eyes. My heart stammered and stuttered. His heartbeat seemed very far away now. I couldn't feel it in my chest. The wind screamed through the ruins like a living creature. My heart fluttered inside. With a quick movement, he turned me onto my stomach and gently smoothed my hair away from my eyes.

The tenor of his voice changed again. His authority was unmistakable. He picked up the ruby-handled knife and touched its tip to a place on my shoulder blade. It burned like a brand. Shocked back to awareness, I screamed and tried to jerk away, but I was completely frozen in place. His voice rose and fell with the words, but I was beyond understanding them now.

"*Diame a satinae et diamae!*"

"*Satinae et dios a cthuli!*"

He lowered the blade.

My back burst into flame.

The agony overwhelmed me and I curled within myself. I couldn't escape the pain or the images. In my mind's eye, I saw my back blazing with white fire. I smelled burning skin even as my mind tried to shut down. White flames licked my skin and smoke curled around us.

Killian's voice echoed off of the stone walls, but I couldn't hear the words over my own screams.

I was burning alive.

My pale golden *saol* was destroyed by the white-hot fire. It melted over the altar and the flames consumed me until I raised my hands to the sky and begged for death.

"Easy, baby," a soft voice spoke in front of my face, "the pain will be gone in a minute."

Blessedly cool water covered me. It lapped at me, tugging the pain away. Like a gentle waterfall, it washed over my body and then my hair and face. Warm fingers stroked my hair and dribbled sweet water over my cracked lips. I parted them and let the water flow through me. I don't know how long I lay in the water, but I slowly became aware that I was alive.

"I'm not dead?" I asked the blackness around me.

An amused snort greeted me. "God, I hope not. I'm exhausted."

I opened my eyes to see his clear blue ones staring into mine. It was then I realized he was cradling me in his arms, and we were standing in the ocean. That explains the waves and the water...

"Don't tell me this is holy water?"

He shook with laughter, "Close enough."

He shifted me in his arms and pressed me against him like he'd never done before. Saying nothing, he rubbed his hand down my wet spiky hair and rested his chin against the top of my head. There was a sense of desperation and relief in his gesture. Finally, he took a breath and asked, "Do you think you can move now?"

"I think so. Are you going to tell me what happened?"

"Can you keep a secret?"

"Cross my heart."

I wanted to slip on my clothes, but they were still drying on a rock near the fire. After tonight, I had mixed feelings about lounging completely naked in front of Killian. But there weren't many options. I had on wet panties to preserve some modesty but kept worrying about yeast infections. Noticing my frown, he finally took pity on me and loaned me his t-shirt. It came to the middle of my thighs so I took off the panties too.

"Come here to the light. I want to look at your back." He pulled the shirt off of me and held the little bowl of light up. He was looking so closely I could feel his breath on my skin and the rough texture of his chin. I tried not to twitch. He was very quiet and then grunted with satisfaction.

"Well?"

"The demon's marks are gone now." He looked at me with sympathy. "He won't be able to hurt you again."

"What a toll I'm taking on your lifespan. You'll have gray hair soon." My hand shook as I reached for the shirt.

"You've no idea." He took the shirt from me and slipped it over my head. When he was done, he pulled me down to sit on his lap.

"Would you like to hear a bedtime story, little girl? It's about a princess and her knight."

The demon had marked my back while I was unconscious in the underground room. The guys hadn't seen all of the symbols because I had been whipped as well. The bloody crisscrossed scabs had hidden some of the marks. These symbols gave him access to my head. He could reach into my thoughts or to my dreams. With time, he could twist my thoughts or force me to jump off a cliff. Luckily, he hadn't had time to play too much since Killian brought me here so abruptly. That explains why the guys were so horrified when they saw my bare back.

The beatings were bad enough, but to mark a human with these demonic symbols was the height of evil. To do this and be discovered meant death when the Primani caught up with you. It was an abomination against God himself. This was one of the reasons Killian brought me here. The magic was stronger than in our plane. Here, there was nothing but ancient magic and Killian. His magic was greater than other Primani because he had been a high priest in his own right well before he was chosen to become Primani. This had been his temple. It still served him well. No one could come here without him, and I was one of a very select few.

I studied him with clear eyes and knew I had to ask the question even though I knew the answer. "If I ask you something, will you tell me the truth?"

"If I know the truth."

I paused to find the right words. "Were you explaining the magic of this place to me by the ocean earlier today?"

He scratched his cheek and answered, "I started to but you fell asleep in the sun. We didn't finish talking."

Oh, thank God! It was just a dream after all. I knew it wasn't him.

"No secrets, remember?"

I sucked in a deep breath and blurted out, "Did you say 'Fuck it, one kiss won't hurt' and then throw me down on the ground and rape me with a grotesquely huge and freezing cold you-know-what until my insides fell out?"

His mouth dropped open and he stared at me. After endless seconds, he said, "That explains the screaming. It's a good thing we don't have neighbors here. Someone would've called the cops." He tried to smile, but his face fell instead.

It was my turn to comfort him, I guess. He was torn between horror for me and mind-blowing fury at the demon. He alternately wanted to hold me like a kitten or dump me back in the penthouse and tear off on a demon-killing streak the world had never seen. While ranting some interesting curse words, he paced back and forth and occasionally blew up a piece of pottery with his hands.

"I didn't realize you had the laser beam thing too. Thought it was just the others. Can I learn that? Guns are bulky."

He laughed in spite of himself and said, "You're crazy. How would I explain that to Sean? This is already going to piss him off. If I bring you back with killing powers, he'll take my head off."

"Oh, and speaking of Sean. We haven't done anything wrong here. So don't feel guilty about all those sexy thoughts you had about me and confess everything. Those feelings are beyond our control here. It's the magic of this place." He shrugged like it couldn't be helped.

"I'm taking you back tonight though. It's harder to resist the longer we're here. If we stay much longer, I won't be able to resist your pull, and we would spend day and night making love on every available surface." He paused and smiled wickedly for a minute.

"Where was I? Oh, my point is I *didn't* make love to you against a tree, *in* the ocean, *by* the ocean, on the floor, *near* the altar, *on* the altar or any other place the two us have fantasized about."

"*On* the altar? Ewww!" I closed my eyes and pictured him standing naked and erect with the golden amulet hanging from his neck. My entire body clenched at the sight. I crossed my legs, tightly.

"What? The altar's too creepy for you?" He leaned forward and ran his fingers up the back of my neck until goose bumps broke out and chased after the shiver running down my spine.

Smiling as my eyes rolled back in my head, he lowered his voice to a velvety purr. "You see? It's part of the magic of this place. In the beginning, God created the Garden, but there were no humans to worship Him. So God created Adam and then Eve. Together, they created mankind...you know the story." Completely serious, he added, "We're on another plane here."

"The Garden of Eden?" I giggled at such a crazy notion.

"Do you still want to repopulate the world from scratch?" He leaned in close and stroked my cheek with a fingertip.

I purred like a cat and rubbed my face against his hand.

"My point exactly."

Chapter 13: Facing the Music

"READY?"

"As I'll ever be."

"It's going to be okay. I promise." He grinned down at me and actually winked. I was going to miss this relaxed version of Killian.

"Hold on," he said and before I could blink twice, we were back at the penthouse.

He'd brought us to the rooftop garden instead of the foyer. Glancing around, I could tell it was very late. The sky was dark and most of the lights were off in the looming buildings. The streets below us were quiet. Thunder rumbled above me, and I caught a flash of lightning from the corner of my eye. The air smelled of rain and ozone. A storm was coming. Killian didn't move towards the door as I expected he would. He was concentrating on something unseen. He frowned and stopped me from touching the door handle.

My hand froze just before I grabbed it and I realized something was wrong. I felt it too. My stomach tightened uneasily and I reached for my gun. No gun. Crap.

"What's happened?" I whispered.

"Shh." He pointed a finger at his temple.

What's wrong?

There's been a fight. I smell demon. Don't touch the door. It's been marked. Wait here for a minute.

He vanished into the night. Antsy, I paced around the garden. Something was wrong here. Large drops of rain plopped on my head and a gust of wind nearly knocked me over. I grabbed onto one of the chairs and swore under my breath. After what felt like eternity, Killian was back.

Take my hand.

As soon as I linked my fingers with his, we were in the kitchen. Whoa! The kitchen was a mess. Chairs were overturned and splintered. Some of the cabinets were hanging open with their doors blown off or hanging by a hinge. The marble top of the island was…melted? How's that possible?

What the heck? I gestured to the marble. *Can we talk now?*

"Yeah, it's okay. The house is empty." He nodded towards the marble. "No idea, but it can't be good."

"Where is everybody? I don't sense them at all. Was anybody hurt?"

He frowned and answered, "There's blood in your bedroom. It's one of ours, but I don't know whose it is."

He reached out and grabbed my wrist as I started for the hallway. "You don't need to see that!" In a low voice, he added, "Don't worry; it's not enough to kill someone."

"We need to find them."

He leaned against the counter and said, "Let me think for a minute and we'll go. It's probably not safe to stay here since it's been compromised."

"Dec? Declan? Where are you, Dec? Can you hear me?" I looked at the ceiling as I called his name.

Killian snorted rudely. "You don't have to look up for it to work. Why do humans always assume that helps?"

I scowled at him and said, "Oh, shut up!"

A new voice spoke from the hallway. "Well, well. Look who's back."

James.

Preternaturally alert, Killian peeled away from the counter. His shoulders swelled with barely leashed power. He would kill James at the first hint of violence. We'd had a long talk about James and Killian was itching to have a chat with him.

"Nice timing, James. I don't suppose you can tell us what happened here?" His voice was dangerously even.

Sauntering into the room, James ignored me completely and shrugged. "I've got no idea. I just got here myself." His expression was full of concern as he took in the destruction.

"Of course, if you would've been here, you would know what happened. How was your *vacation*?"

I didn't see him move, but in the next instant, Killian had James up against the wall with one hand wrapped around his throat. James' eyes bulged as he struggled to breathe while clawing at Killian's hands. Killian held him in place effortlessly and I marveled at this. How powerful was he that he could subdue other Primani? I thought they were all equally strong. Well, I guess you learned something new every day.

James was turning an interesting shade of eggplant.

"Hey, you may want to let him breathe...unless you're planning to kill him. That works for me, but you'll have to explain it to Alex." I shrugged and turned my back.

The sound of ragged breathing told me he let James go. Probably that was the best move for now. James was an asshole, but we didn't have any proof he was dirty. Why would he be? After all, a Primani had the perfect life. It would be crazy to jeopardize that.

With a look of pure venom, James vanished.

Killian cracked his knuckles and commented lightly, "You've gotten so bloodthirsty, Princess. I'm proud of you!"

The whole incident with James had taken about a minute, and I barely had time to turn around when Dec appeared in the doorway. Sean was right beside him.

"Oh, thank God! You're all right!" I started towards them and hesitated. They didn't look especially happy to see me.

Dec's face brightened but he said reproachfully, "Of course, we're all right. No thanks to you."

Ouch.

Sean's eyes met mine and I stiffened. His eyes were hard as stone as they swept over me. His expression insolent as he raked his gaze over my body from head to toe. His lips were pressed together in a hard line and anger radiated like the sun. The muscles in his arms corded with tension as he unclenched his fists. 'Pissed' was an understatement. He was furious and was about to explode. I wisely took a step back and he smiled. This was definitely not the smile I wanted to see. This was the feral smile they displayed just before they killed someone. It always reminded me of a predator with the canine teeth bared. Rarely did I see it on Sean, though Killian had perfected it.

Bravely, or maybe stupidly, I held up my hands and tried to talk to him. I started with, "Baby, I--" That's all I said before he cut me off.

"Shut up, Mica." There was no mercy in his voice.

I took an outraged step in his direction and he lifted his hand. I bounced off an invisible wall and fell onto my butt. No one moved. Dec was frozen with shock. It didn't hurt anything but my pride and my own temper caught fire then. Who did he think he was? Since when did he get all physical with me? I stood up and snarled right back at him.

"You bully! I will *not* shut up. And don't even *think* about cutting off my audio!" I advanced to the invisible shield and glared up at him from there.

"I've been through hell and back because of you and you will *not* be pissed off at me. Do you hear me?" I emphasized my words by jabbing my finger at his chest. He could throw me back to Plattsburgh if he wanted, but I wasn't going to put up with this self-righteous attitude.

Suddenly, he snatched my hand and flipped it over. The scabbed outline of the rune stood out like a brand.

"No, it can't be," he whispered.

The raw fury in his eyes vanished and a look of wonder replaced it. Without a word, he closed his eyes and traced the rune over and over again. Each touch of his finger drew my blood like a magnet and the rune was soon outlined in pale gold. When he stopped, my hand tingled warmly. He lifted his eyes to Killian.

"*Sgaine Dutre?*" His voice was hushed with awe.

Killian met his gaze gravely but didn't speak. He didn't actually move, but it felt like he was suddenly closer to me. The air itself shifted faintly and I felt a breath of air slip over my chest. After a minute, he lowered his gaze to my heart and closed his eyes. Looking a little dazed, Sean reached for my shirt and carefully pulled the shoulder down. He stared at the rune and back at Killian. Then, to my surprise, he bowed his head respectfully and said softly, "*Sgaine Dutre dio*, my brother."

I woke up to the sound of people talking, or yelling from the sound of it. Maybe they need a referee? I stretched and reached for my clothes. It felt good to be back in the farmhouse. We'd left Manhattan immediately after Sean and Dec got there. I slept most of the drive back and crawled into our bed as soon as we pulled into the driveway. Sean slept on the couch, I think.

Now I tried to do something with my hair, but it was impossible. It was so unevenly cut I couldn't keep it pulled back. It lay in shiny brown chunky spikes all over the place. It accentuated my eyes though…Great, I looked like freakin' Tinkerbell. There was no help for it, so I headed for the living room.

Sean and Killian were talking when I walked in. Both glanced in my direction but didn't pause in their conversation. Dec waved at me from the table.

"So what's all the yelling about?" I asked him.

"We got word from Alex that Jordan is still missing. It's crazy. No one's seen an angel just disappear like that. Nobody has seen him, and there's not much we can do about it. No idea where to look." He scooped up a bite of scrambled eggs and popped it into his mouth.

"There isn't anything at all?"

He swallowed some milk and said, "Rumors here and there. Alexandyr and Dimitri swear they saw Jordan in LA a few weeks ago. They were down low in one of those swanky nightclubs stalking Sarin. They were ghost inside one of the private rooms when they saw a guy who looked like Jordan. He disappeared before they could question him."

And who are these people? At my puzzled look, he elaborated with an irritated tone. "Sarin's a pain in the ass. Part human, part demon. He's been on our list for a hundred years. Sean's probably pissed he wasn't there. He's got a personal issue with Sarin. Alex and Dimitri are Primani. You'll meet them eventually, if you're really lucky!"

"Ghost?" I prodded.

"Oh, sorry. Invisible, unnoticeable, blending in as an extreme sport...no one can see us. Etcetera, etcetera."

Oh, that's what they called it. Cool.

"So...the yelling?"

"Oh, that." He waved a hand like it was no big deal. "Sean was thanking Killian for bringing you home...among other things." He said the last part under his breath.

"Huh. I could swear I heard the f-bomb an awful lot. Funny that he'd add that to a simple 'thank you.' But what do I know? Maybe that's how you Primani talk."

He blushed and stuffed more eggs into his mouth.

I helped myself to a bowl of cereal and munched a spoonful. Hmm. Jordan was still missing so that means I really did see him hurt on the kitchen floor. That means that wasn't a dream or a trick of the demon. That's bad since he was really hurt...I liked Jordan and I was really hoping he wasn't dead.

"I still think James did it."

Dec whipped around and said vehemently, "I wish we could prove that. He's such an asshole! I would love to bring him down. But there's no evidence at all and no motive."

"Fingerprints? DNA? Did anyone check that stuff? It could've been humans for all we know. Maybe a robbery?"

He laughed, "Nah, not likely. They can't get inside unless we let them in. The place was protected. Jordan wouldn't let anyone in that he didn't expect or know."

"Protected? Cool. But how did I get in?"

"You're one of us now. You have privileges. Though after last night's attack…we'll have to purge it of demonic tracers and add new protection to it. Good thing we've got this place."

"All the more reason to wonder about James," I said thoughtfully. Hmm. "Does James know about this place?" We *had* been attacked here once before.

"I don't think he knows about it. He's never been here. And Ramon was working for a run-of-the-mill human loser who was working for a lower-level demon. Ramon never heard the demon's name, so we still don't know who that was." He finished a last bite of toast and swigged a glass of milk. I watched the strong muscles work in his neck as he chugged the milk. I had to smile at the sight. Dec was beautifully made. I was surrounded by eye-candy.

"Are you starving, Dec? You just killed about a dozen eggs and a half pound of bacon." I started to laugh but then realized my mistake. "Oh, I'm sorry, sweetie. Killian told me you haven't been eating. I feel like such a jerk."

Unfazed, he patted my hand. "No worries, darlin'. You can't help yourself. I get it."

"Hey, I'm really sincere here! I didn't realize how much you worried about me until the last few days. Killian helped me to see. I remember how it was when Sean…" I broke off my maudlin train of thought.

"Sooooo totally changing the subject since I'm not an emotional guy…where did you go when you guys left?"

Thankful for his understanding, I said, "Eden. How long were we gone?"

His eyebrows went straight up at that. "How long do you *think* you were gone? You don't know?"

"I don't know...maybe three days?" I really didn't know. It was another plane for crying out loud. Who knew how time flowed there?

He burst out laughing and didn't stop. Killian and Sean broke off their conversation and looked over with surprise. What's so funny? Killian and Sean finally got up and wandered over to stare at us with concern. Maybe Dec had finally lost it?

Seeing Killian, Dec got himself under control and threw him a challenging look. "Uh, Killian, do you want to tell Mica how many days you two were gone?"

Killian glared at him for a minute and said grudgingly, "A month, give or take a day."

"What? How is that possible? No, don't!" I held up a hand. "I know, I know, different dimension...but a month? Wow..."

"And while you were gone, we were busy. Let's go for walk and I'll catch you up," Sean suggested.

He seemed in a good mood, so maybe he'd forgiven me. I hoped so. I was getting tired of being in the doghouse!

Killian added, "We have to get some plans together so don't take too long. Things are about to get ugly around here."

I saluted him smartly and said, "Aye-aye, Captain!"

The leaves were changing already. I loved the smell of fall and took a deep breath as we entered the woods behind the farmhouse. It was crisp and sunny today and I wistfully thought of apples. I wondered if there was time to find a farmer's market before we headed out to kill demons. Sean led the way towards our favorite spot by the creek. I followed him on the narrow trail and enjoyed the sight of his muscles working under his clothes. He had a great butt...I was a lucky, lucky girl.

He took my hand and helped me over the rocks until we came to our favorite boulder in the middle of the creek.

Sean leaned back in the sun for a minute before saying, "I'm glad you missed the attack last night. It was brutal. It was touch and go for a little while." He sat up and grinned mischievously. "Dec lost it. He was so pissed off."

"What happened?"

"One of the loser demons actually slashed his arm-- that's the blood on your wall--with a razor. It was a small razor...it's a little like amateur hour to be hurt that way."

"Are you serious? What, it's too mundane? What's he want? A fireball in the gut?"

He just laughed and said, "That's exactly it. He was insulted. Getting blown up is much better. We're warriors for crying out loud. I think he was mostly mad at himself though. He got distracted for a split second and that's when it happened. He'll never do that again!"

"Poor Dec!" I would stroke his ego later. "So what were they doing at the penthouse? That seems weird to me." I stopped and sat up suddenly. "They weren't looking for me, were they?"

He rubbed his eyes. "Maybe, but I think they were looking for something else."

"*Sgaine Dutre?*" Ignoring his surprise, I was thinking out loud. "That's it, isn't it? But I'm thinking it's not here..." Something tickled my brain. Wait a minute...

"It's in Eden!"

"Where? What are you talking about?"

I stood up so I could move more. Movement always helps me think...hard to pace on a boulder though. "Killian's...place."

He looked sideways at me and said sarcastically, "Eden. It has a name?"

Waving him off, I said, "I named it that. It fits. Anyway, *Sgaine Dutre* is the knife, isn't it?" My eyes misted as I remembered the heat of the fire. But the fire healed me in the end...and the knife was the vessel...a very ancient and very powerful vessel. It had also carved these runes into my skin...what power did it leave behind? What did the demon want with it?

He was quietly studying me and I felt a small pang of guilt. Here I was going on and on about this thing and we haven't even made up yet. Most boyfriends would be pretty upset if their girlfriend left for a month in the company of a wicked-hot powerful supernatural warrior slash magical high priest. Probably I should try to make up with him...I plopped myself down so I could sit between his knees and leaned back against his chest. He rested his arms around me and just sat there. I supposed he was getting his thoughts together like I was.

Finally, I said, "I understand if you want me to go. I disappeared not once, but twice, and scared you to death. I haven't been the greatest girlfriend...I can't leave now though; there's too much to do and it wouldn't be fair to Dec and Killian." When he didn't respond, my heart sank. This was the part where he's supposed to beg me to stay. "I'll move into the other bedroom for now and start looking for my own place. Maybe Dani will get a place with me. I'll have to get a real job--" I was babbling now.

"Mica. Stop. Please." His voice sounded hoarse. "Turn around and look at me."

Like facing a firing squad, I twisted around very slowly. He sounded mad and I didn't want to see the anger in his eyes. Instead, I looked into the trees, and the sky, and any other place. Grumbling, he turned my face so we were nose to nose.

"You are killing me," he enunciated each word distinctly. "Every day is a new crisis with you. I'm surprised I have any hair left." He gave me a not quite gentle head butt.

"Ow!" I rubbed my forehead.

"That's what you get for being stupid. You're not going anywhere." He sounded stern but his eyes sparkled. "How many years have you known Killian?"

Nonplussed, I said, "About four or so, why?"

"I've known him for a few thousand. So I think I know him better than you do. Do you honestly think anything could stop him from doing what he wants to do?

"Well, no, I guess not." I turned my face away as thoughts of Killian's personal sense of morality intruded in the back of my mind. He lives by his own rules and no others.

He threw a rock at the creek saying with some irritation, "Do you think I *liked* having you disappear with him for a month? No, I didn't. Was I jealous? Absolutely! I'll admit that. But, and this is important, I trust that he knows what he's doing. I've followed him into more battles than I can count and he's never let me down."

"He's very good at what he does, isn't he?"

He laughed with real humor. "Sweetheart, you have no idea! I wouldn't follow anyone else." He paused and said a little shyly, "I don't want to press you, but if you feel comfortable...I'd really like to hear about the ceremony. It's very old and it's been lost in time. Killian's the only remaining descendent who can use the powers of *Sgaine Dutre*. It's been tied to his family forever. I wish I could've been there to see it."

Yeah...somehow I didn't think he would've been happy with the process. Too much skin, too much blood, too much screaming...

"Do we have time? It's a long story."

Tightening his arms around me, he told me we had all the time I needed. Letting the sun warm my face, I sighed and began my story with, "Once upon a time, there was a princess..."

An hour later, I dried my eyes and wiped my nose on his shirt. I wasn't the only one who was affected by my story. Sean's emotions went up and down like a roller coaster, but he did a good job of hiding it. He'd been respectfully quiet while I shared my experiences in Eden. He was astonished that I instinctively knew it was another plane, and I didn't freak out over the isolation. He was angry when I described the demon's attack in my dream and shared my pain and horror during the cleansing by fire and water. I don't know how long we sat there, but the sun was getting low when he stood up.

"Are you going to give me a proper kiss hello or do I need to toss you into the creek?" He punctuated the question by hanging me over the boulder by my feet. Chilly water bubbled up and splashed on my face.

Squealing at the cold, I yelled, "Okay, okay, I'll kiss you!" He dangled me a little lower.

"Are you sure?" He lifted me like a yo-yo.

"Yes! Pick me up, you jerk!"

Laughing, he pulled me onto my feet and said, "I'm waiting." His face went blank and he dropped his hands, waiting for me to kiss him.

I stood on my tiptoes to kiss him and hesitated. I stopped a few inches from his face and he winked at me. He was so sure I would kiss him now, and why not? More fun to make him wait though. Instead of kissing his mouth, I started with his fingertips. After all ten fingers were kissed I pressed his palm against my mouth and let it rest with a small kiss. Like we were made for each other, the curve of my jaw fit precisely in the palm of his hand. Inhaling his scent, I nuzzled the soft skin on the inside of his wrist and was rewarded with the rush of heat that rose to the surface. Taking my time, I spread tiny butterfly kisses up the muscle of his arm and across his collarbone to the base of his neck.

Instead of kissing his neck, I buried my face against it and wrapped my arms around his waist. I was on my tiptoes again when I finally pulled his face down to me.

Pulling back with a sexy grin and drowsy eyes, he breathed, "Well, now, that was a proper kiss. Good girlfriend." He patted my butt and ducked when I swung a right hook towards his nose.

Sniffing in mock indignation, I left him standing alone on the rock. Head held high, I strolled off like I owned the place only to break into a full sprint when he suddenly appeared beside me. I keep forgetting about the super powers...laughing and gasping for air, I claimed victory at the driveway.

"You're getting slow in your old age!" I crowed in the middle of my happy dance.

Not even breathing hard, he announced. "I let you win."

"Oh, yeah? Let's see how fast I can pack?" I started for the door handle when he stopped me with one word.

"James." He didn't sound pleased.

"O'Cahan. I see you've got your girlfriend back all in one piece." His voice grated on my nerves. He added as an afterthought, "Nice to see you again, Mica."

Sean's expression was carefully neutral as he talked to James on the front porch. He was always good at masking his emotions and was doing it now. The only telltale sign that he wanted to punch James was the tiniest twitching in his little finger. The rest of his body was draped loosely over the railing as he considered James with guarded eyes.

It was odd. James had changed recently. He'd been a little condescending when we met last year, but he was nice to me. He's been more and more obnoxious every time I see him now. He was weirding me out with his strange covert glances. He was doing it now; looking at me from the corner of his eye like I was something nasty stuck on his shoe. What was his problem with me? I saved his life last year for God's sake.

"I'm going inside. I'll let Killian know you're out here," I said in as bland a tone as I could muster. I started towards the door but then stopped. I couldn't help myself. Maybe the devil made me do it, I don't know...but I kissed Sean full on the lips, with tongue, and sauntered into the house.

And ran smack into Killian's chest just as he was about to open the door. I hit him, ricocheted back into the door, and bounced back into his chest. He caught my elbow before I could bounce anywhere else. With Dec's hoot of hilarity echoing through the house, Killian smirked down at me.

Still gripping my elbow, he said, "Your exits suck."

I didn't even blush this time. He was right. My dramatic exits always ended in disaster. I should stop trying. Instead of a snappy comeback, I simply said, "Kitchen, now." I stalked off grabbing Dec on the way.

Once safely in the kitchen, I said, "*What* is he doing here? Now he knows how to find us? We can't trust him and he's creeping me out! He keeps looking at me!"

Killian said, "Orders from Alex. James is going to be working with us on the Dagin problem. Since Dagin was the demon who held him hostage last year, he might have some unique perspective to offer us." He lowered his voice and added, "Plus, he wants us to keep an eye on him." He gave Dec a stern look and ordered, "We are *not* to eliminate James--Alex's orders. I mean it, Dec, no killing James!"

Dec looked positively angelic and said with a broad grin, "Oh, but I'd so like to strangle him on behalf of all Primani."

Chapter 14: Death and Destruction

THE FRONT DOOR SLAMMED and Sean's voice echoed as he hollered for us. Dec pushed open the kitchen door and waved them inside. James checked out the kitchen like he was memorizing the exits. Why was he so interested in this place?

He sensed my suspicion and returned a glance that said 'prove it.'

Sean started to ask Killian about orders from Alex when the doorbell rang. Startled, we all looked at each other with a question in our eyes. Everyone shrugged. We weren't expecting company. The doorbell rang again and Dani's voice came faintly through the door. What was she doing here?

"She knows we're here, so you might as well answer the door." Sean was right. "Go see what she wants. I'll fill you in later."

She was hurrying back to her car when I ran onto the porch yelling for her to wait.

"Dani! What are you doing here?"

Her eyes filled with tears and her face crumpled. "Oh, Mica! I'm so glad you're home!"

"What's wrong? What happened?" I led her to the porch and sat down on the swing.

She didn't look at me right away. Instead her gaze was somewhere high above the tree line and very far away. With a sob, she leaned into me and cried as if her heart was broken. I gathered her into my arms and held her while she cried. A slight tingle on the back of my neck alerted me that I wasn't alone. I lifted my eyes to see Sean peering out of the doorway.

He lifted a hand in question and quietly mouthed, "What's wrong?" at me. I shrugged helplessly as Dani continued to sob.

Rubbing her back, I waited for a lull and asked carefully, "Sweetie, what's going on? Is it your mom?" God, please let her mom be okay. She was all Dani had left.

Sniffing loudly, she struggled to stop crying and managed to catch her breath. "It's Aric!" Her breath hitched again. "Oh, God, he's dead! Mica, he's dead!" With that, she broke down in sobs again.

Aric? No, it couldn't be true! He wasn't sick...there was nothing wrong with him...how could he be dead? I cried with her as I thought about the handsome boy who had been the love of Dani's life. Aric was everything to her. He was perfect for her; they were so happy together. How could he be dead? I don't know how long we sat on the swing wrapped in each other's arms, holding each other up, struggling to deal with the overwhelming pain. Eventually, she leaned her head against the back of the swing exhausted from too many tears and too much raw emotion. Her haunted grey eyes were vacant as she stared out into space. She was completely shattered and I felt her agony tie me into knots. I held her hand and wished I could fix this.

Trying not to intrude, Sean slipped out and with a look of profound sadness, touched Dani's shoulder and kissed the top of her head. She didn't blink. My heart tightened and I squeezed her hand again.

After a few minutes, she seemed to come back to herself and shook her head to clear it. Smiling a weak watery smile, she blew her nose and said, "I'm so sorry I sprung this on you. I was going to call...but that seemed wrong."

"Oh, Dani, don't apologize to me! That's what I'm here for, remember? Best friend?" I tried a smile, but it felt awkward on my face. Instead, I said, "Do you feel up to seeing the guys? Dec's been staring out the window for an hour now, and I think he's about to come through it."

Sitting up stiffly, she closed her eyes and took a shaky breath. "Let me wash up first. My face is numb."

I watched as Dani closed the door to the powder room and then bolted to the living room where everyone else waited. Wanting only my family around me, I skidded to a stop when I saw James lounging on a chair.

"You shouldn't be here right now. This is a family emergency."

He looked apologetic. "Oh, I'm sorry, I had no idea. What's happened? Can I help?" He sounded sincere, but I didn't trust him.

"Can you raise the dead?" I asked bitterly. "That's the only thing that would help right now."

He blinked and paused before asking, "Who's dead?"

Sean growled under his breath and towed James to the door as Dani came into the room. Soap and water had worked minor miracles on her tear-ravaged face. Her eyes were still red and swollen but the pink in her cheeks looked healthy and her naturally pouty lips were even prettier. Those haunted grey eyes only emphasized her pale skin making her look like a china doll. Hovering in the doorway, she sent Dec a trembling smile as he rose to greet her. He was on his way to her side when James stepped between them.

Taking her arm, he said, "Here, let me help you to the table."

Dani gazed up at him with surprise and just a little gratitude. She allowed him to lead her to a chair. Like a gentleman, he pulled the chair out for her and smiled into her eyes.

Dec wanted to kill James on the spot.

Killian spoke up. "Well, James, thanks for stopping by today. I'll call you when we need to talk again." It wasn't a subtle order and we all waited for him to leave.

Flushing angrily, James made a sulky exit. Sean followed him leaving Dec to glare holes into his back.

Dani was oblivious to the tension in the room and stared vacantly at the window. The wind tugged the maple tree's branches back and forth in front of the window. The leaves were splatters of blood against the stark grey branches. It seemed a bad omen and I shivered. Dani was mesmerized by the branch, and I left her alone with her thoughts.

"James is scum, Dec. But Dani really needs you right now. Go and sit with her; her mind is in a bad place."

With considerable effort, he rearranged his face and tamped down his anger. Grinding his teeth as he stood, he said, "He really needs his ass kicked."

I snorted lightly, "True, but not today. I promise I'll hold him down and you can beat the shit out of him some other time."

"Deal." He turned his attention to Dani and I left the two of them alone and went to find Sean.

Killian followed me out and said, "You're a good friend, Mica." He touched me lightly on the arm. "I have something to tell you. Let's find Sean first."

Sean was waiting for us on the porch staring at the air where James had vanished. He took one look at my face and said, "Did you tell her already?"

"No, she's already upset. I wanted to wait for you."

"What's going on? You might as well tell me; this day can't get any worse."

Sean grimaced and said, "Yeah, it can."

Killian hesitated and that freaked me out. Whatever it was, it was really bad.

Sean suggested I sit down. "No, I'm not going to sit. There's nothing you can tell me that is going to hurt more than Aric's death."

"Two more brunettes were found murdered. Both were in their early twenties and had athletic builds."

My stomach cramped and I said very carefully, "That doesn't mean--"

"The last girl's hair was hacked off."

Stiffly, I touched my hair. "But--"

"Just like yours."

My mind just sort of stalled out. I was awake but I just stood there like a zombie. This was too horrible to think about. It could only be one person, but how would he know about my hair? I haven't seen him. Was he spying on me? When would he have done that? I've been surrounded by Primani since they rescued me. That's crazy. Why would he do that?

"It makes no sense..." I whispered to myself.

Sean's voice snapped like a whip. "Where is your gun?"

The change in tone confused me. "My gun? What's that have to do with anything?"

Holding my shoulders tightly, he ordered, "Get your gun and load it. Keep it on you at all times--I mean it. You don't pee without it. Do you understand me?"

He was in solder-mode.

His tactic worked.

The brusqueness snapped me out of the numbness of shock. He's right! I'm not a sitting duck here. I'm a trained killer. Between my gun, my knife, and my lethal hands and feet, I could protect myself pretty well. I've fought demons! One stupid human wasn't going to kill me. Angry now, I pushed away from the wall and stalked into the house.

I knew exactly where my gun was.

Behind me I heard Killian comment, "That went better than I thought."

Dani stayed for dinner and we all listened as she told us what happened to Aric. His mother called her this morning to give her the bad news. He'd been in a car accident coming home from work. The police thought he might have fallen asleep because his car ended up wrapped around a telephone pole in the middle of a sharp curve. There weren't any skid marks, so they thought he was most likely asleep. She told us the story with tears in her eyes, but the hysterical weeping was gone. Dec's magic again. Dani would never realize how he calmed her down, but she would feel better because of it.

"Stay for the night. You're too tired to drive and I need your company." I pleaded my case. It was after 10:00 now and her eyes were bleary.

She started to protest, but Sean cut her off. "Come on, Dani. You're exhausted."

I stifled a grin as I caught him with his hand on the small of her back. Catching my eye, he winked. In the space of a heartbeat, Dani's eyes fluttered and she sank into his arms.

I pulled the blanket over her and smoothed her hair back. Her lashes left little shadows on her cheekbones as she mumbled peacefully in her sleep. She looked so innocent. Thanks to Sean's help, she would sleep dreamlessly for about 12 hours. He was a miracle worker when it came to overwrought females. She'd wake up refreshed and strong. I kissed my finger and pressed it to her forehead.

"Sweet dreams, my sister."

Sean whispered, "She'll be all right now. Do you want to sleep here?"

I leaned into him and soaked in the steady warmth. "I need some peace too. Let's go to bed."

In our room, I slipped off my clothes and crawled into Sean's open arms. I curled up and fell immediately to sleep.

"Mica!" A loud crash startled me awake but sleep tugged at me and I closed my eyes again. Sean shook me with one hand and grabbed his gun with the other. Domino growled softly near the door. Another crash and a shout brought me completely out of bed and into a crouch.

"Get your gun!" Sean hissed.

A high-pitched scream reverberated through the house and Domino went ballistic. Dani! I snatched up my Sig and bolted for the door. Sean was already gone. The hallway was in chaos. White smoke filled the corridor and people were everywhere. I couldn't tell who was who in the smoke but tried to dodge them so I could get to Dani. Her room was at the other end of the house.

A hard blow from the side threw me into the wall and I saw stars for a second. Not wanting to waste time struggling, I pointed the gun at the shadowy shape above me and pulled the trigger. My reward was the meaty splat of blood and body parts hitting the wall. Without a sound, the man fell against the wall.

"Domino, get to Dani!" I sent the dog ahead. She took off like a flash in the darkness.

My ears were ringing so loudly I didn't hear the man come up behind me. He grabbed me around the neck and started to walk me towards the door.

"I don't have time for you!" I gritted out.

He grunted in surprise when I jammed my blade into his thigh. Letting go of my neck, he grabbed at his leg. I yanked the dagger out and shoved it into his chest before he could react. I took off at a sprint.

The smoke had cleared a bit by the time I made it to the living room. I saw Dec kicking the crap out of someone over by the couch. Dani screamed again and his head lifted up automatically. Her screams were punctuated by vicious barking. I nearly tripped over two sprawled bodies when I rounded the corner. Stumbling forward, I lurched into Sean. One look at his expression and I knew we had to move fast. Dani's room was right in front of us now and I threw myself into the door before he could stop me. Sean and Killian were right behind me. The scene that greeted me was worse than a horror movie. Domino had pinned a very ugly demon against the wall, but he wasn't alone. There was a man straddling Dani's legs in the middle of the bed. He held a gleaming blade above him and was about to bring it down into Dani's chest.

"No!" I screamed and threw myself at him.

The man vanished and the demon exploded with a loud whoosh. Domino's barking cut off with a startled yelp. Confused, I looked for my prey, but he was gone.

Dec vaulted over me to get to Dani. Her eyes were black as she shrieked in mindless terror. Without bothering to check for wounds, he drew his hand over her face and her screaming stopped. She lay as quiet as the dead with eyes staring at nothing. Gently, he closed her eyes.

"God, Dani! Is she okay? Is she hurt?" I ran over to help. She was bleeding from several cuts on her arms but none seemed very deep. Her clothes were bunched and twisted around from her struggles. My heart sank and a cold fury took hold of me.

"So help me God, if they…"

Dec caught my gaze and looked at her bare midriff. He lightly ran his hand over her and shook his head slowly. "They didn't." He tugged her t-shirt back down and exhaled loudly.

"Animals! Monsters!" My voice rose with each syllable. "What is *wrong* with these people?" I swung around fully intending to kill anyone who was still alive in this house.

"Mica, wait!" Sean looked like he wanted to stop me.

"Get out of my way!"

Stepping aside, he waved me forward, and I stalked out of the room. I was hunting now. Someone was going to pay. Flipping on the lights room by room, I was only vaguely aware of the destruction around me. Bodies were everywhere. I counted three before I got back to the living room. A soft groan caught my attention and I searched for the source. There, near the kitchen, was a familiar face. What the hell? He was on his feet, but hunched over a chair. He was having trouble standing.

"Balin?" I said. Surprise stopped me from shooting him in the head on sight.

He turned my direction and I gagged. His arm, shoulder, and half of his chest had been blown away and black fluid ran freely from the gaping wound. Before I could say anything, Sean stopped beside me. He took one look at Balin and raised the silver knife. What had once been Balin disappeared as the knife struck true. As the body vanished, the knife clattered on the tile.

"Nice throw," I complimented.

There were two more dead guys near the front of the house, but the rest of the place was clear. That was unfortunate. I was still boiling mad and really wanted to blow up another demon or two. Practically howling with frustration, I caught my breath and rubbed my stinging eyes.

There was no one left to blow up. Damn it.

I settled for kicking a dead guy in the head before sprinting down the hallway to check on Dani. Dec glanced up when I walked in.

"She'll be okay. I've healed the cuts and put her into a deep sleep." He looked miserable. "I'm going to erase her memories."

I looked down at her pretty face and the bloody sheets. "I think that's best."

Supernatural energy is useful not only for killing demons, but also for housework. I was on my hands and knees drowning blood splatters with a bottle of bleach. This house was one massive crime scene. Cleaning was going to take weeks. Maybe we should just burn it down and move? It was nearly dawn when the guys came looking for me. I had no idea what they were up to. I'd assumed they were getting rid of the bodies.

Something in the hesitation of their footsteps made me look up. Killian had a peculiar expression on his face. It was a cross between respect, confusion, and fear. A sense of dread tightened my stomach, and I steeled myself for more pain. What else could go wrong today?

"What is it?" I reached out to Sean, and he wrapped his arm over my shoulders. He touched me like I might explode. His face was white but he didn't say anything.

Killian said, "Come outside. There's something you need to see." His mouth twitched in the tiniest imitation of a smile.

"Okaaaay..." My stomach clenched again and I swallowed the sudden rush of saliva that signaled imminent puking. Cold sweat broke out on my forehead and the light got very dim.

"Hey, hey!" Sean shook me gently. "No puking or passing out right now. This is important." He lifted me up and carried me out to the yard.

Dec was already there. He was kneeling over something that held his undivided attention. He didn't even turn when we approached. We stopped behind him and he jumped as if surprised to see us there. I got the feeling he was blocking my view of something. He stood directly in front of me with his arms spread out. The light behind him cast his face in shadows. I couldn't read his mood.

"What's going on? You guys are freaking me out."

"You and me both," Dec said as he stepped to the side.

I stared. I turned my head to the side to see it from a different angle. I stared some more. My brain couldn't comprehend the message my eyes were sending it. I shut my eyes and opened them.

It was still there.

How was this possible?

Behind me, Sean's chest vibrated with silent laughter. Unable to hold it in, he finally burst out laughing.

"Well, that's one mystery solved," he wheezed.

"What mystery?"

"Who vaporized me."

I stared at the body in front of me. He was bent backwards and sprawled like a rag doll. He'd been thrown on top of the fountain he lay on. The whites of his eyes gleamed dully in the misty early light. Something glinted on the grass and I reached for it. It was his knife. I dropped it like it burned me.

How did he get out here? It made no sense to me...and yet...What about the time the demon tried to kill Trevor? He'd blown up and both Trevor and Domino ended up outside in the snow. That was just a weird fluke, wasn't it? But there was also the demon in the rest stop...All the people in the rest stop! And most devastating of all...Sean exploding in the basement...I wanted to deny it, but the truth was right in front of me.

"No...I..." My stomach rebelled, and I ran to the bushes.

"Dec, get rid of him." Killian's voice barely penetrated the ringing in my ears.

I retched until my stomach was empty and still couldn't hold down the waves of nausea. It was me? Oh, God. I vaporized my soul mate! Gagging, I retched again and still my stomach roiled. There wasn't much left to puke but I thought I could do it again. Memories overwhelmed me and I curled into myself. All the hell we went through...all of us, but Sean most of all. We were so lost without him, but he was scattered.

I am the world's worst girlfriend--ever!

"Mica? Let's go. I'm not going to stand here and watch you torture yourself over this. It's not your fault." Dragging me upright, he said, "Get dressed. We're going for a run."

"A what? Are you nuts?"

"You heard me. Get your running clothes on. We're getting out of here." He nudged me towards the house. To Killian he said, "I hope you don't need us right now."

The first mile was the hardest. My breath wouldn't come through my clogged nose, and I was still struggling not to throw up. Ignoring my distress, he left me behind when I slowed down, so I had to sprint to catch up to him. He kept the same relentless pace we always had and took the familiar route through the trees and down the dirt road. I had to focus on the path to keep from twisting my ankle and soon I had no room for thinking at all. By the end of the third mile, I was breathing normally again and feeling the boost of endorphins kick in. Looking over his shoulder at me, he slowed down a little to let me run beside him on the road.

I tried to gauge his mood but his expression was neutral. If anything, he seemed pretty relaxed. At the end of the fourth mile, he slowed to a walk and stopped near a tree stump to stretch. This was part of our routine too. We always stopped here to stretch. Bending down, he tied my shoe for me and smiled at my surprise.

"You just don't get it, do you?" he mocked me gently. "This isn't your fault. You always want to blame yourself, but it's not your fault." He gave me a playful kiss on my open mouth and laughed at me.

"You keep forgetting your powers came from me in the first place, and let's not discount your destiny...You always think you have control, but you don't. The angels have been generous with your powers. Whatever this is, it's a new power. You get new powers when you need them and not before. But you *do* have to learn to use them, and that's where control comes in." He stressed the last part with a hard look at me.

"But you could've died!"

"But I didn't. Did I? No. Your powers sent me away and brought me back. *You* did that, Mica." He was sitting on the ground stretching now. He looked up at me and asked, "You didn't *intend* to kill me, did you?"

"No!"

"Okay then, the fact that you brought me back here tells me that we're supposed to be together." He rolled his shoulders. "Otherwise, why bother to give you the strength to bring me back?"

Pulling me to him, he kissed my forehead and said, "I forgive you, but you have to forgive yourself. Okay?"

Curling my fingers in the soft material of his shirt, I thought about that. He had a good point. Maybe my vaporizing him was a mistake and the Power that hands out powers decided to help me fix it.

Watching me carefully, he grinned at my conclusion and said, "That's my girl. Now, we have to get back. God only knows what's going on at the house."

Dani was still sleeping and Dec was cleaning when we got back. All the windows were wide open and candles were burning all over the place. I sniffed and my nose curled in on itself. Yuck! It smelled like cinnamon and a slaughterhouse in here. It was so hard to get the smell of incinerated demons out of the furniture.

We really needed to figure some things out, but no one wanted to risk Dani overhearing anything. So Killian left to report the attack to Alex and the rest of us cleaned the house. It was good to be the boss. Dani finally woke up and stumbled into the kitchen about 3:00 in the afternoon. Wrinkling her nose, she asked about the horrible smell.

Dec smiled guilelessly and said, "Mica's cooking. We had to throw out the whole thing, pan and all. It's amazing what she can do with perfectly good cow."

Dani rubbed her eyes and asked, "Since when do you cook?"

"My point exactly!" Dec thought he was very clever.

"Oh, ha ha. Don't you have something to do...someplace else?" I hinted.

"Not really--" he started to say but then the light bulb went off. "Oh, yeah, you're right! I have to fix my door." He leaned over and gave Dani a hug and told her to hang in there.

She seemed better today though. The haunted look in her eyes was gone and she had some color in her cheeks. I searched her face for any signs that she remembered the attack.

"How are you feeling?"

She sighed and said, "I keep forgetting that he's gone. Is that horrible? It's so crazy, Mica." She wrung her hands and looked over at me for reassurance.

"It's just happened and you haven't had time to get used to it. Don't beat yourself up about it. You'll know he's gone soon enough."

Her face fell.

Geez, I'm so insensitive! Quickly, I added, "What I mean is, this is such a shock. You haven't had time to get used to it. It's going to suck for a while, but you'll get through this. We're here for you, whatever you need."

She wiped her eyes and glanced at her phone. "I need to get home. My mom is freaking out. She's called me four times. I'm glad you're here. I feel better when I'm with you."

She glanced down the hallway that Dec had disappeared into. "It's funny, though…"

"What's funny?"

She smiled crookedly and said, "Every time I'm around Dec, I seem to lose time. It's odd. I just can't remember things." She looked over at me with a question in her eyes. "Have you ever noticed that?"

I nodded seriously. "I blame it on his sparkling personality. It's easy to get swept away by him. He's such a sweet guy." I was sure he was listening. "And you can't ignore the power of the dimples."

Her own dimples made a reluctant appearance at that. "He does have amazing dimples, doesn't he?"

I hoped the smell of fried chicken would replace the disgusting burnt demon smell that still lingered in the air. It was comforting to putter in the kitchen after the drama of last night. After Dec's funny little comment about my cooking abilities, I felt challenged to prove I could cook something from scratch. Frozen lasagna didn't count. In the interest of a well-rounded meal, we were having mashed potatoes and biscuits with the chicken. I was flipping chicken and poking at boiling potatoes while

Sean and Dec stayed out of ear shot. Apparently there was some concern that they'd be asked to help...

"You okay?" Killian's question broke through my thoughts.

He must've traveled in since I didn't hear the door. He was dressed in jeans and a Candlelight Red t-shirt. I wondered if he appreciated the irony of their latest video called "Demons." He took the tongs out of my hand and poked at the chicken. Well, this was new. Killian, cooking?

He looked up at me and winked. "What's wrong with you? You look surprised. I've been alone for a long time, Princess." He gestured at his well-maintained body. "Do I look like I'm starving? I *can* cook, you know."

I had nothing to say to that, so I reassured him that I was mostly okay. "I'm not sure, really. I'm just trying to separate all of the crappy things that have happened in the last 24 hours. I don't know what to deal with first." I nibbled the crispy coating off a wing and thought about that.

Crossing his feet and leaning back, he considered my answer over his own wing. He blew on the meat before stripping off an entire side in one bite. Licking grease off his fingers, he narrowed his eyes and said, "Hmmm. Aric first, right? Dani's your first priority."

At my nod, he continued, "I liked Aric. He was a nice kid. It's a shame he's dead, but death happens. His family will have a funeral and Dani will grieve. You'll help her grieve because that's what you do. You help people."

"After a few months, Dani will start to forget the pain of losing Aric and she'll move on to someone else." He shrugged at my snort of outrage. "You know she will. Come on, Mica, she's a pretty girl. Do you think she'll become a nun and hide from men for the rest of her life?"

Probably he was right. But did he have to be...so, so, right all the time?

"Yes. You should just accept that I am always right. You'll feel better if you do."

I had to laugh at that. "You kill me. You know that? I can't understand how you fit through doors with that ego of yours!"

Stripping another wing, he smirked at me. "I've earned this ego."

Sean and Dec walked in before I could answer. Dec said, "I thought I smelled chicken. Need help?"

Rolling my eyes at the suspicious timing, I said, "No, I don't. I'm done. Just bring the bowls to the table and we'll eat." I dumped the steaming biscuits onto a platter and grabbed the butter.

Living with three large males had taught me that the quietest part of any day is the first five minutes of mealtimes. The only sound ever heard during this magical time is the clanking of silverware. No matter the stress in my life, I had to smile at the three of them wolfing down dinner.

"I hate to bring this up, but can we talk about my wonky vaporizing power? It's bothering me."

Sean grinned evilly at me and gestured with a drumstick. "Feeling guilty?"

"Dude, I used to be a little jealous that Mica liked you. But now? I am sooo glad she picked you!" Dec confessed to Sean in a loud whisper.

"She does have a wee bit of a temper these days."

"Careful Sean, you might find yourself sleeping with Dec from now on," I said in a syrupy sweet tone.

"Oh, come on, darlin', we've already talked about this." He grinned over the chicken.

"Questions of my guilt aside, I still don't understand what I'm doing and I think that could be a problem." I looked around the table at their blank faces. "Am I the only one who thinks that?"

Sean cleared his throat and said seriously, "No, you're right. We're just not panicking about it. Do you want to hear what I think?"

I nodded and he continued. "It's translocation--pure and simple. In a split second of panic, you unconsciously moved the person out of danger."

"But that doesn't explain how I've been blowing up demons." I told them the story about the demon with the fireball at the rest stop and reminded them about the one that attacked my brother. Both times, the demons had gone up in a cloud of smoke. Not the typical ash, just smoke.

"And it doesn't explain how you vaporized Sean," Dec added thoughtfully. He was listening to us, but his eyes were glazed as if he were seeing something else.

"Tell me something. Why didn't you move Dani out of the way? You chose to move that human instead. Good choice considering how he ended up dead...but still, you didn't intentionally throw him down on the fountain, did you?" Killian asked.

Startled, I said defensively, "No, I didn't throw him on top of the fountain! Geez. It was an accident!" The image of his eyeballs glistening in the light made me shudder. So gross!

He raised an eyebrow at me and crossed his arms. "Don't get touchy about it. Just answer my question. Did you consciously pick the guy over Dani? Think about it. This could be important."

"I think so...this time. With Trevor and Domino I just wanted them away from the fireball. I totally panicked. This time, I wanted the guy with the knife away from Dani."

The room got very quiet. No one said a word for a few minutes. All of us were lost in our separate thoughts as the sunlight began to fade. I hadn't turned on the lights and the room suddenly seemed very dark.

"I've got it!" Dec announced. "You didn't *blow up* those demons, Mica. You *scattered* them! You vaporized them! Don't you see? They have a totally different molecular structure than humans do. When you tried to move them, the energy released must've overloaded their bodies and *poof!*" He made a gesture to mimic an explosion. "Up in smoke!"

Horrified, I said slowly, "That makes perfect sense, Dec." I turned towards Sean and was assailed by the familiar wave of images that played like a movie in my mind. I knew every part by heart. After he'd disappeared, my brain had refused to rest and replayed these images for days.

For the thousandth time, I watched as Sean grabbed for Dec and turned at the exact moment the demon fired his weapon. The red flame of the weapon collided with the white blast of the chemicals as they ignited and exploded. Caught between them, the two blasts hit him at the same time I had screamed his name in sheer terror. Over and over the image of Sean's body twisting and falling played inside my mind. Totally tranced out, I sat there and let the images come to me. There had to be something I wasn't seeing.

Gentle fingers closed my eyelids and the images stopped. More thought than sound, he said, "I know what you see." He kissed both of my eyelids and pulled me against him in a hard hug.

"You have to let this go. Listen, our molecular structure isn't the same as humans, but it's also not the same as demons. It's possible you could move us without vaporizing us." He rubbed his hand over his chin and looked into my eyes, his eyes clear. "I saw what you saw that night. You know that I was caught between two explosions at the exact second you tried to move me. You know that as fact, right?"

I agreed with him and he said shakily, "It was an incredible force. In that fraction of time before you moved me, I felt like I was going to implode from the pressure. It was crushing me. I would've probably died from the trauma if I'd been left inside that basement. For all we know, you *saved* my life. The point is we *don't* know, and we won't know. So we need to get past this.

We've got more to do and we need you focused." He messed up my hair and added, "Just don't do it again!"

He looked at Dec and Killian and asked, "Anyone else have anything brilliant to add?"

"Can I have a new partner?" Dec asked Killian and then ducked when I threw a biscuit at him.

"Okay, I think we have other things to talk about tonight. Starting tomorrow, Sean, you and Mica run through some drills and get her in control of this new power. Practice on anything, but each other. We can't afford to lose you again." He gave us both a meaningful look. "Dec, you need to pair up with James from now on. I don't trust him with Mica, and I'm not sending him with Sean."

"Killian, I can handle James," I offered. Dec wasn't happy with this change at all.

He frowned and said, "Not a good idea. Something bothers me about the way he looks at you. Until I figure that out, you stay with Sean."

"Sean, you need to know James has been acting strange. He's been conveniently there each time someone was hurt at the penthouse, and he was here yesterday before all hell broke loose." He stabbed a finger at the air for emphasis.

I hadn't thought of that and gasped out loud. "No, he didn't! You don't think James had anything to do with that? It had to have been Balin."

I filled them in on my time with Balin in the park and the burn of his kiss on my hand. It was embarrassing to have been fooled by his disguise. The stupid dog was a Trojan horse...

Sean slammed his hand down on the table. The glasses rattled and I jumped. "Damn it! Is she still marked?" He threw the question at Killian who shook his head.

"Absolutely not." He lifted my hand for them to see. "This rune is mine--I put it there to protect her from psychic attacks. They can't trace her anymore." To emphasize the rune's power, he traced the rune slowly. As before, my blood rose to meet his finger and the rune was outlined in pale golden light. The rune on his own hand responded and began to glow.

Sean snatched up Killian's hand in disbelief. He flushed, struggling to control his temper. Between his teeth, he said, "What is this?"

To his credit, Killian didn't punch him in the face. Instead, he looked him straight in the eye and said with great patience, "My blood to protect her blood. The runes are twins and have even greater protective power because of it." He glanced at me then.

How much do you remember?

Every last second.

His lips curled in a sexy smile that I felt wash over my mind. I covered my rune with my hand.

In the reasonable tone of a history professor he said, "Calm down, Sean. Look, you know the magic is very old. Blood is always required." He said this with a trace of pride. "After what happened with the demon, I had no other options. Keeping her alive and sane were my only priorities. You should understand that."

Killian reiterated the dream I had when we were in Eden, leaving out the part about the demon masquerading as him, and the terrible voices they put inside my head leading up to that. Clearly the demon was planning to use me to get to *Sgaine Dutre.*

When Killian mentioned the blood, I noticed that Dec turned a bit green and I went over to him and whispered, "It was a really big knife too. Actually, there were two of them. Very sharp. In fact, they were so sharp that I didn't feel it at all when Killian carved the runes into my hand or over my heart. I didn't notice until the blood dripped onto the altar." I cocked my head as if thinking of something else. "It sort of undulated down my stomach...very strange in the firelight."

His face had turned the color of moldy cheese and his eyes were squeezed tightly closed. So I added one more little detail to push him over the edge. "You know, now that I think about it, it didn't hurt at all until he set my back on fire. That sort of st..."

Dec bolted to the sink and lost his dinner. All conversation stopped as the three of us listened in shocked silence. It sounded like someone was killing him in there; I almost felt sorry for him. Almost, but not quite. Smiling to myself, I thought, yep, payback is a bitch.

"How much of your blood did you share with her?" Sean sounded pained.

"A bit, why?"

"I don't think we can stand *two* of you."

The stars were out again, but I wasn't in the mood to appreciate them. I was still thinking about Balin and how he'd tricked me into spending time with him. He didn't look like a demon, and he'd brought bait--the dog. That was pure genius and I fell for it. He'd nearly tricked me into going to dinner and God only knew what would've happened. Probably he would have brought me to the underground room that night instead of the next. In hindsight, he'd probably followed me and bided his time to grab me.

I'd forgotten about the green-eyed doctor who'd helped save my life. Sean filled me in on him in our meeting. After bringing him back with me, they turned him over to Alex for more...thorough questioning. Apparently he was an undercover fed. He'd been working to get information on someone who was trying to create new biological and chemical weapons. Before I showed up, he'd worked with petri dishes and test tubes. He was supposed to be a scientist, not a medical doctor. He'd been horrified when they sent me back to him broken and bloody. He'd wanted to help but didn't want to lose his cover. So he gave me injections to help me zone out during questioning and then pain injections when things got ugly. It turned out that he was one of the good guys. According to Killian, Alex had someone adjust his memory and they released him. I said a prayer for him as I supposed demons had long memories and would look for him. He'd be completely at their mercy.

We still didn't know the name of the demon who'd tortured me; I assumed he was in charge though. He had too much arrogance to be a lower-level demon. Others deferred to him there, so he had to be the boss. He was still out there too.

Absently, I rubbed the rune against my cheek for reassurance. I trusted Killian's magic. If he said I was protected, then I was going to believe that. My mind was safe for now, but what about my body? I wasn't indestructible…The door opened and a sliver of light crossed over the rug.

"You're still up?"

Turning away from the window, I pulled the curtains and curled up on the bed. "Couldn't sleep. Are you coming to bed now?" I patted his pillow in invitation.

He pulled his shirt over his head and tossed it carelessly on the floor. Completely unaware of how sexy he was, he stood there for a minute, apparently thinking. Not for the first time, I caught myself drooling a little and licked my lower lip. I could have a million problems, but they all vanished the minute he took his shirt off. The jeans came next and he crawled into the blankets with me. The sheets were cold and I burrowed against his side.

Pulling me close, he whispered against my ear, "How tired are you?"

Chapter 15: Killers, Serial and Otherwise

"NO WAY."

"What's wrong with what I'm wearing?" I turned around to see my butt in the hallway mirror. "It's the perfect stakeout look. Black, black, and more black."

Dec chose that moment to stroll into the room and whistled in male appreciation.

Sean's teeth clacked together, and he asked pointedly, "See?"

"Dec, what do you think?" I twirled around for him to see all sides.

I was wearing black stretchy jeans with steel-toed thigh-high leather boots with a black under-armor V-neck shirt tucked into the jeans. It was all topped off with a bad ass black military jacket. I thought it was very practical...lots of pockets to stash important things like extra magazines, pepper spray, rope, and essential beauty products like a nail file and lip gloss. My gun and its new partner were stashed happily on my black web belt. I thought I looked good.

Dec laughed uncertainly and swiveled back and forth between us. Backing away from Sean, he said, "I'm just gonna say you look *hot* in those boots!" Raising his hands peacefully, he added, "Not sure you should be hot on a stakeout though. Might be a wee bit distracting."

Sean gave him a fist pump and smirked back at me, "Are you going for hot or practical? Seriously, babe, you look hot--too hot for a stakeout. Shit, you're supposed to blend in wherever we are. In that?" He waved his hands over the general direction of my cleavage. "No way. You have to change."

He had a point.

But that was beside the point.

I worked really hard to put this together and wasn't giving in that easily. "Come on, Sean!" I batted my eyelashes, but he still looked stubborn. "Fine. We'll let Killian decide. He's on his way. I can sense him."

"Is that new?" Killian asked as he appeared out of thin air in front of me.

I posed like a super-secret agent and said, "Yes! And it's awesome, isn't it?"

He frowned in confusion at my comment and said, "I was talking about your ability to sense me before I got here." He gestured in amusement at my clothes and added in an offhand way, "You're not wearing that on a mission. You look ridiculous."

Three hours later, Sean was still feeling victorious and was in a great mood while I sulked in the other seat. He was drumming his fingers on top of the steering wheel in time with his iPod. The new car had a fabulous sound system, and he completely tuned me out as soon as we were parked. Two cars mysteriously appeared overnight a few days ago. I couldn't get a straight answer from anyone, so I still had no idea where they came from. We were sitting in the one Sean insisted on driving tonight. It's a faded blue 1967 Camaro. The paint was so faded it was nearly white in patches. It probably had the original paint. Judging from their condition, the vinyl seats were the originals. The stupid car is older than I am so it's a classic. Yay. I don't know why the Car Fairy couldn't have brought us a new Charger. I shifted my butt again and grouched to myself. My seat wasn't keeping its springs to itself.

Turning the volume down, I complained, "I still don't see what's so great about this car. No power steering, no power brakes or windows! How am I even going to be able to drive it? It's got a gear shift, for crying out loud. Why couldn't we take the other car?"

He rubbed his hand lovingly along the top of the steering wheel and closed his eyes in apparent bliss. "You will never understand, love." He stretched his legs and yawned while looking at his watch.

"Heads up. It's time. Are you ready?" He'd turned the stereo off and put on his alert face once more.

"I'm ready." I dragged my window closed so no one could see inside and slunk down in the seat.

After a few minutes, Sean said, "There he is now." In a lower voice, "Damn, he's got a girl with him." As planned, he started the engine and we got ready to follow our target.

Scott Flynn drove a red pickup truck with raised wheels and a gun rack. The rack had multiple occupants. The bed was covered with a black tonneau cover so the contents were hidden. I wondered what he had under there. An axe? Garbage bags? Scissors? As we watched, he smiled charmingly at the brunette he was with. She had a pretty smile and used it often as he walked her to his truck. His dark hair was still long and floated away from his face with the breeze. The deep-set dark eyes were exactly the same as I'd seen them in my nightmares. He had a heavy brow bone that gave him a slightly uncivilized appearance. Heavy brows and cheekbones with a hard mouth and mysterious hooded eyes all worked together to create a face that was both handsome and frightening. Like the devil himself I'd thought on more than one occasion. In the right light, he was terrifying.

"What are we going to do with that girl?"

Sean shrugged and answered, "We'll see what happens." He slowed the car to fall back some and I felt the transmission shift with a rumble. The vibration surprised me.

Scott was driving straight through town, and we were three cars back. It was close to 11:00 now and he'd just left work. It was Friday night and he was taking some girl out for a good time. He pulled up to a convenience store and ran inside. Idling down the block, Sean was deep in thought. Fingers drumming, he said, "Can you get a read on him?"

"You want me to get inside his head? Eeeww!" The man was a horrible excuse for a human. The inside of his head probably squirmed with worms. I'd have to bleach my eyeballs after going in.

He reached over and squeezed my leg gently. "You're safe from him now. There is no way he will ever touch you again." Squeezing once more, he added, "We have to know what he's planning. It would cut out a lot of guesswork if you can read him. Try, babe." His eyes met mine and he nodded in encouragement.

"Okay, I'll try. But you'll have to stay closer."

Scott swaggered out of the store with a 12 pack of beer in one hand and a lit cigarette in the other. He surveyed the street like he owned it before getting back into his truck. His hand hung partly out of the open window as he dangled the cigarette. He drove directly towards us, and I dove across Sean's lap to hide. Sean turned the other way as Scott drove by. As I slid back into my seat, Sean peered at his lap with a sigh and started the engine.

Now that we were back on the road, I tried to reach out to Scott and his slimy mind. Ignoring the sounds of traffic and the motion of the car turning corners, I concentrated and...nothing. I took a deep breath and sent my mind out again. I couldn't even sense him. There was nothing, just a void as if he wasn't there. Maybe we were too far away from him? I was about to try again when I felt the car brake and stop.

The sounds of teenagers laughing and having a good time greeted me as I got my bearings. Ah, Peabody's. A place I knew well. Scott parked down the street and walked over to the passenger side to help his girl out of the truck. He started to help her down and then stopped her partway down so she was pressed against him in the doorway. He had one arm wrapped around her holding her up and the other casually braced on the doorframe.

His back filled the door so I couldn't see what her face looked like. He was relaxed though and seemed to be kissing her.

Suddenly his head snapped back and he stiffened. But then just as quickly he stepped back and pulled her out of the door with a laugh. Even from here, I could tell that wasn't a sincere laugh. The sound was off and his shoulders were stiff as he draped an arm around her.

"Let's rock. We're up." Sean grabbed the keys and started to open the door when I reached over to stop him.

"Wait! How do you want me to act in there? I'm nervous now."

He pulled me over and kissed me thoroughly. I was glowing slightly by the time he leaned away from me.

"There. Now you look like a girl out on a date." Just as fast, the soldier was back, and he was all frowns again. "Act like we're on a date and you're gonna get laid tonight. You focus on me like I'm your whole world. If he's the one we're looking for, he'll react. He won't be able to stand watching you with me. Just don't go anywhere without me." He kissed me again, sweetly this time, and said, "I'll keep an eye on Flynn, and we'll wing it from there."

Peabody's was packed with college kids, and we had to wend our way through the crowd. Sean took my hand and cleared a path leaving startled faces staring after us. I smiled to myself. He could put off whatever vibe he needed to get what he wanted. If it was cooperation he wanted, he either went with suppressed violence or affable party goer. Tonight, it looked like suppressed violence was taking the lead. I sighed to myself. There would be trouble later. No doubt. For now, I clung to his hand like he was my only thought in the world and pasted a vapid smile on my face.

I spotted Scott and his date before Sean did and tugged his wrist to the left. Without making eye contact with Scott, Sean sauntered across the room to a place opposite our quarry. So far, I didn't think Scott had seen us. It was really crowded, and he had both eyes and his hands all over his date at the moment. He was showing her how to hold a pool cue. Who knew it was a full contact sport? Sean pulled up a bar stool and hovered over me like a good boyfriend would. With one eye on Scott, he focused his hands and the rest of his body on me. Strong fingers linked in mine and pulled me closer still. I leaned back against him and nearly melted.

Fanning myself, I tilted my face towards his ear. "You are ridiculously hot," I said under my breath.

He raised his eyebrows at that. "That a compliment or a complaint?"

I elbowed his ribs playfully and smiled up at him. "You're burning up. Are you okay?"

He leaned into my ear and whispered, "I hate to tell you this, darlin', but you're the one who's burning up." He pulled back slightly, and his eyes went round. In a very low voice he hissed, "Your eyes are glowing! Stop that!"

To cover my surprise and well, my glowing eyes, I closed them and pressed my face against the muscles of his chest. Deep breaths, deep breaths, I chanted to myself. To anyone who was watching, I was just snuggling with my man. Nope, there was nothing weird to see here. Why were my eyes glowing?

After a minute or so, I cautiously peeked up at him, and he leaned in to kiss me. Taking his time, he kissed me in that special way that proclaims to the world that we're having sex later. Just in case any foolish mortal guy thought to hit on me tonight. Claim staked. I laughed against his mouth and pulled back grinning.

"I thought we're acting here. You're excited." I dipped my finger inside the top of his jeans. Rock hard stomach muscles contracted at my touch.

"Of course I am. You're setting my blood on fire." He leaned back nonchalantly on his elbows, and I quickly stood in front of him. The ladies didn't need to have their questions answered. "Besides, who says we're not having sex later? I think it's a great idea."

"Do you two want drinks or a room?" an amused voice interrupted my witty comeback. A waitress appeared next to us with a tray of empty glasses. She was a cute little redhead with green eyes and alabaster skin. Only about five feet tall, she had a good view of Sean's assets and her smile widened wickedly.

"Back off, sister. He's mine!" I joked with a real smile. "I'd kill for some water though."

She laughed and said with an exaggerated shiver, "Mmm, I'm gonna let you keep this one. He's a little scary."

"You've no idea," I told her in a stage whisper.

Sean winked at her and said, "I'll take a Sam Adams."

I thought it was safe to sit down again and looked around the bar. I recognized a couple of old friends from high school, but no one else looked familiar. I scanned the crowd while pretending to send text messages on my phone. Sean had his big body draped behind me as he pretended to read my texts. Every so often, he'd whisper something to make me laugh out loud. We'd been there a half hour, and Scott hadn't taken the bait. I had to pee.

"I'm going to the bathroom."

"Not alone, you're not."

"You can walk me there and wait, or you can stay here and watch Scott."

We threaded our way to the hall where the bathrooms were and there was a long line of girls waiting. "I'll be fine here. Why don't you go back and wait? It's packed with witnesses. What could happen?" I stood on my tiptoes and kissed his worried frown.

The wait took about 20 minutes, and I was bouncing up and down by the time I got into the bathroom. Hurrying to an open stall, I closed the door in profound relief. As soon as I flushed and buttoned my jeans, the room was plunged into total darkness. All around me girls started screaming in the dark. Any second now, the lights should blink back on. Power surges were no big deal. I opened the stall and felt my way through the tiny room. Drunk and panicked, girls started shoving to get out of the room and the screaming got worse.

Not wanting to get trampled by idiots, I slipped back into a stall and waited for the herd to cull itself. I had my purse with me and dug out my cell phone. It had a flashlight app. I also had my gun. Not good to pull out a gun in a bar though. It's not exactly legal here. Putting the gun back, I slid my knife into my front pocket. The screaming was down to a dull roar outside in the hallway, so I thought I could get out of here now. Sean had to be worrying out there. I was a little surprised he hadn't already found me.

The scene that greeted me when I came out of the bathroom was so bizarre I couldn't understand what I was seeing at first. The emergency lights were on and blinking red and white in the corners but white smoke filled the rooms. The smoke had a slight ammonia odor which seemed out of place here. Surely that's not from a trash can fire? Eerie shadows flickered here and there like some kind of demented ghosts. Groans and occasional shouts punctuated the muffled silence. Most of the people were gone, but there were bodies lying on the floor and sirens screaming outside. I couldn't see more than a few feet in front of me, but I ran down the hallway, dodging bodies as I went. I had to find Sean and get out of here. There was something very wrong. I had a really bad feeling about this. As I came to the doorway to the main room, my brain screamed a warning, and I reacted automatically.

Knife in hand, I whipped around in a crouch to defend myself. I nearly dropped the knife in shock as he moved towards me with a greasy smile. Knowing I couldn't outrun him, I planted my feet and yelled for Declan, Killian, and Sean as loudly as I could. Swallowing my terror, I stood my ground and waited.

"I was very disappointed to find you'd left me alive, Mica." His reptilian eyes adjusted to the light with shrinking pupils. He seemed in no hurry as he stalked towards me. "How is your memory *now*?" He seemed to hiss the words so quiet was the sound.

He knows I know now? How is that possible? I held the knife higher and said, "This knife will protect me from you. It's killed demons before!" Come on, come on, Dec, where are you? What if he can't come? *Killian! Help me!*

He considered the carvings on the knife with narrowed eyes and paused. "So you think you can destroy me? Silly woman, you can't hurt me. You're powerless against me." His voice rose as he got closer to me.

As he approached, he straightened each finger so that the three-inch claws popped out of the ends one at a time. The effect was paralyzing. I couldn't take my eyes off the claws. I knew exactly how it would feel for them to dig into my skin.

"You are going to die now, and I will forget you as soon as you're gone. You are nothing but a loose end to me. I have what I wanted." His smile showed his two rows of fangs.

Stalling, I said, "Congratulations. What are you going to with it now? Should I be worried?"

His laughter pierced my eardrums like claws on a chalkboard. He was slowly shedding his human façade as he moved. The skin peeled away to show the black scales underneath. Like a snake shedding its skin, it flaked off and fell in long tendrils. One half of his face was already bare and gleamed in the dim light.

He bragged, "You'll be dead. Your precious Primani can't undo that. But I can. I will bring hell to earth for eternity." He considered me with lust in his eyes. "Perhaps I will bring you back to entertain me."

He was right in front of me now, and I turned to bolt just as he reached out to grab my throat. As soon as he touched me, my runes crackled like lightning and he flew backwards. By the time he landed on the floor, Killian and Sean were standing between us.

"I've been waiting for you," Killian snarled in his throat as he raised his glowing hand.

Sean shoved me down the hallway as Killian lunged.

"He did what?" I asked for the second time and tried to brace myself.

Sean was driving the car like the demons were chasing us. I flew sideways into the door and yelped when my elbow got smashed.

"He vanished. Instead of fighting, he vanished. It was crazy." Slamming the car into a lower gear, he skidded to a stop in the driveway. He grabbed my hand and in a heartbeat we were in the living room. This was different from traveling. This was just moving really fast, and he'd never done it with me before. I didn't like the feeling, my head was spinning and I sank to my knees.

"Sorry, babe. Put your head in your hands for a minute." He was agitated, running a hand through his hair and looking at the clock. "Where is Dec? It's been more than half an hour."

The dizziness was gone and I worried with him. Dec was out with James tonight. They should've been back by now, and Dec should've been able to respond to my call, unless something had happened.

Killian stalked in from the kitchen just then. Eyes burning like lasers, he was practically glowing with fury. Out of all of them, he was usually the most controlled. He rarely showed any outward sign that he wasn't just an ordinary young man. The only time I'd seen his eyes burn was when he traveled or in the middle of a serious fight with demons.

"Sean, Mica, what happened tonight?"

Sean briefed him on tailing Scott to the bar and watching him and the brunette. They'd both been at the same table when I went to the bathroom and Scott was there when Sean got back from the bathroom. I filled him in what the demon said. He watched my face intently while I spoke.

"And the last thing he said was, quote: *You'll be dead. Your precious Primani can't undo that. But I can. I will bring hell to earth for eternity.* Then he looked at me like he wanted to have sex with me and said this creepy line, *Perhaps, I will bring you back to entertain me.* What the hell does that mean?"

I was freaked out all over again and walked over to the window to release some tension. "Bring me back from where?"

Killian had stood very still while I repeated the demon's boasts. When I said the last part he flinched back and his face went blank. The expression on his face turned my blood to ice crystals. He didn't move, didn't blink, didn't breathe for what seemed like hours. The blood drained from his face and his lips turned bluish.

I clung to Sean's side and said, "What's he doing?"

Sean was as clueless as I was and just whispered, "Wait."

Killian? What's wrong?

Nothing. No answer. No comment. Silence inside my head.

Please let us help! Let me in, please.

Silence.

Suddenly he sank to his knees as if a great weight was dropped on him. He stared out at something we couldn't see, his lips moving in soundless incantation. His pain was breaking my heart. He was still a million miles away, so I reached out to him and squeezed his hand to show him we were still here for him. Maybe the physical contact will reach him and bring him out of this shock. But just as I held his hand in mine, he vanished into space.

The first thing I noticed was the roar of the ocean as it hurled itself against the rocks. The second thing I noticed was the pain in my hand as my knuckles were ground together. Attempting to yank my hand away only provoked an already angry man. Eyes burning like twin stars, he was definitely out of shock and fully pissed off now.

Before I could say a word, he yanked me to him and snarled down at me, "What the hell are you doing here?"

Wincing, I cried, "It was an accident! I didn't mean to come!"

"You can't be here now! Oh, fuck, Mica!" He shook me so hard my teeth rattled. "It's not safe for you to be with me right now. This is very bad. I need to do some things, and I can't do them with you here."

"Look, I'm here and I'll just sit by the rocks and let you do your thing. I might be able to help or I can just keep you company." I hesitated but touched my rune to his. They glowed on contact. "See? I belong with you."

Still very distracted, he gave me a weak smile at that and gave in. "Come on, we need to get to the ruins." He took off ahead of me, and I jogged to keep up.

True to my word, I sat on the soft grass just outside the opening to the ruins. The sky was entertaining me. There wasn't any breeze at the surface but humongous rolling clouds sped at super speeds in the sky. They flew along in great streams of white and occasionally grey. It was like Mother Nature hit the fast-forward button. Killian had gone inside a few minutes earlier and hadn't come out yet. I was giving him the space I promised. I would wait right here.

An inhuman roar of fury reverberated through the stone, and the hair on the back of my neck stood up. My very human instincts told me to run; run far, far away from this place. Even my fingertips filled with adrenaline, and I almost bolted.

But I knew better.

This was Killian.

I needn't fear him.

Without warning, the world exploded into chaos. An immense wall of solid black clouds formed out of nowhere and rolled across the ocean towards us with supernatural speed as violent blue lightning speared the huge waves. Frigid wind howled around me and I clung to a rock to keep from falling down. Edging into a sheltered niche near the entrance, I huddled, waiting. Killian's voice raged above the roar of the storm, shouting in his ancient language. The cadence of his words rose and fell with the wind and I shivered in the presence of something much more powerful than I'd ever seen.

A great bolt of lightning crashed to the ground a few feet away from me, and I felt the crawl of electricity go up my leg. My skin burned with the slight shock of it. Not wanting to be barbequed, I slipped into the ruins and tried to be invisible. His voice was more powerful inside the small room, and it reverberated through the stone. He stood over the altar with hands outstretched and head back calling to the powers he served. He was magnificent and a rush of heat spread across my chest as I stared in awe. The face I loved was transformed into something fierce and cold. He might have been carved from the same stone as the altar near which he stood. His body was lit from within as he called out in demand. Heat shimmered in waves around him.

Outside, the storm unleashed its full fury, and the stone trembled and screamed as it absorbed the energy itself. Killian raised his knife and slashed a long cut on the inside of his forearm. Holding it aloft in offering, his voice was compelling as he spoke the next words. Lightning struck the top of the ruins; blue electricity sparked in one corner and crisscrossed the entire roof like a spider web. As it traveled down each of the walls, more lightning struck and the pattern repeated over and over again. Each powerful bolt ended in the outstretched hand of Killian. He called the lightning and it answered him.

Mesmerized, I sank to the floor and held my knees to my chest. His mercurial blue eyes were closed as he abruptly stopped speaking and bowed his head. Leaning against the altar, he remained still and silent. His entire body pulsed with the blue fire of the lightning. His chest rose and fell, the golden amulet gleaming in the faint glow from the fire. His forearm dripped blood. Unable to take my eyes off of him, I watched the blood slowly trickle across the glowing rune on his hand. My own rune tingled oddly, and I glanced at it. It glowed softly against the brown of my skin. It took a minute for me to realize the ozone was overpowering my senses and my ears rang loudly. The hair on my arms was standing up as the lightning continued to flow through the rocks. Probably I wasn't safe in here, but I couldn't seem to get up.

Hot as a lightning bolt himself, Killian came over and wrapped his arms around me. Protecting me from the power that still arced across the stone all around us, he held me against him until my heart stopped racing. It didn't matter that he was so hot I was getting burned. It didn't matter that his blood was smeared all over my arm. No, none of that mattered. All that mattered was that he was in control again. I'd been terrified at the house; his shock and pain were more than I could stand. That's not who he is. He's never afraid; he's never unsure or out of control.

This powerful and terrifying high priest commanding the elements is who he is. I had no idea what happened, but I knew he would fix it. He could fix anything and the rest of us would be here to help him. He might want to be alone, but he'd always have me, even if I had to come back from the dead to help. I leaned my face against his shoulder and breathed in his scent. Musky, woodsy…It sent my blood racing, but at least his heartbeat was steady again and everything was better.

He chuckled tiredly against my neck and said, "All hell is about to break loose. Everything is most definitely not better."

Then he kissed me softly between my eyes and looked intently into them, calling to me, pleading with me. His own were crystal clear and blue as the midnight sky. At a loss for words, he hesitated. Intending to kiss me again, he stopped and pressed his lips against my skin and groaned softly. Automatically, his hand wrapped around my waist, and he pulled me closer so I was leaning against his chest.

"I'm sorry you were afraid. I...heard you, but I couldn't answer you. I was trying to find *Sgaine Dutre*. I was looking for it, but couldn't sense it...Then I felt it, but it was in someone else's hands. I knew it was gone then. I had to come here to be sure." His voice was soft and husky.

While he spoke, he lightly dragged his lips across the delicate skin along the side of my face and stopped just below my jawline. Still not kissing me, he didn't break the contact, and my skin sizzled with the touch of his mouth. His eyes were closed now, and his hand rested lightly on the bare skin of my back. He wasn't fooling me; every muscle in his body tensed in anticipation and my body responded to his call.

Afraid to move, afraid to breathe, tingling with the force of the raw sensations that were coursing through me, I froze. Just the feel of him so close to me made me want to throw myself against him and to hell with the consequences. My slightest movement brought my cheek against the roughness of his and I turned into him instinctively seeking more. With barely a sound, he whispered my name and slowly slid his mouth towards mine. He was giving me a chance to move, to change my mind. I lifted my face towards his and felt my world slide sideways when his mouth crashed down on mine.

"I'm not going to remember any of this, am I?"

"It probably wouldn't be helpful if you did." He caressed my face with his as if memorizing every curve. I felt his eyelashes flutter against my cheekbone and my breath caught with a rush of love for him.

"Killian, I..."

He smiled a bit sadly and pressed a finger to my lips. "Shh. Do you think you should? Say it out loud, I mean."

Serious now, I pulled his face back down and kissed him as if I'd never see him again. If I wasn't going to remember this night, I wanted to make sure that he did. Later, when we lay face to face and our hearts raced out of control, the tears that slid down my cheeks were tears of sadness for what would never be.

Kissing the tears off of my cheeks, he whispered, "Baby, don't cry for me." He kissed my bruised lips with some force then. He ran a fingertip over the rune on my chest. "You're never far away from me."

The altar was still smoking with the remains of the fire. While I watched, Killian opened a small brown satchel and placed several items from the tiny storage box under the altar. He was bringing out the instruments he used for the ancient ceremonies. This place didn't feel secure anymore, and he didn't want to risk anything else getting stolen. I recognized the ruby-handled knife, but he also added the bronze cup and a couple of other knives and a small leather-bound book. It had been hidden apart from the other items. With a last look around, he declared it was time to go. We stepped outside the ruin and he stopped me with a hand on my arm.

"One last thing before we go." He started to say something else and I interrupted him.

"Killian, please, don't do this! I want these memories. I feel like this will be all I have left someday. I need to remember you...here...when you're gone."

His expression was sympathetic, but he refused to listen to my argument. "It's for the best. Trust me."

"But it's not fair! I don't think it's for the best. Best for who? Me? Or You?"

"Listen to me! Nothing can come from this night. You and I both know that. I warned you the magic is strong here--It's my fault it happened and I'm sorry. I don't want to hurt you."

He's sorry? Did this mean nothing to him then? I loved him in ways I would never love Sean and that sucked. Sean deserved more from me. And I deserved more from Killian. With eyes shooting daggers at him, I told him to get on with the memory snatching.

"And be sure to get rid of any lingering feelings I have for you. We wouldn't want them to get in the way."

He actually flinched away from me as if I'd slapped him. "Mica, please. Don't be this way. You have to understand," he implored. I was done talking. Resigned, he placed his hands on either side of my face and proceeded to wipe out my memory.

"Why is she covered in blood?" Sean was not especially happy to see us when we appeared suddenly in the farmhouse. "Every time you leave with her, you bring her back bloody. I thought you liked her?"

Killian reddened slightly and said, "Sorry, I forgot about that. She's not hurt. It's mine."

Sean's eyes narrowed even more at that. "Okay, that begs the question of why she's covered in *your* blood. Did you roll around on her or what?"

Good question. How did I get covered in his blood?

"There was a bad storm, and I grabbed ahold of her to keep her from falling. It's nothing to worry about. It'll wash off."

That sounded right. I remembered a big storm and the wind blowing me around. I needed a shower. As much as I liked adventure, I didn't appreciate wearing Killian's blood. It was gross. I didn't even like him that much. I headed off to the shower without another word. Sean was waiting for me when I came out of the bathroom. He eyed me with appreciation as I dug out clothes to put on. Since it was actually morning, I asked him what was on the agenda for today. We still needed to stop this serial killer.

"Get dressed and we'll slip by his house." He reached out and tugged my hand. I curled up against him and finished pulling on socks. He waited until I was done and turned into me for a kiss. "I have the sexiest partner ever. It's a wonder I can focus at all." He helped me up and laughed at my pout.

"Later! Let's get out of here."

"Do you think I can drive this thing?" I asked as he shifted gears and pulled out of the driveway.

Glancing over at me, he said, "Sure. It's not hard. Do you want to practice now?"

He drove a few miles towards town and pulled over into the half-empty parking lot of the electric company. Shifting into first gear, he turned off the engine and handed me the keys. He unfolded himself from the driver's seat and walked around to my door.

"Come on, you have to get out before you can drive it." He held the door open and waved me out.

"Okay, if you say so. I'll try it." I slipped into the driver's seat and wiggled around in the seat. I adjusted it so I could see over the dash but it still felt odd. I was too short for this car. The hood stretched out for a mile and messed with my depth perception. Totally not sure about this, I turned the key and started the motor.

Patiently, he said, "Take your foot off the clutch at the same time you push down on the gas. Do it smoothly so you don't stall the car."

I followed his directions and stalled out the car...several times. Every time it stalled, Sean's lips clamped a little tighter until finally, after the fourth or fifth time, he snorted impatiently and gestured at me to get out.

"What?"

"Out! We don't have all day." Again with the hand gestures!

"Are you serious? I thought you were supposed to have unlimited patience!"

Rolling his eyes, he asked, "Seriously? How long have you known me? When have I ever been patient?"

"But you're an angel! Isn't infinite patience one of those holy traits you all have?

Now he snorted *and* rolled his eyes. "Where do you get these ideas? I thought we covered the wings and harp crap already?"

With very bad grace, I shoved it into first and stalled it on purpose. The engine died with a relieved groan. It was glad to see me go...

After 15 minutes of practice, I was back in the passenger seat. Sean apologized to the car as he started its engine again. Seeming to understand its master was back, it purred to life under his hand and roared through the winding turns on the way into town. In just a few minutes, we pulled up across the street from Scott's apartment. He lived in one of the dumpy places near the lake. It wasn't the best part of town; these roach motels were run-down but very cheap. It was rumored there were a lot of drugs to be had in a few of them. Was Scott on drugs? That could explain things. Though I secretly thought he was crazy enough without any pharmaceutical assistance.

He lived in a side apartment that we couldn't see from the street. Since Sean was memorable no matter what he was wearing, I volunteered to walk around to see if he was home. I pulled my army green hood up and slipped on a pair of wire-framed glasses. With my hair covered and the glasses in place, I looked different enough that I thought Scott wouldn't recognize me. I was wearing oversized grungy jeans with torn out pockets and scuffed combat boots. I was going for the broke-ass-crackhead look and thought I'd done a good job with my disguise.

Sean wasn't thrilled with my plan, but the mission came first. "Okay, just go see if his truck is there and come back."

I walked with my head bent against the wind coming off the lake. It was pretty cold today, so it was natural to slouch into my jacket and keep my head down. I turned the corner and left Sean behind. Looking for the truck, I walked through the parking lot as if I belonged here. No red pickup truck. I took shelter under an overhang and lit a cigarette. Trying not to inhale, I lounged dejectedly for a few minutes. Scott lived in apartment 32A. It was two doors down from where I was loitering. Hmm.

Five minutes later, I knocked on the door and nobody was home. Probably he didn't have an alarm system either. Carefully, I turned the door knob and the door opened. Huh. Unlocked? This didn't seem too smart. Who leaves their doors unlocked around here? Someone with nothing to lose or in a hurry to leave. I pushed the door open and poked my head in. It seemed empty enough. I shut the door and pulled out my Sig. The apartment only had two rooms. It couldn't hurt to look around. I didn't see anything serial killer-ish in the living room. There was a couch and a beaten up wooden coffee table. That was it. The kitchen was mostly empty. There were a few bags of ramen noodles in a cabinet and a few bottles of beer in the fridge. The sink was filled with dirty dishes and a smelly orange dishcloth was thrown over the faucet. It stank like rotten trash in here.

I tried not to inhale...

Sean will kill me if I get caught in here. I need to move faster...With this in mind, I lifted the gun and pushed open the bedroom door. The bedroom had a single mattress on the floor and a couple of plastic laundry baskets. An upside-down box pretended to be a table by the bed. There was a clock and an ashtray sitting on it. I moved into the bathroom and nearly dropped my gun. The bathroom itself was a disgusting mess, but the thing that caught my attention was the curled picture of me stuck to the side of the bathroom mirror.

With scattering nerves, I looked closer at it. It had been taken at the beach a couple of summers ago. Whoever had taken the picture had been close enough to zoom in on my face. I was laughing up at someone above me, but that person's face was cut out of the picture. Ragged edges suggested it was torn not cut. My bathing suit straps were just visible at the lowest edge of the image. This was not good. Nervous now, I glanced around the rest of the room and saw some stains on the floor. Crouching to avoid touching the dirty tile, I peered closer at the rusty stains. Rust? Blood? Hard to say without my trusty CSI tool kit. Improvising, I crumpled a wodge of toilet paper, wet it, and rubbed at the spot on the tile. It was the best I could do at the moment. I shoved it into my jacket pocket and took a picture of the mirror and tile with my phone. I was about to leave when something told me to open the vanity doors so I hesitated.

The scratched wooden doors called to me.

For one second I seriously thought about ignoring the feeling. I was starting to hate that annoying prickling feeling…It usually meant something bad and I wasn't sure if I could deal with more bad right now.

Sighing with resignation, I yanked open the door, and the rusty smell of old blood rushed out. Smashing a hand over my nose, I flinched back in surprise.

Oh now that's just gross was my first thought.

My second was I had to get the hell out of there-- now!

I yanked open the car door and threw myself inside. "Go, go, go!" Taking gulping breaths of fresh air, I tried to settle my adrenaline buzz.

Without asking questions, Sean drove smoothly, but quickly, away and after a block glanced sideways at me. "What did you do?"

"Oh my God, Sean! It's him! He's got a picture of me in his bathroom, and I think he cut Stefan out of it...shit! Does anyone know if Stefan is still alive? And there's blood on the floor, and there's a bloody hunting knife under his sink." I blurted this out in a rush of exhaled air.

His eyebrows met his hairline. He started to say something but then stopped. Instead, he drummed his fingers on the steering wheel and slammed the Camaro into another gear. I could hear his teeth grinding together.

"You were *supposed* to be in the parking lot. How the hell did you get inside the apartment? Do you have a death wish?" The last question came out as a shout.

We were out of the city now, the last of the houses fading from view. He slammed the car into another gear and it shot forward like a rocket. My head bounced off the head rest, sending bright lights ricocheting behind my eyes.

"Killing me with whiplash isn't going to help!" I said sourly.

Instead of answering, he glared at me and slammed the car into Park in the driveway. Throwing his door closed, he left me standing there and stalked inside. Well, hell. I guess he's mad. Geez. It's not like I *want* to die! These things just happen to me....He was still fuming when I walked in. I guess he'll need more than 30 seconds to get over this. Sighing over his temper, I ignored him and went to the kitchen for a drink. Dec and Killian were both gone, so it was just the two of us. I chugged some water and steeled myself for the wrath of the boyfiend...er, uh, boyfriend. Deep inside, I knew he had a right to be mad, I was reckless. I couldn't play the victim here. Gritting my own teeth together, I went to face the music.

He was sitting on the couch pushing buttons on the stereo remote. He set it down and the distinctive opening guitar of Soundgarten's "Rusty Cage" blared out of the Bose speakers. I swallowed a smile because I knew that he picked his music based on his mood just like I did. It was one of the things we had in common, and it tied us together. Music was powerful in its own right, but when it reflected your mood and spoke to your heart, it could be therapeutic and downright empowering. I leaned against the doorway and listened to the music watching his face all the while. He tried to stay mad and stubbornly refused to look at me at first. But by the middle of the song, I noticed his lips twitching just a little. By the end of the song, he finally looked at me and patted the couch in invitation.

I raised my eyebrows in question and he smiled a real smile at me. "You may as well sit down. I can't be mad all night. We have work to do."

Sitting cross-legged across from him on the other end of the couch, I shared the details of my trip through Scott's wonderland. He asked to look at my phone, and I showed him the pictures.

"It's just creepy! What is he doing with that picture?"

"My first guess is he still has a thing for you. Really, who wouldn't? And my second is he's using it to fuel his anger before he kills."

I hadn't expected that answer, and my mouth dropped open in surprise. "What about the blood?" I pulled the wad of bloody toilet paper out of my pocket.

"There's no help for it. We're going to need to take that sample to our lab rats. We don't know if it's blood or if it's his blood or someone else's. For all we know, it could be his." With this statement, he stood up and stretched. "Let's eat and then we'll go."

"We're going to The City? Now? We can't leave Domino here alone."

"We'll travel in and out in an hour or so. I'm not leaving you here alone, and it'll take too long to drive." Frowning slightly, he rubbed Domino's silky ears and she licked his hand. "I'm sorry, girl, we can't take you this time." She looked disappointed.

A bit later, we rematerialized in a side lobby of what smelled like an old hotel. My nose twitched in protest as soon as I took my first breath. It was musty and stale. The walls were covered with ugly beige wallpaper that was plastered all over old hotels. The floor was tattered and stained linoleum the color of split pea soup. This place was nasty. This was our lab? Yuck. You'd think we could do better than this.

Sean read the disgust on my face and gestured to an elevator further down. We got in and he pushed the fifth floor button. Ah, the penthouse suite. Curious, I looked around and waited quietly until the doors opened with a squeal. The hallway we landed on was also non-descript and worn. Sean led the way down the corridor. Stopping at an unmarked door, he placed his hand against a black glass pad and a buzzer sounded from inside. With a click, the door swung open.

Oh! Much better! The room was brightly lit and thoroughly modern with bright blue walls. The chairs and couches were white leather and the tiny tables were chrome and glass. The artwork in the waiting room was modern and vivid. The paintings captured the warrior angels in battles and tender moments alike. They were breathtaking. Now *this* was more like it! The small reception window was covered in smoke-colored glass. Sean waved me to one of the lush chairs scattered around and headed to the window. I didn't want to miss a thing, so I ignored his gesture and followed him to the window. He announced us through a small opening and a woman asked us to please sit and wait for a lab technician.

I couldn't contain my excitement any longer. "Wow! This place is so awesome! And there's a woman here? I didn't think Primani had women. That's so cool."

I was gushing. It didn't take much to impress me.

Archly, he said, "Why wouldn't we have women? There are a lot of female angels. They aren't Primani though. Most female Primani were killed a long time ago. The receptionist isn't Primani; she's just a regular angel."

"I just haven't seen any women since we've been together." That brought up an interesting thought. "Sean, have you had any, uh, more supernatural girlfriends before me? Did you ever date another angel?"

Nearly swallowing his tongue, he burst out laughing. "You want to talk about ex's now? After all this time?" He was still laughing as he said that.

"You're avoiding the question. So yes, I do want to talk about ex's." I was serious now. "So spill it, Secret Agent Man."

Looking at his watch, he shook his head and laughed some more. Seeing my look of determination, he finally said, "Okay, but you're not going to like it. Where do you want me to start?"

Totally intending to mean it when I said it, I promised, "I totally understand you had a life before me. I won't get mad." Warming to the subject, I foolishly suggested he start with his first girlfriend.

He began with 130 A.D. "Mata was my first. She was a serving girl in the Great Hall. Then there was another girl, well, two more, that I spent time with that summer. Let's see, then I went on the road with..." Scratching his head, he paused to collect his thoughts. It was a lot to remember. Twenty minutes later, he had made it through 1000 A.D. when I finally threw up a hand and told him to stop.

Lost in his memories, he was confused by my interruption. "I thought you wanted a list? I wasn't finished yet."

Steaming at my own stupidity, I snapped at him instead. "You're a slut! I can't believe you!" I had to ask, didn't I? Of course he had women! What was I thinking? I had no idea he was such a slut, pure and simple, or maybe, not-so-pure and simple. Why did I assume he was angelic just because he's some kind of angel? *Clearly*, there are codes of conduct that don't apply to Primani. I smacked myself in the forehead with my hand. Ugh. I was an idiot to ask. Simmering and refusing to speak to him, I tapped my fingers on my leg counting the minutes. After about a decade, the receptionist announced in a low throaty voice, "Sean? You may go in now." The inner door buzzed and swung inward.

He smiled cautiously at me like he expected me to bite him. "You coming?"

Still sulking, I debated whether or not to get up. With a shrug, he walked into the open doorway ahead of me. Mumbling to myself, I jumped up and slid through the door right before it swung shut. There was no way I was going to miss this. As I rounded the corner, I stopped in surprise. My teeth clamped together as I watched the receptionist greet Sean with a totally unprofessional lingering kiss on the lips.

Her perfectly manicured nails gleamed in the subdued light as she caressed his face and exclaimed, "Oh, Sean! I thought that was you! Still gorgeous, I see." She punctuated this with a throaty, sexy laugh. Her nails traveled down the front of his chest to hover just above the top of his jeans.

Steam had to be coming out of the top of my head as I thought of various ways to kill her. That tramp! And what was he doing? Oh, nothing. Sean was grinning like a cat about to stick his tongue in the cream. His eyes were lazy as they roved over her tight sweater and silk skirt. Looking down at my ripped jeans and hoodie, I felt like dirt next to this beautiful polished blond. Of course he slept with her. What guy wouldn't? Too surprised to move, I stood there like an idiot gawking at them. The blond finally noticed me and glanced curiously in my direction. I'd hesitated too long to join them now, but I didn't want to leave him alone with her either. Kicking myself for feeling self-conscious, I willed my face to stop blushing and ground my teeth together.

Sweeping past them both, I called over my shoulder to Sean, "I'll just be in the lab, partner. Clock's ticking so hurry up." I kept walking until I was out of their line of sight. Pausing to get my bearings, I noticed I was in a small hall with two windows that opened into the labs. Equipment was set up on tables, and there were computer stations and oversized flat screens for viewing images. Distracted by this cool techie stuff, I forgot all about Sean and the blond for a few minutes.

"Can I help you, miss?" a friendly voice asked.

A young man in a Rangers hockey jersey and baggy jeans came up behind me. He had a mop of red hair haphazardly shoved into a ponytail. Wire-framed glasses gave his face a definite nerdy look. His badge identified him as Chris. He seemed friendly enough so I told him I needed to drop off a sample.

"A sample? Blood, hair, fiber? Whatcha got?" he asked pleasantly. His pale blue eyes twinkled in anticipation of a new mystery. This was a guy who loved his job.

Fishing out the toilet paper, I said, "Blood, we think. We need to ID it first and then see if we can find the donor in the DNA database. Am I in the right place? I'm new…" I smiled in genuine appreciation of his helpfulness and he grinned back at me revealing a missing front tooth. Maybe the jersey wasn't all show.

"Undercover?" He eyed my ripped up jeans.

"Yes!" I breathed with relief. "Broke crackhead." I offered my hand for him to shake. "Nice to meet you, Chris."

I was leaning across the lab table with my nose buried inside a centrifuge when the atmosphere got a little chilly. The jolly bantering between Chris and the other lab tech, Ben, stopped abruptly. I sensed him before he invaded my personal space.

Sean.

"I see you found the lab. Have you got any results yet?" he asked me in an even tone.

Flexing my fingers to keep from smacking him, I kept my own voice light and said, "I see you've finished with your reunion. Plans for later then?"

He laid his hand flatly on top of mine. "Don't tell me you're jealous of Lara? I've known her forever. It's nothing." He spoke in a hushed voice to keep Chris and Ben from overhearing.

I'll bet he's known her forever! Tugging at my hand, I glared up at him and gritted out, "Chris and Ben are working on the sample now. Chris thinks they'll be able to have some results in a few more minutes. It'll be longer before we get a hit in the database though." I smiled stiffly at the two lab techs, and they both nodded their agreement. They seemed uncomfortable with Sean for some reason.

Taking my elbow, he led me farther out of earshot and said, "Oh, it's *Ben* and *Chris* now? Since when did you become a CSI?"

Smiling sweetly, I commented, "Well, partner, there are a lot of things you'd know about me if you'd ask. I've had *a lot* of experiences without you."

"Don't play games with me, Mica."

"You hypocrite!" I hissed under my breath. I twitched away from him and stalked back to the lab table. Ben and Chris both turned very pale and backed away from me a little.

"What's the matter with you two? You look like you've seen a ghost!"

Ben stuttered, "You...you dare talk to him that way?" He looked shocked.

Chris was watching Sean like he might explode any second and whispered to me, "Don't you know who that is?"

"Of course I do! He's my boyfriend, and he's on my last nerve." I looked between the two of them and asked, "What's the problem?"

Ben's voice was hushed with awe, "He's a legend! He's one of the greatest Primani of all time." He shook his head at me and said, "There's no way you're his girlfriend. You're human."

With my very last scrap of patience, I said between my teeth, "And what is wrong with that?" My fingers were tingling, and I knew what that meant.

Uh-oh, too late!

With twin gasps of fear, both lab rats scuttled away from me. The glass screen magnified my reflection.

Guess I'm not so human now, now am I?

Back at the farmhouse, Sean was still chuckling at my anger, and I was about to knock him out. His condescending attitude was getting on my last nerve. As soon as my eyes had started to glow, Sean excused us, and we made a dignified exit. I was still huffing about it. Oh sure, it's okay if your eyes glow *blue* fire, but not *white* fire. The fact that my eyes occasionally glowed with a white hot light didn't bother Killian. He found it amusing in some probably demented kind of way. Then there was the blond...

"I have an idea," I purred.

"I'm listening."

"Let's go spar. I feel like I need to work out." I stretched nonchalantly and batted my eyelashes innocently.

He considered my idea with a huge amount of suspicion. He clearly wasn't an idiot, but we had time to kill and nothing to do. "Uh-huh, sure you do. Do you want to go outside or to the basement?"

"Oh, definitely the basement."

Five minutes later, I was sitting on the mats stretching out. Sean's footsteps on the stairs alerted me and I shifted position enjoying the buzz of adrenaline singing through my veins. Sometimes when we sparred, we played music. It made it more intense. I had already loaded the music and pressed the play button. Godsmack blared out of the speakers. We'd also enjoy Disturbed,

Sick Puppies, and Linkin Park before I was finished today. I had a lot of anger to work through...

He just raised an eyebrow and went to the punching bag. I watched him hit the bag and some of my anger disappeared. Just watching him move was a distraction. The loose t-shirt couldn't hide the bunching of his muscles as he swung at the bag. The stupid blond was right; he was gorgeous. Irritated even more, I strapped on my gloves and waved him over. It was time for some sparring. We had a routine for this, and we worked through the first steps. After a few minutes of warming up, I started swinging as hard as I could. His supernatural powers made him faster than me and he always managed to block my punches with his gloves. It was pretty rare for me to land a shot on his body.

Throwing my weight into it, I pounded his gloves with a strength he'd never seen. He stood his ground and absorbed my strikes, but his eyes narrowed as he caught the new intensity. He didn't block one of my swings and grunted with the impact on his ribs. We switched to Krav Maga and as the lyric *I will not be ignored* screamed across the basement, I kicked him in the ribs and sent him flying across the mat. He rolled back onto his feet and looked at me warily. Reading his body language, I anticipated his move to sweep my legs. When he swung his leg towards me, I jumped up and brought the arch of my foot down on top of his knee. The resulting crack was louder than the music. He crumpled to the mat holding his knee, and I dropped to his side.

"Oh, my God! I'm so sorry!" I was trying to pry his hands away so I could see his leg. "Let me see if it's broken."

"It's broken! I don't need you to look at it." Sucking air in between his teeth, he groaned and his face turned bone white. The last thing he said before he passed out was "women."

"I can't heal that," Dec said flatly. "It's splintered into pieces. He needs a real doctor, probably a surgeon."

"Can he heal it himself? I healed my broken elbow, remember?"

Sean was still unconscious but not in a good way. We'd put a bag of ice on his knee, but it looked horrible. It was swollen like a gigantic eggplant. The pain had to be excruciating. I thought he was in shock.

He considered that for a second. "He's probably able, but we don't know how that's working since he, uh, was vaporized. Oh, and that was you too," he said with some asperity. "Good God, woman, I thought you loved him!"

"That's not fair! I didn't mean to break his leg! I had no idea I could do that! And you know I didn't vaporize him on purpose! How can you even say that?" Sean groaned and I grabbed Dec's arm in panic. "What about Raphael? Can't he do it?"

"I'll see if I can find him. It'll take a little while. Keep him warm and keep ice on the leg. Give him one of these pills if he wakes up. It'll knock out the pain."

I nodded with each direction and glanced desperately back at my patient. He groaned and tried to sit up. Dec and I both ran to him.

"Don't try to move! You'll make it worse," Dec ordered.

Glassy-eyed with pain, he was sweating and more than a little green. I handed him the pill and some water.

"Dec, please hurry!" I whispered as he turned to go.

I made Sean as comfortable as I could. I put a pillow under his head and replaced the ice. He was shivering, so I covered him with a blanket and wiped the sticky sweat off his face. His face lost some of its green tinge as the pain killer took effect. His eyes were still glazed though, and he was groggy. He slipped in and out of consciousness. Domino curled up beside him and gently nudged his arm with her nose. He smiled faintly at her.

"I'm so sorry. Dec is right. I *am* the worst girlfriend ever." I sat near him, but I really wanted to curl up to him. I was afraid he wouldn't want that. So I hovered just to the side.

He whispered, his voice slurring the words, "Dec didn't say that." His hand fumbled for mine, and I squeezed it carefully. He squeezed back and smiled a little. "I'll be okay. It's just a broken bone. No one dies from that."

"I'm afraid I'll have to disagree with you there," a cold voice drawled from the staircase.

Chapter 16: Welcome Back From the Dead

"BALIN?"

Where did he come from?

"Aren't you dead?"

His golden eyes twinkled as he enjoyed my shock. Smoothly, he said, "Oh, I'm sure you have a lot of questions for me, but now's not the time." As he spoke, he came down the stairs never taking his eyes off of Sean.

Domino threw herself in front of Sean and snarled at our unwanted guest. He waved at her in dismissal. "You and your dog! You think she's actually protecting you, don't you? I could kill her if I wanted to." He looked at her for a long moment and shrugged. "There's no point, though. She can't hurt me *now*." He smiled and a cold chill crawled down my spine.

Sean was sitting up, but his color was green again and beads of sweat ran down the side of his face. "Didn't I put a blade in you? Why aren't you dead, demon?"

I sidled closer to him and helped him stand up and lean against the wall. I knew without any doubt that he wouldn't want to die lying on the basement floor. There were two other things I was positive about. One, Balin would try to kill Sean before leaving our house and two, I would die protecting him. This night wasn't going to end well for any of us. Where were Raphael and Dec? A little backup would be great right now.

Balin's handsome face twisted with humor at Sean's question. He purred in that creepy silky demon voice, "Oh, but I *was* dead. And don't think I don't owe you for that. That's why I'm here. First, I'll kill you, and then I'll take her. My boss has a soft spot for her and wants her back."

He was about 10 feet away from me now. Mentally, I groaned at my predicament. I had no gun, no knife; no weapons handy at all. Sean was struggling to rally his killing powers, but I could see he didn't have the energy. His body had been drawing the *saol* to his broken leg, and there was precious little extra to rally into his hands. The bones in his face were white with the strain of keeping upright.

"You don't look too bad for a dead demon, Balin. Why don't you tell us how you got a new lease on life?" I was stalling and furiously thinking.

Could I vaporize him, on purpose? We hadn't practiced that yet. I wasn't sure I could do it without blind panic. Plus, he was too close to Sean…

What if I missed?

"Let's just say I have your friend to thank for that. I'm sure he'll be glad to know we've worked out a few kinks. Now, let's go." He reached for me intending to grab my arm and I let him.

As soon as he grabbed my arm, I flipped him onto his back and kicked him in the head. Jumping back out of his reach, I looked around for something to use as a weapon. There wasn't anything sharp. I was on my own. He got up and in a heartbeat was standing next to Sean. He wrapped his hand around his throat and squeezed. Sean dug his fingers into Balin's hands trying to pry them off, but Balin had the advantage. Sean's face turned red and then purple as they struggled. My vision went completely white when Balin started laughing and let Sean drop to the ground. His laughter pushed me over the edge, and I sent all of my power towards him expecting to vaporize him in a cloud of smoke. Instead, a beam of white light shot out of my hand and cut him in half where it landed. The half that was cut away slid off to the side. The other half looked at me incredulously. His mouth was working to form words, but nothing came out. With one last burst of energy, I vaporized him into smoke.

Only half of him was gone though. The smaller half was still lying across Sean's feet. He was sucking in oxygen and trying to slide away from the stinking remains, but his knee gave out and he sagged against the wall with a moan of pain.

"Wait! I'm coming." I stumbled over to him and pulled him away from Balin and we collapsed in a pile together. My breath was coming in gasps, and my eyes burned like they were literally on fire. I squeezed them closed and lay my head on his shoulder. He was drenched in sweat, but I didn't care. I was exhausted and fell asleep on him.

Someone shaking my shoulder woke me up a few minutes later. My eyes flew open, and I pushed myself up to stand in front of Sean again.

"Get away from him!" There was a crazy edge to my voice that caused him to take a step back. My eyes started to burn again, and this time I embraced the fire and let it grow. Glaring at him, I flexed my fingers in warning.

"Whoa! Relax! I was looking for Killian. Have you seen him?" James sounded less sure of himself than usual. But then he realized how hurt Sean was and a slow smile spread over his face.

"Looks like your boy took one for the team. He's not dead, I hope."

"Are you *enjoying* his pain?"

He rolled his shoulders and smirked, "It's about time the big man feels some pain. He's overdue."

"Overdue?"

My blood actually started to boil like effervescent bubbles floating through my veins; my fingers pulsed with new life, with new power. I looked down at my hand and noticed without surprise that my hands were glowing and the light was spreading up my arms. I let it take over and relished the pleasure of the *saol* coursing through my blood, giving me strength and the will to use it. My vision turned white again, and I met James' arrogant stare with one of my own.

The smirk vanished and he began backing towards the stairs. Relentless, I stalked after him without breaking eye contact. Every detail of his face was clear. Every pore, every line was magnified, as were his thoughts which were running around in circles inside his head. He was panicking and trying to get out of here. He was afraid of me now; it was the eyes. The white light was freaking him out. He didn't understand how it was possible. So he backed away...

"I don't like you, James. If you even think about coming near Sean I will blow you to pieces." To emphasize my words, I raised my hand and blew a hole in the wall just off to his left. Concrete splinters flew like shrapnel sticking in the arm that he raised to protect his face. Confused and afraid, he stared at the blood running down his arm.

"That's right, James. Be afraid. Be very afraid." I didn't recognize my own voice.

He left without another word.

A sound from the other side of the room surprised me, and I whirled around ready to do battle. It was Raphael and Dec. They'd finally showed up and were staring with open mouths and raised hands.

Raphael raised an eyebrow and frowned at Dec accusingly. "Did you know about this?"

Dec shoved his hair back and answered, "Uh, not *this* exactly. She's been gaining power for a long time now. Just a little at a time though. *Nothing* like this!" He looked at me with appreciation and added, "Wow, you were amazing. Can you be my partner again?"

"Anything you want, Dec. Just make it stop! It hurts-a lot!" I was still glowing and it was getting really painful. My skin was too thin to hold it all inside, and I felt like I was about to burst at the seams.

"Go to her, Declan. I'll see to Sean." Raphael sighed and said, "It's a good thing you found me when you did."

"Dec, I'm melting!" I was getting frantic.

He scooped me up and dropped me into the shower. Stepping back out, he turned on the cold water, and I squealed with shock. "What are you doing? Drowning me won't help!" I tried to climb out, and he blocked the exit.

Laughing hard, he wheezed, "It'll bring your temperature down faster. Just stay there for five minutes, and we'll do the rest out here."

So I stood in the shower and watched in amazement as the white light faded and my skin returned to normal. My eyes felt better too. Without the supernatural fire heating me up, the water was too cold and I was shivering. Shutting off the faucet, I begged for a towel.

"All right, come here then." He wrapped a blanket over my shoulders and led me to the living room. "Sit down and stay covered."

"What possessed you to turn yourself into a road flare?" he asked.

"I don't know. I was so furious...It just happened, kind of. I've been getting more powers and more strength. I don't know why. I don't know where it's coming from either. It's really freaking me out."

"Okay, we'll talk about it in a minute. But for now, breathe evenly and deeply. Tell your body to cool off, *control* your temperature--use your mind. If you allow your anger to rule you, darlin', you'll burn yourself up." He reached out and touched my cheek. I leaned my chin into his palm, and he rubbed it with a small grin.

"You know you can tell me anything, right?" he asked with a worried look.

I fidgeted and said, "Yes, but some things are too stupid to talk about."

"If they're so stupid, why do you let them make you mad?" Chafing some color, *human* color, back into my hand, he said, "Tell me what's got you so upset, Mica. Please."

I stalled and stared at the lamp on the table. He's right. I needed to talk to someone about this, and I couldn't share any of my life with Dani or anyone else for that matter. How would I explain these things to them? They'd never understand. Dec would though. I clung to his big warm hand and told him about everything that was bothering me. I was jealous over Sean's girlfriends and the receptionist. He'd hurt my feelings when he let her touch him like he was available. I was confused and afraid of my new powers. Where were they coming from? What if I hurt someone innocent? I was getting more and more afraid of James and what he was doing. I was terrified that Scott Flynn and his bloody knife would kill some innocent girl just because she looked like me. I had so many things to worry about and no control over anything anymore.

He listened intently throughout my rambling and only asked a few questions to help me clarify my worries. He tried not to laugh when I ranted about the slutty receptionist.

"Oh, Lara? Everyone's had sex with her. It's like a rite of passage or something." He tapped a finger on the side of his face, thinking. "Except for Killian, I think; no one ever knows who he sleeps with." Seeing my narrowed eyes, he chided, "But Mica, Sean wouldn't do that now. I can't believe you'd let her make you jealous. You should know better."

"Yeah, I'm so awesome. I just broke his leg in a temper tantrum, and then he was almost killed by a zombie demon that I let into our lives," I snorted. "Yeah, I'm a prize worth keeping."

He didn't laugh; instead he pulled me down to the couch and said, "What's really bothering you? All of these worries are valid, don't get me wrong, but you're dancing around something else. I can feel it."

The problem was I didn't know what was bothering me. I was just angry. In any event, I was saved from trying to explain that by Raphael.

"Declan, come and help me put our young Sean into his bed. The worst of it's done now, but he'll feel better in a bed and off the basement floor." Turning back to me, he said, "Oh, and Mica?"

"Yes?"

"Would you mind fixing this old man a cup of tea? Earl Gray, if you have it."

Earl Gray tea? Raphael was a surprise every time we met. Always elegant and charming, he treated me with great respect. His impeccable old-fashioned manners masked an old and tremendous power within him. I'd only seen him use this power for healing, but I suspected it hadn't always been that way. He was still lean and tough as a warrior though not quite as muscular as Sean and Killian. He was older than them though. I thought he was in his late 40s. I was just guessing about that since I wasn't sure how old he was. For all I knew, he was 5,000 years old...

"How is he?" I asked as I handed him the tea cup and saucer.

He spooned a bit of sugar into his cup and stirred before answering me. "He'll certainly live; however, he was in considerable pain." Setting down his spoon with a clink, he asked, "Might I ask why you felt he deserved to have his leg crushed?" His eyes were cool as he looked deeply into my own.

I resisted the urge to gulp; instead, I frowned into my own cup. "I didn't mean to break his leg, I swear. I just wanted to..."

"Hurt him?" he finished for me.

"No! Yes...but not like that! I was so mad I just wanted to blow off steam and have a good sparring match. He's always been stronger than me so I thought he could handle anything I threw at him." I was miserable again.

He was quiet for a moment and then said, "Sean feels that you're stronger than a human girl of your size should be. Do you think that's true?"

I glanced at him in surprise. "I don't really know. But lately, I feel as if I'm changing on the inside." I smiled awkwardly and chewed on my lip.

"Did he tell you I've been able to translocate people? Usually when I try to do that to demons, they end up vaporized. Today though, I was afraid to blow up Sean by accident. So I tried to focus the *saol* towards the demon by channeling it through my hand, and a white light shot out of my hand and hit him. It cut him in half! It was like a laser! I was shocked. I have no idea how that happened."

Raphael seemed shocked too. He looked steadily at me as if looking for holes in my story. Suddenly my rune began to tingle, and I idly rubbed it with my thumb.

"May I?" He indicated my hand. I nodded and he picked it up and examined the rune carefully. "Hmm." He lifted a finger to touch it and I flinched.

"Don't do that!" But I was too late. As he touched his fingertip to it, my blood rose to meet it in an outline of pure golden light. He nearly dropped my hand in surprise.

Closing his eyes, he traced the rune murmuring, "Fascinating." Setting my hand back on the kitchen table, he asked levelly, "Who's got the twin?"

"I do," Killian answered from the doorway. "Am I interrupting?" He nodded respectfully to Raphael. "I can come back later."

"May I?" Raphael gestured at his hand.

Shrugging, Killian offered it and watched quietly while Raphael examined the rune. Raphael seemed strangely interested in the connection between the two runes. Killian's rune had been glowing when he walked into the kitchen. The sight of it unleashed butterflies in my stomach. Did I want to be connected to Killian in such a physical way? The twin runes felt too...intimate? Yes, intimate. An odd feeling of history snuck up on me, and I had the strangest feeling that I knew him in ways I couldn't define. Déjà vu? I gave myself a mental shake. I had no idea, but I had more important things to do than to wonder about Killian. I excused myself to go and check on Sean.

Killian asked, "Will you let him know I'm back, and I'll check on him in a little while?" He idly toyed with the gold ring on his finger while meeting my eyes across the room. His were worried.

Politely, I said, "I'll let him know. Just don't come too late; we're going to bed early. I'm really tired tonight."

Sean was lying on the bed staring at the ceiling when I walked in. The curtains were closed, and the nightlight was off. It seemed unusually dark to me, and I resisted the urge to turn on the light. Instead, I washed up and changed into a clean t-shirt and perched on the edge of the bed. He smoothed my hair back with a half a smile.

"You're beautiful when you've gone psychotic. You know that, right?"

"Nice. Thanks for reminding me." I felt badly enough without reminders. "It wasn't one of my shining moments. I'm so sorry about your leg."

He gave me an amused look that promised payback but just leaned back. "I wasn't talking about my leg, though you were a little crazy when you broke it," he laughed softly. "I was talking about the way you handled Balin and James." He looked impressed with me and turned on his elbow to watch me.

I smiled hesitantly and worried, "Did I do the right thing though? I don't know the rules yet. I wanted to kill James on sight, just in case he deserved it, but then I thought that was probably bad form." I looked hopefully at him.

There was always the next time.

That got a real laugh out of him. "Good thinking. You really shouldn't go around killing angels...it can lead to some really atrocious karma problems later. Leave James to us."

I sat up and hovered over him in agitation. "But Sean, you didn't see the look on his face when he saw you laying there helpless. I swear he wanted to kick your leg or something. He was so…smug. He said you had it coming. I wanted to slap the crap out of him. What is *wrong* with him?"

He face hardened into an angry scowl. "It's worse than I thought then. We'll deal with him in any case." Pulling me closer, he nuzzled my neck. "Now before we go to sleep, do you want to tell me why you wanted to beat the hell out of me today? Is this about my ex's from 2,000 years ago?"

Well, when he put it like that, it *did* seem a little dumb. It's not like he's getting back together with them…

"Dec told me about Lara tonight. How many times did you sleep with her?"

Turning his head away in frustration, he pushed up to sit against the headboard. Running his hand over his jaw, he groaned and rolled his eyes. "Are you serious right now? I don't know! Once, maybe? It's been a really long time. I don't even remember the year."

"It's not that so much as what happened today. How could you let her touch you like that? Right in front of me? That's so disrespectful to me!" Huffing a bit, I made a point of tamping down my anger and said more evenly, "You deserved getting kicked in the ribs but not getting your leg broken. For that, I'm sorry. But I'm not sorry for being mad at you in the first place."

Ignoring my apology, he touched the locket resting against my chest. At his touch, it picked up the rhythm of his heart and the tiny vibrations made my pulse quicken. His eyes softened and he slowly wrapped his fingers around the back of my neck and pulled me down for a kiss. He kissed me with a tenderness and softness that spoke of love and caring and amends. I let go of my anger and let it drift away into the night. There was nothing as important as the two of us together.

He cupped my chin and said, "I have no real excuse for today. I was trying to annoy you. I'm sorry though. I didn't realize how much it would hurt you. I'm an idiot." He stroked a trail around my jawline, following it with his mouth. "You are the most important person in my world, Mica. I need you to believe that."

I shifted so I was curled on top of him with my head on his shoulder. He hugged me closer and asked, "Do you?" His voice was soft but demanding nonetheless. He wasn't going to drop this until I answered him.

Leaning back on my elbow, I said seriously, "I do. My heart almost stopped today. I came so close to losing you again." My emotions overwhelmed me, and I kissed him with all the pent up fear and frustration of the day. Rolling me onto my back, he was kissing me into oblivion when Killian's voice penetrated the door.

He yelled, "Is this a bad time?"

I yelled "yes" just as Sean yelled "no." Without waiting for an invitation, Killian walked in and flipped on the light. Shrinking against the brightness, I dragged the covers over my head and fumed underneath them. I caught the slightest hint of a knowing chuckle inside my mind.

Ooohh…he did that on purpose!

More chuckling.

Holding the sheet up to my nose, I peered out at him. He was dressed in black commando gear and armed to the teeth. An automatic rifle hung ominously over one shoulder. He looked unusually tense. The crease was sharp between his eyes while he and Sean had a hushed conversation.

Looking over at me when they were done, he asked, "Tell me again what Balin said about being dead."

"Well, he said Domino couldn't hurt him now and that we could thank our friend for the new life. Oh, and they've managed to work the kinks out of it, whatever that means."

Accepting my words at face value and finding them problematic, he was grim and hostile. I scooted back a bit and leaned into Sean for protection from his sudden scowl.

Killian thought for a moment and finally said, "I've got to find *Sgaine Dutre* before they figure out how to control it. I'm going to be gone for a while. Sean, you're in charge here. You know what to do. I'll check in when I can." He caught my eye and held my stare.

"Do me a huge favor and stay out of dark places!" He seemed to consider this an impossible task and frowned in advance of anything I might do.

"Killian, what did the demons do with the knife?"

He was making me very nervous.

He and Sean shared a look and he stood to go. "They raised the dead."

Chapter 17: The Problem with Vengeance...

"OH, NO! NOT AGAIN! Sean!"

The TV was on in the living room while I threw egg whites into a skillet and blended some smoothies. We were all on a health kick at the moment. My appetite just evaporated with the early morning news though. Damn it!

"What's happened? You look like you've seen a ghost." Dec had come running in at the sound of the blender.

Sean took one look at me and said, "It happened again, didn't it?" I nodded, unable to trust my voice. "Was it the girl from the bar?"

"Raped, beaten, and throat cut this time. I didn't recognize the picture they showed on the news." I leaned against the couch and wrapped suddenly cold fingers around my coffee cup.

Her hair was hacked off again.

"Can't you just call the lab and get the results? We could at least rule him out if there's no match in the database." I was mentally slapping myself for not stealing the knife from Scott's apartment; but I guess he could've just bought another one, if he really wanted to use it.

"I'll call in a few minutes, and we'll see what they've got. It's Friday. My guess is he'll be out with his girl again since he didn't kill her." He smiled evilly and asked, "Who wants to go hunting tonight?"

My head was aching from the frustration that was gradually building in all of us. We hadn't been able to do anything to stop the killing and were no closer to proving anything. It was making me crazy.

"Hey Dec? Will you work out with me?"

Lifting one blond eyebrow, he asked, "What's wrong with Sean?"

"I don't want to break him again."

"But you don't mind breaking *me*? Who's going to heal me?" He was backing away with a desperate expression.

I couldn't help it. I burst out laughing. "I promise I won't hurt you, Dec. I just need to burn off some energy so I don't accidently blow up something important later!"

To the compelling music of Staind, I kept my word. I didn't go psychotic and break him. We worked out hard though and were both drenched in sweat by the time Sean called a time out. He'd been watching and coaching as we sparred. Sean was the most amazing fighter I had ever seen. When he joined us on the mats to demonstrate this move or that, I found myself mesmerized by the way he moved. I couldn't copy his grace. I could do the same movements but never with the same fluid motion and controlled power. He always reminded me of a black panther hunting. Dec, with his beautiful golden coloring, was more of a leopard but just as graceful.

And just as lethal.

"What's the matter? Why are you staring at me?" Sean asked when he realized I was gawking at him.

Blushing, I said, "Nothing…I was just…uh, admiring you two."

Astonished, they both stared at me. Dec spoke first. "What are you admiring? We're a sweaty mess over here. Dude, you ripped a hole in my shirt!" He held out the wet material to prove his point.

They really had no idea? Intrigued by their complete lack of awareness, I ventured, "You have no idea how you look when you fight, do you?" I bent over in a pseudo-yoga pose and tried to appear graceful and elegant.

Puzzled, they looked at each other. I got up and tried to mimic the way Sean moved when he stalked prey.

When I finished and rolled up to my feet I said, "You don't see it?"

Both shook their heads like they thought I was crazy. Laughing at them, I went to Sean and lovingly ran my hands down the hard muscles of his shoulders and said in my best Tarzan impression, "You Jaguar."

Then I did the same to Dec and said, "You Leopard."

"You're comparing us to cats?" Dec's mouth twitched and one dimple popped up. Sean's face was red with the effort not to laugh.

"Geez, you two can't take a compliment. Never mind!"

Sean asked with less laughter, "That's really how you see us?"

Seriously, I said, "Yes, always. You move with a grace and overwhelming power that takes my breath away. You don't see it, but I *always* have and it's a beautiful thing to see. I'm really so proud of you both...like beautiful predators when you hunt." I smiled a little bigger at Sean then. "It's one of the reasons I was so attracted to you when we first met. It's how you move."

Neither said a word and when I glanced over at them they were grinning hugely at me. They both draped their arms around me and we walked upstairs together, laughing as we bounced unsteadily up the steps. When we got to the top, Dec pulled me into a hug and squeezed me harder than usual. My diaphragm was about to scream in protest when he finally let me go.

With twinkling eyes, he said, "Do you remember all those years ago when we adopted you?" Without waiting for an answer, he added, "I'm so glad we did, darlin'!"

It was nearly time to go into town and spy on Scott again. I was slipping on a top when Sean came out of the shower. He was sporting a towel slung carelessly around his hips and was brushing his teeth and petting Domino at the same time. Her nose was at towel level.

"Don't even think about it!" I warned her.

Domino blinked and wagged her tail. *A girl can look, right?*

Who could blame her? He was still wet and spiky strands of black hair clung to his face. Drops of water sparkled on his chest as he shook out his hair. His eyes were very blue as he caught my eye. With his free hand, he pointed to the towel with a question in his eyes.

Tempted, I said, "No way. We haven't got time for that. We have hunting to do."

He rinsed his mouth and combed his hair before coming back to me with a sexy smile. "Are you sure? Fighting always gives me a terrible--"

Hands over my ears, I said, "La, la, la. Can't hear you!"

I beat a hasty retreat and waited with Dec in the living room. He could never sit still and wasn't now. His lean hands darted back and forth as he teased Domino with a stuffed dog toy. Reaching out, I pulled one of those hands to me.

"What are you doing, you crazy wench?" He tugged, but I held onto it. He grinned indulgently as I ran my fingernail over the back of his hand tracing the blue veins that kept him alive. He had perfectly shaped hands with long fingers with slightly squared tips. The pads of his fingers were calloused from their love affair with his Gibson guitar. Amused, he graciously let me play with his hand while Sean took his time.

"Watch," I ordered and then ran my finger across the top of his hand just to see the golden light rise to the surface and shimmer gently. The lightest sprinkling of fine blond hair reflected the light.

He peered closer and smiled wistfully at the sight. "You must be a magical wench. I haven't seen that happen since..." He stopped and reddened. Refusing to say any more, he squeezed my fingers and reclaimed his hand.

Sean finally showed up and we opened the garage to leave. It was snowing hard. Big early winter snowflakes that stuck to everything.

"Oh, look! It's like a Christmas card!" I twirled in the snow appreciating the way it sparkled in the dim light from the porch. A few inches covered the porch railing and the bushes. The pine trees at the edge of the property were fluffy white and glowing in the darkness. It was breathtaking.

"Yeah, yeah, great. It's snowing," Dec grouched on his way to the driveway. He was kicking at the snow with the toe of his combat boot. He was dressed in his typical jeans and button-up shirt with the sleeves rolled halfway up his forearms. This one was white with dark purple stripes and was un-tucked. It fit him like a glove. The only nod to the cold temperature was the leather jacket slung across his arm. It was his turn to drive the SUV and I rode in the back. Sean got to ride shotgun simply because he was faster than me. The streets in the center of town were busy even with the snowstorm. It took more than a little snow to keep college kids inside on a Friday night. The bars would be packed. Dec drove up and down the main drag until Sean spotted Scott's truck at The Angry Lizard. Oh great, my favorite place! I hoped I didn't blow it up later…

On our way to the door, I asked Sean, "Are we using the same plan as last time? I act like a horny girlfriend, and you pretend you're getting laid later?"

Bursting out laughing, Dec said incredulously, "*That* is your usual plan? No wonder you can't catch him. Who could concentrate?"

Sean gave him a superior look and said, "I have iron control. Watch and learn from the expert."

As before, we spotted our prey first and sidled over to a good place for spying. Dec went to the bar, and Sean and I got situated at a table. Scott had the same brunette with him tonight, and they were sharing one of the tiny tables near a wall. The music was thumping and she

danced with her back against him. Judging from his sloe-
eyed expression, he was probably going to want to leave
soon. We needed to work harder to get his attention
tonight.

Inspired, I moved over to stand in front of Sean and
wiggled to the music. I closed my eyes and let the rhythm
take me. After a few minutes, Sean pulled me back
between his legs and whispered at me to keep going. He
bent down and kissed the back of my neck like it was
foreplay. Even though I was supposed to be acting, I still
went weak at the knees and saw little stars behind my
eyes.

The stars evaporated when he nipped my earlobe
between his teeth. "Pay attention, he's finally noticed us.
He's watching you. Show time." Without warning, he
turned me around and pressed my face against his neck.
Taking this as a hint, I let my hair cover my face and
pretended to kiss his neck while he ran his hands down
my back. I assumed Dec was watching Scott.

"He's looking." Sean murmured with a devastating
smile. I nearly melted onto the floor.

Dec interrupted drily, "Dude, you really do have iron
control. You look bored. I'm impressed! Mica's about to
pass out though..."

"Shut up, Dec! I am not. It's an act."

That gave me an idea. Scott was used to seeing me
with Sean...but what about another guy? How would that
sit with him? Would he lose his mind? Leaning over to
Dec, I draped my arms around him familiarly and gave
him a big kiss on his very surprised mouth. Startled, he
tried to push me back towards Sean, and I hissed at him
to play along. He glanced helplessly at Sean who was
watching Scott's reaction. Nodding his approval, he
turned so he could watch us and see Scott at the same
time.

Out of the corner of his mouth, he observed with a
lazy smile, "I think you're pissing him off now. Kiss him

again. Just don't use your tongue; I have to kiss you later!"

Before Dec could react, I forced a loud laugh and wrapped my arms around him like we were old lovers from way back. I pouted and batted my eyelashes until he tipped his face down so I could reach him. Poor Dec was really not happy but went along with me. After a sharp nudge from Sean, Dec pulled me closer and kissed me like he was sampling the goods. His lips were lazy against mine and his eyes were closed like he was just toying with me. It wasn't passionate but more teasing as if he wasn't sure he liked me enough to really kiss me. I played along and made a big deal out of flirting with him and curling my fingers in his hair.

"Well?" Dec said under his breath. He'd stopped kissing me and was idly playing with a strand of my hair, pretending to flirt with me.

Sean's voice was grim when he spoke again. "He just got up and went to the bathroom. He's furious. His eyes were shooting daggers at you." He glanced at Dec's red face and said without mercy, "I think now's a good time for you to take a leak, little brother."

Dec bolted from the table like he was on fire. Bemused, I crawled back onto Sean's lap. We had to keep up the appearance of...being really slutty, I guess. The irony was hilarious. Sean was the only guy I'd ever been with and would ever be with. But the entire population of this bar thinks I'm a slut. When I wanted to go undercover, this wasn't exactly what I'd had in mind. Smiling at the irony, I watched the abandoned brunette across the room. She was a pretty girl with a small heart-shaped face and wide blue eyes. Her lashes were long and swept across her cheeks as she sighed into her drink. She had a pouty mouth and the fuller bottom lip was in full pout position at being left at the table alone.

It was like looking in a mirror.

"Sean, do you think we should warn her?"

Before he answered, Dec came rushing back with a worried frown. "Flynn wasn't in the bathroom. I didn't see him anywhere."

"Shit. Where did he go?" Sean stood taller and scanned the room.

"I think he's out back. I can sense him. He's still here."

"Hm, he's probably smoking. Okay, Dec, let's go. We'll walk that way and see what shakes out."

He leaned into my ear and ordered, "No blowing anyone up! Do you hear me?"

"I won't if you don't. Let's get this over with."

Sean opened the patio door to the smoking area and looked around at the scattered groups of smokers. The snow was still falling so there were only a handful of people sitting there. The patio was open to the sidewalk without any kind of borders; easy in and easy out. That was perfect. Where was he? He was still here, but I sensed another familiar mind.

Gripping Sean's sleeve, I pulled him back into the building. Dec had to back up quickly to keep us from running over him. "What the hell?"

"James is here," I announced.

"Really?" Sean breathed with anticipation.

"Whoa! What happened to not blowing things up?" I laid a calming hand on both of them and suggested we try subtlety before a full frontal assault.

I was stretching to sense James and Scott again while the guys whispered about what we should do. Finally, I said, "I think they're in the same place. It seems like it. Maybe they're together."

Coming to a decision, Sean ordered softly, "Mica and I will go in from the sidewalk side and distract them. Dec, you slide up from the other side in case they try to bolt."

With a nod, Dec vanished like a ghost into the snowy night. Sean wrapped his arm around me and led me towards the other side of the patio. There wasn't any cover so we had to walk boldly towards them. Scott was talking to a couple of his buddies and smoking a joint. Their voices were muffled by the falling snow. Like an animal scenting prey, Scott's head snapped up as we approached. His eyes were murderous when he recognized me. He said something to his friends, and they all turned to stare at us. My knees were shaking, but Sean kept a hard grip on my arm and sent a spike of his own *saol* zinging through me. Like a shot of adrenaline, it made me preternaturally alert and ready to fight, or run away. Unlike Sean, I wasn't immune to the flight response.

Scott stood and slowly approached us, one hand reaching into his jacket pocket. Sean crossed his arms and waited. My own hand had a death grip on the Sig in my purse.

"You left your date inside," I said.

He sniggered rudely, "What's it to you? Jealous?"

"I couldn't help noticing she looks familiar to me. Do I know her?"

He squinted and took another hit off the joint in his fingers. Laughing unevenly, he said, "Man, Mica, you used to be a nice girl. What the hell happened to you?" He waved a hand in the general direction of Sean. "Now you're nothing but a nasty slut bangin' those freaks of yours. What are you, their pet? Are they sharing you now?"

I smiled seductively and fondled the muscles in Sean's shoulder. "Freaks? I wouldn't say that, exactly. They have some...unique talents that any girl would appreciate. What's wrong with a little fun? It's all legal. Besides, I was a nice girl until you came along. You sort of ruined that for me. Thanks though, I'm so much freer now that morality isn't an issue."

His friend thought that was hilarious and broke into loud laughter. Scott's eyes widened a bit when Sean spoke, his voice dripping with innuendo.

"Mica's a special kind of girl. She needs a little extra something to be *content*." He ran a hand familiarly across my back and smiled in a way that said he was getting laid later and we might have company.

There's that lack of patience again. Sean was tired of playing games with Scott. Pushing him to the breaking point seemed like a good idea at the time...

I bit my tongue and Scott's eyes went cold as a snake's. Then I felt him on the other side of me.

Dec.

Cocky as always, he wrapped an arm around me and leaned down to kiss my temple.

"Hey, darlin', are you ready for me?"

Like an enraged bull, Scott lunged at Dec, and they went tumbling onto the ground. Sean and I both jumped out of the way as they rolled around in the snow. Scott was unhinged and trying to kill Dec with his bare hands. Dec was struggling to get to his feet in the slippery snow. After cracking his head against the concrete, he was motivated to kick Scott's ass. Scott landed a few really hard punches before Dec got a good grip on him and slammed his head into the concrete-just once. He was out cold and very still.

The silence was absolute.

With a grunt of annoyance, Dec wiped a hand under his nose to catch the blood that was dripping over his lip. He leaned over and caught his breath before pushing himself to stand up. Scott wasn't moving.

"You better see if he's dead!" I hissed to Sean.

Dec shook his head and put a hand to his skull. After a second, he nodded and got up again. Unfortunately, Scott wasn't dead.

Dec glanced up at the other people hovering nearby and smiled what could have been a reassuring smile if it weren't for the blood covering his pretty white teeth. He resembled a very pretty and well-fed vampire at the moment.

He said wryly, "He'll live, people. Shit."

Together he and Sean dragged Scott to a chair and plopped him next to his friend. Sean assured him that Scott wasn't going to die and warned him about picking fights in bars. I suggested we go check on the girlfriend. Walking around to the front entrance, I was thinking of what I could possibly say to this girl to get her to leave without Scott.

"Damn it." Sean's voice was unhappy as he pulled me to a stop in the middle of the sidewalk. He was staring at something farther down the block in front of us.

"Freakin' James!" Dec growled next to me.

He was right. There was James…leading Scott's girlfriend by the hand and looking chummy with her. They were too far ahead of us for me to yell at them, and I looked helplessly at Sean. His mouth was set in a grim line as he watched them get into a car and drive away.

"What's he doing?" Dec asked somewhat rhetorically.

The ride home was quiet as we were all lost in our own thoughts. Once in the house, I plopped down on a kitchen stool with my head in my hands. What was going on with James? I was so confused. Obviously we were missing something, but what?

Completely absorbed with my own thoughts, I hadn't noticed Dec come in and wash the blood off of his face in the kitchen sink. I glanced up at him now. His white shirt was probably ruined, a casualty of the night. I was sorry to see it go. It was my favorite. It fit him really well and the color was great with his eyes. He was such a cutie. Every now and then, I nagged at him about finding a girlfriend, but he told me to save my energy. He'd do what he wanted, when he wanted. It was a shame though. He really was adorable, and I couldn't help thinking about his kisses earlier. They were nice, but no fireworks for me. He had a beautiful expressive mouth though and someday some girl would appreciate it.

I was rudely dragged out of my reverie by a cold shower of water. "Are you nuts? What's the matter with you?" I snapped slapping water off of my arms.

With an expression that was a cross between disgusted and amused, he gargled with mouthwash and with an arched eyebrow, pointedly spit it into the sink with a metallic splash.

"Like kissing my sister, that was." He gargled again. "Don't *ever* make me do that again." Spitting out the last mouthful, he added, "Gross."

"What's gross?" Sean asked as he made his way to the fridge for a glass of water.

Amused, I answered, "Kissing me." I puckered my lips towards Sean.

Kissing me thoroughly, he smacked his lips and said thoughtfully, "Nope, not gross."

"You're hilarious. I'm going to bed. I can't think any more and my brain hurts." I gave Dec a very sisterly hug though and a kiss on the cheek. "I love you, Dec...just like a big brother."

"Okay, babe, get some sleep. I'm going to stay up and talk to Dec. We'll figure some things out and talk to you in the morning."

By the next morning, the driveway was impassable. Mother Nature had been generous with her powder and we'd gotten at least 10 inches of snow. Judging by the heavy clouds skirting the treetops, she wasn't through with us yet. Leaning against the porch railing with a steaming cup of coffee, I watched as Domino bounded through the deep snow. Apparently she woke up this morning and thought she was Bambi. Her spotted coat stood out in sharp contrast against the brilliance of the snow as she leapt up and over the bulk of it. With ears flying and tongue lolling, she had given in to her baser instincts and romped with complete abandon. Smiling at her antics, I thought about the freedom to romp.

I wanted to romp...When was the last time I romped?

Had I ever been that free? I couldn't remember a time that I was. I wondered if I'd ever be that carefree again...

"No smile for the snow, Princess?" a soft voice interrupted my maudlin thoughts.

Turning, I smiled absently and gestured towards the winter wonderland. "I have to go to work. I don't think I can get out of the driveway."

He considered that for a moment and stepped closer to me. He paused several feet away, but I felt the heat from his body. Still dressed in commando gear, he loomed larger than life and I took a small step back. With a knowing frown, he turned away from me and whistled for Domino.

With head up, she came bounding over and rubbed all over him. He was clearly worthy of her attention as her big brown eyes sparkled up into his. He brushed the snow from her coat and pressed his forehead against hers affectionately. I was surprised by the depth of love it hinted at, and a small smile formed on my own lips. By now, my coffee cup was empty, and I was shivering in my blanket. The wind was picking up and fresh snow began to fall. A sudden gust found its way under my blanket, and I reluctantly went back inside.

Sean was still asleep. Not wanting to wake him yet, I held my breath and watched him sleep from the doorway. With one arm flung above him, he was sprawled on his stomach with most of his back bare. His face was turned towards me, and my heart swelled as my eyes soaked in the features I knew so well. The turn of his cheek, the feathering of his brows, the fullness of his mouth...I knew and loved every inch of him. Breathing in a steadying breath, I had to still my pounding heart. Telling myself that he was really here and I wasn't dreaming again, I closed my eyes against the heat building behind them. So close...so close to losing him forever. What would I have done if he'd never come back to me? Unable to stop the panic, I let the tears come...and turned towards the window to hide them from the one who should see them the most.

"Tears so early, baby?" He wrapped his arms around me and gently turned me against his chest. With a feeling of relief, I clung to him as an anchor in the storm.

"I wanted to watch you sleep...but...I wanted you to wake up and look at me. I wanted you to be real." Leaning away, I said fiercely, "Don't ever leave me again!"

Puzzled by my outburst, he nodded seriously and held me tightly against him. "I'm not going anywhere. You're my world now." He kissed me with exaggerated tenderness, and the panic in my heart quieted down again.

It was after noon and still snowing. The drifts were piling up against the house and the weather report called for another six inches today. My boss wasn't thrilled that I didn't show up for work, but couldn't really argue the fact that I couldn't get out of my driveway. Still haunted by a disturbingly maudlin mood, I drifted around the house like a ghost. Everyone else settled in to wait out the snow. Dec built a huge fire in the living room and Domino curled up in front of it watching him play. He dragged out his guitar and plucked a wistful song that summoned visions of Irish maidens and dead highwaymen. Leaning against the cold window, I closed my eyes and listened to him play. As clear as a memory, I watched the handsome highwayman gunned down by the king's soldiers. The screams of the landlord's daughter echoed through the night. I had to shake my head to clear the images from an old story I'd heard somewhere along the way. Dec's fingers tugged on my heartstrings as he plucked out the melody. I sighed and thought of Scott's girlfriend. Every instinct told me he was a killer, but something in his eyes was different when he was with her. The cynicism was gone; they seemed warmer when he looked at her. Could we be wrong about him? I hoped we were. Sean watched me for a bit and finally handed me a cup of hot tea.

"Talk to me. I've never seen you like this," he said with concern in his voice. Killian glanced up from his laptop.

Sighing heavily, I accepted the cup and touched his hand in thanks. "I'm not sure what's wrong. I just feel...heavy, somehow. Maybe it's just the weather, or maybe just my hormones." I tried to lighten up a little.

Alarmed, he gripped my hand in his. "Explain that to me."

"I don't know, Sean. Maybe I'm pregnant?"

Dec missed a string. The discordant note hung in the air for endless seconds. All three males stared at me with undisguised horror. Sean actually sat down on the arm of the couch.

Taking pity on him, I clarified, "I'm not pregnant. I was trying to make a joke..." The severe expressions around me told me they didn't find that even a little bit funny. "Sorry, guess that's not funny right now."

Cautiously, Sean said, "Is there a chance you could be pregnant?" His eyes were round with something like astonishment. Didn't he realize that happens when you have sex? Geez.

Rolling my eyes, I said, "Well, you tell me. Can you get me pregnant? Do you, uh...have um, you know...sperm?"

No one said a word for so long that I got nervous. Sean finally shook his head and said, "I hadn't thought of that...but I don't think it's possible...I don't know. The condoms should work though." He shrugged helplessly and glanced at Killian for help.

Killian scowled at the both of us and snorted with impatience. "There's always a chance. I have hunting to do. I've been here too long."

Without another word, he left.

Dec raised his eyebrows at that and picked up his guitar. Who knew what went on in Killian's mind? He was an enigma on the best of days. We spent the rest of the afternoon in strained silence. Dec kept looking at my stomach until I snapped at him and threatened to break his nose if he didn't stop.

"For the last time, I am not pregnant! I promise if I was, you two would be the first to know." I stomped back to the bedroom after that little outburst.

A tap at the door woke me out of a fuzzy dream. I snuggled deeper into my blanket not willing to let go of the softness of the dream. In it, I stood on a heather-covered slope with my hair whipping behind me. The sun warmed my face as I breathed in the salty air. The ocean crashed against the rocks and I watched as...The tapping came again and this time Sean opened the door and came inside.

"Mica? I hate to wake you up, but we need you." His voice sounded strained so I sat up and rubbed some life into my eyes as the dream drifted away.

His own eyes burned cobalt, and he was all but vibrating with the desire to fly out of here. It was a small miracle that he even knocked on the door.

"What's going on?"

Taking my hand, he practically dragged me back to the living room where Dec was pacing in front of the windows. When he saw me, his mouth tightened into a line and he stopped pacing. I hesitated as a feeling of dread began to creep up on me. Judging by the looks on their faces, it was pretty bad. I glanced between them and then noticed the TV remote lying on the coffee table. A lump formed in my throat sending me into a coughing fit.

Tensing for the worst, I begged, "Please tell me you were watching the weather."

Sean answered for both of them. "No. I'm afraid not." His eyes were bleak, but he continued, "Her name was Lia."

Shaken to the core, I whispered, "No, not her. Please tell me this isn't Scott's girl!" Neither would say that. Her little heart-shaped face swam before my eyes. She was just a baby...She was so pretty and so young...just waiting for Scott alone at the little table. She was just waiting for her man to come for her but he didn't. He was unconscious on the patio when she left. My legs didn't want to hold me up; I sat down heavily on the edge of the couch.

"Same as before?" I asked between my teeth, desperately clinging to logic when all I wanted to do was scream and break things.

Dec's clenched fist crashed down on the table. "No! It was a hundred times worse. She was..." His voice broke and he sucked in a ragged breath. Squeezing his eyes shut against the images, he choked out, "She was...hacked to pieces."

His shoulders shook with his efforts to hold it together. Shocked past words, I raised my hand to comfort him and he shrugged me off. "Don't touch me right now," he said between clenched teeth. He was the true avenging angel, both beautiful and frightening...deadly. I backed away.

Sean stood closer to me, but he was also tightly coiled and wanted to rip someone to shreds with his bare hands.

What happened last night?

I had no facts to back up my imagination, but I saw it clearly in my mind. Scott would've woken up humiliated and furious. But would he take it out on Lia? He'd been insane when he saw me with Dec on the patio. He tried to kill Dec in a murderous rage. Was he so unhinged he went after Lia and killed her in some kind of frenzy?

Oh, Jesus. This is our fault!

Our plan was to provoke him to act.

We provoked him to act all right, but this wasn't supposed to happen! He was supposed to attack me! That son of a bitch! He was going to pay for this. Rage bubbled up from inside and I let it take over. He'd have to answer for what he's done. That poor girl! As sorry as I felt for her, now wasn't the time for crying; I'd cry later.

Right now I need to stay in control and do what needs to be done.

And that means taking him out.

Now.

Heading to the door, I said, "Let's go hunting." I was out of the door and in the driver's seat before the two of them could stop me. I gunned the engine as Sean jumped in the front seat. Dec climbed in the back.

The ride into town was tense. They were absorbed in their own thoughts again, and I was intensely focused on not killing us on the slippery roads. They were a mess, but the SUV had good tires so we only slid a little bit. Driving carefully, it took us 30 minutes to get to Scott's apartment by the lake. The SUV slid the last 10 feet into the side of a dumpster. The shattering of the headlight echoed in the stillness. On autopilot now, I jumped out and strode across the parking lot towards the door. I slowed down long enough to pull my Sig from my holster and wait for them to catch up. We were only a few yards from the apartment when the muffled blast of a shotgun froze us in place. Sprinting the last few feet, Sean and Dec hit the door with their shoulders. The flimsy door splintered off its hinges. The acrid smell of gunpowder hit me as soon as I ran into the room. As bad as it was, it couldn't mask the gagging reek of alcohol that hung over the room like a toxic fog. The floor was littered with empty tequila bottles.

Scott was lying slumped over on the mattress. A sawed off shotgun lay next to him on top of an empty bottle. His head lolled against his chest, and I was sure he was dead until he moaned. Looking more closely, I realized that his head was intact. Gently pushing his head back, I gasped. Oh, my God! Sean and Dec looked away, lips pressed tightly together.

The 12-gauge had blown apart the center of his abdomen, shredding his intestines and several major arteries. The overpowering smell of pumping blood made me light headed. Jamming my hand against my mouth to keep from vomiting, I pressed a pillow against the gaping hole to stop the bleeding.

It wouldn't be an easy death.

"Hang in there. Help is coming." Dec went outside to call 911.

Sean squatted by the side of the bed and said, "Man, what happened?"

Scott wheezed, "Missed..." He tried to joke, but his face twisted in pain. "Fuck, it hurts." Eyes glazed with pain and tequila, his breathing was shallow. It wouldn't be long now.

Blindly he groped for my hand with more strength than I thought possible. "Lia?" His eyes searched for her, but she was already gone...

"Lia?"

Sean's expression was compassionate as he looked at the dying man. He nudged me and mouthed "Be Lia" to me.

Squeezing his hands in my own, I said, "I'm here. We're going to stop the bleeding. Hang in there. You're going to be okay." I was babbling now, but I didn't know what else to say.

I had wanted him gone for so long, but now I was frantically trying to keep him alive. I'd wished him dead before, but now...

"No," he rasped. "Don't...save me. Need to...die." A single tear ran down the side of his face.

The light in his eyes dimmed and I said, "No, no, you have to hold on!"

Sean reached over and laid his hand on mine. My hand shook as I crushed Scott's, trying to force him to cling to life by not letting go of him.

Scott's voice was barely a whisper, "So...sorry...Lia...my girl." He drew in a ragged breath and the sound gurgled ominously. Bright red blood ran from the corner of his mouth, and I wiped it with my shirt.

Sean leaned over and asked urgently, "Why did you kill her, Scott?" His ear was close to Scott's mouth trying to hear anything he said. The sirens screamed outside the apartment now. They drowned out the faint whispers making it nearly impossible to understand him when he answered Sean.

Suddenly agitated, he slurred and tried to lift himself up, "I killed...no...loved her..." His voice drifted off and he lay very still. After a second, he whispered, "Mica?" and relaxed in death.

His hooded eyes were bloodshot and shadowed but compelling even in death. Once upon a time my heart did backflips when those eyes looked into my own. Now my heart felt crushed in my chest and I struggled to breathe. He'd once been someone I cared about. He'd been worthy of my care then. He'd chosen the wrong direction for his life, but he hadn't always been this way. Was this agonizing death justice for what he's done?

Who's to say what vengeance should be?

Heavy boots broke the silence as the paramedics burst into the room with a police officer right behind them. With tears streaming down my face and blood on my hands, I shook my head silently at their questioning looks. Unable to resist, I gently closed his eyelids and whispered, "Go in peace."

Sean's hand closed over my elbow, and I let him lead me away. The policeman had questions for us, and I stood numbly while Sean and Dec described how we'd found him. Shivering in the cold wind blowing off of the lake, I hugged myself and turned my face towards it. The icy air numbed my skin, but it would take more than that to numb my heart.

I wanted to feel nothing.

I wanted to drift off into the snow and lose myself in it. After all these years of wanting Scott gone from my life, I realized that I never wanted him dead. Death was permanent; it was unforgiving. What he'd done to me was terrible, yes; he'd scarred me for years. But it was his attack that changed my destiny and brought Sean into my life. Scott had changed my life in ways I wouldn't ever trade.

I'd forgiven him.

I was having a hard time reconciling him to the brutal murders of my look-alikes. His dying was excruciating and watching him suffer reminded me that I am human, and therefore, fragile. Sitting beside him, I felt his suffering with every heartbeat that ended his life. When he spoke of Lia, I sensed his grief even cloaked as it was by tequila. He truly cared about her. He might have even loved her.

How could he murder her so brutally?

How could I have forgiven someone who was capable of that? That didn't make sense in my heart. I felt no sense of victory, no sense of righteousness.

Scott Flynn was dead and I was hollow inside.

Chapter 18: Bah Humbug!

"YOU HAVE TO GO see your parents. They'll be upset if you blow off Christmas." Sean was subtly nagging at me again. It was nearly Christmas, and I still haven't committed.

"They'll survive." My voice was curt. Side-stepping the issue, I pointed to the dishes and asked why I was stuck with them again.

He flushed, with anger or embarrassment, I couldn't tell for sure. "I'll do them. I was going to do them earlier, but I got sidetracked." His patronizing tone was irritating me.

"Is it safe to come in?" Dec asked from around the corner.

Grinding my teeth, I snapped, "Are you afraid I'm going to blow you up, Dec?"

With a hurt expression, Dec slowly edged into the room. His eyes met Sean's and they did their silent communication thing. Sean sighed and said, "You're right."

Sighing heavily, he said, "This has to stop, Mica. We're walking around here on eggshells." He took me by the hands. "Let's sit down and talk. You haven't said a word to either of us since Flynn died."

Feeling cornered, I backed up. "I don't want to talk about it. There's nothing to say."

"I think there's plenty to say. We know you, remember? Shutting us out isn't helpful. Don't make me intrude on your thoughts. You know I can read them if I want to." He added uncomfortably, "Don't make the mistake of thinking I won't do that if I have to."

"You said you'd never do that!"

He corrected me, "No, I didn't. I told you I didn't *want* to do that and I haven't so far. But damn it, Mica! We can't afford to keep secrets in this family! You, of all people, understand what can happen inside your head."

Dec added quietly, "You're tearing my guts out walking around here like a zombie. It's been two weeks. I can't stand it. It's like you've died too."

I didn't know what to say to that. Guilt nudged at me though, and I looked at them, *really* looked at them, for the first time in a couple of weeks. Dec wasn't exaggerating about his feelings. His puppy-dog eyes were pleading as they met mine. He was always more sensitive than the others and tended to feel extreme emotions as if they were his own. Sean would walk through fire for me if that's what it took to snap me out of this mood. Worry was clearly etched on his face, but he wanted to give me room to work through my feelings. He did know me well; it would take time for me to sort things out. At the moment, I was still struggling with what my feelings were...I thought back to the funeral last week.

It had been freezing cold, the air heavy with the threat of another storm. The cemetery was on the outskirts of Hope Falls in the middle of the Adirondacks. Feeling disconnected and fragile, I wanted to go alone so I wouldn't have to talk to anyone. Sean and Dec had flatly refused to let me go alone. The drive had been endless as the grey and white scenery blurred past the windows. I struggled to wrap my mind around Lia's senseless death. Her face intruded in my mind's eye when my guard was down; big blue eyes staring sadly into her drink waiting for Scott.

Had she known what was going to happen?

Was she dead before he ripped her apart?

My imagination gladly filled in the details, and my dreams were plagued by her eyes bulging in terror as she died at the hands of the man who died in my own. In the worst of these dreams, my own face blended with hers until I wasn't sure which of us was dying. I couldn't seem to move on from this, and my mood had been bleak in the week leading up to the funeral.

Due to the terrible weather, the funeral service was held inside a tiny chapel instead of near the grave. Stained glass depictions of Jesus with his disciples lined one wall while an image of the angel Michael was centered on the other wall. The dim winter's sunlight washed out the colors so they seemed lifeless and cold. Michael's unforgiving eyes followed me, and I averted my gaze. A cold chill crawled down my neck and I pulled my coat more tightly around me. Not wanting to intrude on her family's grief, we sat in the back pews. No one noticed us and no one spoke to us. Lia's family was devastated and hollow-eyed in the front pews. She had two older brothers whose angry eyes promised vengeance as they held up their heartbroken mother. I looked away.

I couldn't look them in the eyes knowing we could've saved her. There must have been a way we could've saved her...

Dec and Sean sat on either side of me trying to bolster me up. Dec leaned against me and tried to calm me with his *saol*. I put my hand on his knee and shook my head. I didn't want anyone to mask my pain. I needed to feel it. Lia's death had been vicious; the least I could do was feel miserable for a little while. Seeing my stubborn expression, Dec withdrew his energy and just loaned me his body heat.

Sean held my hand when the service began. The gray-haired minister spoke of Lia's beautiful young spirit and of loss too soon. He spoke of God's love and forgiveness for the one who'd taken her life. Among the murmured protests, her mother's keening wail of pain sent shivers down my neck, and I struggled for control of my own emotions. Abruptly barraged by waves of intense emotions swirling around the chapel, I dug my nails into the back of my hand trying to distract my mind. Rage and sadness bombarded me from all sides, and I tried desperately to block it out. But like the impending storm, the grief came relentlessly and threatened to swallow me whole.

As Lia's family bowed their heads in grief, many praying on their knees, I wept into my own hands. Sean pulled me against his shoulder and held me while I cried. I heard nothing of the rest of the service, closed inside my own mind as I was. Feeling like I would shatter into a million pieces, I closed my eyes and said my own prayer. Oddly, it was Michael's face that came to me when my pleading became desperate.

Terrifying and beautiful, his eyes burned as his answer seared into my mind.

You pray for peace, little warrior? There will be no peace for you.

His cold words tore my heart out, and I raised my eyes to the stained glass image and whispered, "No!"

Falling to my knees, I prayed desperately, "Please, Michael, I don't know what you want from me. Tell me what you want!" Tears ran down my face as my heart twisted with the pain of knowing he spoke the truth. But why was there no peace for me? What had I done to deserve this?

Was I damned?

"I need...peace...please!" My voice shook with the effort to hold back the grief of Lia's family before it swamped the rest of my thoughts completely.

I pressed my hands over my ears to shut them out. His voice came to me again. This time, the fierceness was softened by the hope of his words.

Do not fear the suffering. It is the pain of others that will strengthen you for what you must do. You will do well.

Later, as the gleaming wooden casket was lowered into the ground, I stared straight ahead without seeing. With both Dec and Sean holding my elbows, I nodded my head and said the appropriate words at the graveside. Afterwards, they helped me to the car, and we headed for home. Like all of the mourners there that day, I was forever changed.

Sean's soft prompting brought me out of my reverie. "Mica? Please…"

With a shuddering breath, I said, "Michael came to me."

Sean said, "Michael? *The* Michael? What did he say to you? Do you remember?" His tone was even, but his little finger was tapping against his thigh.

Sitting on the counter, I finally explained what had happened at the chapel. When I'd finished with my story, they exchanged a knowing look.

Dec was the first to say something. "You do know what an honor that is, don't you? Michael spoke to you…that's amazing. He's never even talked to me!" He dragged me into a hug and added with a crooked grin, "No worries, darlin'. This just means we have some work to do with you if we're going to help you learn to control this."

Sean agreed. "At least we know you're not going to fail." He winked and smiled easily. "He doesn't lie."

The mall was packed with last minute holiday shoppers. I couldn't find a parking spot anywhere near the entrance and ended up walking blocks to get to work. I came in at 10:00 and had been standing behind the cash register ever since. I shifted my weight to the other foot and glanced longingly at the clock.

"Will these people go home already?" Gina grouched under her breath. She and I were the only ones on the registers and the line was out the door.

"I know, right? Why are they still shopping?" I agreed. "It's two days before Christmas. They should be done by now." I plastered a smile on my face and waved the next lady forward. She had a basket full of bottles and maroon hair. I did a mental eye roll and sighed. The line was still growing.

With my attention focused on ringing up endless bottles of body lotions, I nearly missed Dani's tentative wave from the back of the store. Gina elbowed me and told me I had company.

"Dani! Come up here." I waved and invited her to the register.

She stepped around the counter, gave me a quick hug and said, "Are we still on for tonight? I'm dying to talk to you!" The sparkle in her eyes hinted at something juicy.

Uh-oh, that usually meant a new man. I gave the customer her change and waved the next one forward. I had only one more hour to go. I told Dani I'd meet her and she took off. As I handed my customer her bags, I noticed Dani talking to someone in the entrance of the store. His face was in profile, but I wouldn't mistake him from any direction. Growling under my breath, I stared holes into his face until he turned around. With a look of innocence, he draped his arm around Dani and led her away into the sea of people.

An hour later, I was finally free. I wished Gina a Merry Christmas and stepped into the back room to call Sean. Sounding out of breath, he picked up on the fourth ring.

Smiling to myself, I teased, "Whoa! Don't you need me for that?"

I felt him laughing through the phone as he replied, "Nope. I've gotten along without you for years! Jealous?"

Geez! Dork. "Not hardly. It's just more fun for me when I get to help."

Long pause.

"Is that so? When are you coming home tonight?" His voice was silky with a promise that curled my toes. Suddenly it was very hot in here…

"I'll be home in 20 minutes if you're promising something interesting."

"No way, babe! You go finish shopping and hang with Dani. I have things to do with Dec." He paused and lowered his voice to nearly a whisper, "Bring home something sexy for later!"

After making an absurd promise to go to the Victoria's Secret store, which was jam packed with people, I finally took off to meet Dani. She saw me coming and got up to wave me over. Her face glowed with a look I knew was written on my own. Linking arms, we took off to dash in and out of some stores during the dinnertime lull. I hadn't done much shopping, so I had to get a lot of presents. Luckily cash was an acceptable option for my siblings. We ran into Macy's and I picked up some perfume for Janet and cologne for Dad. Dani's gift was already wrapped. I'd gotten her a really cool black and white photograph of an underground tunnel with a backdrop of the Manhattan skyline at night. The shot was surreal and I knew she'd love it. For the guys…I made them each something special. I'd worked on their gifts off and on since the beginning of summer. I was bouncing up and down already thinking about their faces when they opened them.

"Okay, so now will you tell me what's so exciting?" I asked after we'd finally stopped to eat. We were sitting in the food court surrounded by a tableful of toddlers who were too exhausted to do anything but scream. Rubbing my pinched toes, I thought I could relate.

Scanning the huge food court like she was expecting someone else, Dani's attention had wandered. She craned her neck towards the front entrance. I snapped my fingers under her nose, and she jumped with a hand to her throat. Her tinkling laugh was contagious, and I found myself laughing with her.

"It's a guy," she announced.

No shit.

It always starts out with the same three words…it's a guy. Mentally straightening my expression to look supportive, I asked, "What's his name? Do I know him?"

Please don't be James; please don't be James!

Gushing with excitement, she said, "He's so sweet! You wouldn't believe how much he understands me. It's like, he just gets me. You know? He knows what I'm feeling before I do. It's like we're…soul mates. I think I'm falling for him."

Please don't be James, please don't be James…

Forcing my mouth to form a smile, I prodded, "Wow! He sounds awesome. Does this perfect man have a name?"

Shooting out of her chair, she squealed with delight, "James! Over here!" Her entire face lit up like a roman candle as she watched him come over.

Why am I not surprised?

My heart sank like the Titanic. With a loud mental groan, I watched as he made his way around the tables. With both eyes on Dani, he moved with a tension I recognized. He was hyper-alert, but kept his smile lazy. What was he up to? Why Dani? Since when did he date humans? I thought he was tied up with Alex's missions these days. The whole special ops division was out looking for Dagin and *Sgaine Dutre*. Surely he didn't have time for a girlfriend?

He ignored me completely as he pulled her into his arms and kissed her possessively. Her face was flushed by the time he set her away from him. He whispered something against her ear that brought a rosy blush across her chest and up her neck. She quickly glanced at me and replied under her breath. I couldn't hear what they were saying, but the eye contact and body language was pretty obvious.

"What's the matter, Mica? You look pissed," James commented drily.

Dick.

"I just got a text from Killian," I lied, holding up the phone. "*Get home now!*" I made a show of typing a text message and dropped the phone back into my purse.

"He's such an asshole. Why do you let him boss you around?" Dani asked. She was speaking to me, but her attention was clearly on James. He had a hand around the back of her neck and was running his thumb up and down. Her eyes were about to roll back in her head. Oh, my God! Really people? In the food court?

James' eyes met mine but he continued to stroke her. He asked, "Yeah, Mica. Why *do* you put up with Killian?"

Something in his insinuating tone sent a warning bell ringing in the back of my mind, and I absently rubbed my rune. He caught the movement and gave me a chilly smirk. Without taking his eyes off of mine, he leaned over and whispered in Dani's ear. She blushed hotly and giggled. Unable to look away from the train wreck, I was horrified to see his hand graze the top of her breasts. Instead of slapping his hand or snapping at him, she gazed at him with love in her eyes. Ewww. I was going to puke.

Standing abruptly, I announced, "Hey, gotta go. Duty calls and I have to wrap. Dani, I'll talk to you later. Be careful driving home." I disengaged her from James and gave her a very sisterly hug. "Behave yourself!" I hissed with a fake smile.

The sound of raised voices greeted me when I walked through the door. Amused, I stood in the doorway listening as they argued over the best way to kill demons.

Dec's accent grew stronger as he argued with Sean. I wasn't even sure they were speaking English at all. He was saying, "...and blowing them up scatters them. You know they can't bring themselves back together again!"

Sean stood with arms crossed and looked down his nose. "Oh? And if that's such the best idea then why do we have the silver knives to begin with?"

"Think about it, aye! You can always blow them up if your hands are tied." He snorted with derision at the thought of relying on a weapon.

Sean's tone turned a bit surly. "Oh? And at what point would you have your hands tied? It would be the height of stupidity to get tied up."

I interrupted, "I thought you needed your hands to blow up the demons. Don't you have to focus the power through your hands?"

"No, sweetheart, you don't," Dec confirmed.

As soon as he heard my voice, Sean decided to light a fire in the fireplace. He kept his back turned as he arranged the logs and kindling. Carefully feeding the fire, he took his time as I got more and more suspicious.

"Why do you always look so suspicious?" Dec asked with a grin. "Come on, lass. I'll help you put away your bags." Without waiting for an answer, he walked me back out to the porch.

Snow was falling again. Tilting my face skyward, I let it melt on my skin. There was something about the dusty wintery smell of fresh snow settling on the pine trees that made me nostalgic. Christmas was two days away, and I was trying to get excited.

"Can I stand with you?" Dec asked companionably in my ear. At my nod, he wrapped his arms loosely around my waist and stood just behind me. Fingering my locket, I let my eyes glaze over and blur the snowy scene into something magical. The gold warmed my fingers, and I let the vision come to me as it would. I smiled at the sight of Sean laughing down at me from his snowboard. I was flat on my back with the wind knocked out of me. That had been a perfect day with him. Normally so serious, he was free as an eagle on the slopes. I'd wanted to drown in those eyes...as the snowy scene blurred into the farmhouse, Dec's blond hair filled my vision as he knelt over me holding my head. With gentle fingers, he'd rubbed my temples and reminded me to breathe right after I'd thrown up in the sink. The musical lilt of his voice calmed the kaleidoscope spinning in my head that day and many after. His crooked grin and boyish dimples had stolen my heart from the first moment I'd seen him in the bar. He was a real angel, a miracle…I squeezed his arm and sighed as the vision shifted again.

Mist curled along the creek bank as I turned to watch the sun rise through the trees. The pale light shadowed his face and accentuated the sharp angles. Killian's eyes lingered on my mouth as he pressed my cold fingers against his lips. A sudden gust of wind scattered the mist and snow replaced it in my mind.

"What's wrong, darlin'? What did you see?"

Shaken and confused, I struggled to grab onto the vision, but it was gone. I blinked to clear the rest of the fuzziness and stared hard into the trees.

He was out there, somewhere.

Was he alone?

"Let's go inside. I'm cold."

The next morning, I had a text message from Dani telling me that she and James were going skiing at Gore Mountain. It wasn't an invite, exactly, but I wanted it to be. My suggestion that we go boarding for the day was met with mixed reviews. Sean felt the need to point out that we were supposed to go to my parents' house in the morning, and I was supposed to bring something for Christmas dinner. I hadn't figured out what to cook and I hadn't wrapped gifts yet. He was such a downer! I had a feeling Sean and Dec were up to something, but they kept their faces as innocent as two angelic super-secret agents could. Since he didn't have to cook or wrap, Dec thought a day on the mountain was perfect. Sean was being more practical.

Leaning up on tiptoes, I nibbled on his neck to sway him my direction. "Oh, come on, I have a need for speed…"

A few hours later, we had lift passes and had jumped onto a chairlift. At the top of the trail, Dec stood against the sun and waited for us. He always wore charcoal gray board pants and a gray and white jacket. Like Sean, he kept gloves tucked into a pocket but never wore them.

His Oakleys had vivid blue lenses that stood out against his skin. I'd never lose him in a crowd. As we approached the ramp, I was stunned to realize I could see his halo. Blinking against a trick of light, I looked again. There it was. The *saol* that flowed inside was subtly outlining his body. It was as clear to me as his sunglasses.

"Oh, wow! Sean! Do you see that?" I gripped the sleeve of his jacket and pointed to Dec.

Shaking his head, he said, "I don't see anything. What's up?"

My mouth fell open. "You don't see the halo? It's clear as day."

With narrowed eyes, he looked again. "It's always there. Don't tell me this is the first time you've ever noticed?"

He was truly surprised and lifted his sunglasses to see me better. He had on the same blue Oakleys but wore a black jacket with black pants. The only color was a single red stripe along one arm.

"Do you have any idea how wicked hot you are? I'm such a lucky girl!"

After kissing me until my fingers glowed, he said, "Yep, you're pretty lucky. I'm a catch in multiple dimensions."

With that, he lifted the bar and got ready to drop off. At the end of the ride, we both smoothly slid down the ramp and off to the side to strap in. It was gorgeous up here. The sky was grey but no new snow was expected so we could relax and ride. I was waiting to hear back from Dani so we could meet her. In the meantime...Dec and Sean flew past me while I dawdled with my phone. With a loud whoop, Dec was airborne over the drop with Sean on his right.

Oh, no they didn't!

Like a shot, I was right behind them. The Lies was a black diamond run and we liked to hit it first. The trees blurred greenly as I focused only on staying upright on the vertical trail. Falling at this speed would hurt...a lot. I leaned slightly to turn left onto the Mica trail, for obvious reasons, then another quick turn onto the Open Pit. The guys were slightly ahead of me and didn't hear me when I screamed.

I tumbled end over end until my board flew off and took my boot with it. When I finally stopped bouncing, my Oakleys were gone, and I was barely conscious. Lying on my back, I opened my eyes to a green sky.

Why is the sky green?

When my brain caught up with things, I realized I was looking at a tree branch and that my leg was probably broken. A now too familiar pain was shooting through my tibia. Well, hell. That's just great! I started to push myself upright when a voice shouted at me.

"Don't move! You might have hurt your back or something!" A man leaned into my face and shouted at me. He was very young, probably only 19 or 20. His face was very serious as he scolded me.

"Okay, I'm not deaf. Stop yelling at me. What happened? Did you see what happened?"

Looking around us, he sounded confused too. "Yeah, I was right behind you...it was crazy, dude. Some guy just appeared in the middle of the trail in front of you. I don't know where he came from. You swerved to go around him and wiped out. It was spectacular! Do you remember hitting that tree? You bounced off and kept going." He grinned down at me, sharing in my pride. Snowboarders were proud of their wipe outs.

That sounded familiar. The man had been wearing white and yellow. That's all that registered before I fell. "Where did he go? Did you see him leave?"

Shrugging, he said, "No, sorry. I was more worried about you. It took me a few seconds to stop so I wouldn't hit you. By the time I looked up again, he was gone. I'm going to go flag down a ski patrol. You're not walking down this mountain."

My phone chose that moment to buzz in my pocket, but I couldn't reach it. "Could you grab my phone for me? Right front pocket."

"You get a signal up here? How's that possible? My phone sucks. I never have a signal." He dug around in my jacket and pulled out the little phone Killian had given me last year. It was a cell phone...and so much more.

Steeling myself against the pain that was rapidly making itself known, I tried to smile at him. "It's a super-secret agent phone. Cross my heart. Just hand it to me, please. My boyfriend's on the other end of it."

He sat back on his heels and waited while I called Sean. We both flinched as Sean's voice bellowed from the earpiece. I did a whole lot of nodding and said a lot of yesses before he hung up. Feeling evil for deceiving this nice guy, I groaned convincingly and sent him down the mountain in search of a ski patrol person. Thirty seconds after he cleared the trail, Dec and Sean appeared next to me in the trees. Glancing around for witnesses, they both raced over to me.

"What hurts? Tell me so we can get you out of here."

"I think my leg's broken again. I don't know about anything else. I'm kind of numb. Apparently I wrapped myself around a tree or two, so I'm not sure about a concussion." I stopped Sean's hand when he was about to pick me up. "Sean, this wasn't an accident. A guy in a white and yellow jacket appeared out of thin air and disappeared the same way. It had to be James. Get him away from Dani."

Dec was fuming but busy skimming his hands over my body. Frowning, he said, "Her leg's definitely broken and I think a rib or two. I'm going to take her to the house so I can check her out. You go find James and Dani and drive the car back." He gave Sean a reassuring look and added, "Don't worry, I'll heal her and if I can't, I'll take her to the hospital and text you."

Sean's eyebrows went straight up. "You'll *text* me? Jesus, Dec. Use your damn telepathy for God's sake. You're killing me here."

Bending over me, he kissed me lightly and said, "I love you. I'll be there as soon as I can. Hang in there."

Dec knelt beside me and carefully scooped me into his arms and we vanished into thin air.

"What the hell happened to you?"

Killian's worried question greeted us as soon as we landed on the living room rug. He sprung up and caught me before my shoulders hit the floor. Dec filled him in while they worked to slide my jacket and board pants off. I had thin under-armor leggings and a turtleneck on under my board clothes and shivered in the cool air.

Domino came in and sat back out of the way. Her eyes watched us as they hovered over me. Once I was situated they went to work on checking me out. All in all, it could've been worse. I had several bruises and a separated shoulder. My back, thank God, was unbroken. My ankle was badly twisted and my leg was broken. Fixing my leg hurt a lot. With teeth clenched, Killian held my leg still above the break while Dec pulled it to straighten the pieces of bone. I bit my lip to keep from screaming. As the two pieces of bone slid together, my vision shrank to a thin tunnel and I tasted blood in my mouth.

All business now, Killian used his own energy to boost Dec's healing power. Feeling nauseous, I closed my eyes while they helped me heal. It didn't take very long, but I had the strangest sense of déjà vu. We'd done this before...but with all déjà vu moments, I couldn't decide if it was past or future.

Leave it alone.

The order came from inside my head, and I blinked up at Killian. His eyes were hard, his face carefully blank. I started to reach out to him and hesitated. His eyes softened and he wrapped his big hand around my cold one and rubbed feeling back into it. His hands were scratchy with callouses but hot as he worked on my wrist and arm.

"I think she's in shock, Dec. Feel how cold she is? Why's her body temp so low?" The crease between his eyes was back as he tried to warm me up.

"Hmm. That's odd. She shouldn't be." He pressed his lips against my forehead like my mother did to check my temperature.

"I'm fine, mom, really. Stop worrying. I'm just cold. Someone get me a blanket or take me to bed."

Was it my imagination or did both of them hesitate for a split second when I said that? Killian helped me up, and I swayed against him as a wave of dizziness washed over me. Scooping me up, he headed to my room. Stopping partway down the hall, he listed awkwardly into the wall. He squeezed his eyes shut and sucked in a breath of air. Without warning, the rune on his hand burst into life and mine followed. His face contorted with pain.

"What's wrong? Put me down; you're hurt!"

Instead of putting me down, he took a deep breath and staggered the rest of the way to my room. Sweat ran down the side of his face by the time he set me down on the bed. Afraid now, I reached out and tugged on his hand. "Killian! You have to sit down. You're scaring me."

"It's nothing--" he started to say when he suddenly clutched his chest and sagged forward. His fingers grabbed at an invisible blade, fluttered, and then went still. The rune over my heart burned like a brand and I yelled for Dec.

He came running in to see Killian on his knees clutching his chest. "What is it? Demon? James?" His head swiveled as he looked for the enemy.

Killian's eyes rolled up in his head, and he slid over to his side. Domino galloped into the room and froze in front of him. She pressed her nose against his chest and growled low in her throat. With raised hackles, she looked pointedly at me and then back to Killian.

Fix him.

Puzzled, I gawked at her for a minute until Dec touched my collar with a question in his eyes. I pulled the fabric over so he could see the rune. It was glowing hotly against my skin and stung like crazy.

Thinking hard, he proposed, "You have his blood...so you have his power. You're an empath...hmm, you're drawing his pain into that rune." Running his fingers over my hand, he did the same with Killian's hand. Both runes glowed...

"Mica, listen to me. This is demonic magic that's hurting him. He can't fight it alone. We have to find the demon and destroy his connection. In the meantime, you can help him."

"Tell me what to do. I'll do anything."

Considering the two of us for several seconds, he finally said, "You have to harness his powers to push this demon's magic away. Do you think you can separate Killian's powers from yours and focus it back onto Killian?"

I thought about it and considered the words of Michael.

Do not fear the suffering. It is the pain of others that will strengthen you for what you must do.

I didn't know if that applied here, but he *was* suffering and I would take his pain as my own if I could. Nodding at Dec once more, I said a short prayer to Raphael hoping he'd lend me a hand. Dec helped me lay Killian on his back and pulled off the t-shirt. There was an angry red mark over his heart. It was the size and shape of a knife wound. It wasn't an open wound, but more like a scar.

"Hold our two hands together for me. I think it helps." He did as I asked and waited.

Thinking about how to do this, I had Dec place our joined hands on top of Killian's heart. Closing my eyes, I waited. Come on, Killian, where are you? There it was. Killian's heartbeat flowed through our hands and I felt it pulsing over my own heart. My heartbeat slowed to match his strong and steady rhythm.

We were truly connected. Wow.

I smiled in amazement, and Dec looked at me quizzically. Closing my eyes again, I called his magic to me. It lived in my blood, but I didn't recognize it yet. It wasn't a part of me. I had to let it come to me on its own.

Come on, it's okay…come and take over…

Gradually, it bubbled up inside, tentative at first, then building, growing, gaining strength.

That's it, take over…

Once the floodgates were opened, his power thrummed through my veins, dominating me, enhancing me, making me stronger in every way. It didn't hurt exactly, but felt like I was stretching out of my own skin. My arms and legs stretched to compensate, my toes curled with the pressure. There wasn't enough of me to contain it all.

Ignoring the warning signs, I channeled that power through our hands and into Killian's chest. Whatever lingering evil there paled in comparison to Killian's ancient power and dissipated steadily.

Killian's mind had been hidden behind a black wall of pain but as he regained consciousness, his memories surfaced again. Our connection was so tight that I was bombarded with his memories. Before I could pull my mind away, I was swept up in an image of him holding me against his chest as a summer storm raged around us. The crash of lightning echoed in my ears as my tears ran with the rain.

Yanking my mind away, I cracked my eyes to see him looking up at me. Did he see what I saw? Was it just a random memory I stumbled into, or did he want me to see it?

How was it a memory if *I* didn't remember it?

Maybe it was just a dream. Maybe I imagined it...my brain was fuzzy and the wild burst of energy was in free fall. I was about to crash. Exhausted, I glanced at Dec who was staring at me with a hundred questions in his eyes.

"Is he better now?" I asked in a shaky voice. I rubbed my chest and held up bloody fingers.

"Dec, I've got this. Leave us for a minute. Please." Killian was sitting up again with clear eyes. Dec reluctantly left to give us a few minutes of privacy.

Resigned, Killian said, "Sit down, Princess. Let me look at you."

With gentle hands, he pulled my sticky shirt away to look for the source of the blood. Completely ignoring my cleavage, he focused only on the rune over my heart. There was a ragged tear in the skin underneath it. It had ripped from the inside. He touched the tear with the pad of his finger and it tingled. After a minute, the tingling stopped and the cut was gone.

"I'm so sorry. I didn't realize this would happen to you," he said regretfully.

"I'm confused. What's happened?"

"I'm afraid you're not strong enough to handle my power and it will hurt you. It could kill you."

Kill me? Could this day get any worse?

Aloud, I said, "There is no way your powers would kill me. You love me. That love is part of your power over me. It's our connection. You'd never let me die at your own hand."

As soon as I said it, I realized that I shouldn't know that. I broke off and stared at him with new eyes.

Stunned by my words, Killian was speechless. His sudden paleness was the only outward sign of his feelings.

Stuttering with embarrassment, I apologized. "I'm sorry. I don't know where that came from."

With a frightening ferocity that I hadn't seen in years, he yanked me closer and growled into my ear,

"You need to forget that for your own good. Do you hear me?" Flinging my hand away from him, he stalked towards the door.

"But why? Why should I forget that?" Angry too, I grabbed his arm and pulled him back to face me. My voice rose until I was yelling again. "Isn't it true? Am I wrong?"

"Just let it go! Why do you have to push?" With lips clamped shut, he pried my fingers away from his arm.

"Tell me I'm wrong!"

The split second's hesitation gave him away. He couldn't deny it but the knowledge didn't give me any pleasure. Instead, I was more confused than before. How had I missed this? I had no memory of him loving me...

Snatching up my wrist, he pressed the rune against his heart and hissed, "This was a mistake!"

Before I could respond, he whipped out his silver blade and slashed the rune in half. Its twin burned hotly for a second and then faded into a pale white scar.

The connection was broken.

Breathing heavily, he wiped a hand over his eyes and refused to look at me as he wiped my blood from the blade and jammed it into its sheath with a metallic hiss.

"Which one of you plans to explain this to Sean?"

Neither of us heard him come into the room. Dec stood with arms crossed in the doorway. His expression said he'd heard most of the conversation, and judging by the resignation in his eyes, he wasn't shocked. What did he know?

"Dec, you know this is for her own good. She can't be tied to both of us. It would be a disaster." His face softened only slightly and he said to me, "It had to be done. I won't watch my power destroy you."

Dec seemed much older as he watched my face while I cradled the rune to my chest. It was still bleeding but I didn't care. I was in shock over what just happened.

Mute, I stared at Killian's eyes and wondered what was behind them. What was he thinking? Didn't I used to know?

Why couldn't I see now?

I felt oddly adrift as if I'd been cut away from a dock and left without a rudder. I tried to clear my mind and look for him but he wasn't there.

Where did you go?

Don't look for me. I won't let you in.

I don't understand...what's going on?

I don't love you, Mica.

You're lying.

After that silent exchange, I lifted my chin and said, "Don't disappear like you always do. The least you can do is open your Christmas present." I got up to get it and he started to protest.

Dec laid a hand on his arm and ordered in a deadly voice, "Stay here. It's the least you can do for her." Under his breath, I thought I heard him say, "I hate this."

By the time I'd gotten back to the living room, I'd put a Band-Aid on my hand and washed my face. I looked perfectly happy as I made my entrance. With a forced show of Christmas spirit, I sat a tiny wrapped box in front of Killian. I had painted the wrapping paper myself earlier in the year. Each box was unique according my visions of them. Killian's was covered with tiny white-capped waves cresting in a brilliant blue sea.

He frowned at it.

"You've known me for how long now? You should be used to me giving you a present for Christmas. Don't look so angry about it." I tried to keep a light tone, but it sounded flat even to me. Dec hissed with frustration and got up to pace.

Instead of opening the box, Killian balanced it on his palm and said quietly, "I don't deserve this, Princess. Save your thoughtfulness for the others."

That hurt. Suddenly I was furious at him and snapped, "Who do you think you are? Who are you to tell me who to care about? Am I too stupid to know who's good and who's bad now?"

I jabbed a finger towards him and glared at Dec. "You two idiots saved my life more times than I can count. And you want to tell me that you don't deserve a stupid Christmas present?"

He flinched at the intensity in my voice and possibly the white light that caught fire behind my eyes.

Ever the peacemaker, Dec reached out a calming hand and said, "We don't think you're stupid. You're family! I'd throw myself in front of a bus for you. I think Killian's just trying to take a step back and...I think he's right." They exchanged a look that spoke volumes. "You can't be tied to him and Sean both. It's a disaster waiting to happen."

"What aren't you guys telling me? Why do I feel like I'm missing something?" My voice climbed several decibels.

Killian frowned and said, "I'm really fucking this up."

For the first time ever, he was at a loss for words and Dec took over. Dec said, "Look, I know what happened between you two was unexpected, and I don't blame either of you for it, but once we got Sean back it had to end. We all know that."

"I heard what you just said, but I have no idea what you're talking about." I was drawing a blank. "Are we still talking about the runes?"

Dec whipped around and glared at Killian for several minutes. Killian's scowl grew deeper and he flushed with anger. Dec threw up his hands and said sarcastically, "Well, that explains a lot."

To me, he said between clenched teeth, "Yeah, the rune had to go." He looked like he wanted to shove Killian's teeth down his throat.

"Uh, okay. You two are keeping secrets from me-- again. I'm too tired to argue about it right now. Will you please just open your present?"

Killian actually smiled a little when he lifted the pendant out of the box. It was a tiny teardrop-shaped glass pendant wrapped in beaten gold braiding. I thought it looked very pagan or at least rustic. The glass was as close as I could get to the color of his eyes. It hung on a thin braided chain of leather with one strand of gold running through it. There were three strands of leather and one strand of gold. I thought it was very symbolic. I had asked the angels to bless it and I hoped they did. Although no one had popped down to tell me they had.

"Do you like it? I made it myself."

Gruffly, he answered, "It's great. I don't know what to say."

Delighted, I said, "Don't say anything. Just wear it. It'll keep you safe." I came around behind him and closed the clasp. My fingers grazed the fine hair at the nape of his neck, and I had a vivid image of kissing that spot. I froze just as my lips pressed against his skin and he jumped. I backed away from him and into Dec.

"Wow, I don't know why I just did that. Um, Christmas kiss?"

Holy shit! What was I thinking?

Kissing Killian wasn't right! But it didn't feel exactly wrong either. I made a mad dash for the kitchen to cover my embarrassment. I took a few minutes to get us all something to drink and was on my way back into the room when I heard Dec's voice. He was giving Killian a hard time. It's wrong to eavesdrop, especially around supernatural beings, but I couldn't help myself.

"This is going to get worse, you know! You underestimated the strength of her mind." His warning had an ominous ring to it.

"Damn it! Don't you think I know that now? I just wanted to shield her. With the added influence of the runes, it would tear her apart. There was too much connecting us, Dec. I had to cut her loose."

"Yeah, good work! Better late than never, I guess. Do you know how angry she is right now? She doesn't even understand why she's angry, but that anger is influencing her powers and that's scaring her to death. She has got to understand the source of her anger so she can get control of these powers. Do you know why she's angry? It's because of you."

"What are you getting at?" Killian asked tiredly.

Before he could answer, the sound of the garage door announced that Sean was back. Thank God. My brain needed something uncomplicated to focus on. I met him in the kitchen just as he came through the side door. His expression was unguarded as he entered the room. He looked tired but other than that, not especially upset. Good sign.

Wrapping my arms around him, I said with a smile, "Merry Christmas!"

"Isn't it early for that still? It's not that late, is it?" He sounded a little distracted but hugged me back. "Are you okay?" He glanced down at my leg.

"I'm fine now, just a little ache in my shin. I'm so glad to see you! Did you find James and Dani? Are you freezing?"

He raised an eyebrow at the question. Of course, he's not freezing! Duh! "Uh, no, I'm fine. But I'll grab a beer and fill you in. Is that Killian?" Voices were drifting into the room, but I couldn't make out what they were saying. Sean would be able to though.

I yelled a warning. "Killian, Dec! Sean's back." Then I followed him into the living room.

"So, what happened?" I prodded.

His mouth twisted into a sardonic smile and he complained around the bottle top. "It was a wild goose chase. I never saw Dani and I followed James from one point to another but he never stayed long enough for me to grab him. It's like a freakin' game to him." He drained the bottle and added, "I'm going to strangle him when I finally catch him." He said it lightly, but there was an underlying resolve that raised goose bumps on my arms.

"I'm still worried about Dani. What does he want with her?"

It was Dec who answered me. "There's only one way to find out."

Rolling my eyes, I caved. "I'll bite. How do we find out?"

Sean winked at me. "Ask him, of course."

Ignoring their silliness, I sent Dani a text message and worried some more. I sat lost in thought until someone turned on the stereo and "Silent Night" broke the silent night. I hadn't noticed but the sun had set and it was dark outside. Except for a bright glowing light...

With a whoop of complete abandon, I skidded through the hallway and out the front door to the winter wonderland that the window only hinted at. Turning around in a circle I was enthralled by the transformation. Some elves had hung white lights from the porch and the little pine trees around the house. There was a golden angel with a lighted halo on the front door. The plastic angel was so cheesy it brought tears to my eyes. It was such a sweet gesture though and my heart nearly burst with joy.

I loved my elves!

"You've a glory of a smile, love." Sean's smile was brighter than the lights when he crossed to my side. "Merry Christmas, Mica." He kissed me and I thought I'd never be happier.

I looked for Dec and Killian, but they were standing on the porch giving us some space. Both laughed at me when I broke away from Sean and threw myself down to make a snow angel.

"Come on! You know you want to!" I challenged.

When they resisted, I threw snowballs at them. Eventually, they had to fight back and chased me around the yard. Dec finally tackled me and shoved a handful of snow down the back of my neck. Screaming with the cold, I broke into helpless giggles when he rubbed more snow in my face. He stopped when Sean and Killian squatted on either side of me and began discussing the best way to turn him into a snow angel for torturing me.

Finding the idea of any of them turning into a snow angel hilarious, I broke into fresh giggles until I had to stop to breathe. Then I thought about the old saying about eating yellow snow and broke into giggles again.

Killian held out a hand and pulled me up. "You look happy, Princess." He actually gave me a very chaste kiss on the cheek and added, "You deserve some fun. Merry Christmas."

"Wait! Are you leaving?"

He stopped and turned back.

"Now?"

"I have things to do, babe." He shrugged casually at that.

"But…" I glanced at Sean for help. "You can't go now. It's Christmas Eve. Tomorrow's Christmas!"

He hesitated but his mind was made up. He shook his head and said, "This is *your* holiday, remember? It's not mine. You have a full day tomorrow anyway. You won't even be here."

"Yeah, but…"

I had nothing to say that would convince him to stay. He was old enough to make up his mind and do whatever he wanted on Christmas. It wasn't up to me to tell him what to do. I just didn't want to think of Killian alone on Christmas. It made me sad to think of him alone.

"But you'll be alone."

He grinned wickedly and said, "Maybe I'll have Lara keep me company."

Chapter 19: Many Kinds of Gifts

I AWOKE SLOWLY out of a dream in the darkness right before dawn. With one arm under my cheek and the other tucked into his side, I was curled against a very warm Sean. Peering up at his face, I was surprised to find his eyes open and staring at the ceiling. Noticing the change in my breathing, he looked down at me and his mouth curled into a sleepy smile. Shifting positions, he tucked me back against him and sighed contentedly. Neither of us wanted to get up, and I dozed off again. The dream gradually took shape as my mind drifted into unconsciousness once more.

I was walking along a rocky coast with the sun rising behind me. My shadow was long and thin as it stretched out across the grass. The waves lapped gently against the shore below me and I breathed in the salty air. It was peaceful and lovely here. A person perched at the edge of the cliff in front of me. As the light grew brighter, I recognized the curve of a woman's body. She turned around and proudly held up a small baby wrapped in a blanket. The baby's blue eyes regarded me with curiosity and my heart contracted in recognition. The woman smiled serenely at me and told me I was very lucky because the baby was perfect.

The woman was me.

"Hey you, wake up. You're dreaming." Sean's voice was warm and mellow in my ear. He hooked a finger into my bodice and peered interestedly into my nightgown. I felt him smile against my shoulder and smiled in response.

"It was a good dream. Do you want to hear it?" I asked softly enjoying the warmth of his skin sliding against mine.

He rubbed his scratchy chin against my shoulder as a 'yes.' I pulled his fingers into mine and kissed them. I murmured happily, "I had a baby and it was beautiful."

"Did you happen to see the father?" His laughter abruptly turned into a whoosh of air when my elbow connected to his diaphragm. "I'm kidding! Really!" He was still laughing.

Leaning over him with a pillow, I threatened, "You might get smacked with this if you crack another joke like that!" I tried to keep a straight face, but couldn't help laughing too.

"Okay, okay. You win. No more unwed-mother jokes." He yanked the pillow away from me, pinned my hands to my side and said seriously, "You'll be a great mother, love. You're a natural." With a sexy grin, he suggested, "Shall we practice the baby-making part? Maybe if I get this part right, you'll let me be the father."

As the sun rose on another Christmas, I sent a grateful prayer to God and his angels. If ever a life was perfect, mine was. With Sean's fingers linked through mine, I closed my eyes and let his timeless magic sweep me away.

A knock at the door woke me up for the third time this morning. I sat up and nudged Sean, who was sleeping like the dead. Instantly alert, he sat up and scanned the room for intruders. I smothered a grin at his fierce expression and he frowned at me. The knock came again and this time Dec yelled through the door.

"Hey! It's late. Don't we have to be there in, like, 10 minutes? It's 9:15."

We were so late! My dad was going to kill us. Bounding out of bed, I did a drive-by shower and yanked my hair into a clip. While slapping on some mascara so I wouldn't scare any small children, I realized I'd need a turtleneck to cover the tiny bruises on my neck. I went weak in the knees when the vivid image of exactly how I got them flashed in my head. Mm, I so wanted to go back to bed…I think my eyes actually rolled back in my head.

"Can I come in or are you planning to daydream all morning?" Sean's amused tone matched his grin as he watched my face in the mirror.

I made him laugh out loud when I pulled him against me and kissed him. By the time I let him up for air, I was visibly glowing around my fingertips.

"Sweetheart, if you do that again, we're skipping Christmas!" Shoving me out of the bathroom, he said, "Finish getting ready so your parents don't kill us."

A few minutes later, we were in the car heading down the snowy road. Dec was still chuckling every few seconds and I turned around and gave him a dirty look.

"Do you mind?"

Throwing his hands up, he said, "Don't yell at me! I'm not the one who's glowing." He playfully smacked me on the head and scolded me, "I thought you had that under control? Wait a minute. You did." Peering intently into my eyes, he said, "You're letting your control slip again. What's in your head that caused you to let your guard down?"

I flushed scarlet and glanced guiltily at Sean. Sean, the jerk, just smirked and winked at Dec.

Deciding that honesty was the best policy, I said, "*Sean* is in my head, Dec. I woke up this morning and realized my life is perfect. Besides the fact that I love him, something crazy happens when he touches me." Both of their mouths dropped open at that. Dec flushed and looked away from me with a sound of dismissal.

Enjoying embarrassing him, I continued in a seductive tone, "His mouth, his hands, his scent consume me until I can't think of anything else." I leaned over and kissed Sean on the cheek. "Do you want to pull over?"

Bursting into laughter, he nearly swerved off the road. I yelped and grabbed for the armrest. He was still grinning at me when we pulled into my parents' driveway. Jumping out, I pulled Dec over and told him to stop scowling. He tried to resist but scowling was against his nature, and by the time we got to the door, he was smiling again. Domino ran ahead of us and barked for admission.

It was Trevor who met us at the door. His eyes were a little unfocused as the Christmas morning sugar rush had already kicked in. Chattering like a squirrel, he led us into the den. The whole family was sitting in there with the tree and a mountain of wrapped presents. Dad and Janet rose to greet us and fussed over our lateness. I smothered a snarky comment at my dad's traditional Santa sweatshirt. This one showed Santa drinking a beer though, so it was a step closer to cool. As soon as he caught sight of the guys, he pulled the furry Santa hat off his head though. Guess he knew that was WAY not cool!

Dad raised a paternal eyebrow at Sean and Dec. "I see you're still hanging around. Well, come on in and make yourselves comfortable. This usually takes a while." He waved a nonchalant hand in the general direction of the mountain of presents.

Janet spoke up. "Honey, that's no way to greet Sean. Where are your manners?" She gave both Sean and Dec a light hug and a kiss on the cheek as a greeting. "Why haven't we met you before?" She addressed Dec with a warm smile and assessing eyes. Women just couldn't resist him. He was yummy to women of every age. I resisted the urge to grin.

"Oh, I'm sorry! Janet, Dad, this is Sean's brother, Declan. He shares the house with us."

That was our cover for anyone who needed to meet them. Killian was also a brother, but I wasn't sure my dad would let him in the house. Probably it was a good thing he wasn't with us today. Everyone liked Dec though, angelic-mood-altering powers notwithstanding, he was just a nice guy.

Trans-Siberian Orchestra Christmas music played in the background as the time-honored tradition of passing out gifts began. Dad reigned as our Santa Claus and doled them out one at a time. Each person got a gift and we all watched as they were opened. The twins had taken one look at Dec and flanked him immediately. He treated them with a courtly deference and helped them with their wrapping paper. Completely unable to help themselves, they giggled at everything he said. I rolled my eyes at him when I noticed his Irish accent had mysteriously deepened as he told funny stories of Christmas in Ireland. I wondered how many were true...

Sean whispered behind his hand, "He was a bard in a former life."

"Really?"

Huh, a bard? I considered Dec with thoughtful eyes. That would certainly explain a lot.

Digging into my bag, I drew out two tiny wrapped boxes. One box was decorated with tiny golden halos on blue paper and the other was covered with tiny sail boats. I commandeered Dec from my sisters and handed him one of the boxes. He whooped with exaggerated excitement that made the girls giggle.

Aside to them he said, "Your sister gives the best presents." To me, he said, "Can I open it or do I have to wait for Sean."

Sean was running a fingertip across the paper. "Tell me you didn't paint this?" he asked with a little bit of awe in his voice.

I blushed and nodded. "Guilty. I also made what's inside. Go on, open them. I can't stand it."

They opened the paper and pulled out the identical braided wristbands I'd made them. The single strand of gold wire gleamed between three strips of soft leather. In the center was a blue glass teardrop wrapped with strands of beaten gold. The three strands of gold curled under and around the glass to hold and protect it. The symbolism was obvious to them. Dec crossed over to me and knelt beside me.

"It's perfect. I love it. Can you put it on me now?" He held out his wrist, and I slipped it over his tanned skin and slid the clasp to tighten it. The blue glass winked in the lights from the Christmas tree.

"Merry Christmas, partner." There was just the slightest little catch in my voice.

I think he forgot we had an audience then. With his usual sensitivity, he wrapped one of his big hands around the back of my head and kissed me on the forehead. "Merry Christmas, darlin'."

His eyes held mine as he acknowledged our history that made up those bonds of leather and gold. A tear threatened to slip down my cheek and he wiped it with the pad of his thumb.

My dad cleared his throat and adjusted his glasses. "I'm confused. Which one are you dating, Mica?" Pale blue eyes twinkled as he bit down on a grin.

"Geez, Dad. We've been through a lot together. Dec's a little sentimental." Dec displayed his best angelic smile, and my dad stopped grumbling about weirdness.

Sean held out his own wrist and said, "My turn."

After slipping the clasp closed, I dawdled a bit with my fingers on the stone. I wanted to say something more, but we had an avid audience that wasn't privy to our magical leanings. Instead, I winked at him.

"I think you've outdone yourself this year. It's perfect."

Happy with my success, I leaned back against his side and watched the kids open the rest of their gifts. As the gifts dwindled to the remaining few, Sean draped his arm around my waist, and I snuggled into his shoulder. He kissed the top of my head and Abby squealed with delight. Winking at her, Sean kissed me again and then held out his hand. Barely controlling waves of giggles, Abby ceremoniously presented a small golden box to Sean. Conversation faded out and everyone stared at us.

Turning to face me, Sean held out the box in one hand. With the other, he lifted my chin so I was looking into his eyes. He said formally, "Four years ago I looked into your eyes and found my heart. You've been wearing it around your neck for two years." He stroked the locket and it picked up his heartbeat.

Dec sucked in his breath. I stopped breathing completely.

"Today, I offer you the rest of me." Without breaking eye contact, he opened the tiny box to reveal a twisted gold band with a pair of glittering blue stones at the center. "Will you take me?"

I could barely see through the tears as I looked from the beautiful ring to the serious, beautiful face of the one who offered it to me. His eyes were grave as they searched mine. He wasn't just offering marriage; he was offering his love, his life, and his soul. With shaking fingers, I took the ring out of the box and held it to my lips as if I could feel the two tiny souls that I knew made up those stones.

Breathless, I whispered, "Yes, I will take all that you offer."

With perfectly steady hands, he slid the ring onto my finger and pressed my hand against his lips. With closed eyes, he sighed with relief and then lifted my face for a kiss. It was a chaste kiss to seal our commitment.

"I love you," he whispered against my ear, bringing a rush of color to my pale face.

"I love you, too," I said with a sappy smile.

The silence was absolute for about a minute as the whole family sat spellbound. It was Dec who finally broke it. In a bit of a daze, he pulled me up into his arms and held me tightly against him. The gesture was oddly intense. In tune to him already, I recognized the energy thrumming through his muscles as his arms held me against him. He was shaking with the effort to control his power. I had the feeling he was clinging to me to keep from snapping. His face was deadly serious when he looked down into mine.

Alarmed, I whispered, "You're crushing me! What's wrong?"

He whispered harshly, "All hell is about to break loose. We have to go. Make excuses." Then he smiled hugely for the benefit of my family, and added under his breath, "You have no idea what you two have just done. But I like it!"

I smiled at him and ordered between my teeth, "You're vibrating. Take it down a notch."

Sucking in a deep breath, he hugged me again and I felt him relax ever so slightly. At least his eyes weren't glowing. By the time he turned away, he was visibly calmer and made an excuse to go to the kitchen for a minute.

Dad cleared his throat and reached out to shake Sean's hand. He assessed Sean with a grudging new respect. "That was nicely done, Sean. I guess you can't be that bad if you love my daughter that much. Welcome to the family." He cleared his throat again and gave me a hug. "You'd better be good to her or I'll hunt you down myself."

Sean's eyebrows went straight up at that, and he struggled to keep a straight face. With as much gravity as he could manage, he assured my dad I was in good hands. "I can promise you she will be safer with me than with anyone else. I'll be good to her."

Janet and the girls were wiping tears from their eyes and blowing their noses. Janet was awestruck by Sean's proposal and kept saying it was the sweetest thing she'd ever heard. The girls clustered around Sean and Dec like little blond butterflies. Dec's face was kind as he teased them, but he caught my eye and motioned to the door. Sean gave me that look and I knew we had to go for now. Something bad was definitely up.

"Janet, Dad, we're going to run for a bit. We promised one of Sean's cousins that we'd come for a visit this morning. We'll see you later though."

Although they protested us leaving early, they bought my excuse and sent us away with our gifts and congratulations.

As soon as we got into the car, the two guys immediately switched into soldier-mode. I was aware of the change, but didn't want to leave my bubble of complete joy. The twin stones sparkled in the sunlight, and I tilted my hand this way and that to catch the light.

Sean's tone was regretful when he interrupted me, "Babe? I hate to do this to you, but we're going to need your help. Can we get you to focus for now?" He reached over and squeezed my hand.

With a huge overburdened sigh, I said, "I know, I know. I can't marry you if I'm dead!"

Dec drove as fast as possible on the way to the farmhouse. The roads were cleared so he wasn't worried about sliding into a ditch. Apparently Dagin was sending a team in retaliation for Dec and James taking out some of his crew a few days ago. Killian had picked up chatter during his search for *Sgaine Dutre* and sent a message to Dec and Sean. Since Sean's mind had been completely focused on me, it evidently went straight to telepathic voice mail. Good thing Dec was paying attention...

Facing a team of thugs ought to be a piece of cake for the three of us, but Sean was worried about the numbers. If there were too many demons, we'd get overwhelmed. He didn't like the odds. His face was grim as he walked me through our options. The more we planned, the more pissed it made me. It was freakin' Christmas for God's sake! I just got engaged! There had to be some kind of waiting period for demon attacks around major life events. I was going to bring this up the next time I saw Alex. Growling under my breath, I mentally catalogued my weapons.

"Sean, don't worry about me. My runes will protect me from demons, remember? They can't touch me."

He frowned and pointed out that I was missing half the rune on my hand now. My heart sank. I had thought I'd be protected. Why would Killian strip my protection? Did he even realize what he'd done? Maybe the rune still worked to protect me, but didn't connect me to Killian's powers? I mentioned the theory and both guys considered it.

Dec said, "That might be true, but I don't want to make that assumption. Stay away from them. Kill them before they can touch you and don't underestimate them. Demons can come out of thin air and get you from behind. Keep Domino at your back. Don't rely on walls either. They can come through them."

Gee, that's a cheery thought. I was getting less happy by the minute. By the time we pulled into the driveway, I was ready to blow up the first demon that showed its ugly face. Before going inside, I took a minute to see if I could sense anyone on the property. Nothing popped up on my psychic radar. It was clear for now. We had about 40 minutes to get ready. We knew the routine and split up as soon as we hit the front door. In our bedroom, Sean methodically changed into his commando gear and loaded his guns. Without a word, he added extra magazines to his pockets and slipped on his knives. He had the Primani blade sheathed on one side and a wicked-looking military blade on the other. He nodded with approval when I came out dressed like him. I had my mic attached too and slipped in the earpiece. Domino paced by the window with her nose in the air sniffing for anything odd. I bent down and hugged her against me.

"I love you, girl. Be careful, I don't want anything to happen to you."

Sean ruffled her fur and patted her rump affectionately. "Okay, Princess, you take good care of your momma. Mica is your only priority. Do you hear me?"

She pricked up her ears and rolled her eyes. *Isn't she always?*

With that order, we met Dec in the living room. We split up to check the doors and windows. Yep, all unlocked; no sense in locking them. The humans would break them to get inside if we did. We wanted it to be easy for them today. Cell phones were turned to silent mode and we tested our headsets. Everything worked. We were as ready as we'd ever be. It was time to get into position. With one last glance at us, Dec vanished.

I knelt and scooped up Domino tensing as Sean wrapped his arms around us both. Instantly, the three of us were in the trees at the edge of the property. In anticipation of an attack like this, we'd built several natural-looking blinds, like hunters used, on the corners of the property. This one looked like a brushy pile of overgrown blackberry canes; the second one looked like a pile of firewood, and the other like a tangle of grapevines choking a sycamore tree. I was pretty impressed with the job we'd done. You couldn't see them in the summer or winter. Domino and I squeezed inside, and I adjusted the slits I used for my rifle. After checking that I had everything I'd need, Sean patted Domino one more time and pulled me against him for a hard kiss.

"Listen to me now. If you get *any* face time with these freaks, tell us on your mic. Do not, and I mean this, do not think you can handle these demons on your own. If they spot you, you're a target they'll take out." He shook my shoulders gently. "Do you understand me? Don't get cocky!"

"Don't worry. I'm okay. You let me know what's happening though. I freak out if it's too quiet. I need to hear you. Promise me?"

"Promise. Okay, I have to go. Keep your gun down and don't fire unless you're sure you can hit them." With that, he left.

I whispered for Dec and he hummed softly in my earpiece. Reassured, I hummed the next line. It was an old Irish folk song he'd taught me on one of our endless stakeouts. I closed my eyes and searched for incoming. My main job was to search for targets and use remote viewing to see what they were doing inside the house. The guys would pick them off one at a time.

"Show time! I'm picking up four humans coming in from the east side." That was Sean's area.

"Two more pulling into the driveway. Wow, that's bold." That's my area. I could see the driveway and the road in front of the house.

The sound of shattering glass startled me and I hissed into the mic, "Freakin' demon just broke my mirror! It was an antique! Someone kill him before he breaks anything else." Carefully watching the house, I said, "Three demons just popped into the second floor, going room to room. They're dressed like people. The one in our room's wearing a Devils jersey, the biggest one's got a black leather jacket on, and the third idiot's wearing a ski mask." I snorted and added, "Moron."

Sean whispered, "I've got eyes on the four. They're fanning out and going around to the back door. Probably split up and take the back porch and basement. I'm ready. Mica, where are they now?"

"Two at the back porch and one out of view now. He's going to the basement. The third is hovering at the corner of the porch on my side."

"I'm gone," Sean said.

As I watched, he reappeared behind the two near the back door, and with two quick thrusts of his knives, they crumbled silently into the snow. Without blinking, he grabbed their collars and vanished. I wondered where he dumped their bodies. In another second, Sean was back and surprised the thug in the basement. He'd been foolish enough to consider the unlocked door an invitation rather than a trap. He was partway into the room when Sean rematerialized behind him. Without hesitation, he slid the blade into his kidney and vanished with him.

"Dec, you've got the other two. One's in the kitchen tearing apart the pantry. Get him before he destroys everything."

"Gone."

He caught the guy by surprise too. Wrapping his hand over the guy's face, he twisted his neck until it snapped. No blood, no mess. I liked the way he was thinking. After all, I usually ended up with the bleach.

"Watch out! Company in the hallway...uh, two demons."

Dec whirled around just as they rounded the corner and came within eye shot. Using the element of surprise, Dec raised his hand and blew up the Devils fan. His partner had a split second to react and fired a shot at Dec. The fireball went wide and set the curtains on fire. Damn it!

"Sean! The house is on fire!"

"What? Where?"

"The kitchen's on fire!" I looked down at the dog and growled in frustration. She growled back in sympathy. "Ski Mask is running to the kitchen."

Dec and the demon in the leather jacket were close enough to smell each other now and Dec palmed his Primani blade. Crouched to spring, he passed the knife from hand to hand and taunted the demon.

Leather Jacket grinned confidently and pulled out his own blade. It was black and glittered dully in the firelight. Come and get me, he seemed to say. Moving closer to him, Dec smiled wickedly and the demon backed away. The demon was still wearing his human façade, but it was crumbling with the stress of fighting. Part of his face had melted away to show the black scales underneath. His eyes were yellow and narrowed in concentration as he feinted to the left. With lethal precision, Dec lunged and buried the knife in his abdomen. Shoving it upwards, he snarled in the demon's face and yanked the knife out. With a gasp of pain, the demon collapsed and dissolved into ash.

Sean rematerialized behind him and managed to rip the curtain down into the sink and turn on the water. Smoke filled the room reducing the images to shadows. This wasn't good.

Where was that third demon?

Methodically, I searched every room but he wasn't there. Domino growled softly in warning. I dragged my eyes back to the yard in front of me.

"We've got a runner! He's going for the car. I've got him." I slid the barrel of my rifle out of a slit and watched him through the sight. In a blind panic, he scrambled for the car, his shotgun bouncing against his back.

Sorry, dude. No witnesses allowed.

I rested my finger on the trigger and exhaled slowly.

You've got to go.

He fell over like he'd been hit by a baseball bat. Pulling the rifle back into its hiding place, I quickly looked around for company. No one popped up in the yard so I closed my eyes again and searched that way. We were still short one demon and one human. I'd counted them and two weren't accounted for.

"Nice shot," Sean said in my ear. He clapped his hand over my mouth to keep me from yelping.

"Jesus! You scared the hell out of me! I could've killed you!" I nudged his thigh with the tip of the knife I'd been holding.

Smirking, he said agreeably, "You could've tried. Where's the other human?"

"I lost him. I can't see him anymore."

"I'll go look around. Stay here for now and keep watching. There may be more on the way." He stopped just long enough to kiss me again before vanishing.

"I thought he'd never leave," a sarcastic voice said outside the blind. "You might as well come out, girl. We've got you covered and we could always just shoot you from here."

Domino growled and alerted. Well, well, our missing trespassers. Obviously, they had no idea how much I wanted to kill a demon right now or they'd be bothering someone else. After making sure my mic was on, I palmed my knife in my left hand and gripped my Sig in my right.

"Oh, I'm so scared!" I muttered snidely into the mic. "Idiots."

Brazenly throwing open the door, I leveled the Sig at the human and shot him in the chest before he could twitch. His gun fell out of his lifeless fingers and hit the ground. His body followed. The demon lunged for me at the same time Domino threw herself in front of me. She bit his leg and he howled in agony. Smoke curled from the bite marks and Domino spit demon skin into the snow.

"Do you have a name, demon? I'd like to know who I'm about to vaporize."

Instead of answering me, he laughed softly. It was an evil sound that made my skin crawl. I looked closer at his face, watching in horror as it shifted and morphed into someone eerily familiar to me. It was the eyes...they weren't reptilian or yellow.

They were ocean blue as they pinned me in place.

No, no, no. It could not be.

He smiled easily and I backed up a step. The smile was the same.

No. It wasn't possible. Not here, not now.

Then he started to talk, his voice making my heart pound. It was his, but not his. "Oh, come on, darlin', aren't you glad to see me again?"

The silky tones froze me in place and I started to panic. I couldn't fight him! I wasn't strong enough before; I wasn't any stronger now.

He said, "I'm happy to see you. I've missed our time together."

Domino still growled and snarled but was confused by his appearance. He'd morphed completely into an exact copy of Sean. He smiled down at the dog and she hesitated. Lowering her tail, she glanced at me, unsure. He took advantage of her distraction and kicked her hard in the ribs. She cried out in pain and landed several feet away in the snow. With a whimper, she lay still.

He turned to me and I couldn't move. I stood there holding the knife in my hand but was unwilling to use it. My brain screamed at me to run, to fight, to scream, to do something. Instead of moving, I was paralyzed by my fear as wave after wave of memories crashed over me. He laughed obscenely and plucked the knife out of my hand. Then he pulled my arm behind my back until it snapped. I tried to scream but my voice was gone. Instead, I could only stare at him as he smiled lovingly into my eyes and broke my finger.

"I'm going to kill you this time and there's no one to save you. Your Primani are being occupied at the moment. Oh, they'll come back here looking for you in a bit. Sadly, it'll be too late. You'll be dead and I'll be gone."

He kissed my neck and broke another finger. I bit my lip and tried to recoil from him…from Sean's face. His voice went on and on, but I retreated into my head where he couldn't touch me. I huddled inside my mental room and prayed for a miracle.

Michael, Raphael? Someone? Anyone? Help me! Killian? I can't fix this. He's too strong. I can't move. He's breaking me into pieces…

Enraged at my lack of response, he slapped my face and yelled at me. From a distance, I saw his eyes change to slits as his mask slipped. Sean's eyes were gone…that was better. I started to black out when someone spoke sharply to me. It was Raphael.

Mica! Pay attention!

He is the target of your anger. You know this! Don't hide from him. You have Killian's powers. You must use them now or you will never be free of this demon.

No, I can't. I can't even move, I thought, cringing further into the little room.

Yes, you can! Use Killian's powers!

Rough fingers jerked my chin up and he slapped me again. "Wake up, bitch! I'm almost done. You don't want to miss the finale."

He was running out of patience with me. I was running out of fingers. I needed to make a decision. Could I use Killian's powers? I pictured Killian's face and knew he'd kill me himself if I didn't at least try to defend myself. He'd know that I gave up and let this monster destroy me. Somehow, he'd know and he'd be furious. Did his anger matter to me? No, but his sacrifice mattered. He'd given me his blood to protect me. He'd given me his powers, too. But he'd taken them away...

Would it still work?

With great effort, I forced myself out of the little room that protected me and faced my demon head on. It helped that his eyes weren't Sean's anymore. The face was the same though and he smiled the same sexy smile that normally turned me into Jell-O. A rush of hatred curled up from my gut. I was just about sick of these games. I took inventory of my body. I thought my nose was broken and at least six of my fingers. My arm was broken again and my eye was swollen shut.

The bastard thought it was funny. He thought it was a game. Let's see how long we can play with the stupid human before we kill her. Dressing up like Sean was just sick. That was seriously twisted and cruel. Raphael had to be right, didn't he? If he was, I could stop this.

I was helpless once before, but things were different now.

I had a little help from Killian...

He ranted and raved while I stoked the white fire deep inside of me. I called to Killian's powers like I did before and felt them bubble through my blood.

Come to me. Take over and make me stronger. Hurry!

The power had come slowly before, but this time it rushed to fill my veins. Surging into my muscles, it flowed like a tsunami into my heart. My broken fingers vibrated even through the pain as the energy turned into raw power. My vision went white and I saw clearly what was under the mask. He was hideous. Black scales covered sharp angular features.

He was nothing like my Sean.

Nothing like him!

His flimsy mask could never replace the real Sean. I embraced my rage and let it overwhelm me for once.

In a voice I didn't recognize, I snarled, "You're not him! You'll never *be* him."

Stunned, he stared stupidly at my mouth.

I felt his puppet-master control slipping and very deliberately raised my hand. He struggled to hold me in place, but I was stronger than him. With a slow smile, I raised one hand and then the other. He didn't back away but he hesitated.

He should've run.

"I've had enough of you!" I blew off one of his arms. It landed without a sound in the snow. "You think you can tear me to pieces? You filthy piece of garbage!"

I blew off his hand.

His mind was racing as he tried to control me. He was still arrogant enough to think he would win this. After all, he could grow another body.

Advancing on him, I purred, "There won't be enough of you left to squeeze into another body by the time I'm done with you."

He took a step back and I raised my hand. He jerked to a stop like he'd backed into a wall. Terrified, he could only stare at me while his human mask crumbled away.

"Uh-oh! It looks like somebody can't move."

Thanks, Killian!

With laser precision, I sliced off one piece at a time while cataloguing all of the horrors he'd put me through. "...and this is for breaking my nose. And this is for implanting tracers in me. And this is for breaking my leg."

Off went his nose, his shoulder, his leg...Oh, yes! This felt great!

After working my way through all of the things he'd done to me, I was panting with the effort of controlling the power that was raging through me. I was burning hot and my eyes felt molten. I was dangerously hot and needed to wrap this up. What was left of the demon lay on the ground staring up at me with resignation in his eyes. I almost felt sorry for him, for just a second. Almost.

Until I remembered his worst offense.

"And this is for dressing up like Sean and trying to seduce me." I sliced him in half where his penis would be, if he had one. "You sick bastard."

I wiped my hands on my pants, and said cheerfully, "Well, now. I feel a lot better."

And with one final burst of power, he disintegrated into smoke.

Okay, now I was really hot. I sat down in the snow and rubbed a handful over my face and eyes. Of course it melted promptly, but it did cool me down. I did what Dec told me and closed my eyes and forced my temperature down. Once I wasn't the same temperature as a road flare, I took a deep breath and stood up. I had to find Domino. With this thought in mind, I turned around to look for her. There in the trees were Sean and Dec.

Dec raised his hand in greeting and said, "Uh, nice work, Carrie!" Sean elbowed him in warning and he said innocently, "What? Did you see what she just did?"

"Where's Domino? Have you seen her?" I didn't have time for Stephen King humor.

"She's alive. We just checked on her."

"My poor baby!" I crossed to her and kissed her little face. She whimpered and licked my hand. "She's hurt though. Give her to me."

I still had Killian's power running unchecked through me, but more importantly, I had the gift that Raphael had given me. Cradling her against me, I gave my fierce little warrior the last of my *saol*.

Suddenly drained, I sat down heavily. My legs just wouldn't hold me up. Sean scooped me up and brought me into the house. I was a bloody mess again, so he sat me on a blanket to keep the couch clean.

I started to tell them what was broken and Sean held up a hand. His eyes glittered as he said, "Baby, I heard you down there. I know what's broken." Shaking with the force of his own fury, he struggled for calm. "I didn't know. Why didn't you tell me what he did to you?"

Shrugging tiredly, I said, "It would've just hurt you and there's nothing you could've done. He used you like a weapon to torture me. He tried to make me forget he wasn't you and...he was very convincing...He seemed so real to me. He'd hurt me and then try to seduce me to make the pain stop. It was cruel...but I had a plan of my own. I retreated inside my head to hide from his seduction."

The demon's face swam in front of me and I shied away from the reminder. Shoving the image out of my head, I said fiercely," I wouldn't let him use you that way! If I'd let him touch me like that..." I left the thought unfinished and glanced down at my engagement ring. A lump in my throat nearly strangled me. Needing to feel him, I curled against his chest.

"God, it would've destroyed me. I'd never be able to love you again. Every time I looked at you, I would see him. I knew that. He knew that, too. That's what he wanted. It was a game to him...So whenever I retreated, he broke something."

"He never...forced you?" he asked in a calmer tone. Calm was relative at this point. He wasn't about to go nuclear now though. That was better.

Shuddering at how close it had been, I said, "No, he didn't. Apparently he wanted me conscious." I tried to laugh but it sounded off. "I was unconscious a lot. You saw how many broken bones I had?"

Dec said, "That's not funny, Mica! Don't ever joke about this." He took my broken fingers in his and healed them with tears of his own running down his face.

I sniffed and smiled. "We're a mess. Look at us."

Both guys sniffed and grumbled. Sean said, "I'd say the one person we love more than anyone being sadistically tortured and then having to kill the monster is a pretty good reason to be emotional. Don't worry, it won't happen next until we get married and then when we have our first beautiful baby. I get to cry then, right?"

"Absolutely." I smiled tiredly at them both. "Do I have time for a nap before we go to dinner?"

"You still want to go out? Are you sure?"

"Are you kidding? It's Christmas!"

Chapter 20: And the Plot Thickens

"SO, YOUR DAD STILL doesn't like me?" Sean scanned the price tag on the mirror and stuck it in the cart. He seemed irritated with this latest revelation about my family. Not that I could blame him, really. He'd been the perfect boyfriend and now fiancé. My dad just had no idea how many times he'd kept me alive...

I tried not to smile because I knew he was frustrated. To kill that urge, I pretended interest in the shelf of assorted nails and screws. Picking up a box that seemed to be the right size, I held it up for his inspection. I had no idea how nails worked...he took the box and tossed it into the cart.

"Well, it's just that they don't seem to remember how long we've known each other. It's some kind of weird parental denial mechanism, I think. For some reason, they keep thinking we just met. It's not that he doesn't like you. He just thinks it's too soon. And then there's your *brother*, Dec." I did crack a smile at the memory of my dad's shocked face when Dec kissed me on Christmas morning. "I guess he's a little too intense for Dad's old-fashioned sensibilities."

He snorted with half a laugh. "Yeah, sure. That's totally it. Remind me to banish Dec when we get home." He pointed the cart towards the checkout lines.

"Wait! We still need to get new kitchen curtains. Let's see if they have any here." I commandeered the cart and took off towards the other side of the Home Depot.

The house was a wreck and I had officially gotten tired of looking at it this morning and dragged Sean to the store. The demons had attacked a week ago, leaving the house in ruins. I'd guilted my Primani into helping me clean up the next day, but the repairs had to wait until now. The three of us were busy with new assignments courtesy of our temporary leader, Sean. He and I had gone to The City to see Alex about the attack. After listening to Sean's report, Alex was angrier than I'd ever seen him before. He'd called Raphael in from wherever he exists.

When he saw me, he'd lit up with pleasure and taken my hands in his. He wasn't really a hugger, but hand squeezing was an acceptable affectionate greeting. Hey, I took what I could get. I had the impression he was a high-level angel. I really should ask Sean about that one of these days. Seeing that Sean and Alex were deep in conversation, Raphael steered me into the beautiful kitchen for tea--Earl Gray to be exact. Out of deference to his considerable age, I fussed over him and made him the perfect cup of tea. I even scrounged up a box of cookies that smelled fresh.

"Did Alex get a new house manager?" I asked as I set out the tea things. "We've got new cookies."

Spooning in a bit of sugar, he smiled fondly at me. "You, my dear, are very observant. You are quite right about both things. The new house manager's name is Jonathan and he just went shopping today." With impeccable manners, he served me the best cookies from the selection.

I'd wanted to see him badly since Christmas, and now that he was here I felt unsure. I knew what I wanted to say but the words didn't seem quite right. So I blew on my tea and fiddled with my spoon until he gently pushed me to spit it out.

Blushing shyly, I said, "I have something for you. If you'll accept it, that is."

His dark eyebrows lifted in surprise but he nodded graciously. I went to my purse and pulled out a tiny wrapped gift. The paper was only a simple sky blue though. I hadn't had time to decorate it for him. The gift, though, I made at the same time I'd made the others. Something had told me even then that I would continue to owe my survival to this kind being sipping tea with me. I sat it down on the table and put my hands in my lap so I could fidget privately.

"Raphael, I have no words to thank you properly. It seems I am to be forever seeking your help." I smiled shyly and added, "I hope you like it. I made it for you."

His face was carefully blank as he considered first my words and then the tiny box. Seeming to decide that gifts were acceptable, he un-wrapped the box. Inside was a tiny glass heart encircled by strands of beaten silver and gold. The result was a shimmering halo protecting the blood-red stone. The pendant was strung on a braided chain of silver and gold. The chain wasn't heavy but I thought it was masculine enough. It had taken me three weeks to get the pendant right. The halo wasn't perfectly shaped. It listed a little to the right...Maybe it's not good enough for him. I should've started over again. He hadn't said anything yet. He must hate it. I dug my nails into my hand waiting for him to say something. Instead, he closed his eyes and bowed his head.

Unable to stand the silence, I apologized awkwardly. "I'm being presumptuous, aren't I? I'm so sorry if I've offended you." I reached for the box intending to take it back. "I'll just get it out of your way..."

He laid his hand on top of mine and said with feeling, "No! It's quite beautiful." He smiled wistfully. "Do you know that I've never had a Christmas present before?"

Completely surprised, I blurted, "How is that possible? You're so amazing. That's terrible!"

Chuckling, he squeezed my hand gently. "Mica, my dear, you are such a beautiful soul! I will wear your gift proudly if you'll just show me how to put it on."

Sean and Alex walked in just as I fastened the clasp for him. Alex and Raphael exchanged a look that caused him to peer closely at the pendant.

Alex joked, "Why Raphael, I do believe Mica's given you her heart!" He nudged Sean and laughed, "Competition, son!"

I stood back and warily eyed the trunk of the Camaro. There was no way that mirror was going to fit. I'd mentioned that twice already, but the male circling the car had other ideas. I could imagine the wheels turning as he cocked his head and used his hands to measure out the size of the trunk. Refusing to admit defeat, he switched his focus to the back seat. I tapped my boot impatiently. There's no way the mirror will fit in that back seat. Rolling my eyes, I shifted the bag to my other hand.

"I've got it. We'll just take it out of the cardboard. It'll fit then." Energized by the brilliance of his plan, he quickly tore the protective cardboard away from the mirror and slid it into the trunk. It just fit although one edge was dangerously close the lid.

I had a bad feeling about this.

Cheerfully peeling out of the parking lot, Sean gave me a smug look of male righteousness and turned up the radio. The ride was uneventful until he pulled into the driveway. There had always been a slight dip from the road into the driveway and the heavy snow had made it worse because we now had ruts to deal with. As the car bounced over the ruts, a loud crash came from the vicinity of the trunk.

Groaning with irritation, I looked over at him and said, "Seven years."

Puzzled, he asked, "Seven years, what?"

Pointing at the shattered mirror, I hung my head muttering, "Dude."

I left him to deal with the mess and toted the plastic bags through the front door. The rich meaty smell of chili greeted me. Yay! Dec was back.

And cooking!

"Dec? That smells amazing!" I went straight to the kitchen to sample it.

The chef was loosely bouncing a hacky sack in one hand as I walked in the room. Ignoring me, he tossed the soft ball to Domino who leaped and neatly caught it with her front teeth. She pranced around in a victory dance before bringing it back to him. When he reached for it, she shook her head and backed just out of his grasp. He laughed and lunged for her. Anticipating this move, the dog launched herself over his back and bolted to my side. With mock fury, Dec circled the two of us and finally tackled Domino. After a mad wrestling match complete with un-angelic swearing and yelps of indignation, Dec emerged covered with scratches and not a few bite marks.

The dog kept possession of the hacky sack.

"All right, all right! I give up. You win." He waggled a finger at her and said, "You cheated. I'll get you next time."

Domino dropped the slimy wet object at my feet and sashayed to her water bowl. *Whatever...*

"You might want to wash those scratches out. I hear dogs carry a lot of nasty diseases on their feet. They're not too clean, you know."

Domino turned to me with narrowed eyes. *Excuse me?*

I corrected diplomatically, "You don't wear shoes, ergo, your feet are dirty." Turning back to Dec, "I'd wash them out if I were you. Did you hear any news while we were out?"

Dec was supposed to try to contact Killian while we were shopping. He sucked air between his teeth as running water flowed over the scratches on his forearm. Focusing only vaguely on his arm, he filled me in on his morning. Unfortunately, Killian was off the grid, but he had heard something strange on the local morning news.

"Shae's Funeral Home reported two corpses stolen this week," he said.

"Shae's? Is that local?"

He shook his head and elaborated for me. "It's down near Albany. And that's not the only thing. I remembered what Killian said about bringing back the dead and a light bulb went off. I called Jonathan and asked him to snoop through local police reports around The City and..." He paused to perform a drum roll on the marble island top.

Rolling my eyes, I tapped my fingers and stared at him. He gave in first and leaned across the island with barely suppressed excitement.

Oh, this was going to be good.

"This is really bizarre; you'll like this. The police found a man roaming around a neighborhood in Queens. The neighbors thought he was drunk and called the cops. When they got there, the guy was staggering in someone's yard. They tried to talk to him, but he was really out of it. They were about to tase him when he fell over."

"What's bizarre about that? Was he on experimental drugs or something?"

"Not even close. Here's the good part. They called an ambulance because he was out cold. The paramedic nearly had a heart attack when they got him inside and got a good look at him."

A tingle of premonition made me shiver. I know what he's going to say next. I wasn't going to like this. Sean walked in and started to say something. We both shushed him and he clamped his mouth shut with a frown. Waving a hand at Dec, I said, "Spit it out."

"The guy was visibly dead. As in, like, rigor-mortis-and-gray-chalky-skin dead. No pulse and squishy, smelly tissue...clouded eyeballs, etc."

Red lights and alarm bells clamored loudly inside my head and I could tell by their expressions that they came to the same conclusion I had...

Zombies.

Holy shit.

No one said a word until the timer on the stove went off with a loud beep. I nearly swallowed my tongue and dropped my glass. The shattering glass, on top of the abrasive beeping, finally broke through the collective

283

shock in the kitchen. Everyone moved at once. Dec turned to the stove to check the chili while Sean and I bent to clean up the glass.

"Wow," I said finally.

Sean's expression was mocking as he half-heartedly swept up glass shards. "That's not the word I'd use, but it'll do." He dumped the glass into the trash and looked at the two of us. "We're going to have to call for reinforcements. This is much bigger than Dagin's greed. He's lost his mind. Humans aren't ready for the zombie apocalypse."

"Are we?" I had to ask.

Dec wielded the chef's knife he used to cut up the vegetables for the chili and proclaimed, "I'm ready! Let's go kick some undead ass!"

Unable to resist, I picked up a mallet. "Sure, why not? I'm in!" We both stared at Sean with identical expressions of blood lust until he finally rolled his eyes and shook his head at me.

"And you used to be so innocent."

It was nearing 10:00 and I finally leaned back and stretched. We'd been talking over possibilities for hours and had drawn up plans and to-do lists. I'd somehow become the secretary and dutifully typed up our brainstorming notes. We'd come about as far as we could on our own and would have to talk to Killian and Alex to get help. After all, Manhattan wasn't really our jurisdiction. There were other Primani who were supposed to be keeping it safe. But because of our past experience with Dagin's operations and Killian's *Sgaine Dutre*, we expected to play a big role in finding the source of the zombies and taking Dagin out once and for all. I took advantage of a lull in their conversation to point out that it's New Year's Eve and we, at least I, was young and should be out celebrating.

Always up for a night out around humans, Dec agreed with me. Sean didn't really want to go out, but agreed we could check in on Dani on the way. Throwing him a kiss, I ran to the bedroom to throw something pretty on. Twenty minutes later I walked into the living room and both of them stopped talking to stare. Twirling for the full effect, I stopped and waited with dramatically downcast eyes. My dress settled at the top of my thighs and had no back at all. My front, er, assets, were completely covered by the high collar. I wore a black and red tribal cuff on one arm and my engagement ring on the opposite hand. The thigh-high leather boots provided assurance that I'd be steady on my feet if any demons attacked. Peeking up at Sean, I winked and he broke into a huge grin.

Sighing dramatically, he said, "I'm going to have to kill somebody later, aren't I?"

Dec laughed and agreed. "Dude, I can almost guarantee it."

The bar was packed by the time we got there. My two bodyguards looked like they wanted to drag me back to the car as soon as we walked in the door. Two of Scott Flynn's friends were standing by the entrance and spotted me immediately. They sneered and made gross comments to each other until their drunken brains realized I had company. Sean draped his arm possessively around me and said, "Why couldn't you be ugly?"

I burst into laughter and craned my neck to kiss him. "Don't be cranky. This is supposed to be fun."

Running his hand all the way down my back, he commented, "I'm liking this dress more and more."

Feeling pretty safe from zombies in here, I made it my mission to lighten up and force these two to have a good time. It was New Year's Eve, after all--the end of one fairly crappy year and the beginning of a new one full of possibilities. Sean didn't love to dance, but I pulled him onto the crowded dance floor with a determined grip. The music was loud and the lights were low setting the right mood for a party. Hardly able to move without hitting someone, I let the bass soak into my blood and swayed against him.

With a sensuous smile, he crooked his finger at me saying, "Come closer," and fitted me tightly against him so we moved together.

My ring sparkled in the strobe lights and I tilted my head to kiss him. With one hand pressing the small of my back and the other behind my head, he kissed me until I forgot where I was. My head spun with the music and the lights and the blood pumping through my body. His hips moved against mine with perfect rhythm, filling my mind with nothing but sensations. There were no angels, no demons, no zombies. We were alone in the crowd. With fingers clenched in his shirt, I fought an overwhelming urge to take him and fly away somewhere where no one could ever find us.

"Do we have to stay till midnight?"

"Fuck no!" With that, he took my hand and led me off the dance floor.

Laughing at his sudden urgency, I asked about Dec.

"He'll be home later. He's busy right now."

Groups of partiers thronged the sidewalks in spite of the freezing cold. I didn't need a coat thanks to Sean. I was plenty hot enough. He opened the car door for me and leaned in for a long kiss before slamming the door and vaulting into the driver's seat. The drive home was endless but I kept myself amused by whispering in his ear and letting my hands roam. By the time we pulled into the garage, he was ready to toss me down on the concrete. Scoffing at this suggestion, I ran into the house making him chase me. He caught me at the top of the stairs and spun me around into his arms. My dress was too short to be any kind of obstruction and it wasn't.

I was lying on my back floating someplace in another universe when he splayed his hand across my belly. Very gently, he traced his fingers across the muscles of my abdomen. Leaning down, he nuzzled my belly button and I twitched.

"What are you doing down there?"

He smiled into my eyes and said, "Just thinking about your dream. You're so beautiful." He kissed my belly. "You're sexy and strong, but soft and delicate too." He was running his hand over my skin and I was trembling with the urge to giggle.

"Let's run away," I suggested.

Bracing himself on his elbows, he looked into my eyes and smiled. "I wish we could. I want to take you someplace far away from demons and violence. I hate seeing you in pain. Someday, I will take you away from this and give you a normal life."

I started to reply when I caught a glimpse of a face in the window. Choking on a scream, I could only point and scramble off the bed to lunge for my gun. Sean whipped around to confront our intruder but the face was gone. There was nothing there now. Buzzing with adrenaline, I threw up the window and looked outside.

Sean said, "There's no one there. He's gone."

"Did you see that?"

He shook his head and said, "I only saw a reflection. It was gone before I could see what it was."

Taking the gun from me, he tucked it into his waistband and strode out the door. Jumping up too, I threw on a robe and followed him. We went through all of the rooms and then walked around the outside of the house.

"Damn it!" The footprints led from the back porch to the middle of the yard and stopped.

Slowly looking up at our window, he gritted out, "Consider this your warning. If you come back, I will blow your ass to dust."

"What are you looking at?" Dec rematerialized next to my elbow. "What's going on? Why are you outside in your robe...and barefoot?"

"We've got a Peeping Tom. And he's got *powers*," I explained. I filled him in while Sean pondered the situation. His scowl was nearly as scary as Killian's so I sidled a little closer to Dec.

Dec was just as mad as Sean. "I'm getting sick of this crap. I'm going hunting." He disappeared leaving me envious.

Chapter 21: The Walls Have Eyes

"I'M SORRY, MICA, really I am. James already made plans for us this weekend." Dani handed the manicurist her bottle of polish and turned back to me. "I can't cancel on him."

Studying my nails to keep from saying something rude about James, I swallowed my disappointment. "No, but you could bring him with you. It's my 21st birthday party. It's not like we haven't been planning this since we met."

She looked a little sheepish at that. "I know! But I totally forgot. James and I have been so busy these last few months. He's crazy about doing things together. He's like the Energizer bunny!" She smiled blissfully and I wanted to smack her. "Honestly, I'm exhausted! I haven't had a night to myself in months." She laughed and blew on her nails.

Ah, the opening I'd been hoping for...

"I've noticed you two have been together a lot. Are you getting, uh, serious about him?"

"Oh, my God, he's..." She broke off and blushed furiously. The manicurist gave her a curious look and left us to dry.

Already knowing what she was going to say, I hesitated to ask. "He's what?"

Giggling with her secret, Dani leaned over to me and whispered, "God, he's amazing in bed. I can't say no anymore!" Finally chortling out loud, she added, "Damn, I don't want to either! He adores me, Mica. I feel amazing when he's with me. I swear he's the perfect man!"

Okay, count to ten first. I took a deep breath and asked, "Good in bed is good. Does he, uh, have any...unusual *skills*?"

It was my turn to blush, but I needed to know if James had shown her his powers. He could be good in bed without sharing his powers with her. After all, they all had the ability to read thoughts and were bound to use that for pleasure if they were inclined to.

She was re-braiding the tiny braid that hung by her cheek so didn't answer for a minute. Finally, she secured the end and asked, "Special skills? Other than knowing my every thought? No."

I knew she was telling the truth and breathed a sigh of relief. Sean would be glad to hear that. I hadn't spent any time with Dani since before Christmas and it was February already. Every time I tried to do something with her, she had plans with James. I was beginning to worry about her, but couldn't quite put a finger on the problem. Back in December, Dec and Sean had suggested we ask James about his relationship with Dani. At the time, I thought they were joking. But Dec's plan had been sneakier than that and I was still thoroughly impressed with it. Thinking back to the last update I'd gotten from Dec, I was just slightly reassured.

It had been very late one night in early January. Dec came in covered with ash and assorted disgusting fluids. I'd taken one look at him and pointed to the bathroom.

"You smell like barbequed demon. Get that nasty crap off of you before the whole house reeks."

Exhausted, he hesitated as if he was going to flop down on the couch. I glared at him and he reconsidered and shuffled off to the bathroom. Twenty minutes later, he was clean and ready to fill us in.

"Where have you been? You look tan," I asked.

Rolling his shoulders tiredly, he said, "Rome first, then Madrid. I swung by Los Angeles for a couple of days and took out a couple of old *friends* I ran into." He took a long drink and continued, "Do you have any idea how many demons are in LA? It's ridiculous! I was having such a good time I had to stay a few extra days."

Rolling my eyes, I said, "Geez. I'm sorry I missed it. Next time you should bring me. I've never been to California."

"Maybe someday, but I actually just stopped in to give you some info on Dani and James. The bug worked. He's been staying with her a lot and they're not very quiet."

Yuck.

"Geez Dec, I don't want to hear about their sex lives..."

Looking down his nose at me, he said, "You have a dirty mind. That's not what I meant. James spends a lot of his time telling her how beautiful she is and how much he wants her for himself. He's really laying it on thick."

His eyes narrowed thoughtfully. "It's odd though. He doesn't sound that sincere to me. I would've thought she'd see through the bullshit. I think he's using his powers to influence her, but I can't tell without being closer." Frowning, he added, "I don't like it."

He'd bugged Dani's room with a device he could tune into remotely using an app on his cell phone. He'd been trying to catch James doing something wrong, but so far it seemed like he was only guilty of too much flattery and questionable motives.

I guess my worrying wasn't productive, but I'd learned to trust my intuition and something about Dani and James was off. We were done with our manicures and I had to finish my other errands. Leaving her with a promise to do lunch, I left the shop. I was on the way to my car when a furtive movement caught my eye. I dropped my bag and bent down to pick it up. Out of the corner of one eye, I saw him. Tingles of recognition teased my memory. Hmmm. Dark pants with a leather jacket. It was too nice a jacket to be a student even though I was leaving the college bookstore. He turned away to talk on his phone but stayed exactly where he was. I started towards the parking lot and pulled out my own phone. Using the mirrored screen, I watched him nonchalantly enter the lot. Instead of getting into my car, I called Sean and put him on speaker. With the phone sitting on the roof, I turned around and crossed my arms.

My tail looked up to find me studying him and stopped. We weren't exactly close, but I could see his face clearly. He was probably in his mid-thirties with close-cropped red hair and green eyes. His ruddy face was square and he had a scar running down his cheek from his eyebrow to his chin. It looked like a sword wound. Ouch. Even though he was clearly busted, he was a professional and tried to play it off.

"Hey there, I hate to bother you, but I've lost my directions. Can you tell me how to get to the old base from here?" He smiled easily as if he was just a new guy in town.

"Cut the bullshit. Why are you following me? Are you stalking me?"

He looked stunned at the accusation. "Stalking you? You're crazy!"

I'd give him an A for effort if it weren't for my enhanced intuition. He was totally lying. Pulling away from the car door, I picked up my phone and took a picture of him before he could flinch. To Sean I said, "It's on the way. What do you want me to do with him?"

The man hesitated while I listened to Sean and finally murmured a response. It was his turn to be angry now. He wasn't faking it either. "You're in a lot of trouble, Miss Thomas!"

"I don't know what you're talking about. I'm perfectly fine."

Warming to the subject, he pulled out his own phone and handed it to me. "Does this man look familiar to you?"

My brain nearly froze in surprise. It was a grainy picture taken in the pouring rain, in the dark of night, in the deep shadows of a wraparound veranda. The man's face was pretty obscured but my heartbeat quickened at the sight of him.

I scoffed, "I can't see a thing in that picture. It's black."

Unconcerned, he passed me another one. "How about now, Miss Thomas?"

Uh-oh.

This one wasn't as blurry. Even with my hand shaking, it was impossible to miss the resemblance.

Instead of answering him, I posed a question of my own. "So what kind of trouble am I in?"

Smiling like he'd won, he purred, "Oh, conspiracy to commit acts of terrorism, arms smuggling, and murder are the top three. As you can see by these pictures, you and this man are clearly involved with known terrorists and arms dealers."

Okay, this had gone on long enough. I needed to get out of here before anything bad happened. I nodded and closed my eyes for just a minute. When I opened them again, he was smiling at me like I was his new best friend. I shook his hand and smiled back.

"You should be good to go now. The base is just down the street. I'm late for an appointment! Bye, now."

"Okay, thanks again!" He smiled and waved good-bye as I got into my car.

My face was about to explode and I broke out in hoots of laughter as soon as the car turned the corner. "Sean! You're a freakin' genius! It actually worked." I did a little happy dance with my butt and headed towards the house.

Domino greeted me with a big doggy grin when I pulled up. It was a bit warmer today so Sean let her out to romp around the yard. He was lounging against the porch post throwing a ball to her. The snow was melting and the grass was starting to poke through. Spring was on its way.

Throwing my arms around him, I crowed, "You're a genius! No, wait! I'm a genius!" I did a little dance around him just to prove my point.

Laughing, he asked, "What did you actually do?"

"I erased myself from his memory. All he knows is a pretty brunette gave him directions to the old base. Mica Thomas doesn't exist--not face or name. We need to get those pictures though. You can see me with Dec in the trees and it's a good shot."

"I'll call Alex. He's got techies who can make them disappear. Killian wasn't exaggerating when he said your abilities had really evolved last year. You're getting good at this." He glowed with pride and my heart did a little dance too.

"Do you think so?"

"Absolutely! You're impressive, love. There are many Primani who would give their right...uh, arm, to have this kind of psychic power." His voice had dropped as he scanned the forest around us. "Domino! Come!"

Catching his unease, I asked, "Is something wrong?"

Calling over his shoulder, he said, "No, just an odd feeling, like we're being watched. Let's go inside and talk."

"Is Dec going to be back this week? I was hoping he'd be at The Lizard on Saturday." I made small talk while putting away the things from the store and grabbing drinks. I knew him well enough to know he was scanning the property and ready to cross over into soldier-mode at the barest hint of threat. We were all a little edgy these days.

With eyes still distant, he murmured, "I'm not sure. He hasn't found him yet." He suddenly stiffened and moved towards the front room. Domino paced him with her ears alert. Growling softly, she pressed her nose against the front door. I raised my eyebrows in question. He shrugged.

"I'm not sensing anyone...what do you hear?" I asked.

He shook his head sharply and put a finger to his lips. Okay, no talking. I strained my ears and still didn't hear anything. Domino growled deeper in her throat and raised her hackles. He whispered something to her and she trotted over to me and sat. He vanished. Okay...

Ten minutes later, he reappeared, cursing. "I'm going to rip his head off when I catch him!"

"What happened to your eye?"

Instead of answering, he growled at me.

"Who was it? James? Dagin? I'm confused."

Still swearing creatively in multiple languages, including several dead ones, Sean slammed his hand down on the island and irritably swiped at the blood that was running from a cut above his eye. It was a hard blow judging from the split in his skin and the amount of blood pouring out of it.

"Is he gone then?" I asked as I soaked a washcloth in cold water. "This'll sting; hold still."

Irritably, he jerked it out of my hand and smashed it against his eye. He seethed while I watched with a million questions. None of which were getting answered until his temper cooled down.

"Who's bleeding? I can smell it from here."

I snapped, "Don't you knock?"

James shrugged and waved a negligent hand towards the door. "It wasn't locked. You should be more careful about that." He smiled coldly. "Haven't you heard about the serial killer running around?"

Sean tensed but kept his voice even. He said, "Glad to see you finally made it in. Alex wants you back with Dec in Brooklyn." He tossed the wet cloth into the sink. "Things are heating up down there and you have skills we need."

James raised a bushy eyebrow at that. "How soon do I need to go? I have plans."

"There are no higher priorities than our work, James. Cancel your plans. You need to be there ASAP."

My surprise must've been obvious because James sneered at me on his way by. "This is your doing, isn't it?"

"What? I've got nothing to do with this!" I was flabbergasted and stared at him like he'd lost his mind.

"Happy birthday, Mica," he said as he stalked out of the room. He vanished before I could say another word.

"He just gets creepier and creepier…"

Saturday dawned clear and sunny and I thought this was a good omen. My birthday was today and I was officially old enough to drink. I hadn't needed the calendar to change anything though. I'd been getting into bars for years. For some reason, no one ever asked for my ID…

"Stop sulking. He'll be back if he can." Sean leaned over and kissed my lower lip before heading down to the basement. I followed him but I wasn't working out today. My shoulder was stiff and I was trying to let it heal on its own.

"It's been too long." I frowned at the floor, "I'm worried about him."

Slipping on his gloves, he answered me with a casual shrug. "Babe, he's fine. This is what Killian does, remember? He's been in touch. He's just focused and not in the mood to slow down." He patted me awkwardly with his gloved hand. "And he's only been gone a few months. I've gone decades without the pleasure of his company and I've survived just fine. You will too!"

I sat and watched him for a little while, not really seeing him, but taking comfort from his presence. The steady thunk-thunk of his fists on the bag was reassuring in my crazy world. Dec wasn't back yet either and I was trying to keep a brave face. I really, really wanted them to be with me tonight. I felt our bond more than they did and my mood was affected by how close or far they were from me. I got crankier if I went too long without seeing one of them. It wasn't hard to explain this. It wasn't magic. It was simple human emotion. They were my family and I missed them. Sean and I would celebrate my birthday with friends that didn't include Dec, Killian, or

Dani. Other than Sean, these were the three people I cared about most. It almost seemed pointless to try to celebrate anything without them there. With a heavy sigh, I got up to go for a walk.

Sean tracked us down a few hours later. Domino and I had just wandered out of the woods when he appeared on the path. With tongue lolling, Domino ditched me and threw her dignity out the window to chase a stick into the yard.

Shaking my head in wonder, I mused, "Do you think she was one of your ex-girlfriends in a past life?"

Laughing at me, he said, "Could be...Are you okay? You've been gone awhile."

More seriously, I said, "I've changed my mind about tonight. I don't want to go out."

"You don't? Why not?"

"I've been thinking and I realize my birthday just isn't that important anymore. There are much bigger things to worry about and I just don't care that much now. Can we go someplace, just the two of us? We could...travel someplace nice for a few hours."

"I suppose we could do that. Do you want to pick the place or do you want me to surprise you?" He lifted an arm in invitation and I snuggled underneath it.

"Surprise me. Just make sure I'm dressed so I don't freeze!"

Just as I was about to lay down for a nap, Sean asked if I was ready to go. He wore jeans and a heavy wool sweater with the black combat boots that went with everything he owned. The heavy sweater was a clue. I raised an eyebrow and he grinned.

"It *is* February. Dress warm and don't wear girly shoes."

Ten minutes later, I was ready to go. I'd thrown on my own jeans with a couple of shirts layered under one of his oversized wool sweaters. I loved the sloppy look and it was much warmer than any of my jackets. My Uggs completed the winter look. With a last kiss for Domino, he took my hand and brought me to paradise.

Icy wind nearly knocked me off my feet as we landed on a cliff overlooking a coast. The sleet hit me like machine gun fire and I instinctively hid my face against Sean's shoulder.

"Sorry!"

The next time I opened my eyes, we were standing behind a house at the end of a short dark street. The houses were small and nestled together as if trying to keep warm in the frigid air. Curious now, I peeked around with interest. Behind us, a dog barked with authority and I jumped. Sean took my hand in his and led the way.

"You look happy."

"I'm always happy here. This is home." He waved a hand to include the little houses and smiled. "I miss it when I'm gone too long."

"We're in Ireland?" I nearly pulled him off of his feet with the force of my hug. "Oh, wow, Sean! This is so cool!" I swung around and looked at everything at once. It did look like Ireland...

Pulling me into a dimly lit doorway, he leaned down to kiss me. "I hope you like it."

The warm stuffiness of the pub surrounded us the moment we walked in. The rich tang of pipe tobacco floated on the air and the soft sounds of music added to the mellow atmosphere. The pub was clearly very old as the heavy wooden beams and chunky stone walls suggested. There was a large fireplace on one side and several old men sat around drinking beer and keeping warm.

A cheery baritone voice greeted us. "Sean O'Cahan! As I live and breathe, come in, come in!"

Sean's entire face transformed at the sound of his name. He smiled broadly and clapped the burly bartender's back with genuine affection. The older man smiled showing several gaps in his teeth, but he was sincere as he bustled around us. Feeling a little out of place, I hovered behind Sean as he chatted with the man. Remembering his manners though, he drew me forward to introduce me.

"John, I want you to meet my fiancé, Mica. Today's her birthday."

Sean draped his around me and said, "Darlin', I want you to meet one of my oldest friends, John O'Hara. His family's owned this pub for generations."

John's expression was curious as he shook my hand and looked me over. With a cheeky grin, he kissed me on both cheeks and welcomed me to the pub. Sweeping other people aside, he led us to a little table near the fire and left to draw a couple of pints.

After dragging another chair over to our table, John sat down and grilled Sean on how we met. "You've been away so long, son, we've just about written you off as dead. And now you show up with a pretty little American." He nodded good-naturedly at me. "The young ladies will be devastated around here, lass."

Smiling easily, Sean disagreed. "Don't listen to this old man, love. I've never dated any of the girls here." Lowering his voice, he added, "So keep your claws sheathed!"

He grunted as I stomped on his foot under the table.

Under my breath, I said, "Oh? Not in this century at least..."

"You're not gonna let that go, are you?"

Smiling hugely, I said, "No, probably not." My stomach chose to fill the silence with a loud demand for something besides beer. "Sorry. I'm a little hungry."

John grinned around his glass as he drained most of it in one swallow. "I like to see lasses with an appetite, love. Don't worry about a thing. I've got just the dinner for a proper birthday party." Bowing slightly, he lumbered off towards the kitchen.

"He's not going to bring me haggis, is he?" I asked tentatively.

Snorting a laugh, Sean looked down his nose at me. "That's not Irish food. Haggis is Scottish. Either way, I'm pretty sure you're not getting anything that comes from the organs of a farm animal." He reached across the table and took my fingers in his.

"Happy birthday, Mica." He kissed my fingertips lightly and I glowed with normal human happiness.

Leaning across the table, I kissed him and teased, "You called me your fiancé earlier. Tell me, Mr. O'Cahan, does it sound funny to you?"

"Not even a little bit. Although calling you Mrs. O'Cahan sounds a bit odd. I've never been married before."

"Hmmm, Mica O'Cahan…it has a nice ring to it." I tilted my ring finger to catch the glow of the lamp and smiled at the turn my life had taken.

"Nice rock, Princess."

"Dude, the traffic was horrible. Sorry, we're late!"

With a most unladylike whoop of joy, I swung around to find Killian and Dec standing just behind me. Dec raised a few eyebrows when he swung me around in a wide bear hug. John had to dodge my legs on his way to our table. With a noisy kiss, Dec passed me off to Killian who was a lot more dignified.

He held out his hand to me and I showed him my ring. Smiling stiffly, he brought my hand to his lips and kissed it with a slight bow. "I'm happy for you."

"I'm so glad to see you guys! Now my day is perfect. Come on, sit down."

The atmosphere inside the pub had cooled just a little when they settled in. The other people were glancing over at us like we were going to blow the place up. The two old men who'd been sitting next to us got up and moved to a booth on the other side of the room.

"You know how happy I am to see you both, right?" They nodded. I waved a hand over the general direction of their commando black. "You didn't think to change first? I think you're scaring the locals."

Sean stifled a grin and said, "It's not the clothes, love."

Nonplussed, I asked, "Then what's the trouble?"

Killian said, "It's possibly the smell of dead demon that's bothering them."

"What? They know?" I nearly shrieked and Sean clapped a hand over my mouth.

Chuckling near my ear, John leaned down to me and said, "This is the Old Country, love. There are no secrets here." He sat down a plate full of fries and crunchy battered fish. My mouth watered immediately.

"Oh! It's fabulous, John! Perfect!" Passing the plate, I shared my food with Dec. He was always hungry.

"Any news?" Sean asked quietly.

Killian said irritably, "Yeah, but not good news." He leaned forward to keep his voice from projecting. "I feel it, but I can't find it." Absently, he rubbed his chest.

"Has it been hurting you?" I asked.

He shifted uncomfortably and said, "No. It's fine."

I leaned back and crossed my arms. "Really? That's strange because I've been getting these random pains just here." I tapped a finger against my heart. "Do you want to answer that question again or should I just assume I'm under another kind of attack?"

He flushed and scowled at me. "You shouldn't be feeling anything now. I took care of that with the rune."

I placed my hand flat on the table and leaned towards him. The rune was still a pale scar. "Oh, yeah, I remember the plan was to break our connection so I wouldn't be destroyed by your immense power." I smirked at him and Sean squeezed my knee under the table.

"You have something to say?" Killian asked evenly. His eyes were intensely blue as he assessed mine across the table.

Bolstering my courage, I said, "It didn't work. First of all, the rune didn't repel the demon that attacked me on Christmas and second, I was able to channel your power to destroy him--with exact precision. So your plan didn't work. You left me unprotected and still in possession of your power."

"Oh, and the nice demon gave me six broken fingers for Christmas. I blame you for that." I waggled my perfectly healed fingers at him to make my point.

Incredulous, he stared at Sean using that annoying telepathy. Finally, he looked back at me and his shoulders slumped. "I'm sorry you were hurt. I don't know how that could've happened. I miscalculated something. Sean says you were completely controlled though. Did you feel that way at the time?"

Dec snorted rudely. "Dude, she was like a real avenging angel! She scared the hell out of both of us. She sliced that demon into pieces with her *mind*." He paused to give me a high five. "And she knew exactly how to bring her body back to normal by herself."

"Is that true?" Killian asked Sean. He seemed torn between guilt and pride.

"Yes, it's true. She really had it under control. I was proud of her."

Not wanting to hurt his feelings, I reached across the table to soothe Killian's clenched fist. "Hey, I'm not mad about it. I just thought you should know I still have your powers but not your protection. It feels a little unbalanced."

Sighing with resignation, he agreed, "We'll have to fix that at the house. I don't want to leave you without protection."

John approached but hung back respectfully. "Come over and join us, John. What's new with your family?" Killian invited kindly.

The rest of the evening passed in comfortable warmth and camaraderie. The pub wasn't busy so John sat with us and caught up with Killian and Sean. He was obviously used to their ways and wasn't at all surprised when Dec pulled out his blade to clean it off. The midnight hour was upon us when Sean stood up and stretched. His eyes were heavy with fatigue and I knew he was ready to go. Domino was waiting for us at home and we needed to get back.

John gave me a warm hug and whispered, "You're always welcome here, lass. Visit any time." He pressed a small doggy bag into my hands and kissed my cheek. Before I could thank him, Sean took my hand and we landed in our living room.

"Whoa! Is that okay? We just vanished in front of him!"

"He's cool. His place is a sort of safe haven for us. You can always go there if you're in trouble."

"Nice. I have no idea where we were though and I have to take planes," I pointed out with not a little sarcasm.

Killian agreed but added, "I have an idea. Mica, take my hand and project your image of the place into my mind. Let's see if I can find it for you."

"I can't travel. This won't work." I looked dubiously at them. But Sean and Dec agreed it was worth a try, just to see how far my powers were progressing.

"Okay. Here goes." I took Killian's hand and waited for his mind to open to me. I was used to connecting to his mind so I let him slip in easily. I imagined the pub in as much detail as I could remember and let it fill my mind so he could see it too.

I sensed the change instantly. I opened my eyes and we were standing inside the darkened building. It was empty but still warm and inviting. Blinking in the darkness, I wandered around to be sure it was the same place.

Killian breathed, "Damn."

"Wow! That's so cool! Let's try someplace else that you've never been to. Maybe you subconsciously brought us here and it wasn't me at all," I suggested. He told me to think of anyplace I wanted to go.

I held his hand and imagined the sandy beach of a deserted island in the South Pacific. I'd always wanted to see one of those...in a heartbeat I was caressed by the warm salty air of the ocean. Opening my eyes again, I was stunned by the beauty of the sandy cove around us. We stood on a tiny strip of black sand that butted against a tropical jungle. The beach ended in a jumble of rocks that jutted out from a hardened lava flow. Turquoise water gently lapped at the shore and a sea bird dipped its head into the water just off shore.

"Oh, my..." I breathed and looked up at him.

His hard face softened with the wonder of the place. All too quickly the practical being showed up to throw a wet blanket on the fun. "Mica, we can't stay here. This isn't stable. I don't know if this is our plane. Come on, we need to get back." His tone was stern but his mouth curved into a smile.

Turning away, I headed towards the rocks. "I'll be right back. I just want to see what's on the other side of these rocks!"

"Mica!" Killian shouted.

I looked back to see him stagger and sit down on the sand. He clutched at his chest as my own began to sting.

Dropping to my knees beside him, I demanded, "It's happening again, isn't it?"

His eyes were unfocused, the lids fluttering shut. The white color of his skin sent alarm bells clanging in my brain. Uh-oh, he can't pass out!

An animal screamed in the trees and the sour taste of fear filled my mouth. Peering nervously at the trees, I worked hard to keep from panicking. The jungle loomed behind us, its tropical growth nearly pitch black with decay and death. No one knew where we were and we would be stuck here if Killian was unconscious.

Smacking him against one cheek, I yelled, "Don't you pass out on me! Wake up!"

I started shaking him by the shoulders when he grabbed my wrist, grinding the tiny bones together. His eyes were black as the pain in my chest deepened. His must be killing him, but he struggled to stay awake.

"That's better. Get us out of here," I begged him. The animal screamed again, closer this time. "We can't stay here, Killian. Please."

Wrapping my arms around his waist, I shouted at him to take us home and then everything went black.

My world brightened gradually until I squinted against the fire's glow. Fire? Where was I now? I scrambled upright kneeing Killian in the stomach as I did so. He was lying under me with both arms still banded around me. He wasn't completely out though. His eyes were slanted just a bit and he was trying to blink. I peered around us and was surprised to see an altar with a brazier of hot coals. Ah, that explained the glow. It was stone and very old, much like Killian's Eden, but in a different place. It was quiet as only uninhabited places can be. I strained my ears and heard only my ragged breathing. I reached out but sensed no humans. Something odd tickled at my awareness but I didn't recognize it. Not Primani, not demon…something else?

Killian's breathing quickened and I reached down to check his pulse. I wanted to get up but he held me in a death grip. Instinct told me I was running out of time. This place wasn't safe and we were vulnerable.

"Killian? Wake up. We can fix this, but you have to wake up." I patted his cheek but he only blinked at me.

"I'm awake," he rasped. "Stop yabbering; I'm trying to listen!"

"Oh, nice."

Leaving him to listen, I snooped around the cave. It wasn't very large and the altar dominated the space. The glow from the coals cast reddish shadows that reflected some kind of sparkling minerals in the walls. It could be quartz or limestone, I wasn't sure. The sweet smell of water tickled my nose and I swallowed painfully. My tongue wanted to stick to the roof of my mouth reminding me that I hadn't had anything to drink for a while. Killian was still prone so I followed my nose. Near the back of the altar was a small depression, a tiny pool, of clear water. It smelled okay and I stuck my finger in it to taste it. It was slightly bitter but seemed okay. I filled a small metal cup and gulped it down. Filling the cup for him, I moved back to Killian and offered it to him.

"Is it *Sgaine Dutre*?"

Nodding and springing to his feet like a cat, he washed his face in the pool and paced. "Someone is wielding it...someone very powerful." He crushed the cup and threw it into the coals. "But it's fighting."

"That has to be good, right?" Laying my hand on his shoulder, I asked, "Is it here?"

"No, it's not here. We're on another plane...like Eden. Eden's been compromised, so I created a path to this place. It's empty, too."

"Are you sure it's empty? I felt another presence when we got here. Not human, but not quite demon or Primani. Are there other beings that could be here?"

"That's not possible! What did you sense?"

"Just a presence; like something hovering outside the cave. It seemed *unfriendly*."

Clearly unhappy with this news, he ran his fingers over his jaw and glared at the walls. "Okay, let's try this. See if you can sense it again. Can you do that?"

"I'll try."

I closed my eyes to concentrate on locating the strange presence and was hijacked by an unexpected image of Killian waking me up from the grip of a nightmare. He sat on the edge of my bed, smoothing my hair back from my face. As I struggled to wake up, he kissed my forehead with so much tenderness I nearly cried with the memory. Forcing my eyes open, I gaped at him.

"You...no, it can't be." I shook my head to clear the fog. But when I closed my eyes, the image reappeared. This time I'd woken up and he held me curled against him until I stopped shaking.

"What's the matter? Can't you sense it?" His impatience was obvious. He wanted to bolt.

"I can't seem to focus."

He studied my face before saying, "Never mind then; we'll deal with that later. Come over here and let's fix that rune." A gust of wind whistled shrilly across the entrance and he paused to listen. Unperturbed, he waved me over again. "Let's get this done so we can go. I don't want to get stuck here."

I sat and watched while he pulled off his shirt and replaced my tiny pendant with the large gold one he used for rituals. The dying embers cast a glow over his chest and the gold glimmered enticingly. Murmuring, he sprinkled a handful of dried herbs onto the coals. A sweet smell filled the cave and my head began to swim oddly. The walls undulated, shimmering faintly. Killian's voice was reverent in prayer. He held the blue-handled blade aloft and called upon an ancient power to bless it.

"Come, Mica. It's time," he called from the altar.

He reached for my arm and I laid it across the altar stone with my palm down. Holding the knife out in front of him, he chanted firmly,

"A Dios entrante, Dutre gainhi."

"A Dios entrante, Dutre gainhi."

He recited the words and swiftly carved the rune into the top of my hand. Blood flowed freely but there was no pain. His own freshly-carved rune was still bleeding when he raised it to me. I pressed my hand into his and felt a small surge of power as his blood mixed with my own and flowed through my veins. His eyes shone with clear blue fire as the blood flowed and my own brightened in response.

As he spoke the words that would seal my fate, his heartbeat throbbed in my ears, calling me, compelling me, *drawing* me to him. As the ancient magic claimed me for its own, my heartbeat echoed his. Still standing with the altar between us, I closed my eyes and surrendered to the pull of the raw power. Instinctively, I grabbed his wrist and dragged him towards me. Instead of coming closer to me, he entwined his fingers with mine and held on as the magic took effect. We stood linked together with blood running between us and flames searing the walls around us. I locked my eyes to his and felt the tenuous bond crystalize into stone. Our connection was complete and we would not be easily separated now.

His raspy voice brought me back to the present. "I'm not sure that was a good idea," he mused as he rinsed the blood off his hands. The tiny pool gleamed red in the fire's glow.

I looked down and realized I had blood all over my hands. In a daze, I washed up and then studied him as he studied me. Minutes passed while the wind howled outside.

Pensive, he met my eyes and frowned. "I'm almost 100 percent sure that I just made you 100 percent more powerful. Sean is going to be pissed."

"Why is it you absorb my blood *and* my power? No one else does." He tossed another coal on the fire and continued his musing. With a mocking laugh, he asked, "Do you know how many times I've bled on Sean?"

"That's a little gross, really."

Laughing shortly, he said, "In war, babe, bleeding happens."

The hair on the back of my neck prickled in warning. "There's something outside!"

Throwing me a knife, he ordered, "Stay put."

Putting the altar between my fragile human body and the cave entrance, I palmed the silver blade and searched for the source of life I'd felt. It was still out there...a whisper of life...not a whole soul, but a shadow, no, a pale reflection of a soul hovered malignantly nearby. The power it projected was unlike any I had ever felt before. A trickle of sweat slid between my shoulder blades and my fingers tensed around the haft. A slight shift in the atmosphere alerted me and I froze with the blade ready. There, a few feet in front of me, was a shimmering, a disturbance, in the light of the cave. I blinked but it was still there, hovering just out of arm's reach.

"What do you want?" I growled under my breath.

A faint echo of laughter answered me and the shimmering flattened out and disappeared altogether. Killian reappeared just as it vanished. Angrily, he swung around to confront this intruder but there was nothing for him to see.

"Fuck!" He slammed his fist into the cave wall and a small shower of rocks peppered the floor.

With furious movements, he gathered up the wicked blades and sheathed them. With three steps, he went to the altar and said several angry words over it. With one final burning glance at what only he could see, he cursed the unseen presence and banished it from this place. In response to his command, the cave walls sung with a low vibration that began at the altar and radiated outward until the entire cave trembled. A faint blue light crisscrossed the ceiling and the walls until the cave was completely covered in the protective web.

Slowly lowering his hands, he bowed his head and murmured a prayer. Satisfied, and a lot calmer now, he took my hand without a word.

"Well, at least you're not covered in blood this time." Sarcasm greeted me the second we rematerialized. He was leaning against the fireplace with crossed arms.

Dec was draped across the recliner, wagging his head in disapproval. His mouth curled up just a little on one side as he fought back a grin. Evidently they'd been waiting for some time and he'd been stuck with Sean's complaints.

Flushing guiltily, I got defensive. "It wasn't my fault! We got stranded on a deserted island."

Sean sniffed with disbelief. "Why am I not surprised?"

Killian, who had been trying to keep a straight face, finally broke down and smiled. "Mica's got exotic tastes; she wanted to see the South Pacific. We ended up at the cave though." He went on to explain what happened and the silence was leaden when he mentioned the shimmering presence.

"That's freaking creepy." Dec's brow furrowed as he sank deeper into thought. He absently scooted over so Domino could curl up with him. She leaned against his side and rested her chin on his lap. It was past her bedtime.

Sean asked, "Did this feel the same as our invisible Peeping Tom? Maybe it's the same guy."

I thought about that for a few minutes. Was it the same, uh, entity? Not a person, surely. It hadn't felt like an angel either. I didn't sense an aura of goodness that usually surrounded Primani and the other angels I'd met.

"This presence seemed malignant; it gave me the chills and I wanted to run away."

"I asked what it wanted and it laughed at me," I added ruefully.

Dec unfolded himself and stretched. "I'm going to do some research on this. Something seems familiar, but I can't put my finger on it."

"I think we need protection over this house. It's not secure anymore and we need to be able to talk," Sean pointed out to Killian.

"And you should do that now…" I murmured while slowly jabbing my thumb towards the window without turning around. Three pairs of eyes followed the motion…and then vanished along with their host bodies.

Chapter 22: How Hard the Fall

"WHERE IS IT?" Killian's voice was deadly quiet when he questioned the prisoner.

The prisoner squirmed in the chair and tried the bonds around his wrists. With profound dignity, he stared unblinking at the wall in front of him while Killian prowled the room. Sean observed with a blank expression that masked his thoughts. He was reserving comment for later.

Yanking the prisoner to his feet by his neck, Killian asked him again. Again, the answer was stony silence. Frustrated but hiding it with immense control, he dropped the bound demon to the floor. He grunted as his face hit the concrete. Killian's boot pressed down on his back and shoved him harder into the floor.

"I asked you a question, demon, and I'm running out of patience." He bent closer and dragged his favorite knife from its sheath.

The metallic hiss sounded loud to me but the demon stayed cool. He remained silent with his reptilian eyes tracking every move Killian made. The black pupils were unusually large in the yellow irises. The putrid yellow color was only visible as a ring around the huge pupils. Like most demons, he wore a human mask to cover the scaly skin that would give him away. This one had the dark skin and aquiline features of an Egyptian. His thick dark hair was cut close to his scalp and he had prominent cheekbones. Not a bad looking disguise overall.

With a twist of the wrist, Killian slid the blade against the demon's cheek bringing a tendril of smoke curling from the wound. Sensing progress, he held the blade just above the skin on the other cheek and waited.

"Loyalty is an admirable quality. I'm surprised to see it in a demon." The blade trailed down the cheek leaving a pale curl of smoke. This time the prisoner sucked in a breath but didn't cry out. I was impressed with his stubbornness.

I tended to scream when someone cut me.

Killian wrenched him upright again and shoved him back into the chair. Switching tactics, he sat down across from him and steepled his fingers on the table. Apparently bored, the demon considered him without a sound. The clock ticked and the wind screamed outside, but the basement room was silent.

I glanced over at Sean and raised a shoulder in question. He moved over to the stairs and motioned me up them. Once we were out of the basement, he closed the door and stalked into the living room.

"How much longer is he going to go at this? This guy's not talking." I tried to keep the admiration out of my voice, but he noticed.

"Please tell me you're not impressed?" He hissed, "It's a frickin' demon, Mica! They have no redeeming qualities, remember? It's not loyalty that's keeping his mouth shut. Don't be impressed."

Backpedalling, I denied it. "Of course, I'm not impressed. Well, not really. But he's been at it for hours now and this demon is just stubborn." I paused for the right words. "It's like...his brain doesn't realize that Killian's about to kill him..."

Sean's whole face lit up and he sprinted towards the basement calling, "You're a genius!" on his way down the stairs.

What did I say? I caught up with him just in time to hear Killian rumble, "Zombie?"

Zombie?

Did I say that?

Well, that would explain things. Sure, I'll take the credit for this. Why not? I perched on the steps and listened as they talked.

Killian moved around to the prisoner's face and peered into the eyes with a new zeal. He was going to get to the bottom of this little mystery. After a moment, he gave Sean the thumbs up and motioned for me to join them.

"Mica, come over here and see if you can get inside his head," he ordered. He was on the verge of a breakthrough and he was about as excited as Killian ever got.

"Ewww! Why?"

"I want to know if he's got thoughts rolling around in there or if the brain is simply keeping his body alive."

"Okaaaay..." I was not comfortable with this idea. Balin had kept his marbles, such as they were...and I didn't feel like being possessed again. "I don't like this idea. Sean, anchor me?"

"I've got you. Just do a drive-by and come back."

A drive-by was our slang for a quick look around and then out again, in other words, no in-depth snooping or parking.

The demon blinked his yellow eyes and stared straight ahead. I took a deep breath and looked deeply into his eyes. Unlike the multidimensional irises of the Primani, his yellow irises were a flat shade of pus yellow. I peered beyond them to gather some insight into his mind. After a few minutes, I pulled back and blinked to moisten my eyes.

"Well?"

I thought carefully before answering. Nibbling on my fingernail, I said, "Hmm. I'm a little puzzled. There's not much there. Mostly his mind is blank, but I caught a few simple pieces of information. There's nothing complicated, probably just what he needs to survive. I saw a place...maybe where he lives. I also saw the face of another demon and then I saw our house. That's all I found. Everything else seems to be wiped clean."

All three of us turned to consider our prisoner.

His eyes faced forward and he wiggled his hands in their bonds. I waved a hand in front of his eyes but he didn't flinch.

Killian asked, "You didn't see *Sgaine Dutre?*" Disappointment colored his tone. He had to be frustrated with the news but didn't show it.

"No, sorry. But look, here's a thought. If I was Dr. Frankenstein, I'd want to test out my zombies before I made too many of them. I think this one was programmed to come here as a test. You know, come here, check it out, and then return to his home."

Sean finished my thought, "But he wasn't sophisticated enough to escape capture." He considered the prisoner again and asked Killian, "Do you think he's got a tracer?"

"Good question. Let's check."

He and Sean focused their attention and used their own psychic powers to check him for physical or magical tracers. A tracer would allow his Dr. Frankenstein to follow him right to us.

After a minute or so, Killian dismissed him. "He's clean."

"So what do we do with him now? Do you think he can find his way back home? We could try to follow him or put our own tracer on him."

Grinning broadly at me, Sean said, "That is an excellent idea, love."

A few hours later, our demon zombie was tricked out with a tiny little tracer bug that Killian implanted in his back. With any luck, he would find his way home and we would track him down.

If we could get him to leave...

I stifled a laugh as the guys shoed him off the porch--again. They smiled reassuringly at him and firmly pointed him towards the yard. He was confused and stood on the steps looking back at the porch. He turned around and came back to the door again. This time, he just stood in front of it with a blank expression on his face.

Sighing heavily, Sean took him by the sleeve and led him back down the steps and stopped him in the middle of the driveway. He turned around and sprinted back to the porch. The zombie stood there for a minute and then turned his head towards the porch again. His face was puzzled this time. I had to go inside to keep from laughing out loud. Grumbling with annoyance, Killian put him in the car and drove him to the end of the dirt road.

It was like dumping a puppy.

The tiny bell above the door tinkled when I walked into Zen. Dani's mother was hanging some crystal pendants on a cut tree branch for display. Turning to greet her customer, she smiled warmly when she saw it was me and hurried over to hug me.

"Mica! It's been so long since you've come by. I thought you had moved on. It's so nice to see you!"

She towed me to a cabinet so she could work while we talked. Her blond hair was done in little braids again and today she was draped in a heather purple shawl. Although she must be in her 40s, she never seemed to age and was still a pretty woman. She reminded me of an elf.

"I know I haven't been by. I've been busy lately."

"Lately?" she challenged with a knowing glance. "You are one mysterious young woman, my love."

Squirming with guilt, I had to lie again. "Well, it's not so mysterious to work and study. I'm taking an on-line class. Sean and I are--"

She cut me off with a wave of her hand. "Oh, please! Do you think I don't know what you two are doing out there?" Her eyes were suddenly cold. "I'm not ignorant of the ways of the unseen."

Unseen?

WTF?

"I'm not sure what you mean by that," I delayed with more than a little steel in my voice. I didn't like her tone.

She studied me for a heartbeat and turned away. I thought she'd dismissed me and was going to leave when she spoke again. "I'm sorry, sweetie. What you do is none of my business. I'm just worried about Dani and it's making me snippy." Her voice caught at the end.

"What's wrong with Dani?"

Absently toying with a pale pink crystal, she said, "Do you know very much about this James person she's seeing?"

"Some...not a lot. Is something wrong?"

She paused to collect her thoughts. "Dani isn't...Dani when he's around. She's someone else who I don't know and I don't understand. He manipulates her into doing whatever he wants to do and she doesn't see it. She smiles this weird empty smile and prattles on about love." She crushed a bunch of dried flowers into powder and sighed as it drifted to the floor.

Not what I wanted to hear.

Carefully, I asked, "Do you ever hear him talking to her about anything unusual?"

She stilled and quickly glanced up at me. Her eyes were suspicious as they probed mine looking for deception. "What do you know of this?" Her whole body tensed and she seemed poised to reach out and strike me.

Hands out in a gesture of calm, I tried again. "From your reaction, I guess I've hit a nerve. Do you want to tell me what you've heard?"

She eyed me with something like fear then. Backing away, she busied herself with gathering up empty boxes and running them to the back room. She knew something and she sensed it was important and probably knew it was supernatural. But why would she be afraid to tell me?

Was she afraid of me?

When she came back into the room, she was calmer but still very pale.

I went to her and gave her a hug to show I was harmless. "Please tell me what's going on. I'm on Dani's side no matter what. If I can help, you know I will."

"Come and have tea with me and we'll talk."

After the tea was brewed, we sat on the bright floor cushions and she unloaded. According to her mother, Dani had been entertaining James in her room every night. I knew this already so nodded without comment. Her mother had gradually noticed that James seemed to show up late and leave before dawn as if embarrassed to be there. She was outraged that her daughter might be just a booty-call to this man who seemed strangely in control of her. Dani laughed off her mother's concerns at first, which was true to her bubbly sweet personality. Lately though, Dani coldly refuted her mother's concerns and told her to stay out of her business. Her tone and her demeanor were not her own. She'd never been rude to her mother and was now acting more than rudely. She was downright hostile. She was a stranger.

Even more disturbing, she'd overheard a strange conversation between James and Dani. She related it to me with tears in her eyes.

James' soft voice was strangely compelling as he'd said, "Listen to me, Dani. You're special. You don't know it yet, but you will change the world."

Dani had breathed in anticipation and asked, "What could I do to change the world?"

"You'll see. You'll see soon enough. Now lay back and be quiet. We have work to do."

As she finished the story, she took a sip of her tea with a trembling hand. I reached out in sympathy and steadied her. She noticed immediately when my *saol* flowed into her body and her eyes went huge in their sockets. Sending orders to stay calm to her mind, I smiled reassuringly at her. She calmed down and stopped shaking.

"What did you do?" She was wary again as she rubbed at her hand.

"I'm just sending serenity vibes your way--nothing more than that." I was getting better at lying to her. "Is there anything else about James?"

"He's…I don't know how to say this. He's not…nice."

"Nice?"

Growling in frustration, she stood up. "Oh, that sounds so stupid! Nice. That's not what I want to say." Looking at me carefully, she added, "Maybe you'll understand more than I give you credit for."

"Okaaaay…" What was she talking about? Maybe she's lost her mind?

"I sense things, okay? There, now you know. I'm a little bit psychic." She seemed embarrassed as if this was an unpleasant affliction like herpes.

"Go on. What are you sensing that's got you so upset? Seriously, I'm not going to laugh at you. Trust me, I'll understand."

Finally deciding I was sincere, she said, "He's his own twin."

"Come again?"

"When I met him I knew he was divided or torn into two images of himself. I sensed good and…evil. Now…I only sense evil." She shuddered delicately and pulled her shawl more tightly around her shoulders.

It was my turn to shiver. It was uncanny how much she knew without even knowing anything about him. My mind was running in circles. James was Primani. He'd been good when we met. Primani were warriors, yes. They could be arrogant, crude, and obnoxious.

But they were essentially good at their cores.

They were soldier angels and got their powers from God's own archangels. Primani were ruthless demon killers, but they were spiritually good beings with human survival at the heart of their existence. James had been acting mysteriously for over a year and we'd been watching him. Even though he'd gradually hardened into something less righteous, less good, he hadn't led us to anything concrete yet. We had nothing to charge him with. He'd been too clever. James was creepy, sneaky, and a complete dick, but was he evil? That seemed impossible.

How would that happen?

"Mica? Mica? What are you thinking?"

Shaking my head to clear it, I said, "I'm thinking about James. I'm not convinced he's evil. It doesn't make sense to me. Do you have any other ideas?"

She snapped as only a mother could. "Damn it! He's touching my daughter with his filthy evil hands and whispering lies like the devil himself into her brainwashed little ears! He tells her she's special. He loves her. He wants her. But where is he? He sneaks into the house in the middle of the night. He leaves before the sun comes up so no one sees him. What kind of love is that?" She threw herself to her feet and paced angrily.

"He's using her. But for what, I don't know. And every day, my baby grows cold and the light dims in her beautiful stormy eyes." Exhausted by the force of her anger, she started to cry.

I wrapped an arm around her and tried to soothe her misery. Dani was clearly in trouble. I had a niggling suspicion that was freaking me out. I needed to get to Sean now. I couldn't share my theory with Dani's mom. It would destroy her.

If I was right, it was about to destroy Dani.

"I have to go. I need to see someone about this." I held her away from me and gave her a little shake. When she looked up at me with tear-soaked eyes, my heart squeezed painfully. Her pain was palpable, and I felt it all the way to my toes.

"Promise me you won't confront James? He's dangerous and I think he'd hurt you. I'll come back as soon as I can and tell you what we've found out."

She nodded miserably and squeezed me hard enough to crack a rib. "I would tell you to be careful too, but I think you have all the protection you need." Her fingers brushed the rune on my hand and she smiled wistfully.

I slammed the door in my rush to get inside the house. Domino broke into a fit of barking at the interruption and I heard boots crossing heavily across the wooden floor. Killian. Perfect. I needed to talk to all of them.

"Yes, I had to slam the door. Yes, I think I'm the only one who lives here. And yes, I'm gloating because I can totally read your mind." I threw this at him on my way into the living room. After peeling off my gloves and tossing them onto the coffee table, I finally turned around to match his mocking smile.

"Touché." He bowed elegantly to the floor.

"Where's everyone?   I want to call a family meeting."

He pressed his lips together and considered my request and my mood. He said, "You're vibrating. I can feel you from here. What's got your anger up?"

"Is there anything you don't know about me?"

Smiling lazily, he said, "No, not really. Though there are times I tune you out just to keep my sanity. You're a little intense."

I was incredulous. "I'm intense? Look who's talking! Geez."

A shadow clouded his face and his smile faded. Turning towards a window, he said seriously, "Sean is snooping on the feds and Dec is snooping on Dani. Guess we're all in the spook business now. The CIA's got nothing on us."

"And what about James? Any news on him? I have a theory you're not going to like."

"Shoot," he ordered.

"Okay, I think he's turned evil. I think he's working with Dagin and working against us...like a double agent. And I think he's trying to get Dani pregnant." I blurted this out and left it in a pile at Killian's booted feet.

There, the ball's in his court.

I was hoping he'd laugh at me and tell me this wasn't possible. I didn't want this to be true. Time slowed to a crawl while he thought about my theory. I could hear the hands on the clock moving and my own heartbeat racing in my chest. I knew better than to prod him. He was doing what he did best. I'd just have to be patient. My eyes rested on his tense shoulders, and I rolled my own to release the tension. After all these years, he hadn't changed at all. He was still tall and bulky with muscle. If anything, he'd gotten leaner and harder. Even relaxed, every muscle was defined and beautiful. His hair was still military short. Unlike Sean and Dec, he never let it grow out to curl around his ears. The proud set of his head showed the confidence that comes from knowing your blood runs with a power so ancient that there are no others who share it. He had a right to that pride. Once he'd told me he'd earned his ego. I agreed; though I'd never admit that to him.

His head might explode.

With three strides, he was back at my side. I managed a squeak of protest before he dragged me over to the couch and sat me down. He pushed too hard and I bounced up again.

"Hey! Stop manhandling me! I have ears. Do you think you could learn to use your words?"

His mouth opened in surprise and he blinked a couple of times. Breaking into a rare smile, he apologized. "I didn't realize it, but you're right. I'm sorry, babe. I get wrapped up in my head and it's just easier to move you myself...saves time."

"*Saves time*? Wow, you're a caveman! You just take what you want. I just love that about you." I said the words flippantly, but they unlocked a poignant image that stunned us both.

Like a photograph inside my head, I saw him with an arm draped around me as we watched the tide come in on a rocky shore. My head rested against his shoulder. We were naked.

He sucked in his breath with a sharp hiss.

Just like that, the image was gone, almost as if it didn't happen. The image was gone but the lingering feeling of loving him settled around me like a fine mist. I felt the weight of it against my skin and inside my heart. But my brain denied all such ideas. I searched for some memory that supported my feelings but nothing appeared. I remembered Killian helping me train, helping me grieve, and helping me heal. Nothing in his actions had been romantic. I had no memories of us as lovers...and yet...there was something between us that I couldn't see now.

He cleared his throat and prompted, "James?" He stood just out of reach and eyed me like I was dangerous.

I was suddenly acutely aware of the heat and scent of him and stepped back even further. Flushing, I started to ask him about this feeling but stopped. He looked coolly at me now as if daring me to give voice to my thoughts. I could push the issue, but I wasn't sure what I would get from it.

What did I want to get from it?

The rational part of my brain said I needed to know what was happening so I could deal with it and put it behind me. The irrational part of my brain, aka my heart, shied away because it knew there was only pain to be found. For once I was siding with my irrational nature-- now wasn't the time for this conversation. I was more concerned with Dani than my own screwed up memories.

With a business-like attitude, I pushed these thoughts out of my head. I'd play along with Killian for now. I said, "James. Okay, tell me I'm wrong. Please."

"I wish I could, but I'd be lying to you. It's probably worse than you think too." His expression was grave as he spoke. "We have a word for Primani who slip into darkness...who choose evil over good and who use their powers to do harm."

"You're freaking me out a little now. What happened to James?"

"He's fallen." Choking on the word, he cleared his throat.

Surprised by the word, I asked, "As in fallen angels?"

It seemed so....well, biblical.

I struggled to apply it to a situation happening in front of me.

Smiling grimly at my surprise, he nodded. "Yes, as in fallen angel. The term is appropriate; if James has turned to evil, he'll be stripped of his powers and he'll be barred from Heaven for eternity. He'll be trapped on earth until his body gives out and then he'll spend eternity with his new friends in Hell." His eyes gleamed as his mouth spit out the words that seemed to burn his tongue. He was controlled as usual but his eyes gave away his fury and his pain.

"I feel sad for him. I should be mad, but I'm only feeling sorry for him. Is there any redemption for him at all? Can't we do something for him before it's too late?"

"Listen to me carefully, Mica. James is not a human who can simply be led down a path by a tricky demon. He's Primani and used to be a damn talented one. Primani don't get tricked or coerced into switching sides. When they go, they go with full knowledge of the choice they're making." He wrapped his long fingers around my arm and squeezed to get my full attention. "There is no turning back. There is no redemption. He's damned and he will be destroyed by his choice."

I covered his hand with mine and peered into his burning eyes. "And that troubles you? You're not just angry; you're sad for him, too. Aren't you?"

Tilting his head to look down at me, he answered coolly, "You're projecting again. The only thing I'm feeling is pissed off. I can't stand traitors. I'm going to have to see Alex about this, and we'll end up bringing him in for a talk. It'll be ugly and I'm looking forward to it. As far as I'm concerned, James is dead already."

I started to reply when I felt him coming. "Hold that thought. Here comes Sean. Right...over...there." I pointed to the living room doorway just as Sean rematerialized.

Startled, Killian gaped at me. "You're getting scary, you know that?"

"What's up? You two look intense," Sean asked as he crossed to me for a hello kiss.

I leaned into him and clung for a second longer than usual, reluctant to break the contact. I really needed to feel his arms around me, anchoring me to this crazy place. "I'm so glad to see you. I'm totally freaked out."

Placing a kiss on the top of my head, he glanced over at Killian's hard expression. "It looks pretty important. Want to fill me in?"

Killian filled him in on what we'd already discussed and when he was finished, Sean was grim too. He was quiet for a few minutes soaking it in and finally looked at Killian and said, "When do we leave? I need to call Dec back for this. He'll kill us if we leave him out."

I asked, "What happens now?"

Sean answered, "Like Killian told you, we need to let Alex know and then go bring James in. He'll have to report to Michael himself for sentencing. If Michael decrees it, James will be stripped of his Primani powers and banished from Heaven."

"I'm sorry, but I don't see how any of this is going to solve our problem. He'll still be alive, right? He can still see Dani and do whatever he's trying to do now. He'll still be able to work with Dagin and cause trouble for everyone."

"But without his powers, he can't travel, he can't influence Dani's mind, and he can't spy on us. So some things will be better. Plus, he'll be more vulnerable and could die an accidental human death." He grinned wolfishly at the idea.

"But...what if he's become demonic? Won't he have demon powers? What if he fights us?"

It was Killian's turn to bare his teeth. "Oh, I'm counting on that."

Sean interjected, "Mica, you can't go with us. The rules are strict on this. Only Primani can bring in The Fallen. You'll have to sit this one out."

Killian spent the next few hours planning the mission with Sean and I made dinner. It was nice to work in the kitchen for a change. I had my iPod hooked to the speakers and sung along with my Linkin Park play list. I made a Thai stir-fry with shrimp and rice. It was after 8:00 when were all finished eating. Sean was about to get up from the table when I spoke up.

"Hey, I need to talk to you about something. Can you make it to bed early?"

Killian shrugged and said, "We're pretty much done, Sean. Why don't you just go hang out? We can finish up in the morning."

A few minutes later, Sean tapped on the door and let himself inside. His eyes darkened to midnight as I twirled in front of him. I was barely covered by an amethyst-colored satin negligee. Backless and strapless, the pushup bustier ended with a flounce of fabric that just covered my butt. I'd even invested in a pair of black thigh-high stockings. Candlelight reflected off of the locket at my throat and the twin stones on my finger. I'd piled my waves of hair on top of my head and let just a few heavy tendrils curl around my face.

Never taking his eyes off of me, he moved instantly to my side and dragged me against him with one arm around my waist. I wrapped my hands around his face and guided his mouth to mine and kissed him until his breathing was ragged.

"God, you're beautiful," he groaned against my throat. I arched against him in invitation and he followed me to the bed. I posed across the sheets and watched with sleepy eyes as he pulled off his clothes and threw them in a pile. Standing in nothing but his glorious skin, he drank in the sight of me and I smiled at his reaction.

Patting the bed, I smiled seductively and slid my stockings together just to hear the gentle swoosh of the silk. "Do you remember the first time you kissed me?"

He was running his hand up my stocking and peering interestedly under my flounce. "Of course I remember it. You seduced me on my yacht."

"It was a sailboat and you had no chance. I wanted you to kiss me and I wasn't getting off the boat without one. And then you came to me and scared me half to death. I'd thought it was cute to toy with you. I had no idea about the power. When you touched me, it felt like I was going to burst into flames. I was terrified." Lazily, I ran my hands down his shoulder and added, "But I couldn't look away. I was lost in you."

He raised his head and placed a playful kiss on my belly button. "You were scared of me. I saw it in your eyes. I smelled the fear. I was going to stop until the minute you realized that you were in love with me. That hit me like a cannon and I was stunned. That you loved me was a miracle. I couldn't have stopped if I tried. I was drawn to you like a magnet."

"And I still am." He was level with my face again and tugged on my lower lip with his mouth. I smiled up into those beautiful eyes and realized he was hovering above me on his elbows. His body was just barely touching mine, the muscle of his chest and thighs brushing mine. I trembled with the need to touch him, to hold him inside of me, to feel that connection again.

"Look into my eyes. What do you see now?" I tilted his face until he peered directly into my eyes.

"I see the truth of things between us. I see your love for me and I see your need." He dipped his head and kissed me, his tongue slipping against mine. My hips circled against him, pressing, inviting...He rubbed slowly across my thighs, taking his time, teasing us both. I felt the heat move up from his body to mine and marveled again at the soft golden light that wrapped around us and tied us together. Curious, I consciously pushed some of my own power outwards to see if I could add it to the *saol* that already flowed around us. The effect was immediate. The gentle heat was hotter now and more intensely concentrated.

"What did you just do?" He grinned down at me.

"Too much?"

"Did you want to melt?" He was laughing now.

"Okay, okay, I'll turn it off." I scaled it back and gradually the intense heat faded again.

"Now, where were we?" He grinned as he deftly unhooked the front of my bustier with one hand. The other was busy working magic elsewhere.

"Sean?"

"Yeah?"

"When do you think we should get married?"

Long pause.

"After we kill the zombies."

The trees were skeletal as they clawed towards the heavy grey clouds. I hurried down the path with Domino trotting alongside of me. The wind pushed against my back as the storm barreled down from the west. We were expecting a monster snowstorm and it would hit soon. I wanted, no, *needed* to meditate and felt drawn to my little clearing in the trees. Something was urging at me and I couldn't ignore it. Sean, Dec, and Killian had been gone for two days and I was alone. I'd started dreaming again last night. The dream had scared me and I'd woken with my heart racing and screams echoing in my mind.

In the dream, I was locked in a dark concrete cell with Dani. Dani was glowing with happiness and pregnancy. Her belly was grotesquely swollen but she didn't notice. Her eyes were mad as she crooned to the unborn child in her womb. Her voice gave me chills as she chanted the strange words of a lullaby. Over and over she chanted the words as if in a trance.

This woman didn't look like the Dani I knew. Her once beautiful eyes were jaundiced and ringed by heavy black eyeliner and her lips were painted a bloody red. Someone had changed her.

She stared at me with revulsion before snarling in a voice dripping with venom, "You're jealous! You pathetic freak! You'll never have babies like me!" Then she'd gone back to caressing her stomach and crooning the creepy lullaby.

I said, "No, Dani, I'm not jealous. I'm happy for you! Can't I help you? We'll get out of here and you and the baby will be safe again."

Flinching away from me, she hissed, "Leave? This is our home. I'll never leave here."

Before I could argue with her, she gripped her belly and screamed an inhuman howl. I froze in horror as two sets of claws appeared out of her belly. Her screams reverberated off the walls as the thing inside her clawed its way out and devoured its mother.

The dream freaked me out more because I suspected it wasn't a dream at all but a premonition. I didn't have them often but when I did, they always came true. I needed to meditate and clear my head now so I could get my thoughts together before going to see Dani. I wasn't waiting for the guys to come with me. I can handle talking to her without backup.

The trees in my clearing were bare too, but they were friendlier than the larger ones on the edges of the property. The small trees seemed to protect my clearing as they arched over it like a chapel roof. Reaching it now, I spread the blanket on the cold ground and sat down. Domino curled up by my side and set about the important business of guarding me while my mind was focused inward. I took one last glance around. The sky was roiling above me and a gust of wind whipped the blanket's edges around us. The storm was nearly here.

I needed to hurry.

Closing my eyes, I pictured my tiny pool surrounded with purple orchids and lush leaves of green. The water was so clear I could count the pebbles beneath my feet. Warm floral air caressed my cheek with gentle fingers. I breathed slowly and deeply and filled my soul with calm. My mind cleared of all thoughts but those of sensing. For a moment the physical world drifted away and it was only me in my private world. But the calm was abruptly shattered when something hit me on the back of my head and I fell on my face.

Domino's urgent barking gradually brought me around. I lay on the ground trying to make sense of what happened but my mind was blank. I tried to sit up but a burning pain stabbed into my skull when I moved. Carefully moving my arm, I felt the back of my head and winced when my fingers found a sticky spot. I wasn't bleeding a lot and I could feel the cut was pretty small. The knot, on the other hand, was about the size of an egg. This was going to hurt.

What the hell hit me?

Squinting, I looked around without moving my head. It was like trying to look through a blanket. The snow was falling in huge clumps and the wind was blowing it into swirls even inside the trees. The storm had started. I felt Domino leaning next to me and gave her a weak smile. Okay, it was time to get out of here.

"Good girl. I'd hate to freeze to death out here."

Despite the cocooning snow and howling wind, my psychic senses went ballistic. Suddenly I realized I wasn't alone. Someone was out there, watching me.

Someone who wasn't a friend.

"Domino, who's here?"

She went to doggy soldier-mode and scanned the perimeter. After a few seconds, she growled low in her throat and pointed to the left. I took a deep breath and shoved myself to my feet. The sudden movement left me nauseous and my vision dimmed to a tiny tunnel. I swayed and would've passed out again if Domino hadn't been there. She barked madly and backed into my shins. With hackles raised, she pivoted and barked at something further to the left now. It was moving.

Or there was more than one.

He was on me before I could lift a finger to stop him. I was flat on my back in the gathering snow with his heavy body flattening me and his hand clamped over my opened mouth.

"Don't even think about it. I've been trying to get you alone for too long to let you call for help," James sneered into my stunned face. Something sharp nudged the skin where my jacket had ridden up.

With a smile that would have been sweet if he wasn't evil, he lifted his hand away. When I tried to yell, I found that he'd cut off my audio. Damn it. Why does he still have his powers? He grinned down at me as if this was a flirty game between lovers. All fun and games...Without warning, he kissed my mouth in an oddly gentle kiss.

"Our first kiss. Do you remember your vision in The City? You were meditating and I watched you enter your little oasis. I came to you in your dream and showed you what it would be like. I wanted to pull you into my world and kiss you then, but you didn't give me a chance. I'm patient though. You see, I knew even then that you would be mine. That kiss was destiny. And now, it's happened." His face was calm as he reflected on his brilliance even as the cold metal rested along my rapidly warming skin.

His mood shifted and he frowned, "You've wasted too much time. All because of Sean...your *soul mate!*" Disgusted, he spit into the snow. "You didn't give me a chance, did you? That night...that night I showed you our first kiss...you gave yourself to that cretin. He took your body like he deserved it. The golden boy who gets everything he wants. I watched you spread your legs for him and I cried. Then I killed my first human."

The knife point dug into my skin, and I forced myself not to struggle. "I should've been your first. You deserved me. Then."

Killian! If you can hear me, I've got James for you! I don't know how long I can keep him distracted though. Hurry!

With eyes turning a sickly shade of greenish yellow, James continued to talk. "I would've been good to you. I wouldn't have bailed on you like he did. He said he was *scattered.* Ha!" He looked pityingly at me. "For a whole year? And you believed him. Why don't you ask him where he really was all that time? Your golden boy lies just like everyone else."

Killian's sharp voice snapped inside my head. *Are you in danger?*

I considered the knife in my side and the half-crazed evil demon-thing working itself up to killing me.

Nah, piece of cake.

Nothing to fear here.

Oh, sure, take your time. I'm good. He's spilling his guts though. Maybe you guys should listen to this instead of blazing in and vaporizing him?

James was lying of course. There's no way Sean would've stayed away unless he couldn't get back. I wasn't even going to entertain that story in my head. So I tried for a calm expression of sympathy and grimaced gently. That was the best I could manage...he leaned over and stroked my cheek with the back of his hand.

He sighed dramatically. "What am I going to do with you now? You're everything I've ever wanted. Would you consider leaving Sean for me? I don't want to kill you like the others."

With a soundless cry of fury, I took a swing at his face and he ducked with a sharp laugh and shoved me back down.

He patted my cheek and boasted, "Yeah, that was me. Your old boyfriend was the perfect distraction. He did some side work for us that put him right in my path. He was already a friggin' time bomb. It was too easy."

He shifted his position so he was sitting on me, but the knife stayed pressed into my side close to my kidney.

Furious, I choked on angry tears as I pictured Lia's pretty face the night she walked away with James. She'd trusted his lies and she was dead. He'd butchered her...because of me.

Mica, we're here watching. Keep him talking; we need to know what he's done.

"Why would you kill all those people? I thought you were...nice last year." I was trying to stall but really just wanted to rip his throat out. Killian better know what he's doing.

"Those humans were just cheap imitations of you. You have to understand. I didn't want to kill them, but I couldn't kill *you*...It wasn't your fault, after all. Your golden boy cheated. He took away your will so you'd stay with him. Oh, I thought I could get you out of my system with some substitutes; but no, that didn't work for me."

He glanced around us, waiting, and I tensed to launch myself up. He grinned and shifted the blade to just below the rune on my chest. I froze again gritting my teeth in frustration. Fine, James, just keep talking, you creep.

They say confession is good for the soul.

"And now, here we are. I can't stand him having you while I settle for second best. He makes me sick. Everything about him makes me want to kill him. And the irony is you think he's so pure, so honest. You only know what he wants you to know."

At my mutinous glare, he sighed and pinched my cheek. "Still loyal, I see. Well, since you won't come to me, I'm going to have to kill you. Sorry love, but that's the only way. You see, I don't like loose ends. Killing you is the best solution. Sean won't have you and I'll be able to move on with my Plan B." He winked at me, his expression boyish. "You were Plan A. But you didn't cooperate so I'm moving on; nothing personal."

"Leave Dani alone!" I ground out from between my teeth. Oh, my audio was back on.

"Sorry, can't do that. She's my little brood mare. My family tree needs some new branches. I'm running short on descendants, and she's pathetically eager to climb into bed with me. My blood is now half and half. Combining this with the human blood will give me a child with the best qualities of all three. He'll be unstoppable."

"Three? I don't get it. You're Primani. You should be happy with that."

His arrogant expression sharpened. "Ah, yes. But you see, Primani have limited powers. Our friends from the underworld now, they have their own special abilities. For instance, did you know they can remain invisible and keep all of their physical capabilities?"

"Invisible? It was you, wasn't it? You hit Sean, didn't you?" I asked for Sean's benefit.

"Oh, you should've seen the look on his face! Priceless! Invisibility is oh so helpful." He looked around and shouted, "I know you're there. You might as well show yourselves. You're not going to attack me while I have a blade against her gut."

Slowly, Sean rematerialized on our right. Killian and Dec appeared on the left. The three of them were in full soldier-mode. Sean would rip James in half and not think twice about it. It was reassuring. They fanned out to circle us but kept a distance when James drew blood and I winced.

Sean called to me, "Are you okay?"

"Oh, sure. I'll heal. No worries," I called back.

"Get the fuck off her, James! Your fight's with me. Leave her alone!"

He made an angry move towards us and James thrust the blade against me causing me to jump in alarm. Sean hesitated and glanced meaningfully at Dec who nodded and palmed his own blade. Dec's face was a thundercloud; his eyes drilled into mine pleading for permission to move in.

Confident in his own power, James ignored Dec and Sean. "Being invisible is great for people watching

especially when they're doing things they shouldn't be."
His voice lowered to a conspiring whisper and he glanced
triumphantly at Killian.

My chest tightened into a knot and my heart began to
pound.

I had a bad feeling about this...

He felt it and raised an eyebrow at me. "Sean, since
I'm killing her anyway, I want you to know that it's really
your fault. If you'd have kept your hands off her, she
wouldn't be in this situation now. You didn't even miss
her while you were *away,* did you?" He stroked my cheek
again and his voice took on a sing-song tone. "Though, to
be honest, she didn't miss you. She can't seem to stay off
her back with any of you three."

Shocked, I lurched up to protest and the blade slid
deep into my side. Clutching at the haft of the blade, I
gasped, "What? I never slept with...them. *Only* Sean!" I
held my breath as I pulled the knife out and the pain
reached my brain.

Killian lunged at James and James whipped the blade
to my throat and just the tiniest pressure sent fresh blood
streaming down my neck. Killian froze and fumed, "Let
her go! You have enough blood on your hands. As it is,
Michael's going to banish you. Don't make us kill you."

James chuckled and gloated, "I'm not worried about
that. You won't get your hands on me as much as you're
dying to."

His eyes swiveled to Killian's face and hardened to
yellow glass. "Your control *is* impressive, but not
limitless, eh? How long did it last once she was free? One
month? Four? Six? How long until you had her in your
bed?"

"What? Shut up, James! You're lying!" Looking
wildly at Killian, I cried, "Shut him up!" I struggled to
get up and James laughed at my attempts to throw him
off.

Sean's face drained to white with twin spots of angry
red blazing from his cheekbones. He glared murderously

at Killian and then me. Killian looked like he wanted to die, his face a mask of misery and anger. Dec bounced from side to side trying not to throw himself onto James and rip his head off.

"It's not true! Sean, believe me, I didn't sleep with Killian!" I had tears running down my face now. "He's evil! Don't listen to him!"

The betrayal on his face was breaking my heart into tiny little chips of ice.

Embracing his own form of twisted self-righteousness, James sneered, "No, you only *slept* when you were too exhausted to go another round. Your denials are so sincere; could it be you don't remember?"

As if pondering a great mystery, he pretended to think deeply. "Now how is it you wouldn't remember the *tender* loving of the most powerful warrior priest ever born? Surely you remember your screams as they echoed off the sides of mountains? I know I do--so delicious! I believe there was a tree once. Those memories helped me pass many lonely nights with great entertainment. Oh, and what about the time during the storm? Seems to me, you rather enjoyed the rush of the rain and the lightning crashing around you--"

"Shut up! That didn't happen! Why are you lying?" I was screaming over him, but his voice was supernaturally loud and echoed around us.

Killian! Tell him it's not true!

Silence.

Killian! Please!

I can't.

My face blanched even more as understanding began to dawn. I closed my eyes against the wave of misery that washed over me. Oh, God. It was true?

How could this be true?

Sean would never forgive us.

Cruelly, James grilled me further. "It didn't happen? Let's ask loyal buddy Declan what he remembers. He lived with both of you. Dec, didn't these two have something going on when Sean was out betraying Mica?"

Dec snapped indignantly, "Sean never betrayed Mica!"

"Ah, but did Mica betray Sean?" James purred.

Dec's face crumbled when he met Sean's furious glare. "Nobody betrayed you! We thought you were dead. They were both devastated and...it just happened. We never stopped looking for you though and we brought you back as soon as we found you. Then it was over."

"Did you ever wonder why it took a year to find Sean? It was because he didn't want to be found. Ask him sometime. It's a great story."

"I'm not stupid, James. I know Mica and Killian were close while I was gone. They don't lie very well. But it's over," Sean ground out between his teeth.

His furious eyes bored into mine, and he passed the blade from one hand to the other. There was no forgiveness in his expression. My heart sank.

I tried to get up but James pushed me back down and snapped at me, "I'm not done! Are you in a hurry to be dead?"

Clearly enjoying ruining our lives, he shifted his focus back to Sean and kept taunting him. He was going to make the most out of his moment in the spotlight before he killed me and vanished. "So you think it's over? An attraction that strong doesn't go away overnight. Look at them now--they can't stop looking at each other. In all fairness, Sean, he did try to be noble. Let's ask Killian about Eden. I'm sure *he* remembers it all. Don't you?" He shifted and adopted a sentimental tone.

"It's really quite romantic, isn't it? Didn't she cry when you made love to her for the last time? You told her it had to be that way because you didn't want to hurt Sean. You said her destiny was with Sean and not you. That was very noble of you. But how did she respond? She cried as if her heart was broken. And you kissed away her tears, didn't you? So sweet, you must really love her to let her go. And when she told you she loved you, you did what?"

He spoke to Killian, but his eyes were glued to Sean's face.

"No, no! It can't be true! Killian, please! Tell him it's not true!" I was crying hysterically now, unable to even form words through my sobs.

I had no memories...no memories of any of this.

Why would James keep lying?

Killian was frozen like a statue, his face a mask of guilty misery that matched Dec's. Sean and I both stared at Killian.

Squaring his shoulders, he said bluntly, "I erased her memory."

My heart stopped and I quit breathing. "You what?"

James shouted in victory, "Louder! Say it louder! We all need to hear how the love triangle ends."

Like a man facing a firing squad, Killian sighed with resignation. "I erased her memory so she would never remember that she...cared for me that way. Her place is with Sean, not me. I did it to protect her, and I won't apologize for it." He turned to Sean and nearly pleaded. "I won't lie to you. I took care of her while you were gone and somehow, I fell in love with her. But I never intended to replace you. Once you came back, it was over for both of us. It was always you she wanted, but she settled for me."

Small black spots danced in front of my eyes and my head spun alarmingly. Probably I was bleeding a lot, but I didn't care right then. I was too stunned to think about it, and if I died, it didn't matter anyway. I didn't remember anything that James said. No memories...nothing. A year of my life was gone...stolen.

What the hell was Killian thinking?

Who was he to decide to erase my memories? We could've just moved on and pretended it never happened. But now thanks to James' little game, Sean will never forgive us and will probably leave me as soon as he can go. Killian and Dec will go too. They have work...purpose.

I'll be alone to pick up the pieces that'll never fit together again.

And Dani? Sweet, innocent Dani...his brood mare?

Evil, disgusting demon!

Why did I feel sorry for him? Killian was right; he was damned. There was no hole deep enough, no pit black enough for his rancid soul!

A phosphorus rage settled in my heart and I gathered the power quietly while he and Sean taunted each other. James continued to gloat over how Sean didn't really have me either. He was replaced by Killian! Oh, how did that feel? He needled and Sean was about to explode. He paced like a panther waiting for an opening.

When Sean slipped around opposite us, I saw my chance. With one furious burst of power, I threw James straight towards Sean. Sean reacted with lightning speed and whipped up the shining silver blade. The blade slid cleanly between James' bones and severed his spinal cord when he collided with Sean. He collapsed on top of Sean with an expression of surprise. Dumping him to the ground, Sean gutted him from pelvis to sternum.

James' eyes went black and his body slowly started to smoke.

Chapter 23: Hoards of Demons Come A' Calling

SNOW FELL ON MY CLOSED EYELIDS and slid in icy rivulets down my cheeks. I lay perfectly still and gathered my *saol* to the deep gash in my side. The tissue knit back together as I healed myself. The tiny cuts on my neck and chest could wait. Hell, they weren't going to kill me, so they could just freaking bleed for all I cared. Once the bleeding stopped, I got to my knees and inhaled a steadying breath.

The wind still howled with the fury of the storm and snow flew like a hail. Trees bent against the gusts and I braced myself. Using one hand to shield my eyes, I rapidly searched for Domino, ignoring the stony glare from Sean. I carefully avoided looking for Killian. That wound wouldn't heal any time soon. Searching with my mind instead of my eyes, I found Domino lying under a bush. She was conscious but didn't want to get up. She shook her head and cried in pain. James must've kicked her. Yet another good reason for him to roast in Hell! I picked her up in my arms and stumbled back to the house.

Just once, I was making a dignified exit.

Back at the house, I healed her quickly and put her into my own car. I clamped off the screaming in my mind and the tears threatening to clog my throat.

Not now, not now.

There's no time for losing it.

I drove as fast as I could through the blizzard. My tires slid all over the road, and I nearly ended up in the trees a few times. Luck was the only thing keeping me on the road. It was still early and Dani's lights were on. It was hard to believe my entire life was just ruined in the

LAURIE OLERICH

course of about 15 minutes. Well, now Dani's world was about to crumble, and I got to deliver the shitty news.

Dani's mother opened the door at the sound of my pounding. Relief lit her face until she saw my bloody clothes. "Oh, my God! Sweetie, you're hurt! Come inside quickly!" She hustled me and Domino into the living room and closed the door with a determined slam of the deadbolt.

"What happened to you?" she demanded. "Did you wreck your car?"

"I don't have time to explain. Where's Dani? I have to see her right now!"

Her face wilted. "She's gone. I hoped she was with you…"

Oh, Jesus! My hands shook as I tried to stay calm. My blood heated and the room faded to white around the edges. Gripping her hands too tightly, I asked, "Is she pregnant?"

Tears slid out of the corners of her eyes and she sank heavily to the couch. "We argued…just today. She tried to keep it from me, but I heard her throwing up this morning. She's…not herself." Dragging me into her arms, she clung for dear life. "Mica, what's happened to my baby?"

In no mood to protect any secrets, I told her the truth. "James is a demon, or was. He's dead and back in Hell where his evil rotten pathetic excuse for a soul can burn for eternity."

Stunned, she blinked at me and sat back. "He's a demon? And Dani's pregnant…" Her eyes rolled back in her head as she slipped into a faint.

"I'm sorry, but I don't have time for this," I whispered to her and slipped out the door.

"Where is she?" I asked the dog riding shotgun. She shrugged and looked out the window. I slid the car into the 7-11 parking lot and dialed Dani's cell phone. No answer. I left a message and hung up. Tapping my fingers

340

anxiously on the wheel, I racked my brain for places she'd go. That she didn't come to me for help screamed warnings inside my head. The old Dani wouldn't have hesitated. This was James' doing. Just for a second, I let the rage take over and surge through me like a flood. With eyes closed to hide the blazing light, I let myself wallow in the hatred I felt for James and smiled at the memory of his destruction...just for a moment.

Okay, enough of that. The clock is ticking. Shoving the anger into a box inside my head, I focused on finding Dani again. I thought she might be at James' place, but I didn't know where that was. Ugh. I was going to have to go back to the farmhouse and ask Dec. I so didn't want to see any of them right now. But Dani's life was more important than my pride. Gritting my teeth, I headed to the house.

The walk from the driveway to the front door usually takes about 20 seconds. Tonight it took me several minutes as I stopped and started a few times before I boldly opened the front door and let myself into the empty hallway. My neck ached with tension as I made my way through the house. As I drifted past the kitchen doorway, Dec called my name and I slowed. I wasn't ready to see him yet.

He walked into the hall and faced me with a grim expression. I stared at him, silent.

I had nothing to say.

"Please don't look at me that way! You're breaking my heart." His voice was anguished and he looked like he wanted to cry. "I'm so sorry!"

"You knew?" I accused with angry tears in my eyes. He flushed guiltily and lowered his eyes.

"How could you do that to me, Dec? I trusted you! More than anybody in my life, I trusted you!"

Grasping my arm, he pleaded with me, eyes huge in his face, "Please understand! I did it for you!"

The sound of my palm cracking against his cheek echoed throughout the silent house. White faced, I yelled,

"I'm sick of hearing that lame-ass excuse! You did it for your brothers! You left *me* hanging out to dry. And after all we've been through, how could you?"

Stung, he tried one more time. "I deserved that. Let me explain--"

I held up my hand to stop him. "Are there any other dirty little skeletons in my closet?" I rounded on him again. "Did I sleep with you too?"

"What? No, I swear! It was never like that between us. You're like a sister to me." He stepped closer with his hand stretched out in a gesture of peace. "Don't be like this."

"If you touch me again, I'll blow your hand off. Get away from me, Dec." I turned and left him standing there.

Shaking with fury and disappointment, I headed straight to our bedroom. I knew he was there and I couldn't put this off any longer. He deserved some kind of explanation...though I had no idea what I could say. Without any memory, I didn't know what happened between Killian and me. Apparently a lot if James was telling the truth. Surely he was exaggerating. Why couldn't I remember? Damn it. This sucks. Opening the door, I took a deep breath and slipped inside.

With his back to me, he dug up a handful of shirts and slammed them down on the edge of the bed. I could tell by the tense set of his shoulders that he knew I was there, but he ignored me and kept packing. My gut clenched and I gripped the door jam with my fingers.

How could he just leave?

He was just going to leave without even talking to me? Or yelling at me? Or anything? Disbelief held me motionless as I stared at him. Domino sat by his backpack and whimpered. His movements were jerky as he shoved clothes into his duffle bag. The clock kept ticking and he ignored me. The silence was unbearable and I began to sweat as a shiver of fear crawled down my spine. The room dimmed as if the lights went out and then came back on again.

Suddenly I was too hot.

My emotions were taking over my powers and I was getting overwhelmed. I tried to calm down, but my blood was racing to the frantic beat of my heart. I was about to have a panic attack, and I didn't know what my powers would do about that. My fists were clenched at my sides and the telltale glimmer of light peeped from inside my palms. I was getting dangerously hot between my own raging emotions and absorbing the cold fury radiating from Sean.

"You're just going to leave? Without a word?" I finally said in a voice too curt to be considered apologetic.

Not deigning to answer me, he grunted something manly and finished packing. Finally turning to face me he stopped and considered his words carefully.

"I loved you. I *loved* you and you betrayed me. There's nothing to talk about. You blew it. It's over."

My eyes burned fiercely and I blinked to cool them. Struggling for control over the building energy, I snapped, "How can you just walk away? We're not going to talk about this?"

His eyes were empty when he looked down at me then. There was nothing in them. No fury, no pain...nothing but an emptiness that broke my heart all over again. He didn't care.

He was over me.

"Wow. I guess I didn't mean that much to you after all." I paused to think. "All that time I grieved for you...we all did. Where were you? Do you want to talk about that? Did you lie about that? Or is that okay since it's you doing the lying? Is Dec in on that too?" My voice rose with each word until I was shouting at him.

"Mica! That's not helping." Killian stepped into the room and put his hands between us. "Sean, come on, man. Let's get out of here. We can figure this out."

Sean and I both snapped, "Fuck off!" and glared at him.

Exasperated and upset, he glanced back and forth at us and tried again. "There's a lot more to this than James' version. Don't let him destroy everything!"

Sean stalked to the other side of the room and I turned my back on Killian to follow. He would just have to deal. I wasn't in the mood for him.

With a growl, Killian dematerialized.

"Sean! Aren't you going to answer me? Where were you?"

Narrowing his eyes at me, he growled, "Why don't you just shut up? There's nothing you can say to me that excuses what you did. You know, I could understand needing comfort, but you actually fell in love with him! How could you do that to me? I should've known better to get involved with a *human*. You're weak and pathetic. Now get out of my way or I'll move you."

Planting my feet, I snarled right back, "Try it." At this point, I was throwing off waves of heat that caused Domino to sniff the air.

With a cold glance, he took a step forward and I braced myself. He kept walking and I stood my ground. My eyes bored into his and I tried not to blow him up. His eyes were ice cold as he looked through me and vanished into the night.

With no outlet for my frustrations, my eyes burned and I stood in the same spot panting with the overwhelming power surging through me. I had to get out of there. Without a backward glance, I flew down the front steps and took off in a sprint. It was snowing, it was dark, and it was dangerous for me to be alone in the woods. I welcomed the fool who attacked me tonight. I would rip them to shreds with my bare hands.

Where were the vampires and werewolves now?

I wouldn't mind running into a few of them...I was furious and I was powerful. And, a little voice piped up in the back of my mind, heartbroken.

Don't forget heartbroken...

By the time I cooled down to a human-ish temperature, I'd run for an hour and came back to the house dripping with sweat and melted snow. I wasn't even breathing hard, but at least my temperature was normal again. Slamming the front door, I stalked through the rooms to see if Dec was still there. The house was empty. Not a sound. No one was here. Now what? Sagging against the doorframe, I fought back a lump in my throat. I couldn't believe my life had just spiraled into the ground.

How had things come to this?

Raphael's prophetic words haunted me as I stared at the stairs. *You will be challenged and you will be hurt. There is great pain on your path, Mica.*

Lucky me...

Wandering listlessly to the bedroom, I took a shower and put on a robe. On autopilot, I checked the doors and windows and set the alarm. Suddenly exhausted, I crawled into bed with Domino. Curling around her soft little back, I cried myself to sleep.

It was late in the afternoon the next day when Domino nudged me awake. Groggy, I peered at the clock. For a minute, I forgot what happened yesterday. Then in a rush of painful memories, it all came flooding back.

Oh, Sean...his empty eyes broke my heart all over again.

I loved you. I loved you and you betrayed me. There's nothing to talk about.

He'd said *loved,* as in past tense, so he no longer loved me. How was that possible? After all we'd been through...I'd never stop loving him no matter what he did. How he could just walk away from me. It was so unfair. I didn't even remember what I did. And where was Killian right now? He couldn't take the heat and ran off to do some big bad ancient warrior crap leaving me here to live with the mess. Shit. I was so through with Primani!

Great warriors? Screw that.

Arrogant bastards.

All of them.

I allowed myself one last good cry and then let anger take over. Anger felt better than self-pity. My head ached and my eyes burned. Rubbing them irritably, I sighed to myself. Okay, maybe too much anger wasn't good either. I couldn't live like this; I hated pain. I needed to get up and get my life back together. To hell with all of them! I didn't need them for anything anyway. They needed *me* now that I had Killian's powers. Feeling smug, I imagined the expressions on their faces when they realized the ramifications of leaving me alone...

Furious, resentful, and very, very strong.

They'd be back.

In the meantime, I had to keep busy so I wouldn't accidently go off and kill somebody. First, I would find Dani. My broken heart would have to take a back seat until I figured out where she was and do something about the demon baby. I had no idea what I could do; maybe I could still talk to Raphael. He'd know.

"How do we find Raphael, Princess?" I asked the dog.

Call him? She wagged her tail helpfully.

Duh! "It's worth a shot! Here goes..." I closed my eyes and called his name.

Silence.

Five minutes later, I announced, "Okay, that didn't work out. Probably he's super busy and can't just pop in here. We'll have to call the penthouse and talk to Alex."

She yawned and rested her chin on her paws. I was boring her.

Someone finally picked up the phone after four rings. My brain froze at the sound of his voice. My tongue stuck in my throat and I couldn't get a word to form.

"Mica? What do you want?" Sean snapped at me through the receiver. "I have nothing to say to you."

That did it.

"I *want* to talk to Alex, if that's okay with you, oh glorious one!"

"He's not here. What do you want?"

"Nothing from you! I need to talk to Alex or Raphael." I hung up the phone and fumed. He's taking pissiness to a whole new level.

Stalking to the bedroom, I cleaned my guns and wiped down my knives...just in case. I had no help now...what on earth was I going to do if this place was attacked? I needed to get out of here and move on. The house was huge, too huge for me. I could go back to my parents' house, but that didn't seem like a good fit for my new life skills. No, Dad wouldn't appreciate my demon hunting under his roof. I guess I could give up demon hunting and just work at the mall...that seemed like a waste of perfectly good ancient powers though.

Stay here or go home.

That was it. I had no other options. I had no savings. I had very little cash. My car was on E.

I had no place else to go. Crap. Tapping my fingers on the counter, I took a deep breath to slow down the panic. There was no reason to rush into a plan. I had time. I guess it wouldn't hurt to give Sean some time to cool off. He was mad, but maybe he'd come around. After all, we didn't have a deadline. It wasn't like I was pregnant or anything. With that thought, my stomach lurched uncomfortably and I broke into a cold sweat. Oh, no, no, no. I AM NOT PREGNANT. Not possible! I just made it to the toilet before I threw up my lunch. Glaring at my nicely-shaped abs, I chanted "I'm not pregnant" inside my head until I'd convinced myself it was true.

Days went by and turned into weeks. The snow was gone and spring was here. I was curled up in a blanket on the patio watching it slowly rain and turn the yard green again. Mother Nature making love to the earth again...I dialed the number, again. No answer, again. Listless, I called Dani's mom. She picked up on the first ring. The hopefulness in her voice cut me to the quick.

"Have you found her?" she asked breathlessly.

"No, I'm sorry. I haven't. I was hoping you had." I'd been apologizing for weeks. What kind of a psychic was I? I couldn't sense my best friend who was in big trouble. I had no idea where she was.

She let her breath out slowly. "It's been a month, Mica. Where could she be?"

"The police have no leads?" She'd filed a missing persons report weeks ago, but Dani had disappeared without a trace.

My working theory was that James had stashed her at his place or with the demons somewhere to wait for the baby to be born. He hadn't counted on dying before he could get back to her. For all I knew, she was already languishing in Dante's second circle of Hell. If James was right, I'd end up there myself someday…lustful wanton that I apparently was.

My stomach gurgled unhappily and I held my breath. Counting down the seconds, it took just 15 of them before I hurled myself to the railing and threw up my dinner. Heaving again, I gagged and spit out what was left of the toast.

I'm not pregnant. I'm not pregnant.

Who was I kidding?

The signs were getting more ominous by the day. I was throwing up every day now and so tired I barely wanted to eat. I chalked both of these things up to stress and depression. If I was pregnant, I had to tell Sean and Sean hated me now. How would he feel about a baby? Would he even want it? Would he believe it was his? It was too much to think about, and I closed my eyes for a minute while I worked up the courage to call him.

"This sucks!" I complained to the universe in general. "How could this happen?" I asked rhetorically and shuffled into the house. Domino rolled her eyes at me and stuffed her nose between her paws.

I needed someone to help me and no one would answer the phone. I called the penthouse again. The phone rang and rang. This time no one answered. There was no answering machine and I slowly pressed the end call button. What was going on down there? I really, really needed help finding Dani and no one would answer the phone.

Didn't anyone care about me up here?

And if I was pregnant, and I wasn't admitting I was, well, that would be another complication. I needed to tell Sean. But none of them would answer the phone. I could be dead for all they knew! Well, let's see them ignore me when I show up in Manhattan. With this thought in mind, I started to pack a suitcase when the hair on the back of my neck stood up.

Something was here.

And it wasn't human.

Frozen with dread, I listened. The sound that reached me turned my blood to ice. Scratching, like claws over stone, sent shivers down my spine like so many fingernails on a chalkboard. Domino went ballistic. The house creaked as the scratching grew louder. A shadow in the window caught the corner of my eye. I whipped around and stared into my nightmares. The demon's reptilian eyes were red with lust as he leered at me through the glass. He was joined by another.

Domino lunged and they clung to the frame and laughed. The sound reverberated inside my head. Stay calm, stay calm. The house was protected, right? No one could get inside and my body was protected by the runes.

Was my mind safe?

I could go crazy with terror alone here in this huge empty house. More and more demons landed on the roof. The scratching continued as they tried to peel the walls apart. My blood ran even colder. Snapping out of the paralyzing fear, I raced to the windows and yanked the curtains closed. Panting with exertion, I stood in the kitchen to catch my breath. Suddenly the glass shook and

I screamed as a pair of fanged demons pressed themselves against the kitchen window. Not bothering with a human façade now, they appeared in their true forms. Black and scaly, their reptilian skin dripped black fluid and shimmered in the twilight.

Their sing-song voices came through the glass.

"We've come for you!"

Evil emanated from the black-scaled creatures as they clung and shouted at me.

With hands over my ears, I ran out of the kitchen to the bedroom. I was trapped here if they got inside. There was no place left to go. I would have to fight them or jump out of the second story window. The screeching of claws grew louder and was joined by the howling of hundreds of demons.

The house was completely surrounded.

I was under siege.

God help me.

High-pitched wailing sent fear skittering over my skin and I broke out in goose bumps and a cold sweat. Even as my mind wanted to shut down, my instincts to fight took over despite the overwhelming odds. Adrenaline pumped through my muscles and my eyes burned. Even with Killian's powers, there was no way I could fight off hundreds of demons.

I would die here and not without pain.

Abruptly the lights blinked off and on like strobe lights. Domino whined pitifully next to me and hid her face with her paws. Oh, you think that's funny, do you? I said to the hoard in general. I can fix that! Tuning them out, I marched to the basement and flipped the breaker for the upstairs lights. Now it was dark but at least the lights weren't blinking.

No sooner had I gotten back upstairs, the pounding started. A thousand fists beat the roof and walls of the house with a tremendous force. The walls vibrated and bits of plaster fell from the ceiling. The glass creaked and rattled within the wooden frames.

I was trapped and there was no way out.

It was only a matter of time.

I crept slowly from one door to the next and all exits were blocked. Every time I got close, the excited squealing on the other side sent shockwaves of adrenaline coursing through my body and I was in an agony of readiness. My eyes glowed with heat and my muscles ached with too much power and no outlet for it. My skin felt barbequed from the inside out. The screaming and clawing and pounding went on for hours. I lost track of time as I huddled in the powder room hoping I'd die quickly.

Maybe they'd be in such a frenzy they'd just rip me to pieces.

Numb with terror, I was only vaguely aware of an aching low in my belly. The aching grew stronger as the night wore on. At some time in the middle of the night, I clutched my silver Primani blade and watched as my power brought it to life. The silver blade glowed in my palm and lit the tiny bathroom with its eerie pale light. Fascinated, I gazed at it and prayed to Raphael for the courage to use it on myself.

"Raphael, I'm sorry, but I can't let them take me again. I'll die first," I whispered with frozen lips to the one angel I thought might still care about me.

Though why he should, I did not know.

The sounds of cracking glass and splintering wood jolted me out of my prayers and I poised for a quick death. The demons went into a frenzy of howling as the glass windows finally weakened and shattered.

The protection was breached.

The shrieking grew louder and closer. The pounding of a thousand feet shook the floors.

They were coming for me.

They were *all* coming.

I clutched the knife to my heart and prayed for strength with my eyes squeezed shut.

It was time.

Suddenly, the tone of the howls changed.

The howls turned to yelps.

Then absolute silence.

He was there, prying the blade out of my clenched fingers, whispering to me.

Raphael.

He'd come. He'd come to help me after all.

I lifted stunned eyes to his blazing blue ones and fell apart with relief.

Gathering me into his strong arms, he carried me out of the tiny little room. "Come, child. This is no place for you." Setting me down on the couch, he said, "You're safe now. The demons are gone."

"You came? You came…"

"Of course I did. I would never ignore your cries for help, little one." He carefully pulled out the pendant and let it rest on top of his shirt. "After all, you left me in possession of your very fine heart. It wouldn't do to let you die before your time."

Forcing a watery smile, I sniffed and tried to get my breathing back to normal. A sharp pain crawled across my belly and I pressed a hand against it with a low groan.

His regal features were calm and, well, angelic, as he met my eyes with a reassuring smile. After a moment, he asked, "You're not okay, are you?"

"I'm fine…no, I'm not fine. I can't find Dani and she's pregnant with a demon spawn. I dreamed that it killed her. I'm terrified for her and I can't find her!"

Shaking his head sadly, he said, "We've looked for her for you. There is no sign of her anywhere. I'm afraid that's not good news."

My heart sank. "Is she dead?"

Nodding, he answered, "It's likely; though the alternative isn't much better. She could be dead or under the cloaking of a powerful demon. That doesn't bode well for her now that her protector, James, is dead."

I sighed miserably at the idea of Dani shivering alone and terrified in a cell someplace. The demons wouldn't care about her at all. They'd keep her alive long enough for the thing to be born. They'd kill her if the birthing didn't. I had to find her before it was too late. Raphael squeezed my hand gently and went to check the house for me. With a wave of his hand, the cracked glass quickly reformed and the doors were reinforced with heavy wood and locks. He murmured a protective prayer as he wandered from room to room and then went outside. He came inside and washed his hands in the kitchen.

I wanted to ask him about Sean and the others. He'd know what they were doing. I was dying to know how they were. I missed Sean and Dec. I missed Killian. They were my family. Sean was more. But I was afraid to ask about them. Afraid to hear that they moved on, that they didn't care about me after all. Dec's sunny smile flashed into my mind and I swallowed the lump in my throat. God, I missed him. But they'd made their choices, and they chose to leave me here unprotected.

"Raphael, I--"

With no little sympathy, he interrupted gently, "Your destiny is nearly fulfilled, Mica. There is more to do yet, but you are nearly at the end of your tribulations. There is more pain to come. Can you bear it? Can you bear it, child, for the rewards that will follow?" His gentle eyes probed mine as he asked if I could stand more pain.

I didn't respond because another cramp, stronger than the earlier one, ripped through my belly and a rush of heat poured out of me. I limped to the powder room to find blood soaking my underwear. Stupidly, I stared at it without understanding. Then the cramps began in earnest and I doubled over against them.

After a few minutes, he tapped on the door. "Mica? What's wrong, child? Are you hurt?"

Gritting my teeth against the cramps, I said bitterly, "Is this part of it, Raphael? Is this one of those tribulations?"

Silence.

The door lock flipped open and he peered inside at me. Taking in my ghostly pale face and the fetal position I was curled into, he raised an eyebrow in question. "What's happening?"

Grimacing again, I spoke softly, "I think I'm losing my baby." Another contraction tightened my uterus and I curled up around my stomach. "I don't know what to do."

There was a lot of blood but surely that's normal? I had no idea…but I was getting worried now. What if I bled to death? That could happen.

Raphael's blank stare suggested he was communicating with someone else. When his eyes cleared, he helped me up.

"Come with me. I can't heal you unless the miscarriage is completed. Your body needs to rid itself of all the effects of the pregnancy or you could get a nasty infection and become sterile."

"What are we doing then?" I asked as he led me to the garage.

"I'm taking you to the hospital. That is, if I can remember how to drive a car."

I was numb. White curtains surrounded me like a cloth-covered prison cell and I was numb. After an excruciatingly long wait, I was showed to an exam room where the only thing separating me from the kid with a busted lip and a gangbanger with a superficial knife wound was a thin white curtain. The uninterested nurse helped me onto the gurney and yanked the curtains closed. I was still sitting here with cramps ripping through me and feeling the tiny life drain away.

So tiny…the little guy never had a chance.

Turning my face against the pillow, I cried for the baby who wouldn't be born and the loss of my fragile connection to Sean. Bitter tears soaked the pillow as I curled around the pain. I would never have his baby now. That dream wouldn't come true. He was gone and the baby was just a dream. There was nothing left of us.

"Hey, bitch. Why don't you stop bawling over there? You're giving me a fucking headache." The gangbanger apparently had a death wish as he complained to me in my fragile state of mind.

Reaching deep inside, I drew on my powers and was about to take his head off when Raphael showed up and gently placed his hands over my own. Shaking his head at me, he said, "Oh, no you don't. I'll handle this."

He pulled the curtain back and murmured something to the waste of oxygen next to me. Turning back to me, he said, "There, that ought to do it."

The man started to cry and sobbed painfully for several minutes before quietly falling asleep where he twitched with nightmares.

Raphael's expression was somber when he turned back to me. The crease between his eyes grew more pronounced as he frowned at me. Gathering my hand in his, he said, "I know you're hurting. It will be over soon and you'll be able to heal."

The nurse chose that moment to pull back the curtain. "Sir, are you her father?"

Smoothly, he said, "No, I'm a good friend. What's going on?"

"We're going to take her to an exam room so the doctor can check her progress. You can wait for her here."

Grimly, he nodded. "Thank you. I'll be waiting."

Raphael's deep blue eyes followed me as they wheeled me away.

Suddenly panicking, I called out to him, "Raphael, don't leave me!"

Trotting to catch up to the gurney, he stopped it with one hand. Completely ignoring the technicians who were tugging at the gurney, he leaned over me. "Listen to me, Mica! I'm not going anywhere. I'll be right here when you come out. Now let the doctors help you."

The exam was excruciating and I retreated deep inside my mind to hide from the pain and embarrassment.

After an eternity, it was done and I could leave. I wasn't so sure I could even walk though. Shell shocked and feeling raw and exposed, I let Raphael lead me limping to the car and take me home. Once in the house, he helped me to the bedroom and waited patiently outside the door while I took a bath and changed into clean clothes. My movements were slow and jerky and I fought back tears of grief and pain.

Inside my head, I still heard the screaming and clawing and cracking glass.

My hand rested on my tender belly and I cried some more. I was an emotional mess. The doctor said the pregnancy hormones were to blame and I'd be less emotional in a few days. Huh, what did he know? He didn't know about the hoard of demons...I wasn't likely to forget them any time soon. I tottered back to the bed and sat down gingerly. Raphael was patiently waiting and smiled encouragingly at me.

"I know I can't heal your heart, little one. But let me at least heal your body so you can rest without pain." He held my hand in his and firmly traced the shape of the rune. A feeling of calm settled over me.

"Thank you, Raphael. You're so much more than I ever deserve. Will you keep this our secret?"

"If that is your wish, then of course I'll keep your confidence. Will you tell him?"

"I...I don't know yet. Maybe...what's the point now?" I turned my face towards the window and stared out into the blackness that pressed in on me.

I couldn't stay here, not now.

He kept his thoughts to himself and focused on healing me. With eyes closed in concentration, he rested his hands over my uterus. The warmth of his healing *saol* flowed like honey across my tender skin and into the deeper wounds and raw edges inside of me. As an added bonus, he brought his fingers to my eyes and stroked the aching muscles around them until my headache was gone.

With a ghost of a smile, he kissed my forehead and told me I would be okay. After he left, I sat on the bed with my head in my hands. I was a mess and wanted nothing more than to leave this house and run far, far away. But I was too afraid to go outside now. What if the demons were waiting outside the protective border?

I was terrified to go to sleep.

The nightmares would be worse than ever before. I was just as trapped now as I was when the demons attacked. Where was my family? I needed them and they were nowhere to be found. Sean apparently was never going to forgive me, so I didn't expect him to show up. What would I say to him now? Hey, I know you hate me, but guess what? I was pregnant with your baby but a hoard of howling demons caused me to miscarry. Oh, and if you guys had been here, maybe they wouldn't have attacked me.

Yeah, it's kinda your fault.

To make things worse, Killian and Dec were MIA too. They all talked about family and protecting me...They sucked...I was so afraid and there was absolutely nobody I could talk to. It all seemed like too much to deal with. I just want out. I don't owe anyone anything. Screw this mysterious destiny of mine. Who decided that anyway? I never wanted to be important. I just want a normal life.

Somehow in my wandering, I'd ended up in front of Killian's room. Raphael was right. He couldn't heal my heart. But there was another who could. Desperately trying to hold down the howl building in my chest, I opened the door and flinched as his scent hit me. Surrounded by his essence, I wanted to yell...I wanted to cry...but mostly, I wanted his steadiness to ground me again.

But he was nowhere to be found and I was floundering, lost.

He'd sworn to protect me, but that was so long ago and he'd failed.

With a howl of pain, I finally cried, "Killian! I need you."

Leaning into the wall, I whispered, "How could you leave me unprotected? You promised."

Suddenly the air pressure shifted and his arms were crushing me against him. "Don't cry, baby. I'm here; I've got you."

"You can't fix this…you can't." Unconsciously, my hand rested protectively over my belly and his eyes widened in growing understanding.

With surprising gentleness, he splayed his warm palm across my belly and peered into my eyes. His mouth twisted with sadness and he whispered, "Oh baby, I'm so sorry." Pulling me onto his lap, he cradled me against him and rocked me to sleep.

Sometime later, I rubbed my eyes and pulled away from him. He came to me. When I needed him, when I called to him, he was there. He'd been there for me…before too. He'd been there too many times for me to count. But he wasn't off the hook yet. Meeting his unfathomable eyes again, I accused, "How could you do it? How could you take my feelings away from me like that?"

"I wanted to protect you. Mica, please understand! You love Sean and he loves you. I don't want to come between you two. It wouldn't be right."

"But that's not the point! I *loved* you! I must have! I didn't just decide to fall in love with you on a whim! You *earned my love*! You deserved it. It's mine to give and mine to take away. You can't just erase my memory and expect that to kill my feelings. Am I as shallow as that? Do you think so little of me?" My voice cracked as my anger dissolved into numbness.

Taking my hand in his, he lightly kissed the rune and it glowed in welcome. "I've never thought more of anyone in my life." My hand tingled against his mouth. I licked my lips and he closed his eyes and sighed. "Do you want your memory back?"

My heart skipped a beat and I inhaled slowly. Did I want that? What would I do with those memories? Surely it would hurt more…but maybe I could put them into perspective if I knew what we'd been through. I looked into his clear blue eyes and remembered the color of the sea. He studied me through his heavy lashes and a part of me recognized the expression from another time. There was something between us and my not knowing didn't change it.

"Yes, I think I do."

"Are you sure? You might regret it and I don't think I can tamper with your memory again. I'm going to need you to kill zombies with me."

Incredulous, I said, "You want me to stay?"

Shocked at my question, he asked, "Why would you ask that? Do you think so little of me?" He reached out to touch my cheek but hesitated. "I'd never abandon you."

With a mind of its own, my palm cupped his cheek and I warmed with pleasure at the contact. "Princess, this is dangerous…" he growled softly against my skin and I looked up.

Something primal in his eyes called to me and I was powerless to resist it. I tilted my face and he pulled me into a rough kiss that left me breathless and hungry. My hands wrapped around his neck and held his mouth against mine.

The world spun and swayed around me but I clung to him, his mouth plundering mine. My feet landed on cool wet grass. The sensation of spinning stopped when I opened my eyes to the wild Irish countryside. With gusts of wind tearing at my clothes, he laid me down on the soft summer grass and shielded me with his body.

Leaning on one elbow, he asked, "What will you do with your memories?"

Drowning in his eyes now, my heart already remembered everything it needed to know. What did I need the memories for? The truth was clear to me.

"You know I can't hide anything from you, right?" He nodded. "Surely you must know how I feel about you? I don't need the *memories* of things we did together. I love you without a history. I love you now."

His breath hitched and he gazed at me for a whole minute before he said, "*None* of my magic works on you! You're not supposed to remember! Why do I bother? Your mind's got its own armor!"

Sitting up, he glanced around us in obvious frustration. Pulling me up to walk with him, he took off across the heather dragging me along behind him. The heather was purple here and waved prettily in the gusty wind. Judging from the clouds rolling in, we were about to get soaked.

Gasping for air, I huffed, "I know you loved me before. I've been inside your head, remember? You've never said it out loud though. Did you ever tell me you loved me?"

Without stopping or looking at me, he replied, "I told you I'd never lie to you and I would keep you safe. Do you remember that?"

"No. So how do I know you really made those promises? Not that it matters since you've kind of broken both of them anyway."

"Funny!" Stopping abruptly, he waved a hand at the rocks below us. "Watch your step."

Black and glistening in the pale sunlight, they beckoned with the promise of certain death. As the waves crashed against them, the foam caught in the gusts of wind and sprayed us with fine droplets. I hadn't noticed before, but the sky was darkening with night and the tide had come in with a vengeance. Fascinated by the force of the waves, I stood as close as I could to the edge. Leaning out, I shivered as the wind caught my hair and lifted it off of my bare neck. The movement was enough to shift my weight and I stumbled outward over the cliff.

"Mica!"

A scream died in my throat as I slammed abruptly into a wall of dirt. Stunned, I looked around to find I'd only fallen about 10 feet onto a small rocky ledge.

"Mica? Where are you?" Killian's worried voice came down from above me.

"I'm okay! Just stuck on a ledge!" I called up to him. I didn't think anything was broken. I moved my arms and legs experimentally and they worked. Several things were bruised though and I was going to be sore...

Killian appeared and squatted to scan my level of brokenness. Smiling a little, he said, "Well, this is a first for you. You didn't hit your face on the way down!"

Blushing, I said, "Ha. Ha."

He said quietly, "Your whole face lights up when you blush like that. It's one of the things I love about you." He shrugged in apology for his lapse into sentimentality.

"Tell me more." I suggested hopefully.

"Greedy wench! I have a better idea."

Without another word, he helped me to my feet and shifted us to the back of the ledge where the rocks concealed a small entrance. Intrigued, I held his hand and let him lead me into the crescent-shaped slice in the stone. It was pitch black inside. I waved a hand in front of me and couldn't see it. Killian held up his hand and faint shimmer of light illuminated the walls.

Impressed, I said, "That's a cool talent. Can I do that?"

He pressed his hand against mine and nodded as mine picked up the *saol* and began to glow. Together, we walked farther into the cave. The sounds of the sea grew indistinct once we moved away from the entrance. The only sounds were of dripping water and my own uneven breathing.

"Nervous, Princess?"

"Did I ever tell you I'm a little claustrophobic?"

"Really? I didn't think you were afraid of anything." He sounded sincere.

Snorting a laugh, I said, "Yeah, right! I'm terrified all the time. I'm just too cocky to back down."

Reeling me in closer, his voice grew husky and he asked, "Are you still afraid of me?" He dragged his palm up the cool skin of my arm to my shoulder and curled it around the back of my neck.

I was acutely aware of every inch of him and my heart was galloping in my chest when another vivid memory crashed through the wall in my mind. He was laughing down at me as a wave pulled me out of his arms in the surf. I sputtered and spit sea water at him as another wave crashed over my head.

I could almost taste the salt.

"What did you see?" His eyes stared intently into my own as he whispered the question.

Wonderingly, I said, "You playing with me in the ocean. When...when was that?"

"It was about eight months after we lost Sean. You had a bad night...the nightmares were keeping you awake again. Dec was gone and you were crying in your sleep. I could hear you and it was tearing my guts out. Some nights, I just sat beside you while you slept. Other nights, I put my arms around you while you cried and you'd fall back asleep. That night was really bad. You were distraught and I was exhausted. I didn't know how to make the dreams stop so I took you away...to Eden."

I slipped my fingers into his hand and squeezed. "And then?"

"Well, you stopped crying almost immediately when your feet got wet!" he joked but then turned serious. "I don't know what possessed me to do it, but I scooped you up and dropped you in the ocean. You were so shocked! And when the first wave crashed over you, you laughed with real joy. You laughed for the first time in ages. The smile on your face hid the sun that day and that's when I knew it was over for me."

"I reached down to help you up and you fell against me in the waves. They pushed you against me and I kissed you. That was our first kiss." His voice had gone soft and sexy and brought goose bumps to my skin.

"I remember." I wrapped my arms around his neck and kissed him, his fascinating mouth molding to mine, our tongues dancing, probing. This time the memories all flooded back in a rush. My head swam and I burned for him. Dragging my mouth away, I was overwhelmed by the emotions I'd felt when I'd been with him before. We were intensely in tune with each other. He *knew* me and I knew him. There was a sense of history between us. Our minds were joined even more completely than our bodies had been.

My intuition was working overtime. I sensed the emotions racing through his brain now, in the present, and remembered them from the past. They hadn't changed. The intensity was staggering and I was humbled by his willingness to sacrifice his happiness for mine. He would give me up to keep me safe. He would give me up to keep me happy. He would walk away if that's what it took to give me peace. These things I knew without the memories to show me. I knew him, inside and out. I might not have the actual images in my head, but I knew what magic there was between us.

"I would die for you. But let's hope it doesn't come to that," he answered my unformed question. "Now do you see why I don't tell you I love you? You already know." Skimming his lips over my ear, he murmured, "Can you ever forgive me for taking your memories? I need your forgiveness."

Nearly hypnotized by the sound of his voice, I put one palm flat against his chest and pushed him back. "You're not off the hook yet! You left me alone to face Sean. You walked away and left me all this time. You swore you'd protect me but you left me alone. Those demons would've killed me. I lost the baby! If it weren't for Raphael, I'd be ripped to shreds and we wouldn't be having this conversation."

Frowning, he said, "What do you mean 'alone?' Where was Sean?"

Barking a laugh, I scoffed, "Gone! He bolted immediately. He doesn't love me anymore and he'll never speak to me again. It's been over a month and not a word." I added more softly, "His eyes were dead. He didn't even look at me. He told me I'm weak and pathetic and he's sorry he got involved with me. It's over: For both of us."

Growling low in his throat, he asked urgently, "And Dec? Where was he?"

My lip quivered at that. "He left with Sean. You *all* left me alone." With a burst of fresh anger, I punched him in the arm. "You and Sean dragged me into this world of yours. I didn't ask to have powers! And then you left me alone to fend for myself. No one even checked to see if I was alive. You're lucky I didn't blow up the Adirondacks!"

Rubbing his arm ruefully, he said, "You weren't supposed to be alone. I...well hell, I assumed, that Sean would stay there. I left to give you time with him...so you could work things out. I thought I was doing the right thing. I'd never imagine him leaving you alone. I don't know how he could do that."

"Huh. Well, he wasn't in a forgiving mood that night. He stuck around long enough to pack and then I was stuck holding off hoards of demons alone. You guys all suck. I should hate you."

"But you don't."

"That doesn't mean you don't suck."

Holding back a grin, he ran his fingers delicately over my rune again, sighing with satisfaction when the twin runes glowed brightly in the dim light of the cave. "I'm here now and I'm not going anywhere. I'll say you were right, just this once, and apologize for leaving you alone." He smiled at my surprise. "Yeah, I said it. Don't get used to it. Probably you'll never be right again!"

Suddenly serious, he held my chin and kissed me gently, chastely. Leaning his forehead into mine, he said, "I'm really, really sorry for not being there to protect you. You should never have to face that kind of evil. I would give my right arm to turn back time and erase those memories. I will *never* let that happen again. As of now, we're starting over."

His words were so sincere; his emotions close to the surface. He felt my pain and he felt guilty over it. I knew his heart had been in the right place. He'd done what he thought was right. He'd been sure Sean would stay with me because that's what he would have done if the roles were reversed. But he didn't count on Sean's pride, I guess. I would take his apology and his promises and believe them as much as I believed in him.

Leaning against him, I kissed him back. "It's a deal. Fresh start."

He held me close in relief and finally backed away from me. "Come on, something's here that we need to find. We'll have make-up sex later." He tucked my pouting lip back into its natural position. With improvised flashlight, he dragged me further into the cave.

In a naturally widened room, the light bounced off of glittering walls. The tiny crystals sparkled softly against the faint light of Killian's outstretched hand. With a small cry of pleasure, I looked around in amazement.

"Look!" His voice was suddenly loud with excitement. I jumped.

Dropping my hand, he strode over to what was unmistakably a small stone altar carved into a niche. A misshapen lump of rock sat in the middle of it. It looked like nothing to me but he got very excited. Reverently dropping to his knees, he bowed his head and murmured words of the priesthood. The unfamiliar language no longer surprised me. I didn't know the words themselves, but I knew what he said. He'd asked permission to approach the altar and use whatever we found in this cave to fight the evil that walked on the earth.

Apparently permission was granted.

A loud creaking groan came from the niche and a small shower of rocks peppered the floor as a hidden room was revealed.

"Holy shit!" I exclaimed delicately.

"Really?" He frowned in disapproval at my choice of words. "This is a holy site."

"Sorry...it slipped out." I was chagrined. It was, after all, a very old site. I should know better. "Can I come too? Is it safe for me?"

He was already entering the room and grunted his approval. I rolled my eyes at his distraction. Like Indiana Jones, he was. I picked my way over the scrabble of rock and hovered in the doorway. I was afraid it would close behind us and entomb us inside. Shuddering at the thought, I stayed put. Wild horses couldn't drag me into that room. The interior was smoother than the other parts of the cave. It seemed like something had melted the stone.

"What happened to the walls?"

"Fire. You see, it's like glass. Like mica."

"No, it's not. Mica is layered and flexible. You're mixing up your rocks."

"Huh. When have you been flexible?" He mumbled absently as he poked through stone urns and a couple of crumbling containers. "Ah!"

Holding a small bound book close to his face, he peered at the writing and then tucked it into his pants. Okay...guess that's a keeper. Next he moved on to another little section of shelves dug into the rock. It was hard to tell if they were natural or carved out by some prehistoric temple builder. I couldn't tell from where I was standing. He was very thorough though and checked every inch of the room.

"I'm fascinated just watching you," I observed with some amusement. "You're like a detective."

"Hush! I'm thinking."

At last he found what he was looking for. It was another knife. But this one wasn't silver. He held the faintly glowing blade in front of his chest and murmured a few words to claim it.

"Sgaine a dia seanagh, a dia sgaine ten."

The blade sprang to life and glowed hotly in his fist like freshly-poured gold. Its light cast shadows over Killian's face transforming him into something pagan and wild. The last shreds of civilization melted away and I saw him as he must've been thousands of years ago. His eyes were distant as he listened intently. I strained my ears and caught the faintest note. Like the last clear note of a ringing bell, the blade sang in response to Killian's touch.

I understood how it felt.

With a tiny smile at me, he tucked the now cool blade into his belt and walked over to the doorway. "This'll work. Let's go."

"What? Where are we going? We're done already?"

Patiently, he pointed out that I was claustrophobic and this was a very small cave. "Where do you want to sleep? Do you want to go back to the house?"

"Do you think they'll come back?"

His eyes clouded with regret. "No idea. But we have to live someplace. Domino needs a human and I can't leave you there alone. Sean will have to deal with it."

"So we're going to be alone at the farmhouse?

"I'm not planning to move into your bedroom, if that's what you're afraid of."

"This is serious."

"I'm being serious. You're right about us getting you into this. If it wasn't for us, you'd be getting ready to graduate college and start your life. You'd be marrying some dorky IT guy and popping out 2.5 kids. Good or bad, that's not your life now, and I can't leave you alone to deal with that. I won't."

His voice softened and he promised, "I won't pressure you. We can stay strictly hands-off and focus on getting the zombies under wraps. I'll be busy enough with that and finding *Sgaine Dutre*. I'll need to be gone a lot but I'll be back at night so you won't be alone in the house. I'll be there to chase away the nightmares, babe."

That was a huge relief. They would be back with a vengeance unless I had some magical assistance.

"Don't you think Sean's going to assume we're sleeping together? He's just going to get madder."

He crossed his arms in a typical Killian pose. "He can come back whenever he wants. It's his choice, don't you think? If he really loves you, he'll swallow his pride, forgive you and come back. You'll have a squeaky clean new conscience and you can live happily ever after with my blessings. I'm warning you though. If he doesn't come back in a reasonable amount of time though, all bets are off."

Chapter 24: Road Trippin'

THE LOGS CRACKLED and popped as the small fire consumed them. Holding my hands out, I rubbed them together and let the heat soak in. My fingers were cold and stiff in the chilly dawn air. I could warm them up the supernatural way, but I liked the way the fire smelled. The sun wouldn't be up for a few more minutes and I breathed in the fresh air with a sigh of pleasure. There is something to be said for roughing it. The earthy smell of the woods and the chatter of early morning birds were magical. On the other hand, there was no bathroom...

"Why are you sitting on a mountain top?" a familiar voice interrupted my musings and startled me.

Standing slowly, I eyed him warily, not sure if I was glad to see him or not. It had been months without a word. "Dec. What are you doing here? Has someone died?" I asked evenly.

"Yeah, Sean, a little." His voice sounded strained and I glanced at his eyes. "Not that he'd admit it."

He stood just opposite me with a hesitant, lopsided half-smile that fell short of reaching his eyes. His hair was cut short and his cheekbones were very pronounced. He wasn't eating. He didn't look well. The beautiful blue eyes that captivated me were sunken and hollow with purple smudges emphasizing his pallor.

No, he didn't look well at all.

Grinding my teeth to keep from throwing myself against him in a hug, I met his eyes and raised a shoulder in a shrug.

"He's got a funny way of showing it, now doesn't he? All this time, no word at all. He's done, Dec." I twisted away so he wouldn't see the pain in my eyes. Sean wasn't dying--he was moving on.

"Are you okay?" he asked softly. "I've been worried about you."

As silent as a panther, Killian slid out of the trees. "She's fine, Dec. Safe and sound now." His lips were tight as he considered Dec's question.

Dec's expression hardened and he stood a little taller. He'd aged since I'd seen him last. "Why are you here, really? Just to ask if I'm okay? That's a little lame, considering you ignored my calls for help when I needed it." Killian stood close to me in a show of support. Unconsciously, he laid his hand against the small of my back. I was grateful for the gesture.

"What are you talking about? You didn't ask me for help." He seemed confused about that.

Snorting a rude laugh, I said, "Oh, sure. I only called the penthouse a hundred times and none of you bothered to call me back or check on me."

He started to respond and Killian held up a hand. "Has something else happened? Is it Sean?"

Dec flinched. "More bodies have gone missing from funeral homes around The City. Alex wanted to know if you've got any new ideas about the zombies."

All business now, Killian responded, "How many bodies are we talking about?"

"Twenty or so. The police are freaked out and the news says there's a satanic cult at work."

Killian snorted with derision. "They're partly right. I don't have much news for Alex. We're tracking the zombie we sent home but he's still wandering around. That might be a dead end." He paused and added, "Mica and I had some good luck and found *Sgaine Dutre*'s brother blade. It was a useful find. It'll come in handy when we find the zombies."

"What does that mean?" Dec asked.

Smoothly slipping the golden blade from its sheath, Killian palmed it and showed it to us. Its haft was unornamented except for an irregularly-shaped red stone set deeply into it. It had an oval shape, almost like an eye. I had the strangest feeling that it was watching me and stepped away from its view.

Noticing my movement, he nodded approvingly. "Yes, Mica, it sees you. That's one of its powers. It acts as my eyes and will search for its brother blade even while I'm asleep."

Intrigued, Dec peered more closely and forgot he was mad at Killian. Like a boy with a cool new toy, he grinned and asked, "Does it have a GPS for its brother too?"

Laughing in spite of the earlier tension, Killian said, "It'll tell me where *Sgaine Dutre* is and lead us to it. It should be able to undo the magic that reanimated the zombies. I'm not 100 percent sure on that though. I've only got history to go on. I've never used the blade before."

A chilly wind ruffled Dec's hair and he gazed longingly towards me across the fire. His dimples were in hiding and my own smile refused to make an appearance. I had too many questions for him but there was no point in asking. I had no claim on Sean.

Killian touched my arm in question and nodded towards my backpack. Yes, it was time to get moving again. We had things to do. I dipped my head in answer and Dec caught our silent communication and frowned.

"Mica," he began uncertainly. "Are you sure about this?" He rolled his eyes towards Killian.

"Dec, don't. There's nothing to say. What's done is done. I'm only sticking around to find Dani. After I find her, no matter what happens, I'm leaving all of you. I can't live like this."

Stunned, he spun around to Killian. Killian just shrugged and Dec's shoulders slumped with defeat. "I see. Okay, then." After a few more words with Killian, he left the way he came.

"I'm surprised at you, Princess."

"I don't know what you mean." I paused in the middle of banking the small fire.

"Why won't you forgive him? You love him." His eyes swept over my face and rested on the stubborn tilt of my chin. "Will you punish him forever?"

Refusing to meet his eyes, I turned my back to him and ignored the question. Moving with lightning speed, he was in front of me. Gently, he pulled me upright and forced my chin up so I met his eyes. His steady gaze and disapproving frown worked havoc on my conscience.

He doesn't deserve this. You know that.

I *was* being particularly hard on Dec. I knew that in my heart. I had forgiven Killian. I'd forgiven him out of necessity and out of desire. I needed him to find Dani. But more than that, I didn't feel betrayed anymore. Yes, I'd been furious with him for erasing my memory. Sure, the plan completely backfired...but at least he meant well. Dec, on the other hand, kept secrets from me that left me looking stupid and dishonest as I protested James' accusations. Sean must really think that I played him, and that's what really hurt the most.

In hindsight, I was wrong to hide my relationship with Killian. We were so relieved to have Sean back that we never considered staying together. We just agreed to let things go. We should have told him but the time never seemed right and it didn't seem important since it was over. If I had told him, he could've dealt with it in private which would've left him with his dignity. But I didn't.

Bad decision.

After Killian erased the memories, I had no choice but to deny James' accusations. I believed myself...That vehement denial left Sean feeling more betrayed...I wasn't ready to forgive Dec yet. The wounds were still too raw. Dec was always my healer, but he'd caused some of those wounds and I couldn't forgive him for hurting me. His deception turned my world upside down. Out of the three of them, Dec had always been the one I trusted the most. His boyish smile and warm eyes healed my spirit but I didn't trust them now.

Are you going to answer me?

Irritably, I snapped, "It won't be forever! I'll die before then!" I slung my pack over my shoulder and headed down the trail. Domino trotted next to me and grinned back at my warrior shadow.

As I picked my way down the trail, I let my mind drift. It had been a month already since Killian and I went back to the farmhouse and he'd kept his word. He treated me with great care and respect and hadn't tried to touch me or influence my feelings. He'd promised to give Sean time to come back to me and he'd done his best to leave me with a clean conscience. His eyes followed me though and I knew he wondered what I was thinking. Surprisingly, he didn't pry.

We'd fallen into an easy routine. I went to work at the mall and he traveled on his Primani missions. Most evenings I was home alone and went to bed in the darkened house. I never heard him come in, but he was always there when I woke up in the morning. Since Raphael's visit, the house had been demon-free and I was finally able to sleep through the night. Miraculously, the nightmares had stopped. I strongly suspected, but had no proof, that Killian was affecting them.

Yesterday, I was working out in the basement when I sensed someone rematerialize upstairs. Pausing in mid-kick, I realized it was Killian. He was home early. Heavy boots thunked on the steps and I finished my move and gracefully bent over in a stretch as he poked his head inside the room. He had a full view of my butt and I caught a frustrated groan inside my head. Peering up from between my legs, I enjoyed the rather nice view of his long hard body poised on the stairs.

Black pants, black t-shirt, hard muscle. Yum!

Straightening, I blushed slightly at the direction my thoughts had taken and he smiled knowingly. I blushed all the way to my toes and he laughed quietly. I was

dripping sweat but goose bumps popped up all over me
when I caught the smoldering desire in his unguarded
eyes. My own ignited and my body followed.

Time's up. All bets are off.

Frozen like a mouse with a cobra, I could only stare
at him while my heart beat like a butterfly in my chest.
He crossed to me in three strides. Not touching me, with
palms just a hair's breadth from my bare skin, he waited
for me to stop him and the clock ticked loudly.
Hypnotized, I took a single step towards him and he
spanned my waist with his hands but still waited as his
thumbs stroked my skin. Deep inside of me, something
stronger than instinct ripped my control into pieces and
the ice began to melt.

Voice shaking, he said, "Tell me to stop. If you don't
want this, tell me..." His hands shook as they ran down
my back and gripped my hips. I was melting into the
floor.

Finding my voice, I whispered, "Make me
remember. I need to remember." My heart pounded like a
drum and my head filled with visions of flame and stone
as he glued his mouth to mine.

"Killian..." I whispered to the forest, my heart
thudding against my ribs as yesterday's memories washed
over me.

"Come, nymph, there's something I want to show
you," he said against in my ear.

Taking my hand, he led me down a steep rocky
crevice that led to a clear pool of spring water. Going
back up for Domino, he rematerialized with her and sat
her down carefully. The pool was lovely. Black and grey
granite lined the pool and glittered in the early morning
sun. Two tiny ferns perched precariously at the edge,
their brilliant green an artistic splash against the grey.

"Oh! It's perfect!"

"Perfect for what, witch?"

"For casting spells, of course!" I teased. While slipping a bit, I managed to lean forward and scoop a handful of water. It was sweet and tasted of the earth.

"Are you happy, Princess?"

Suddenly serious myself, I thought for a minute before I answered. Bringing his knuckles to my cold lips, I kissed them and released his hand. It slid to my chest and his fingers toyed with my locket. The locket responded happily with a faint glow and a deep hum. It *knew* him. *I* knew him.

Instead of answering the question, I said, "I remembered everything last night. After we made love, I couldn't sleep."

"I know," he murmured.

"I lay there for hours...just remembering us...remembering you."

Cautiously, he asked again, "Are you happy?"

"Yes."

"So what you told Dec...You're not planning to leave us?"

"Are you kidding me? After last night, you'll be lucky if I let you go to the bathroom by yourself! You were amazing!" I joked and then blushed as my words sunk in and his mouth dropped open.

Grinning arrogantly, he boasted, "Oh, anytime, babe, anytime."

As we climbed back down the mountain, I mused that there was so much more to this complicated creature than I would probably ever know, but I understood him more and more every day. We ended up on this mountain because I'd announced I needed some fresh air and he brought me here. When I asked why he chose this place, he shrugged and said he knew I was a creature of the forest. We'd climbed to the top, set up camp, and spent the night under the stars wrapped in each other's arms. The night was heavenly. This morning, it was back to civilization but I felt strong and ready. Maybe I was a creature of the forest.

He drove the SUV and I relaxed against the seat absently watching the scenery zip by. At some point during the drama of our days, the seasons had changed and spring had finally come. The sky was a clear, bright blue today. Trees were dressed with shiny new leaves and the snowmelt filled the rocky crevasses and poured down the sides of cliffs. It was a wild land and I entertained myself by imagining I was really a wood nymph. Frolicking throughout the ferns and sycamore trees…wearing some strategically-placed flora…now all I needed was a satyr…I peeked under my lashes at Killian. He'd look delicious in a fig leaf…hmm. He clamped his lips together and firmly shook his head. Ok, then, no satyr…maybe Dionysus?

"He's the god of wine, not of wood nymphs."

I gave up my fantasy and enjoyed the silence and lingering scent of wood smoke.

After a little while, Killian reached over and took my hand. It was a comfortable gesture and my hand fit perfectly in the curve of his. He absently stroked my palm and my fingers curled in response.

"Can I ask you a question?"

Interest peaked, I nodded.

"Are you interested in going on a mission with me? I need to go away for a few days and I don't want to leave you. I understand if you don't want to go. It'll be dangerous. There *will* be demons, and it might be too soon for you." His eyes unconsciously dropped to my lap. He was still worried about the miscarriage.

"Do you think I'm strong enough to be your backup?"

"You're tough, babe. I know I can count on you in a fight. That's not the issue. I'm more worried about your emotional state and whether you're ready to face demons again. Can you handle them?"

Sighing, I chose my words carefully. "I can't undo what's happened. The fact that Raphael saved my life and brought you back to me tells me that my work with you isn't done. Like it or not, I'm still needed. I can't walk away from that. I'll kill as many as you want me to."

"That's my girl."

"And Killian..."

"Yeah, babe?"

"Thanks. Thanks for being here...for giving me space. And...thank you for caring about the baby. It couldn't be easy for you knowing it wasn't yours."

Without responding, he steered the truck over to the shoulder and put it into Park. Turning to me, he said mockingly, "Don't put me up on too high a pedestal, Princess. I'm no saint. I want to strangle Sean for leaving you alone to deal with being pregnant and then losing the baby. That was his responsibility and he fucked it up." He rolled his shoulders and continued gruffly, "All I did was come in after the fact and help you deal with the loss. I'm no hero."

"But you--" I started to argue and he cut me off.

"But I *grieved* with you. Is that what you wanted to say?" Taking my face in his hands, he kissed me carefully. "Yes, I did. I still do. That tiny little baby was part of you and it's gone. I would never take that lightly."

"Detroit? Michigan? What on earth is in Detroit?" I exclaimed hours later.

"Dagin's second lab. I've been all over New York and Vermont. There's no sign of *Sgaine Dutre*. I talked to Alex this week and he told me there's a rumor about a second lab. We should go check it out."

"Whatever you say..." I was game for a road trip. A nice long car ride would be great. It would give us time to be together without interruptions.

Later that afternoon, we pulled into my parents' driveway and parked. Domino was sulking and had her wet nose pressed firmly against the window with her butt in my face. She was not happy with me.

"Why don't you wait here?" I suggested to Killian.

My plan was to run inside quickly and drop Domino off before my parents could ask any nosy or otherwise unanswerable questions. Like, where is Sean? Who is that scary-looking big guy driving that SUV? Where'd that SUV come from? Why are you going to Detroit? What happened to your engagement ring? And there were so many more possibilities...I had no answers to give them today. Oh, one, maybe. My engagement ring was sitting alone in the bottom of my jewelry box.

The rap of knuckles against the driver's side window caused us both to jump and whirl around. Ugh. This was not good. My dad was peering interestedly into the truck. So much for running in and out without them seeing Killian...Mentally smacking myself on the forehead, I decided that offense was the best defense and boldly got out of the truck dragging Domino behind me.

"Hey Dad! You didn't have to come outside!" I trotted over and gave him a nice daughterly hug while attempting to steer him away from the truck.

Digging in his heels, my father played along with my forced good humor. He took a second to adjust his sunglasses and said. "Oh, it's okay, hon. I don't mind coming out to meet *you*." Peering over my shoulder, he stiffened and drew himself to his full height.

At 6 feet 3 inches and 220 pounds of solid muscle, Killian towered above my modestly proportioned father. At the moment, he stood loosely in a non-threatening way giving off his best 'I'm not dangerous' vibes and actually smiled pleasantly at my father. Cringing for the fallout, I introduced him.

"Dad, this is Killian. He's a good friend of mine." Killian's fingers dug into my side just a wee bit and I bit the inside of my cheek to keep from laughing.

He offered his hand to my father who seemed confused about why his seemingly normal offspring kept showing up with mercenaries draped over her like accessories. To be fair, he'd just gotten used to Sean...and that took him four years. Killian was a bit more…well, *everything;* taller, harder, stronger, bigger, intimidating and intense.

At least he'd shaved…

Trust my father to make an awkward situation even worse. He shook Killian's hand and asked pointedly, "So are you a friend of Sean's too?"

"Dad!"

Feigning innocence, he asked, "What? I'm just trying to connect the dots here."

Killian smiled easily and answered, "Yes sir, as a matter of fact, Sean and I have known each other for a long time. And now Mica works with us. She's been a great help with some of our tougher projects so I'm taking her with me to meet some out of town clients. She's really good at her work. I know you must be very proud of her."

Having absolutely no idea what kind of work I did, my dad had no choice but to agree. "Oh, sure I am. She's always been a hard worker."

"Well, would you look at the time? We're going to hit the traffic if we don't get moving! Thanks again for keeping the pooch for a few days. I'll call you!" With a last hurried kiss on the cheek, I left my dad standing in the driveway and practically sprinted to the truck.

Killian raised a hand in farewell and smoothly pulled the truck onto the road again. Shaking his head with amusement, he glanced over at me and said, "You *are* a witch. You know that? I can't believe I just played nice with your father…I'm going soft."

Hooting with mirth, I bounced across the console and kissed his cheek. "And I thank you very much for that! It didn't kill you to be nice, did it?"

Scowling, he said, "No, but don't get used to it. Humans are annoying. You're the only human I plan to be nice to. And that, witch, could change if you get me killed in Detroit!"

We were taking the 401 through Ontario from New York to Detroit. The speed limit was higher and it was a straight shot. It would take about 10 hours to get there. During the drive, we finalized our plans for the op. I busied myself with getting the location coordinates together and plugging them into the GPS and my memory, in case the truck blew up or something. Our weapons were concealed under a customized floor panel to avoid any delays at the border. I had brought extra magazines, just in case.

I dozed off halfway across Canada and was dragged back to consciousness by the whispered argument going on beside me. Intrigued, I kept my eyes closed and listened shamelessly.

What was *he* doing here?

"I had no choice! She couldn't handle the truth!" Sean's cold tone set my teeth on edge.

"You don't know her at all, do you? She's stronger than that." Killian defended me.

Sean snorted with derision, "Trust me, she wouldn't understand this."

"It doesn't matter anyway. You blew it."

"Oh, yeah? And are you taking my place *again*? How does it feel to be her second choice?"

Killian's voice was relaxed as he said, "Careful, brother. I can still put you in the ground."

"Whatever, man. I have to get back. I'll see you in Detroit."

Minutes passed. My eyes were closed but my mind raced with questions. What was he doing here? What was he talking about?

"You can pretend if it makes you feel better, but I know you heard us." Killian's voice was kind and he glanced sideways at me.

"What did he want?" I asked.

"Alex sent him to meet us in Detroit."

"Is that necessary? Do we need him? Three's an odd number for the team. It's unlucky."

"Unlucky?"

"Yes, odd numbers are unlucky. New rule."

"It'll be fine."

It was after dark when we pulled into a roadside motel off a highway near Detroit. Wow. This place was a dump. I questioned Killian's sanity for even pulling into the parking lot. There were bars on the windows of the convenience store across from the motel and the streetlights were mostly broken. A couple of young men lounged on the sidewalk in front of a liquor store, their eyes following our every move. Next door, a skinny black girl in a ripped miniskirt and a sequined halter draped her bony body against the doorway of a check cashing storefront and boldly stared at Killian's crotch.

Dream on, baby girl. It ain't gonna happen.

Doing my best to blend, I acted like I lived there and shuffled to the motel lobby. My nose hairs curled in on themselves when Killian pushed the door open and waved me inside. The lobby walls were yellow with old cigarette smoke and the air smelled like unwashed dishes and mildew. Gagging a little, I backed up in full retreat from the stench and he steadied me with a hard grip on my elbow.

"What's wrong?" He stiffened automatically and scanned the lobby for threats. Nonplussed by the lack of armed men or scaled demons, he asked again, "What's wrong with you?"

Holding my nose, I mumbled, "It stinks in here. I think I'm going to puke."

"You're turning green around the edges. Is it that bad?" He inhaled deeply and coughed with revulsion. "Okay, it's not great. Do you have another idea?"

Backing out into the relatively fresher air of the parking lot, I inhaled gratefully and suggested he look for something better. "I can drive if you're tired. I don't mind."

"I've got it. Let's go." We headed back to the relative safety of the SUV only to find it under close scrutiny by three men wielding tire irons.

They straightened in challenge until they got a good look at Killian, then they got a little less cocky. I was always impressed by the transformation when he dumped his human façade. His size and merciless eyes left no doubt he would rip them to pieces. I swallowed a grin and unsnapped the holster for my Sig. I tensed and waited to see how this would play out.

Who would blink first?

One of the men, the largest of the three, stepped forward with a calculating gleam in his eye. He gripped a tire iron in one hand and tried to intimidate us by smacking it against his palm. I rolled my eyes. Amateur! Killian cracked his knuckles. The other two fanned out forming a wedge that cut us off from the truck. I lifted the Sig and the man closest to me hesitated. He couldn't have been much older than me. His face was young but he had the hard eyes of someone who'd lived a hundred years already. His dirty brown hair hung limply and his face was spotted with scabs. Desperate brown eyes fixed on my backpack.

What had brought him to this? Drugs? Hunger?

It was hard to say, but he was hungry now and judging by the intensity of his stare, he was willing to kill me to keep the truck. Well, today wasn't going to be his day. I wasn't dying so some punk junkie could take my wheels.

Killian's voice came to me. *Put your silencer on the Sig.*

With a practiced motion, I withdrew the silencer from my cargo pocket and screwed it onto the Sig. The punk next to me sucked in a breath and took a step back. Killian pulled out his own silenced Sig and shoved the slide back with an ominous metallic click. The men froze and looked at their leader.

Killian said, "Walk away before bad things happen." He leveled the gun squarely at the man's chest. I did the same to the man on my right.

"Don't even think about it," I said to the third man. "I can hit you before you can reach me. I'm just that good."

It didn't take them very long to make a decision. The leader put out his hands in a gesture of surrender and backed away. "Hey man, take it easy! We didn't mean no harm; we was just lookin' at it."

He backed away and his two buddies followed him. We turned in their direction with weapons raised until they were well away from the truck. Without taking my eyes off of them, I went to the truck and climbed inside. Killian planted his feet next to driver's door and stood tensely until they were well across the street. Sliding into his seat, he sat the gun down on the console and started the engine.

"See? I told you humans are annoying," he said with a very tiny grin.

"You're horrible! Angels are supposed to like people."

Shaking his head, he said seriously, "That's not in *my* contract."

Letting it go with a grin of my own, I checked for a tail as he drove down the road in search of more friendly parking lots.

"It's clear," I announced after a few miles. "Can we just stay at the Hampton Inn? I saw a sign for one and it's coming up in a few more miles. They have free breakfast!"

We found it a few minutes later and checked into a third story room with a view of our truck. It was a nice room as far as hotel rooms went. Cream-colored walls and cherry furniture gave the room an upscale feel. There were two double beds and a flat screen TV. Groaning with pleasure, I stretched across one of the beds and flipped on the television. The local news was running and I nearly swallowed my tongue. No way! Killian scowled as the anchorman finished the story.

"Shit."

"Yep."

I patted the bed and he angrily dismissed the invite in favor of pacing and swearing in a variety of languages. I think I caught Latin and possibly Gaelic in the stream of words coming out of his mouth. Was that French? Finally, I gave up and burst out laughing. He paused in mid-pace and gawked at me like I'd lost my mind.

"What's funny? I don't see anything funny about the possibility of zombies in Detroit!"

That reminded of the movie "Shawn of the Dead" and I dissolved into fresh giggles. It was perfect! Sean would be here to fight zombies...his accent wasn't quite British, but it was close...

"You've lost your mind, haven't you?" Killian frowned over me like the warrior angel he was. The glower was wasted on me and I pulled him down to the bed and kissed him until he gave up scowling and his eyes burned with something other than fury.

"Now, isn't that better?" I asked with my lips pressed against his throat. Nuzzling his neck, I moved to his ear and purred, "Don't look now, but your blade is happy to see me."

Startled, he stared at the subtly glowing golden blade. Turning away from me, he fingered the stone with eyes lowered in concentration. Fascinated, I watched as the tiny red stone burned hotly in the haft. His seductive mouth moved in silence as he murmured the words to see what the blade would show him. I couldn't help myself; I wanted badly to kiss his full lower lip right where it curled naturally into a smile. Instead, I showed great restraint and contented myself with remembering how it felt against my own. Damn zombies were ruining my love life!

He hopped up with clear eyes and said, "Got it! Let's go."

"Wait! Where are we going?"

"Manhattan. Come on, get moving. If we leave now, we can be there in a day. Sean can check out the zombie rumors here. I've got a line on *Sgaine Dutre*. That's more important." He was pacing again with an eagerness that was just a little insulting.

Mentally, I was wiped. I was *not* in the mood to drive 15 hours to Manhattan tonight. Knowing he was reasonable, usually, I suggested, "You're right, of course. But would it hurt for us to finish our job here first? At the very least, I need a night's sleep. I'm not Primani...I need real sleep." Shameless, I batted my eyes at him and yawned hugely.

Stopping only to roll his eyes at my theatrics, he reluctantly agreed, "You have a good point. You're still human and need rest. I forget that sometimes." He trailed a finger down my cheek leaving a trail of heat behind. I closed my eyes at the pleasure of it and he kissed me softly. "Maybe you should get some sleep?"

I wound my arms around him and teased, "I can't sleep now. Look, my runes are glowing!"

"What am I going to do with you?"

"How about you make the rest of me glow and then let me kill a bunch of demons tomorrow? It'll be the perfect vacation."

The next morning, I stepped out of the bathroom wrapped in a fluffy white towel and nearly dropped it in surprise. Flushing with embarrassment, I hissed, "What are you doing in here?" The towel felt entirely too small and I clutched it tighter.

Sean's eyes traveled lazily over me and rested coldly on my flushed face. "Nice to see you, too." He waved a hand over my practically-naked appearance. "Were you expecting someone else?"

Letting my annoyance show, I said shortly, "*Killian* left me alone so I could get dressed privately. Again, why are you here?" I tapped my foot.

He was standing between me and my clothes and he knew it. The self-satisfied smirk on his face made me want to punch him.

In one fluid motion, he was standing an inch away from me, so close his jeans brushed my bare thighs. Looking down into my face, he sneered at my surprise.

"What? No proper welcome?"

"Back off, Sean!"

He didn't move but arrogantly looked into my eyes for answers. I threw up shutters and closed him out. He had no rights to my head anymore.

"Intimidation is beneath you. It's sad that you'd stoop this low."

Growling low in his throat, he spun away from me and put some space between us. "Get dressed so we can leave," he ordered rudely. His eyes roved over the beds and noticed that only one bed had been slept in. He glared at me and added, "Already? You make me sick."

"Get out of the way so I can get my clothes, you prick!" I was sick of him.

Grabbing me by the arm, he snarled, "You better watch your filthy mouth!"

Yanking my arm back, I hissed, "I'm not an angel! I'll say what I want! Now get out!"

He stalked out of the room and slammed the door. Trembling with anger and something less tangible, I sat down and took several deep breaths. His anger was tearing me up inside. I got it. He was furious with me. It seemed a little long to hold a grudge though. We'd broken up months ago.

This was his choice, for crying out loud.

He left *me*!

What was he still mad at me about? I'm the one who should be furious. And the little voice in my head reminded me that deep down, I *was* still furious with him.

A few minutes later I was dressed and dreading spending any time with Sean. Where was Killian anyway? I stuffed my things into my backpack and a note fell off the table. It was from Killian.

Mica, I have to do some recon ahead of our surveillance. I'll get in touch with you later. Sean will be there to go with you. I'm counting on you to stay focused. You can yell at me later! Careful and smart, got it?

K.

I held the note to my chest and breathed a little easier. He'd left a note. That was so much better than just leaving with no words at all. I wasn't afraid to admit I had serious abandonment issues at the moment.

"Are you ready to leave yet?" Sean's sarcastic question came from the doorway. He'd let himself in, again.

"Let's get something straight. You don't have the right to just rematerialize wherever I'm at. You lost those privileges when you left me. Don't do it again or I might not be so friendly."

With that warning, I swept past him to the elevators. He kept up easily and scowled at me the entire way to the lobby. I forced myself to get the complimentary breakfast because I needed the fuel. My gut was squirming from the tension so I settled for toast and fruit. Sean sat next to me tapping impatiently on the table top. His eyes scanned the room and returned to glare at me while I sipped coffee.

Halfway through my toast, a woman dressed for business walked into the room. She was very pretty with her shining blond hair falling to the middle of her back. Dressed in a short black skirt and sky blue silk blouse, she was the poster child for sexy American businesswomen everywhere. Her almond-shaped brown eyes lingered on Sean as she passed our table. His eyes followed her with amused interest. She hesitated and smiled over her shoulder at him. He followed her into the serving area while I finished my breakfast. The low rumble of his laughter floated above the decorative half-wall.

What did I care? I had Killian to curl up with. The image of that brought some healthy color to my cheeks and a sappy grin I had to smother. I glanced at my watch. It was time to go so I walked out. He could catch up. Once in the parking lot, I fished out the truck keys and Sean snatched them out of my hand and commandeered the driver's seat. Fuming mutely, I climbed into the passenger seat and slammed the door.

"Where to?" Sean demanded.

I gave him a dirty look and turned on the GPS. The nice British woman had all the directions he'd need. I wasn't speaking to him any more than absolutely necessary. Folding my arms over my chest, I struggled to do several things at once. First, I had to get my emotions under control and hide my stress from him. He was stressing me out and my heart was pounding loudly in my chest. Probably he could hear it, if not actually feel the vibrations. He didn't deserve the satisfaction of knowing he affected me. Second, I had to get focused on this op. My thoughts were scattered and I didn't remember what I was supposed to be doing...Killian's counting on me...focus, focus...

Taking slow, deep breaths, I reeled in my ricocheting thoughts. The mission was to stake out an office that was supposedly a front for Dagin's operations. He supposedly experimented here and created some kind of zombie. Rumor had it the lab was still active. We needed to find proof of demon activity and kill off any zombies we might find. Killing demons was authorized too. Thank you, Alex!

The neighborhood we entered was run-down and scary. Most buildings didn't have windows; they were smashed out. Any windows that were still intact were covered by bars. Nearly everything was spray painted with graffiti. Garbage littered the sidewalks and weeds overflowed in the tiny green spaces. Like sentries, men lounged against stoops and street signs. All eyes followed us as Sean navigated the streets. If I wasn't armed to the teeth and accompanied by my very own Primani, I wouldn't be caught dead in this place. Ignoring said Primani, I checked my weapons again. The silencer remained on the Sig and I tightened it. My backup was loaded and in its holster. Both of my knives were strapped on and the pepper spray hung from my belt. My boots were laced up tight and my hair was braided into a knot on the back of my head. I wore faded jeans and a band t-shirt that had 'Encore!' printed across my boobs. It was hot and sticky already and I fanned myself idly with the *Cosmo* I'd stuffed under the seat.

This day was going to suck.

Without even glancing at me, Sean grunted, "This it?"

He had slowed down near a three-story concrete and glass office building that had seen better days a century ago. Its concrete was chipping off in chunks and stained with rust and mold. The building lumbered above the row houses that drooped sadly against the asphalt streets. They were low squat buildings with covered front porches. Some were duplexes and some were still single-family homes. All had a decayed look about them that screamed for demolition. Two of the address numbers on the office building were broken off, but it seemed to be the right address. Driving past and then turning around, he parked along the street near a grey house whose covered porch was partially collapsed onto the tiny yard. The chain link fence tilted drunkenly along the front sidewalk. The summer rains had been plentiful and weeds grew two feet high. Yellow pollen floated in the stagnant humid air. Sean sneezed and rubbed his nose with the back of his hand.

Settling in to wait, I got comfortable and peered interestedly at the building. An hour or so later, I spotted two men getting out of a car parked at the curb. Carefully pulling out my camera, I snapped the stills and waited.

They were humans…short hair, glasses, satchels…scientists? Not sure, I made a note and took a small sip of water. If they were scientists, it reasoned that the lab was still active. I sent a text to Killian's phone.

Sean watched my every move. "You've done this before?"

"Yep."

Two more hours went by with no movement at all. Stakeouts suck. My butt ached and I shifted in the seat. I needed to pee but would never admit it. Instead, I sunk a bit lower and stretched as much as I could. My eye caught a hint of motion and I used my peripheral vision to watch a demon exit boldly from a Cadillac Escalade that pulled up across from us. He stared right at us and said something to his partner. Both took a step in our direction and Sean reacted automatically to protect our cover. Playing the obnoxious boyfriend, he yanked me across the console and kissed me hard enough to grind my teeth against my lips. I struggled to pull away but his hands were like steel bands and he laughed against my mouth.

He stopped laughing when I bit him.

"You bastard!" I hissed. My vision went white around the edges and he eyed me warily.

The demon studied us for another minute and took a step our direction. His hand disappeared inside his jacket. Uh-oh.

"Sorry…" I murmured to Sean right before I slapped him hard enough to rock his head back, screaming for our audience, "I hate you! Don't touch me!"

The demon paused and elbowed his partner. They just loved pain and chaos…Sean wasn't playing the game now and his eyes went flat. The white handprint filled in with brilliant red and shined like a beacon on his face.

Wrenching my wrist, he snarled loudly at me, "You ever do that again, I'll break your fucking hand."

I morphed into Ghetto Girl, screaming obscenities at him. Letting loose with some colorful descriptions of his manhood, I piled on the drama until our demon shrugged and turned away. After making sure he went inside, Sean jammed the truck into gear and squealed off down the street.

"You bitch! You fucking hit me!"

"Don't call me a bitch! I was protecting our cover! And you split my lip." I ran my tongue around the inside of my mouth and felt a bleeding cut on the inside of my upper lip. The taste of blood made me wrinkle my nose. "I'm bleeding! You're such a dick!"

My phone buzzed. It was Killian. "Hey."

"You sound like hell. Where are you?"

"We're taking a break. Did you find what you needed?"

"Yes and no. Tell Sean to bring you back to the hotel."

"Killian's back. Take me to the hotel."

"Oh, great."

He parked and I left him standing with the truck and stalked angrily to our room. Killian looked up in surprise when I walked in. He took one look at my face and crossed over to me with hard eyes.

"What happened to your mouth? Did someone hit you?"

Sean walked in then. Killian stared at the red handprint on his face and before I could stop him, he grabbed Sean by the shirt, lifted him off his feet and flung him backwards against the door. The force was hard enough to crack the doorframe and I flinched as Sean's head hit the wood and his eyes rolled back.

Crouching over him, Killian said from between clenched teeth, "Primani *never* hurt our charges! If you can't control your anger, you're off this team! Is that clear?"

Flushing crimson, Sean didn't argue the point. Killian held out a hand to help him up and he brushed it off. "I'm taking a walk."

"Good idea," Killian agreed.

After the door slammed, Killian turned to me and said, "I'm sorry you had to see that, babe. But I had no choice. He's too powerful to let his emotions rule his brain. He's got to get it together. Losing control isn't an option for us." He sat next to me and said, "Let me see your lip."

He touched the pad of his fingertip to the cut. The tiny wound knit together in seconds. I ran my tongue behind my lip and the cut was gone. The metallic taste of blood lingered unpleasantly though.

"How do you stay so controlled? I mean, you were really mad at Sean. I could sense it. But you didn't go crazy."

With a mocking smile, he said, "Years of practice."

Later that night, the three of us pulled up to a stop sign a few blocks from the office building. It was late but still not quiet. Police sirens wailed a few streets over and the red and blue lights bounced off the windows of the building beside us. The eerie light gave weird life to the trees growing next to the road. They seemed to twitch back and forth in the humid night air. Weird. The ride over was tense and silent except for Killian's last minute instructions. Mostly it was me and Sean who were tense and silent; Killian was in his element directing super-secret paramilitary operations. The perfect leader, he completely ignored the waves of anger rolling off of Sean and the not-so-subtle flow of annoyance ebbing off of me. With his usual thoroughness, Killian ran us through our jobs and backup plans. Sean would help him with the explosives, but I was relegated to playing lookout again. Back in the hotel room, Killian had taken one look at the mutiny on my face and pulled me aside while Sean idly watched.

Killian had said, "What's the problem?"

Stealing a sideways glance at Sean, I said quietly, "Why can't I help you inside? Dec taught me how to set the timers."

"Mica, we've been through this. You're not ready yet."

Sean wasn't even bothering to hide his eavesdropping and raised an amused eyebrow at me. Pointedly turning my back to him, I tried another approach. "I don't like this set up. What if you need more help?"

I bit my lip before I gave voice to what was really on my mind. I wasn't going to say it out loud. I didn't want to jinx us. But he knew exactly what I was afraid of.

Leaning a closer to my ear, he promised, "We'll be okay in there. It's not going to happen again. I won't let it."

Not trusting myself to say anything, I had nodded with my lips clamped together. Raphael's warning of more tribulations and pain bounced around my head. Could this operation go south too?

Sean interrupted my worrying by tapping the brakes hard enough to lock up my seatbelt. His half-smothered grin mocked me in the rearview mirror. Refusing to rise to the bait, I adjusted my mic and did a final check on the radio.

Eyeing my preparations with approval, Killian said, "Stay in the truck and keep us straight, just like you usually do. You leave as soon as the building goes up. Don't wait for us. We'll meet you at the hotel."

"And if something goes wrong?"

"What could possibly go wrong?" he asked with perfect confidence and slung a heavy canvas pack over his shoulder.

Sean was similarly outfitted and scowled impatiently. They took the easy route this time and simply vanished and rematerialized in the building's cavernous basement.

"We're in." Killian's hushed voice came clearly through my earpiece.

Okay, it was time to earn my keep. Searching the surrounding area should be easy, but I couldn't see like I normally could. Everything was black. Scrunching my eyes and focusing inward, I tried again.

Come out; come out, wherever you are…

Crap, I still couldn't see anything. I didn't like being blind. Tapping my fingers together, I peered out the front window and then it hit me. There were too many obstacles in front of me. I would have to get closer.

Grabbing my Sig and a flashlight, I slipped out of the truck and hurried up the street. Across from the building, the block was open with little cover to get behind. But there was an old boarded up house sitting diagonally across from the building. The faded gray paint and black shingles screamed invisibility. The streetlight was out so the darkness was complete. It would be a good hiding spot. With one eye on Dagin's front entrance, I sidled along the street hugging the shadows until I made it to the porch. Ducking behind the wooden half-wall, I waited for someone to sound an alarm but everything stayed silent.

So far, so good.

Closing my eyes, I searched for Sean and Killian. Oh, much better. They appeared in my mind's eye like bodies in front of night vision goggles. Their heat signatures appeared as a faint halo around their bodies and I could clearly see their faces which were both blank with intense concentration. They worked in unison stringing up plastique and wiring the timers. As I watched, Killian reached out and took a bundle of explosives from Sean and taped it the wall. After he let it go, Sean pulled up his shirt to wipe the sweat off of his face baring most of his torso. A glint of metal winked at me. He was carrying two guns tonight, as was Killian. I smiled into the darkness as I remembered their earlier complaining about not being heavily armed for this. I privately thought they just liked the way they looked with automatic weapons slung across their shoulders…

Reining in that particular train of thought, I refocused on what they were supposed to be doing. There were several pillars in the center and those would be wired too.

The explosion was supposed to take out the building without a large outward blast. I grimly pictured the sad little houses falling like so many dominos. Alex had specifically ordered Killian to limit the blast to reduce collateral damage. I wondered cynically if he had any idea what this crappy neighborhood looked like. A cat squalled shrilly and I jumped with a muffled scream. With heart racing, I peeked over the wall to see a fat tomcat chasing a female over the weed-filled yard.

Stupid cat sex!

Sean's voice hissed in my earpiece, "You all right?"

"Fine. Sorry, false alarm."

"Amateur."

Asshole.

Settling in to wait, I watched as they moved across the basement. Other than the stupid cats, it was quiet. The police cars were long gone. Mosquitoes whined and a dog barked occasionally, but nothing else stirred. The muffled rumble of the first explosion brought me completely alert. Blinking sleepily, I looked around.

Damn it! I'd dozed off!

Where were they?

The ground under my feet vibrated from the basement explosions. Before I could move, the silence was broken by a loud blast and shattering glass from the first story. Frozen on the porch, I was hypnotized by the fire for just a few seconds but it was still too long. Flames lit up the street as more timers went off.

I was too close!

The blast wave from one of the explosions reached me and knocked me backwards into the side of the house. Struggling to keep my balance, I lurched off the steps and stumbled for the truck. By this time, the building was in full flames and I started sprinting down the sidewalk.

Police sirens echoed in the distance just as I threw myself into the driver's seat so violently the keys went flying. Shit!

The sirens were getting closer; the lights flashed between the houses on the opposite block.

Where are those goddamn keys?

Wedged between the seats...Oh, thank God!

Slamming the truck into gear, I floored it and skidded around a corner just as the first cops pulled onto the street.

"What the hell are you doing?" Sean yelled in my ear from behind me.

"Jesus! Are you trying to give me a heart attack?" My chest burned from the surge of adrenaline.

"What are you still doing here?" he demanded while climbing over the seats. "Are you stupid?"

Frantically looking in the rearview mirror, I snapped, "Oh, shut up and watch our back."

I took the next corner on two wheels and he slid across the console into me. The wheel spun out of my hands and we drove up over a sidewalk and ran over a stop sign. The metallic crunch sounded supernaturally loud to me. He grabbed the wheel and yanked hard enough to put us back in the center of the deserted street.

"You suck at driving! Pull over!"

Spotting the freeway on-ramp, I headed towards it. "You can get out any time. I don't need your help."

Grimacing and finally sitting back in the passenger seat, he griped, "No, I can't. Killian would *kick me off the team* if I left you here."

"Is there a downside to that?"

"You're the one who shouldn't be out here. But Killian wouldn't consider taking *you* off the team."

"Well, you *did* tell him to take care of me while you were gone. Too bad you weren't more specific," I pointed out, swerving into the right lane.

"I should've never taken this assignment. You're a pain in my ass."

The hotel was on the next street so I ignored him and focused on driving and parking without hitting anything.

"Later," I called as I sprinted towards the side entrance.

"Where do you think you're going? I'll walk you up to the room." He caught up with me too easily.

I fished out the key as soon as we left the elevator intending to get into the room quickly and close the door in his face. But my hands were sticky with sweat and I fumbled with the plastic card and dropped it. I stooped to pick it up and when I straightened, Sean was standing behind me. In one smooth motion, he reached out and plucked the card from my fingers.

"Nervous?" he whispered against the back of my neck sending goose bumps racing over my skin.

"You wish!" I spun around to tell him to leave me alone but ended up too close.

The fine hair on his forearms tickled my shoulders as he trapped me against the door. With both arms surrounding me like a cage, his lips turned up with a slow smile as the pounding of my heart grew louder.

"Ah...there it is." With one finger, he deftly lifted the locket out of my shirt and held it against his palm.

It glowed happily.

Apparently it didn't realize we'd broken up.

"Sean--" I started to warn him to let me go but the door to the room next to us flew open and a woman walked into the hall.

Busy on her cell phone, she ignored us and hustled past. Sean followed her with his eyes until she got into the elevator. I plucked the key out of his fingers and quickly slid it into the reader. Slamming the door in his face, I whirled around to find him standing right behind me, smirking.

"Really?" He shook his head like I was crazy.

"Okay, I'm safe now. Go away!"

I didn't exactly feel safe...

Not with the way he was looking at me.

Hostility and something a little less ugly surrounded him like a halo. It was all I could do not to back away from him. He was enjoying making me squirm.

He stared at me; I stared at him.

He blinked first and shrugged.

Pulling off his sweaty shirt, he commandeered one of the beds and flipped on the television. I was speechless.

"You're staying?" I nearly screeched.

Not bothering to glance at me, he nodded smugly. "Killian *ordered* me not to leave you alone. And since he's clearly not here..." He shrugged like he had no choice.

"He'll be back soon. I don't need a babysitter." My tone sounded whiny and I clamped my mouth shut. I really wanted a shower and sleep.

"Don't count on it. He went to The City to see Alex. He might not come back if he's given new orders. We'll leave in the morning though." He stretched and grinned mockingly at me, "Just you and me..."

I stomped over to the bathroom and brushed my teeth until the enamel was thin and spit viciously in the sink. Damn him! I was hot and sticky and really wanted a shower. No way was I taking my clothes off with him in the room. Maybe I could put it off...I gave my armpit a tentative sniff and my nose objected. Okay, maybe not.

Stupid Detroit heat!

Not bothering to lock the door since he could pop into the shower if he wanted, I threw myself into the shower and broke speed records. I was in the middle of combing the tangles out of my hair when I realized my clothes were in the other room. Gritting my teeth, I bounced my forehead off of the door. Ugh!

"Could you bring me my backpack?" I called through a crack in the door.

"Sorry? What? I didn't hear you say please."

I hate him.

I should just walk out in a towel and grab my stuff. That would show him. Visions of him pulling the towel off of me stopped me.

"*Please* bring me my clothes."

He tapped on the door. I opened it a hair and he held up a thong and said, "This is all I could find."

Chapter 25: Forgiveness and Promises

IT WAS 3:00 THE NEXT AFTERNOON when Sean finally pulled the truck into a Tim Horton's restaurant off the highway. We were in the middle of Ontario heading towards Plattsburgh. Our plan was to pack up some things and meet Killian in Manhattan. A strong feeling of foreboding had greeted me when I finally woke up from a restless sleep. Distracted and unwilling to rise to Sean's barbs, I spent the trip staring out the window, much to his annoyance. After the thong incident, I shut him out and I had the feeling he didn't like that.

Last night, I had snatched the thong from his hand and marched to my backpack in the towel after all. Fully disgusted with him, I turned my back and defiantly dropped the towel. With furious movements, I yanked on my clothes and then turned to him.

"I can't believe I loved you. What's happened to you?"

He started to reply and then stopped, deflated. Without another word, he shut off the light and took a shower. When he came out of the bathroom, he crawled under his sheets and turned his back to me. I lay on my own bed staring at his back for hours. Memories drifted through my mind...My lips remembered the smooth texture of his back the day he told me they were angels. That same day, he'd told me he loved me. The memory filled my head and I let it play out with tears in my eyes: How had things gone so wrong?

It had been a beautiful day and we'd walked to the creek near the farmhouse. Finally trusting me with their secret, he admitted they were angels, of a sort. Fascinated, I walked around to his back and lifted up his shirt. He sucked in his breath against the sudden cold. I was afraid to look, but when I opened my eyes to look at him, all I saw was smooth muscular skin the color of warm honey. I pressed my face against his skin and kissed him softly between his shoulders.

"Well, did I pass?" he'd asked with a grin.

"No wings?"

"No wings. Are you disappointed?"

"Not really, I think they would get in the way. What do you call yourselves?"

He'd looked relieved by the simple question. "Primani, we're called Primani--Soldiers of the First Legion."

I'd considered his serious, beautiful face. He was a contradiction. When he was with me like this, he was sweet and gentle. When he was in soldier-mode, he was ruthless and deadly. I was more than a little afraid of the soldier in him and shivered.

"Don't! Please don't ever be afraid of me. I would never hurt you; you have to know that." He'd reached out and cupped my face in his hands. The little golden light in his eyes flashing brilliantly as the truth hit him. He'd kissed me with yearning and tenderness. I'd clung to his shoulders to keep from falling. He dragged his mouth away from mine and lowered it to my collarbone. With the other hand, he pulled the zipper of my sweatshirt down. I was bare underneath it. He pulled his eyes back to mine. I searched his eyes but his mind was closed to me.

"What are you thinking?" I whispered.

"You're so beautiful it takes my breath away."

"I love you."

"And I love you," he said wistfully.

What had happened to that love? Where did it go? I was floundering on unfamiliar ground now. He'd vowed he'd never hurt me...but he was, every second he was near me. I was afraid of him, of who he was becoming, of who he might become.

I thought I knew him, but I didn't know this version of him.

I didn't like this version of Sean.

He was cold and his words cut me to the quick. Maybe I deserved his anger, but I didn't deserve this hostility. I thought of James and wondered if this was how he drifted into the darkness.

Did his love get twisted into hate?

How did he lose his soul?

That couldn't happen to Sean. He was the greatest Primani ever...

As I picked at my salad, I wondered what he would have to say if he knew about the baby. I wanted to tell him but there hadn't been a good time. And now...well, the silence had grown into a stone wall between us and I saw no way over it. My heart ached with the knowledge that he was so far out of reach when I needed him most.

I felt his eyes on me and looked up. His expression was carefully blank as he watched me from across the table. The restaurant was crowded and loud with the clanking of glass and silverware, but Sean overwhelmed my senses until there was no one but him in my world. The golden lights in his eyes were muted as if his *saol* was focused someplace else. The ocean-colored irises were opaque to me now. Unable to help myself, I peered into them and found no way inside his shuttered mind.

What secrets was he keeping?

He was closed to me and my throat tightened in response. Abruptly pushing away from the table, I rushed out of the restaurant and climbed into the relative privacy of the truck. Swiping angrily at tears, I swore in every language I knew. But still they came and I groaned in frustration at the human weakness. If only I could be hard and cold...like Sean.

Sean pulled open the door and climbed in. After a minute of awkward silence, he finally snorted impatiently, "Damn it, Mica, stop it."

Turning to face him, I said, "You think it's that easy? Maybe for you! You have no feelings. If you don't want to see me cry, then stop hurting me!"

Incredulous, his eyebrows went straight to his hairline. "Me? What have I done? You're the one giving me the silent treatment!"

I didn't have a comeback for that. Defeated, I drooped. "Once upon a time, you promised there would be no lies between us. Do you remember that?"

His jaw tightened but he answered stiffly, "I remember that conversation." He added bitterly, "But we also agreed there was room for secrets. And now, can you live with them?"

"Mine or yours?" I asked with intensity. My eyes were dry again and I searched his face for some kind of emotion. What was he hiding?

His mouth twisted into a grimace and he ripped his eyes away from my face. Retreating into his head, he tapped his fingers on the steering wheel and looked away from me.

The silence dragged.

"Ah, I see how it is. You can have your secrets but I can't have mine. Well, you know mine now…and you can't forgive me. So I'm asking you. Where were you? And if I knew, would I be able to forgive you?"

He flushed hotly and shook his head in denial. "You don't know what you're talking about! I told you I was scattered." But he didn't meet my eyes.

"I heard you arguing with Killian. You think I'm too weak for the truth. I *know* you're hiding something."

He hesitated for a minute as if wondering what he could say. "You don't know anything."

Tiredly, I said, "Whatever."

Sighing loudly, he started the truck and the road trip continued. The farmland blurred by as I tried to meditate.

The sense of impending doom settled into my bones like a cancer.

Who would we lose this time?

We'd barely slept and already it was time to get back on the road. Morning was not my favorite time of the day and Sean's attitude was a little less fun this early. I resisted the urge to snap his head off as he nagged at me.

"We need to go. Are you packed?" Sean asked.

The deliberate rudeness was gone but the holier-than-thou tone was nearly as bad. I shoved my hand into my pocket to stop it from slapping him again. Geez, he was overplaying the role of victim here.

Rolling my eyes, I lifted my bag and started towards the front door. "Yeah, let's go. We need to get down there. Killian's waiting for us to move on Dagin."

He plucked my heavy bag off of my arm and snapped, "Yeah, let's not keep Killian waiting!" and stalked into the early morning darkness.

Sean drove the Camaro like it was an extension of his body. The muscles in his arm flexed as he steered the powerful car. The car responded to his slightest movement and growled aggressively as we roared down the highway. I stole a peek at his face. His strong profile was set in stone as he lost himself in his own thoughts. The shadows hid his expression but I knew he was painfully unhappy. I'd known his every mood for years...once he would have talked to me, not now...his pride wouldn't let him. I sighed to myself and wondered what he was thinking. His eyes were entirely focused on the road and he'd been silent since we pulled away from the house.

His moods were giving me a constant headache. It was bad enough that I had to deal with my own pain. I was still having flashbacks of the demon attack and bouts of sadness from the miscarriage. I felt horrible about Sean's pain. I missed Dec desperately. I was barely keeping myself together as it was. If it weren't for

Killian's love and caring support, I'd be curled up in a bed refusing to leave the house. Absorbing Sean's emotions was overwhelming me. Rubbing my temples, I pulled out my phone and started to send a text to Killian. I craved some kind of contact with someone who liked me…maybe…

Killian? Probably you can't hear me…but I need you. I really need you. My head aches. Needing its comfort, I stroked the outline of my rune and closed my eyes to shut out Sean's emotions. Gradually, my hand began to tingle and I opened my eyes to see the golden outline shining gently in the washed out light of dawn.

I'm here, babe. Close your eyes.

I closed my eyes again and there he was, standing in the light airy room in my mind. He was grimy with sweat and dirt as if he'd been fighting in the woods someplace. His beard shadowed his jaw sending his sexiness skyrocketing off the charts. His teeth were very white when he greeted me with a slow sexy smile. He held his arms open to me and I threw myself against him. Catching me surely, he held me close until my heartbeat slowed and my headache drifted away. Smoothing my hair back and lifting my chin, he kissed me with a smile.

Better?

I could only smile and nod happily. The slight roughness of his calloused hands warmed my skin as he ran his hands up my arms to cup my face for one last kiss. I moaned happily against his demanding mouth when he deepened the kiss with his tongue. Tiny white lights sparkled behind my eyes and I forgot where I was. Dragging his mouth away, he said he had to go. With that, he vanished.

Sean's dry voice brought me flying back to the physical world. "Do you need a towel?" He waved a hand in the general direction of my lap and peered suspiciously into the air, sniffing. "God, I hope you were dreaming?"

"Yes, a dream…" I murmured and licked my lips.

"I needed a hug," I huffed defensively.

Barking a sarcastic laugh, Sean said, "You could've asked me! I'm a little closer." Something struck him as funny and he burst into a real laugh that he smothered with a cough.

Laughing uneasily, I ran my tongue over my lips and thought I could just taste Killian. His scent lingered on my fingers. What an amazing thing…And my headache was gone, too. Assuming it was a dream, Sean was smiling again and his face transformed into the glorious, beautiful Primani he was. Wide blue eyes glittered against the golden color of his skin. Dark stubble shadowed his jaw giving him that just-rolled-out-of-bed look that usually melted women everywhere. This smile, this rare, rare, smile, lit up his face and softened the hardened warrior that he wore so easily. My heart lifted just a bit. Maybe the sad and angry Sean was gone? Automatically, I reached over and touched his hand. He looked surprised but didn't move.

"Truce?"

Gritting his teeth, he shrugged my hand aside as if he couldn't bear to touch me. Instead of commenting, he pressed the play button and Metallica's "The Unforgiven" blasted out of the speakers.

The parking garage was nearly empty since most people were at work for the day. After easing the Camaro into the reserved slot, Sean lovingly rubbed the steering wheel before removing the keys. Shaking my head, I got out and grabbed my bag. A slight movement caught the corner of my eye and I paused to watch as a shadow slipped behind the wheel of a parked BMW on the other side of the garage. Pretending to dig in my purse for something, I watched suspiciously. The engine roared to life sending echoes throughout the space. Instantly alert, Sean shoved me into the wall as the driver careened towards us. Standing in the lane, he waited as the driver approached and held up his hand. Was he crazy? I yelled at him to move and he shook his head at me.

Unaccountably, the car slowed and drifted to a stop in front of him. The driver's face was slack with sleep and he slowly slid down in the seat. What the heck? I was stunned and watched with my mouth hanging open as Sean calmly searched the car. He stuffed some baggies into his pocket and shoved a handgun into his backpack. He finished the search in about two minutes while I leaned against the wall and did nothing useful. Finally, he tapped the hood with his knuckles and strode towards the elevator. To my continued astonishment, the driver woke up and shook his head in confusion.

Dragging me into the elevator behind him, Sean said, "It's a useful talent."

"Sooooo...?"

"Nothing to do with us; he's just a regular idiot with an unlicensed gun and a bagful of Oxy. He'll be pissed when he realizes his stash is gone."

A familiar voice called out to me as we entered the lobby. "Miss Thomas! Welcome back!"

Jacob Martinelli was one of the concierge attendants. He was in his late twenties with liquid brown eyes and a shock of thick black hair that was tamed only with copious amounts of hair gel. He'd once confided that he wanted to shave it into a Mohawk but he'd lose this job. I'd laughed and complimented him on his good sense. With his usual friendliness, he started to move around the concierge counter but took a good look at Sean's expression and stayed where he was.

Taking pity on him, I detoured to his desk and greeted him with a genuine smile. "I see you've still got your job, Jacob. It's nice to see you again." Leaning a little closer, I lowered my voice, "Anything unusual going on?" I winked broadly to emphasize my meaning.

Grinning conspiratorially, he nodded. "Funny you should ask! Rumor has it that a whole bunch of stiffs have been snatched off their slabs. Got the whole city on edge."

"Huh? That's crazy, isn't it?" I flashed my dimples and squeezed his hand in thanks. "Will you let me know right away if you hear anything else?"

"Absolutely, Mica, I mean, Miss Thomas." He checked that his boss hadn't heard his breach of protocol and grinned back.

Sean's finger jabbed the elevator button a little harder than necessary and I peered over at him. What was his problem now? Geez! The penthouse was on the 18th floor and the ride was eternal in the old elevator.

Tick tock, the silence stretched.

"A friend of yours?" he finally asked mildly. He sounded calmer but his fingers were tapping the side of his leg.

"Well, sort of. We got to know each the last time I was here, before I was kidnapped and killed. He's got friends in some interesting places."

He made a sarcastic sound and crossed his arms. Rolling my eyes at this weird show of jealousy, I followed him into the black and white marble foyer. The little niche by the door was still empty. Making a mental note to ask Alex about the golden cherub, I opened the door and strolled inside like I owned the place. Sean's eyebrows went straight up at my new boldness but he didn't comment. Giving the front rooms a sweeping glance, I was disappointed to find them empty. A note rested on the marble island in the kitchen. It was addressed to me. The elegant handwriting was a surprise and I traced my name with a fingernail before unfolding the heavy paper.

Your angry eyes destroy with their fire,
Will you carve me to pieces?
To lie scattered in the ashes of our friendship.
Am I always to remain,
Unforgiven?

Dec. It could only be him. What have I done? Carefully avoiding Sean's curious gaze, I folded the letter and tucked it into my back pocket. Hurrying towards the rooftop garden, I threw open the French doors and leaned over the brick wall to look down at the city. Turning away from the noise below, I leaned against the wall and drew his handsome face into my mind.

Innocent blue eyes...deadly blue eyes...

He was my protector, my friend, my brother...

It was time to forgive him.

Throwing my arms up, I called, "Declan! Come back!" And I waited with arms open but eyes closed against disappointment.

The slightest shift in pressure and he was there, in my arms, hugging me like I would vanish if he let me go. I don't know how long we stood clinging to each other in the hot summer sun. He was too thin, lanky, and I ran my hands down his lean back with tears glittering on my lashes. I sensed the pain he carried in his heart and the frustration that crippled him. He was frantic over Dani's disappearance. He was devastated over my silence. He was torn between Sean and Killian. We were all tearing him to pieces and he'd never say a word. That wasn't his way.

He would hold it inside until it ate him alive.

He was always the sunny one. He was the one bright spot that sparkled like a single star in the blackest nights. This sad and angry Dec was a stranger to me.

The sun had gone out like an eclipse.

I squeezed him harder like that would somehow make him feel better. I wanted to mother him. I wanted to heal him. I wanted him to be happy again.

He pulled back from me and knelt formally on one knee, with his head bowed in misery. "Will you let me burn?"

My throat tightened at the strain in his voice and I sat down abruptly and pulled him down with me.

"I'm sorry, Dec. I'm so sorry."

Looking into his sad eyes, I threaded my fingers in his hair and smoothed it as his mother probably did 2,000 years ago. His eyes widened a bit when he felt the warmth of my *saol* flow from my fingertips. I shushed him and massaged the tight muscle at his temples and then worked my way down his jaw and around the tender skin of his eyes.

"Let me help you for a change. Close your eyes, baby, just let go," I ordered softly as I leaned my forehead against his. "Don't be sad."

Concentrating on easing his pain, I watched his startled blue eyes soften and shift to the stormy sea as he finally relaxed under my fingers. His careening emotions finally calmed and settled. His anger drifted away, replaced by his natural courage and resolve. He would find Dani and save her. He would tell Killian he was pissed about his sleeping with me. He was relieved to make peace with me.

He felt whole again.

I smiled as he surrendered next to me. His breathing slowed even more as I carefully pushed my power into him. My own breathing slowed and I relaxed for just a minute...

"Wake up, Sleeping Beauty!"

The sun was gone and it was very dark. Where did the time go?

Laughing for the first time in ages, Dec rolled to his feet and offered me a hand. Not letting me go, he tugged me with him to the wall that overlooked the city below. It was beautiful. The city lights sparkled like man-made stars. Here and there blue and red lights flashed as the police stayed on their toes. Sean had once said Manhattan was full of demons...a wicked city, a city of chaos. The screeching of a car alarm echoed in the night and below us a baby cried.

Wicked it may be, but I loved Manhattan!

"You're so far away from me. Where do you go inside that pretty head of yours?" He asked as he leaned down to shield me from the wind. His lean body was warm and he smelled of the trees, green and fresh. I secretly believed Dec was a wood elf...too tall to be a nymph like me.

Snuggling against his side, I sighed contentedly. It was so good to have him back. "I have to say this out loud. I need to say it out loud, so don't interrupt me and don't cut me off."

"You don't have to say anything. You know that."

"Still, I'm saying it." I took a deep breath and continued, "You once made a vow to me. You said, *"You are my sister now and I will always have your back."* Do you remember that?" Without waiting for him to respond, I asked, "Do you have my back? Are there more secrets, Dec? Do you know where Sean was all that time?

Grimacing uncomfortably, he inhaled through his teeth and looked down into my eyes. Trying to gauge my mood, he took his time before answering me. Finally, he said precisely, "He *was* lost, darlin'. I don't know where, but I know he couldn't get back. I don't know anything else." He pushed my hair out of my eyes and added thoughtfully, "It's a mystery, isn't it, though? Can I ask you a question now?"

"I suppose. Go ahead."

"What's going on with you and Killian? You're different now. I can sense your powers are stronger, but you're more fragile emotionally. Is it him? Is he hurting you?"

It was my turn to feel awkward and I blushed before answering honestly. "A lot happened when you and Sean were off decimating demons on the Eastern Seaboard. Let's just say, I had my share of inner and outer demons to vanquish. They damaged me. *Killian* came to me when I needed him most and he's...healed me."

"You're not telling me everything, are you?"

Smiling ruefully, I agreed. "Some things are too painful to talk about. But Dec, never worry about Killian hurting me. He grounds me; he takes away the chaos and that's a good thing. Let's just kiss and make up. I need to see Killian." I leaned up and kissed his scratchy cheek and he kissed my nose.

Arm in arm, we went back inside to an empty house.

"Geez, doesn't anyone stick around this place?" I grouched.

The clock said it was nearly midnight and the place was empty. Suddenly lonely for Killian, I made excuses and went to find my old room. After washing up but still hot, I crawled naked into the cool sheets. Staring at the shadows dancing across the ceiling, I said a prayer of thanks to God. He'd been good to me, all things considered. After all, I was surrounded by angels and fiercely loved by the most perfect being outside of Heaven.

Now, if we could just get rid of these pesky zombies...

A warm hand cupped my mouth sometime in the wee hours of the night. My eyes flew open to bump into the long lashes framing the brilliant blue eyes staring into mine from a nose length away. Without a word, the hand slipped into my hair and warm lips took its place. With eyes wide open, I inhaled his scent and deepened the kiss.

"I've missed you..." I murmured kissing the soft skin of his chest as he fitted me tightly against his side. Like a key into a lock...The palest glimmer of dawn lit the room as I drifted off to sleep.

The faint tolling of church bells gradually penetrated the heavy veil of sleep that wrapped itself so seductively around me. Unwilling to leave my dream, I buried my head under the sheet and drifted off again. In my dream, the church was a great cathedral with soaring arches that reached the heavens and enormous stained glass windows that bent the light into rainbows across my eyes. The tolling bells were melancholy in the misty light near the gardens. Wisteria grew lush and wild along the stone path. I wandered barefoot through the scattering mist, intent on nothing, expecting nothing more.

Pausing to bring the purple blooms to my nose, I inhaled the fragrance and closed my eyes.

The garden smelled of *him*.

Strangely comforted, I tucked the flower behind one ear and wandered into the tiny clearing where he stood waiting for me. The years had not been kind. The rain had pitted his face and it was pocked with bits of green moss. After all these years, he stood in the rain, waiting.

Waiting in his tomb…waiting to be freed.

One day…when he'd served his time. I paused beneath his feet and bowed my head in respect. Once a mighty warrior, he had slipped off his path. The tears surprised me and I reached up to wipe them from the roughness of his cheek.

Only his eyes followed me…only his eyes betrayed his sorrow…

And still he waited.

"You look like hell. Didn't you sleep at all?"

"Not much, no." I glanced automatically at Killian and blushed.

"Leave her be, Sean. She's got enough to deal with. You're not helping," Killian said mildly with an undertone of steel.

"Whatever, man. Let's get started. I'm ready to kill something."

Rolling his eyes at Sean, Dec threw me an apple from his spot at the kitchen island. He managed to devour his in three neat bites. Wow. After demolishing the poor apple, he tucked into a plate of grilled chicken and vegetables. The garlicky smell assaulted my stomach which growled like an angry bear in response. Since the kitchen was clean, I'd guess room service. Forgetting

Sean's sniping, I made a beeline for the covered plates and found a grilled breast and a handful of zucchini and mushrooms.

"You left me the crappy veggies again. You know I hate zucchini. Thanks," I grumped playfully at Dec.

"Don't look at me! I just got up too." He waved a chicken leg at the other two who shrugged unconcerned.

Glancing up at him, I was chagrined again by how thin he looked. His cheeks were too hollow as if he'd lost 20 pounds. I put my chicken on his plate, kissed the top of his head, and fetched him a huge glass of milk. He started to protest and I hushed him and gulped down my own milk. It wouldn't kill me to miss a meal. It wasn't like I needed the extra food anyway...not now...

"Are you all right?" Killian's whisper startled me and I jumped more violently than necessary. Deftly catching my flying hand, he gently steadied me to the interested stares of both Sean and Dec. With his body shielding me, he placed a warm hand protectively over my belly and leaned closer to my ear. "Do you want me to take you away from here? Just say the word and we'll bolt."

Eyes suddenly misty, I coughed to cover the rush of emotion. Trying to stay casual in front of our audience, I looked up into his serious face and knew he meant it. We'd put the zombies on hold if that's what I needed. He held my eyes and nodded. Instinctively craving connection to him, I linked my fingers in his as they lay across my stomach. It was a promise of sorts. It said someday, *someday* I would have that perfect little baby from my dream.

I will give you a child, Princess. I promise you that.

His eyes grew softer as he waited for me to understand. Finally, he gave my hand a squeeze letting his fingers linger on the rune until it glowed.

Chapter 26: Apocalypse Now

NIGHTFALL WAS NEARLY COMPLETE as we made our way down the busy city streets heading towards Lower Manhattan. People streamed by caught up in a current of humanity. Busy, busy people had places to go. They had lives to live and bills to pay. Did they have any idea of the horror that lurked just beneath the pavement? Did anyone know how close they were to death?

Couldn't they sense it?

Pulling my leather jacket closer to my side, I tensed with anticipation and not a little fear. The wind was blowing in fits of anger as Mother Nature planned another stormy night. When we crossed the street at Broadway and 21st, the wind hit me hard enough to rock me into Killian's side. Clearly unaffected by the wind himself, he used this as an excuse to wrap his arm around my waist and pull me close against his side. This public show of affection was unlike him and I peered up at him.

"How's your intuition tonight, babe?" he asked tightly, eyes scanning the sidewalks for any hint of trouble.

I knew without looking that the ruby-handled knife burned against his calf. Totally synced with it, Killian followed it like a GPS in his head. We zigzagged from street to street as it located our prey. He was practically twitching with readiness, muscles tensed and ready to spring.

I said candidly, "I have a bad feeling about this. It's never as easy as it should be, you know that. Raphael and Michael both warned me there would be more pain and suffering ahead. I don't think they were talking about a miscarriage. Something tells me we're not going to get off lightly tonight. Do you have anything you want to say to me before we get there?"

Barking a surprised laugh, he leaned down and said, "You win, Princess. I love you and I want you beside me. No matter what happens tonight, I'll find you."

Without missing a step, he pulled me around a corner and kissed me as if the world would end in flames right then. Ignited by his power, my blood raced through my veins so fast it thrummed like a plucked guitar string. I had to pull back before I spontaneously combusted.

With fingers digging into my shoulders, he captured my mouth again, growling low in his throat, "Don't fight it; let it take you."

The more he kissed me the faster my blood raced and my own power stirred in response. Feeling light and powerful, I clenched my fingers in his shirt to keep from floating away. And still the thrumming grew louder, the notes low and clear as a bell.

"Do you feel that? Your blood sings for me." The planes of his face shifted in the shadows giving the illusion of another, someone ageless and more powerful. He lightly gripped my upper arms and said in that compelling tone, "When the time comes, you will answer my call."

"Always," I promised before standing on my tiptoes to kiss him one last time as Sean rounded the corner. He jerked like he'd been electrocuted and froze in disbelief.

Without a word, Killian released me and continued walking. I trotted to keep up with him while Sean stalked along on the other side of me. His face nearly purple, he huffed impatiently at every tiny delay. At one crosswalk, he demanded, "What did you do with your ring?"

"I pawned it," I lied.

Killian said, "You two have to focus. This is major. We'll talk about this later."

Suddenly he stopped and listened. "Got it!"

He gestured at a rusted metal door crisscrossed with a chain and padlocked. The door was partially concealed by plywood sheets left over from a construction project. A helpful citizen had spray painted obscenities across it to add some local color to the rusty door. Nice work...Very fancy painting in pretty shades of purple and red.

Killian was a thousand miles away as we waited to go inside. He was communing with his seeing-eye knife and I left him to it. I did my best to sense the undead. At the moment, all I could sense were the waves of anger rolling off of Sean so I glared meaningfully at him and he flipped me off. Turning his back to me, he called Dec who rematerialized a minute later. We all waited in varying degrees of readiness while Killian listened with his ears and his mind. Looking around, I noticed we were on 8th Avenue. It was fully dark and the streets were nearly empty now. A skinny yellow dog dug at a McDonald's bag lying in the street and I thought of Domino. I wished she was here with us. She'd have my back without nagging. I sent my dad a quick text telling him I loved him...just in case things went south.

Dec positioned himself in front of the door and the lock mysteriously fell free. The chains hit the concrete with a slithering thunk. Peering around for an audience and finding none, we slid into the darkened building one by one. With a forceful yank, Dec closed the door behind us and I had to remind myself that we could teleport out. It was a dark as a tomb, the air stagnant and warm. Using my tiny flashlight to conserve my personal energy reserves, I followed along between Killian and Dec. Sean brought up the rear in case there was trouble. His body vibrated with restrained power and his heartbeat reverberated in my head. He was close enough for me to feel the heat coming off of him and I moved a little guiltily towards Dec. It was strange to stand so close to Sean after so much distance between us.

The dim light revealed a dusty hallway that eventually stopped at another, much older, door. The red paint had long since disintegrated and rust had taken over.

With quiet precision, Dec cracked its lock and manhandled the door open against the uneven concrete floor. The harsh grating seemed supernaturally loud in the silence of the room.

His teeth gleaming in the darkness, Dec whispered, "Still got that bad feeling, sweetheart?" He'd never been scared in his life and was ready to jump into this night with both feet. I wondered vaguely if he was a wee bit insane...

Killian stood with arms hung loosely by his sides listening to the echoes in his mind. *Sgaine Dutre*'s brother blade glowed triumphantly in his fist, the red eye burning like brimstone. The red light brought his cheekbones into sharp relief giving his face a hard, sinister look. Turned away from me, Sean watched the hallway with an eager ferocity that made me wonder if I'd ever really known him.

He was reputed to be one of the best Primani of all time...and he'd earned that reputation by sheer tactical skill and overwhelming brutality in a fight. It wasn't in his nature to show mercy and he would annihilate the demons we found tonight. The set of his jaw and the rage in his eyes promised a vicious death for anyone on the wrong side of our mission.

Taking a minute to reach out with my mind, I raised a finger to tell Dec to wait a minute. It was creepy and dark, but there was no danger here. And yet, something tickled at the far edges of my intuition and I knew someone, or something, was waiting for us. The feeling of impending doom hung in the air like a noxious cloud of steam.

Fear curled in my belly like poison.

We were going to lose someone.

Nudging Dec's arm to get his attention, I said simply, "This is going to be bad, Dec." Impulsively, I hugged him and whispered fiercely, "I love you! Please be careful!"

Squeezing me hard enough to crack a rib, he whispered against my hair, "I will, sweetheart. We still have things to do, you and I." Then he released me and straightened towards Killian who watched us with thinly-veiled patience.

"Let's go. It's this way." We moved purposely into another hallway.

Killian slowed long enough to reach a hand back to me. I touched his wrist in answer. Yes, I'm here and I'll be ready. His eyes caught mine in a glance, conveying the words he'd said to me on so many missions…*careful and smart*--his parting words for us every time we went out without him. My heart sped up as I digested the words and took notice of our surroundings. This hallway was lined with crumbling brick walls and my stomach churned. The walls gradually became tunnels broken up by occasional metal doors. I knew this place.

One of these doors was witness to my darkest nightmares.

Keep moving. Don't dwell on this place It has no power over you, Killian's voice whispered sharply.

Hundreds of scurrying feet sent shivers climbing up my neck and I choked on a scream when a heavy little body ran across my foot. I stopped abruptly and Sean ran into me with a grunt of surprise.

"Rats," I offered under my breath and kept moving lest it come back to taste me.

We'd gone about a hundred yards farther when a wave of déjà vu washed over me. I froze next to a door. This door wasn't padlocked and had been used recently. The dust was disturbed around the door handle and there were footprints jumbled around in front of it. Cold sweat crawled between my shoulders and I nearly bolted in a sprint, but Sean stopped right behind me and held onto my arm. This was the room. High-pitched shrieks echoed from inside and Killian swore softly in front of me.

The sound of booted feet on metal startled us into action. Killian took off in a sprint towards a tunnel to the right. We just cleared the corner when several men came out of the room into the tunnel where we'd just been standing. Their laughter echoed eerily as they stood outside the room smoking. From their tone, they were flunkies. One of them sounded vaguely familiar to me though. Another scream undulated shrilly from the open door and Dec dug his fingers into my arm.

"Not human; not our problem," Killian's harsh whisper broke through the horrific scenes running through my brain.

Not human…demon? Reanimated corpse?

The eye of the blade burned hotter the deeper we moved into the tunnels and Killian's entire expression changed again. Gone was my lover, my friend, my Primani. The high priest was back and in complete control now. Moving with utter silence, he stalked his prey with single-minded purpose.

Sgaine Dutre must be close.

When we turned to the right, the tunnels abruptly forked into three directions. We stopped to see which way he wanted us to go. In that voice that brooked no argument, he told us to wait. He went to the left and vanished. Right after he left, Dec perked up, his face lit with excitement, eyes gleaming in his face.

"Can you hear that?" He pointed at a pipe in the wall. The mortar was decayed and crumbling around it leaving a gap that seemed black as night to me.

Straining my ears but hearing nothing above the pounding of my heart and Sean's breathing behind me, I shrugged negatively.

"I'll be back in a minute," he promised, bolting down the other tunnel and vanishing around a bend in the dark.

The sense of foreboding grew stronger and I rubbed my arms to hold myself together. "I guess it's just you and me…" I murmured to Sean who was listening to something I couldn't hear.

The darkness was getting oppressive as if the entire city was about to cave in on me. I tried to ignore the small space, the heavy air, the solid darkness. It was a good thing I wasn't alone. I'd really be freaking out.

"Stay here for a minute. I'll be right back." He vanished without letting me argue.

Stunned by this turn of events, I pressed back against the wall and cursed all three of them. What the hell were they doing? Just when I was nearly hyperventilating with anxiety, Sean reappeared from the tunnel darkness.

"Where did you go? Are you crazy?"

Shrugging arrogantly, he replied smoothly, "I had to check something. I was only away a few minutes. I thought you were a big girl now?" He eyed me with a challenge.

Gritting my teeth, I muttered, "Never mind."

Walking back into the darkness, he called over his shoulder, "Come with me. We're going to meet Killian."

The silence was broken by dripping water that must be the East River. We were in an unfinished line of the subway that went from Lower Manhattan to Brooklyn. The river was on top of us right now...suddenly the rats didn't seem so bad. About 50 yards into the tunnel, my flashlight went out. The darkness was absolute. Disoriented by the sudden loss of light, I bounced into the wall and scraped my elbow. Hissing with pain, I stopped and dabbed at the raw skin. Sean halted in front of me. I couldn't see him but I sensed his presence. In half a heartbeat, he was standing very close to me with one hand possessively wrapped around my arm.

Invisible in the black void, he purred in my ear, "Are you afraid?" Slowly, he rubbed his palm along my shivering skin leaving a trail of heat behind.

"What the hell are you doing?" I stepped back only to find the brick wall.

Before I could say anything else, his mouth was on mine in a demanding kiss that bruised my lips and ground my head against the brick. Pressing his body against me, he ran his hands under my shirt even as I struggled to push him away. I bit down on his lip and twisted my head away to break the kiss. I was nearly free when a voice thundered in the tunnel behind us.

"Mica!" Sean shouted. "No!"

The Sean holding me in his arms chuckled and blinked. His eyes changed from brilliant blue to sickly yellow and he grinned at me showing his fangs.

"Surprise!"

No! It couldn't be! Not again!

Screaming in horror, I struggled to push him away and he pressed me to the wall with his forearm and mocked me with his eyes.

"What's wrong, sweetheart?" he crooned in exactly the right voice and blinked his eyes to blue again before turning to greet Sean.

Sean was frozen with shock, eyes wide and unblinking. In his hand, the silver Primani blade gleamed dully reflecting the pale fire of his eyes and illuminating the space. He didn't say a word and he didn't move. He stared at us with a what-the-fuck expression. His mouth worked but nothing came out.

Frantically, I called to him, "Sean!"

Shrugging, the demon said, "Well, that's a bit anticlimactic. I was hoping for more of a fight. What did you do to him?" He dismissed Sean completely and said, "Where were we?"

Reacting out of sheer revulsion now, I twisted and turned trying to throw him off but he was too strong and I couldn't get out of his grasp without ripping my own arms off.

Laughing cruelly, he said, "You can't fight me, human. You caught me off guard once before, but this time I'm ready for you. I didn't get to be this old by being stupid."

Stalling, I said, "I killed you! How are you alive? Who are you?"

Smiling coldly, he said, "In this plane, I'm known as Dagin. Surprised?"

"Dagin!"

I was most definitely surprised. The Primani had been looking for him for years. He was a royal pain in the ass on a good day.

At the sound of this name, Sean reacted like he'd been stung and roared back to life launching himself at Dagin. Dagin turned to meet his attack with his own battle cry. The force of Sean's attack sent them both skidding down the corridor while I watched in stunned silence. I must be having a seizure...a nightmare...something.

How was this possible?

I *killed* Dagin, didn't I?

I cut him to pieces and blew him into nothing but smoke...

The entire scene was so surreal I had to keep shaking my head to make sense of it. The dark tunnel was lit up by the burning heat radiating from Sean and Dagin's eyes. In full soldier-mode, Sean's eyes blazed and his body put off a subtle glow as the energy raced through him. The odd bluish light cast them in creepy nightmarish shadows. With jaws clenched in fury, their cheekbones stood out in sharp relief. Except for the eyes, it was impossible to tell them apart: they both looked like something out of the bottom rings of Hell. I shrank away from them and pasted myself against a wall. The two of them moved so fast I could barely follow the fight. They blurred from one position to the next trying to rip each other to pieces.

Across the tunnel, Dagin's snake eyes gleamed vividly in the dim light. His expression was almost bored as he flexed his fingers. Laughing softly, he shot a fireball at Sean's head that missed by inches. Sean jumped away from it easily and fired back with an energy blast. The blast hit Dagin in the chest and he staggered back but kept to his feet. The smell of sulfur drifted in the air. Hissing loudly, he dematerialized and popped up behind Sean. Sean was ready for the trick and jabbed him hard with the silver blade. Dagin only grunted and grabbed Sean's knife hand.

While twisting his wrist sharply, he snarled into Sean's face, "You little pussy! You're pathetic."

Sean growled, "Fuck you, demon!"

Sean's face was beet red as he struggled, but he was able to break free by head butting Dagin and smashing his nose. Dagin swore viciously and dropped his grip. Before he could regroup, Sean whirled around and blasted him again. The energy beam missed as Dagin rolled and leapt back to his feet in a crouch.

I was so intent on the fight in front of me that I missed seeing Dec rematerialize with a struggling person in his arms. Cursing profusely, he finally dropped the person who landed with an indignant squeal of anger. Dani?

"Mica, help me with her!"

"Dani?" I yelped when I heard her voice. "Oh, my God! Dani, is that you? Dec, I can't see her; can you fix the lights?"

With an irritated sound, he sent a bolt of power to a broken emergency light near the top of the tunnel. It burst into life with a buzz.

I stumbled over to them just in time to see her get awkwardly to her feet and rub at her butt. She was dressed in an oversized cotton nightgown made for an old lady. It was filthy with grime and torn down one side exposing her pale skin. Her feet were bare and also filthy. They had to be cold too...her hair was matted and greasy. She fluffed at it now with a haughty air and scowled at us.

This was bad.

Dec's face glowed like a tiny sun in the tunnel illuminating everything nearby. He stood preternaturally still as his eyes met mine.

"What happened, Dec?"

Between his teeth, he ground out, "She was in a *cell*, Mica, a freakin' cell! No food, no water, a rag...like an

animal! Worse than an animal!" He lowered his voice but
fury hardened every word until they came at me like
machine gun fire.

"My God…"

"Not likely!"

"Didn't she recognize you? What's wrong with her?"

Laughing bitterly, he snapped, "Oh, she recognized
me! Exactly as James programmed her to see me…as her
enemy! She tried to rip my face off when I picked her up
to carry her out of there." He tilted his face my direction
so I could see the bloody gouges across one cheek from
eye to jaw. They seeped blood and he wiped angrily at
them. "We've got to get her to Zadkiel. He can help her
better than we can."

I started to reach out a sympathetic hand and he
jerked away. "Don't touch me! I don't want to calm
down! I want to hunt these animals down and rip their
guts out inch by inch."

I was on board with that idea and it was all I could do
to stay where I was. "We'll get them. It's going to have to
wait a minute though." I nodded towards Sean and Dec's
mouth dropped open.

Grabbing his blade, he jumped up and bolted
forward.

Sean shouted, "No, Dec! This bastard's mine!"

To punctuate his claim, he dematerialized and
grabbed Dagin from behind. Dagin flipped him to the
floor and threw himself on top of him, knife gleaming in
the odd light.

"Shouldn't you do something?" I demanded. This
was taking too long. Sean had to be getting tired, didn't
he? Maybe they didn't get tired?

Shaking his head firmly, he snapped, "Not yet. This
is Sean's kill. We need to see to Dani."

Dani leaned against the wall looking defiant and
angry. Approaching her cautiously, I said, "Dani, we're
going to get you out of here! Don't worry. Everything
will be okay." I reached out to hug her.

She spit on me.

Her mouth twisted in an ugly grimace. "I'm not going anywhere with you. This is my home now." She rubbed a loving hand over the bulge under her dirty nightgown. "James will be back soon so you should leave. He doesn't like you, Mica." She looked down her nose at me. "He says you're a slut and you've been screwing around on Sean. Does he know that?" She pointed a finger at Sean who was struggling to keep Dagin from getting the upper hand.

Gritting my teeth and feeling my temperature rise, I tried for calm. She was obviously brainwashed. This wasn't my Dani. I tried again. "Dani, we need to get you out of here so the baby can see a doctor. You want the baby to be safe, right?"

Snickering behind her hand, she scoffed, "I have the best doctors here. They see to my every need. Look at me! I'm perfectly healthy and so is the baby."

Dec groaned next to me and ground his teeth together loudly. Dragging me to the side, he snapped, "We have to get her out of here! I can't stand seeing her like this!" His voice grew more intense until he finally punched the wall sending showers of mortar around us.

I was used to Sean and Killian morphing into their harder Primani selves, but Dec usually stayed relaxed in a fight. He'd even been known to grin cheekily while dispatching demons. This Dec, though, was unnerving me. He'd morphed completely into that supernatural warrior, looking more demon than angel in the dim light.

"Grab her!" he shouted as Dani tried to make a run for it.

It was too easy to stop her and my heart broke just a little at how weak she was. She slapped at my hands but I forced her to sit down. Dec knelt next to her and cupped her chin in his hand trying to calm her. Wanting only to help, he whispered to her in a compelling voice. She resisted and tried to knock his hand away. Determined, he gripped her chin hard and hissed at her to sit still.

Defiantly, she sneered, "You piece of shit! Get out of my face!"

She spit in his face.

Stone faced, he kept whispering to her, trying to reach into her mind, trying to find her beyond the demon's control. How had this happened? We were all so normal not that long ago...My mind just couldn't understand...Unable to watch any longer, I turned away and blinked back tears for Dani.

But the sense of unreality continued. Sean and Dagin were locked in a battle of strength and wills and Sean hadn't destroyed him yet. It was bizarre how evenly matched they were; neither had gotten the upper hand. They looked identical now, and I couldn't tell who was who. They wore the same face, but one was good, one was evil...

But was it really so black and white?

Remembering those kisses, I thought about how familiar they felt even though I knew it wasn't Sean. Just for a second, it had felt like him...until he hurt me. Sean hadn't ever been violent to me...until recently.

Detroit.

His anger pushed him into someone he wasn't...someone he shouldn't be.

Killian's words came back to me.

He's too powerful to let his emotions rule his brain.

His pride kept him from forgiving me. Now that anger and pride drove him to destroy Dagin.

Would he kill him for my sake or for his own?

Staring intently, I knew which one was the real Sean. He was the one with the underlying desperation in every move. No longer graceful and elegant, he threw himself at Dagin with brute force. He wasn't just fighting one demon.

He fought the lure of darkness, the shadows creeping around him.

He fought his own darker side.

Why didn't he just finish him? It was taking too long...he'd lost the Primani blade and couldn't reach it; the powerful blade lay on the floor in a puddle of murky water.

He threw himself to the side as Dagin slung a fireball at his head. Rolling to his feet, he shot a bolt of energy that collapsed the ceiling near Dagin's head. Back and forth they went; it was almost like they could predict the other's moves. Neither scored a direct hit, both were nearing a tipping point.

A faint murmuring gradually penetrated my brain as I stood transfixed by the scene playing out. Straightening with sudden recognition, I tensed and looked for him. Killian.

His shout drew my eyes to the darkened tunnel as he rematerialized a few feet in front me. He had the golden blade raised over his head and stood defiantly waiting as the first of them shuffled forward like a nightmare in the darkness. The awkward shuffle was so theatrical that I smiled.

This was going to be too easy...

Killian's voice whispered in my mind...persuading, calling...his magic as familiar to me as if it was my own...

Sgaine dios a liane, Sgaine dios a liane.

He called the lightning.

With each word, the tone of his call grew more demanding, more insistent. His voice compelled me, it was impossible to resist. I would be what he needed, do what he needed. I would answer his call. I was part of him...as connected to him as his own hand.

Our bond formed by blood and stone.

Stronger together than apart...we would win this.

It was destined. I saw this as clearly as I saw the faint blue shimmer.

The air crackled and the hair on my arms stood up while the powerful force surged like a current through my veins...readying me for what was to come. Waiting for

428

his signal, I stood by his side. They came forward, one at a time at first. They were different from the reanimated demons; these had been people and death had changed their bodies.

The first zombie had been shot; the gaping hole in his chest ragged with decay. A woman shuffled behind the first one. She had been young; her blond hair still hung limply down her back as she shuffled mindlessly towards me. After a minute, there were six of them moving our direction. As they got closer, I got antsy.

Why wasn't he doing something?

They were 50 yards away and more streamed in to fill the tunnel in front of us. Still he stood, facing them, blade glowing fiercely above his head. Inclining his head slightly, he spoke the simple words that would change the world.

"Sgaine dios a liane, Sgaine dios a liane."

He called the lightning.

Now there were too many to count and they were crowding forward. An ominous murmur grew louder to my right and turning with dread, I found the other tunnel filling with more undead…Two of the three tunnels were blocked. Sean and Dagin were throwing each other against the wall behind me while Dec crouched over Dani's still form.

We had only one way out.

At the moment, the others were too intent on their own battles to notice the beginnings of the zombie apocalypse bearing down on us. Tensing for the fight, my eyes burned and my fingers gripped my Primani blade hard enough to imprint the carvings into my palm. Balancing my weight on the balls of my feet, I felt a strange sense of calm. With my heightened vision, I saw the decomposing grey skin clearly as the first of them were nearly upon us.

Killian's voice rang in a shout of triumph that I felt in my bones.

"Sgaine dios a liane! Sgaine dios a liane!"

He called the lightning and it came.

With immense control, he slowly released a blue ball of lightning from the palm of his outstretched hand, and like St. Elmo's fire, it hovered in a sphere of light. Instinctively, I reached for it and linked my fingers through his. The twin runes exploded into light as the sphere raced into my body. The jolt of electricity sent my heart galloping in my chest and turned my vision white. Time stopped as I relished my sudden strength. I could move mountains...They were nearly on us and still we waited. Both tunnels were filled with hundreds of them. Raising my silver blade with his golden one, I took a deep breath.

"Now!" he shouted and crushed my hand in his.

Channeled through the metal blades, the lightning arced across the tunnel ceilings. Pulsing with heat, I stood perfectly still as it snaked down the walls around us casting everything in its eerie light. As in the cave, the current formed a web across the ceilings and the walls pulsed with the power. Killian's blade burned like a star in his fist. His body burned with the power of the lightning.

Ready?

Nodding, I followed his lead. Together, we drew the web around the stunned zombies and tightened its hold. The lightning arced between us creating a storm of wind and heat that swirled violently around us. Ready to end this, he released a surge of power into my hand that nearly knocked me over. Planting my feet, I took a deep breath and let the electricity pulse and build until it was so strong I could feel my skin splitting across my back. My body shook with the force and my eyes felt like they were melting in their sockets...finally, he nodded at me and we released the lightning with a loud crack.

For the barest of seconds, the blue fire raced up their bodies outlining them in the eerie light. They pulsed for a split second before exploding into the tempest. My hair whipped against my eyes as the winds howled around us.

Killian met my eyes, his expression triumphant. Slowly lowering the pulsing blade, he scanned the two tunnels for survivors. They were empty of everything except bits of dust floating on the air. Bowing his head respectfully, he murmured a prayer to send the undead to their resting places.

He said something to me, but I couldn't hear him. My ears hummed and I shook my head to clear them. He said it again and I just shook my head at him.

Don't you hear that? I asked silently.

Shaking his head like he had water in his ears, he nodded seriously. *It's from the lightning. It'll pass. Are you hurt?*

I'm not sure. Am I bleeding?

Sheathing the knife, he ran his hands up my shirt to look at my back. His fingers stung as he traced an outline across my shoulder blade. When he was done, the burning was gone. Coming around to my front side, he pulled up the material and stopped in surprise. Wonderingly, he traced the undamaged rune over my heart and smiled faintly.

You did good, Princess.

Grinning at him now, I licked my finger and dabbed at a smear of grey ash on his cheek. "We kicked butt!"

"Bravo! Well done!" The sound of someone clapping echoed around us.

Killian pushed me behind him and hissed, "Jordan!"

All motion stopped.

Dec's mouth dropped open and he pushed himself to his feet. Dagin froze and Sean took advantage of his distraction to snatch up his knife and plunge it into Dagin's shoulder. But just as the knife should've sunk into his body, it clattered to the floor and Dagin flew to Jordan's side. All eyes on him now, Jordan smiled ruefully and gestured in apology.

"I do apologize, my dear Sean. But I simply cannot allow you to destroy Dagin." Inclining his head politely, he said, "I've certain...ah, business arrangements that require me to offer my protection. I'm sure you understand."

Furious by the interference, but confused by his sudden appearance, Sean ventured in a formal tone, "I'm not sure I do understand. Would you care to elaborate?"

I twitched against Killian's side drawing his attention. Unconsciously, he stepped slightly to the side so I could see around his back. Jordan's eyes widened at the intimate gesture and he smiled at me. Once I'd thought Jordan to be a nice angel. He'd been gracious and efficient as the house manager in Manhattan. We'd had many comfortable talks in the kitchen. Now though? He made my skin crawl.

His eyes were too knowing, too cynical...creepy.

I edged close enough to Killian that my breasts brushed his back. The steady thumping of his heart calmed my sudden urge to panic, but this wasn't going to end well. Adrenaline zinged around inside of me and I knew this was going to be bad...

"Ah, Mica, sweet girl! I've missed you! I must say you look remarkably well considering the tragic loss you've suffered. The resilience of youth, I suppose." He bowed respectfully. "Please allow me to offer you and Sean my condolences on the loss of your son."

Twin gasps of shock broke the silence.

Dec and Sean swung around towards me and Killian. Sean's eyes snapped to my face and I looked at him helplessly. His eyes were desperate as they locked onto my face. Instead of answering him, I shook my head, unable to find the words. When he realized it was true, his eyes died like a match in the wind.

Defeated, his shoulders slumped.

Dec growled low in his throat. With clenched fists, he tensed to attack. Killian pulled me against his side and firmly restrained me from my darker instincts.

Watching our reactions carefully, Jordan continued in that same insincere tone. "I see you didn't know. Oh, but I am so sorry to spring it on you like that. That was most discourteous of me. Of course, had you been where you were supposed to be, you would've been there the night I sent my new friends to your house. You and Mica would've been destroyed along with the baby you spawned on her. Fortunately, the baby didn't survive; sadly, you both did."

It was my turn to gasp. "It was you? You did that? Why?"

"I do regret having to disappoint you like this. But I have my own--" His voice abruptly stopped and his attention swiveled to Dec who had lunged at him.

With impossible strength, Jordan lifted Dec off his feet and broke his neck with a heartbreaking snap. Seeing nothing but white-hot fury, I threw myself at Jordan only to be snatched back by Killian's hand. Pinning me to his chest, he wrapped his arm around me to keep me there. Out of control with grief, I struggled to get loose, even biting his arm, but he refused to let me go.

"Stop! You can't help him!" he whispered harshly in my ear. With his other hand, he whipped out his knife but before he could hit Jordan, he let go of Dec.

Dec crumbled to the ground, his face ashen, eyes staring.

Oh, God, Dec!

I was crying and struggling to get away from Killian who could barely hold me with both hands. Dec was so still...

His beautiful, terrible eyes were dimming in front of us.

Sean was at his side frantically feeling for a pulse when Dani stumbled to her feet and raced to Jordan's open arms.

"Sean? Sean? Is he alive?" I cried, desperately wanting it to be true.

With his head bowed over Dec's chest, his shoulders shook and I knew it was too late.

He was gone.

My legs wouldn't hold me and I crumbled over Killian's arm.

Oh, God, no. Not Dec…Not Dec…Not Dec…

Shaking me gently, Killian sent his thoughts to me. *Listen to me! Mica, listen!*

I was beyond hearing him.

He dug his fingers into my arm and I gulped at a steadying breath.

Mica, please! I need you to be strong! I have to go after Jordan! I have to. Will you be strong for me?

Still crying, I nodded mutely. *I'm going with you.*

Killian glared into Jordan's eyes and said in a voice so hushed it was less than a whisper, "Why? Why would you do that? What deal have you made with Satan?"

Satan? My ears perked up and my tears shut off like a faucet. *The* Satan?

Jordan stayed silent.

Sensing a soft spot, Killian goaded, "It has to be good. Money? Women? Power? Hmmm. What would a *butler* want?" He said the word *butler* as if it was a filthy word. The effect was electrifying.

Jordan's voice shook the mortar from the bricks around us. His face caught fire with an unholy glow that made me cringe against Killian. "Butler? Butler? I was *never* a simple butler! My family comes from ancient magic; I'm more powerful than you idiots will ever be! I had to bide my time…waiting for you to make a mistake. And you didn't. Not for almost 3,000 years. Not until you let your hormones overrule your Primani duty."

"Yes, yes, we're all very impressed with you, Jordan. I'm going to ask you just one more time. What *deal* did you make with Satan?" His soft tone brooked no argument.

Unimpressed, Jordan crowed, "I followed you to your altar. Once you left, I simply retrieved *Sgaine Dutre* and left the plane. You were so preoccupied with Mica that you didn't sense my presence. It was disappointingly easy. Now *Sgaine Dutre* belongs to me. I will master it and use it to fulfill my destiny."

"And what is that, exactly?" Killian said between his teeth.

"I'm going to replace God. He's gotten too soft. Mankind needs more discipline."

My mouth fell open and Killian inhaled sharply. Several things happened after that. Dec's still form began to shimmer like a mirage. His beautiful soul swirled from his body like gold dust and disappeared into the air. We watched in horror as his body vanished, leaving nothing but his scent trickling through Sean's desperate hands. Devastated, he collapsed against the wall with empty black eyes. Killian swore savagely and yanked me around to face him.

"Anchor him!"

With one hand he threw me into Sean's arms just as Jordan began to shimmer.

Killian's eyes held mine and then he was gone.

As the world spun out from under me, Killian's last words rang in my ears.

Don't let him fall!

About the Author

Laurie Olerich is the author of a paranormal romance/urban fantasy series that started with *Primani* and continues with *Call the Lightning*. Much of the story is set against the wild and beautiful mountains of upstate New York and Vermont. A wood nymph in a past life, she's most at home inside the forest. Laurie spent most of her life in the Northeastern United States and in Western Europe. She now lives in San Antonio, Texas, with her son and Dalmatian duo, Domino and Rambo. Desperate to escape the heat, she lives vicariously through Mica and her Primani by setting their adventures in the mountain coolness of New England. Before throwing caution to the wind and diving into a writing career, Laurie dedicated 20 years to her country by serving in the United States Air Force. Much of her time was spent around men with guns and cool toys...this explains her obsession with both.

Connect with Laurie online:
Website: www.laurieolerich.com
Facebook: Laurie Olerich-Author
Twitter: Laurie Olerich@LaurieOlerich

Five years, full circle. Sacrifices made. Promises kept. Enjoy this excerpt from the next novel in the Primani series: *Stone Angels*

Lucerne, Switzerland:

KILLIAN LEAHY STOOD BROODING on a small balcony overlooking the city. The sun had set for the day and the barest hint of stars brightened the sky. In his hands he held a thin gold blade. Its red stone glowed brilliantly against his hand outlining the strong bones of his fingers like an x-ray.

"Come on, come on. Where are you?" he murmured into the night. He watched the city street bustling ten stories below him and then tuned it out to look inward.

Sgaine Dutre was here. He felt it in his bones. Jordan was using it, wielding it like it was his. Every time he used it, the echoes of its power thrummed through Killian's blood and pierced his heart. Warning him, calling him, searching for him...

Sgaine Dutre was his.

He was its master and it wanted him back.

The golden blade was its brother; they had been forged together, one silver, one gold; bonded by words and magic. But most importantly, they were bonded by blood.

Killian's blood...and a lot of it.

It wouldn't rest until it brought its brother back to its rightful place. Killian closed his eyes and searched with his mind. Methodically, he scanned the city from right to left using a grid map in his head. It was here. He would find it. Searching...searching...

There!

A faint glimpse of blue fire tickled the edges of his sight. He tensed and got ready to move. It was moving away, it was nearly out of his range. Suddenly it was gone.

Poof.

Just like that.

"Motherfucker!" he swore savagely and gripped the blade tightly enough to draw blood. Into the night, he whispered, "Run, Jordan. Run away. I'll find you. It's only a matter of time."

Sucking the blood off his palm, he took a deep breath and reeled in the sharp bite of anger and frustration. Giving it free reign was dangerous. Anger was a tricky emotion and not one that he entertained very often.

The angels let him keep his powers as long as he controlled them. He was unwilling to sacrifice any of his powers for the luxury of rage.

Jordan was toying with him. The sonofabitch had been toying with him for days…some men would be out of control with anger and frustration. That would make them reckless and recklessness led to mistakes. Killian smiled grimly into the night. Jordan had miscalculated this time. Killian was never reckless. He had unlimited patience.

After all, he had everything to lose.

A loud knock interrupted his musing and he glanced at the clock on the bedside table. His stomach growled softly as the smell of grilled steak drifted under the door. It was room service with his dinner. Forcing himself to seem harmless, he pulled open the door. Gasping, the young delivery woman took a step back with her hand over her mouth.

Patiently, he said, "Come in. I don't bite." Waving her politely ahead of him, he stood near the door so she could pass by with plenty of space.

Petite with a choppy blond haircut, she couldn't have been any older than Mica. She flushed prettily and stammered at him while she wheeled in the cart with the food on it. She managed to get most of his beer into the glass but spilled half of it on the table. He sighed inwardly at the wasted beer but kept a straight face. He didn't want to scare her any more than she already was.

Women always lost their minds around him and he'd never understand why. He wasn't interested in hurting them. He was usually too busy to even think about them at all. With the exception of Mica, he thought human women were generally too delicate. If he had to deal with them at all, he'd rather protect them than hurt them. But Mica said he scared the hell out of everyone, especially women. She said humans sensed he wasn't one of them, that he was a predator.

Smothering a grin at the thought of Mica ever being afraid of him now, he tipped the startled girl and shut the door in her face. The steak was overcooked and the beer was warm. He ate it anyway and finished the beer on the balcony. It didn't matter if it tasted good or not. Food was just fuel for his body. He'd need it if he was going to keep traveling around Europe. Teleporting took a lot of energy. Weary, he closed his eyes and thought of Mica. Her heart-shaped face drifted across his eyes and made him smile. She was out there across the continent right now. What was she doing? What *would* she do? He frowned and traced the pearly scar on his hand. Could she handle Sean?

What would it take to keep him from falling?

Was she strong enough to hold him?

To *survive* him?